EDISTO ISLAND is a paradise where people escape from the mainstream world. Yet for newly sworn-in Edisto Police Chief Callie Jean Morgan, the trouble has just begun . . .

When a rookie officer drowns in a freak crash in the marsh, Callie's instincts tell her it wasn't an accident. As suspects and clues mount, Callie's outlandish mother complicates the investigation, and Callie's long-time friendship with Officer Mike Seabrook takes a turn toward something new—but is shadowed by the unsolved mystery of his wife's death.

THE ROAR OF the surf made Callie's steps soundless, her thoughts louder. Two and a half weeks on the job, and she'd lost an officer. Edisto hadn't sacrificed an officer in its entire history, and the first female chief had to be the one to break the record.

She sniffled. Salty breezes began to clear her sinuses, but nothing could assuage the guilt clinging to her like the muggy air.

Sarah lived. Francis died. And somebody had to be disappointed at that freakish turn of events, because she suspected it was meant to be the other way around. Crime was for people who lived across the big bridge on the mainland. But whether the natives liked it or not, the brake lines were cut on Edisto. She didn't want to go down that path, but one of them might be a frustrated, unfulfilled killer.

The Novels of C. Hope Clark

The Carolina Slade Mysteries

Lowcountry Bribe

Tidewater Murder

Palmetto Poison

Newberry Sin

The Edisto Island Mysteries

Murder on Edisto

Edisto Jinx

Echoes of Edisto

Edisto Stranger

Echoes of Edisto

Book Three: The Edisto Island Mysteries

by

C. Hope Clark

Bell Bridge Books

This is a work of fiction. Names, characters, places and incidents are either the products of the author's imagination or are used fictitiously. Any resemblance to actual persons (living or dead), events or locations is entirely coincidental.

Bell Bridge Books
PO BOX 300921
Memphis, TN 38130
Print ISBN: 978-1-61194-706-9

Bell Bridge Books is an Imprint of BelleBooks, Inc.

Copyright © 2016 by C. Hope Clark

Published in the United States of America.

All rights reserved. No part of this book may be reproduced in any form or by any electronic or mechanical means, including information storage and retrieval systems, without permission in writing from the publisher, except by a reviewer, who may quote brief passages in a review.

We at BelleBooks enjoy hearing from readers.
Visit our websites
BelleBooks.com
BellBridgeBooks.com
ImaJinnBooks.com

10 9 8 7 6 5 4 3 2 1

Cover design: Debra Dixon
Interior design: Hank Smith
Photo/Art credits:
C. Hope Clark

:Leew:01:

Dedication

To the dedicated, hard-working, self-sacrificing officers of the Edisto Police Department who do a remarkable job keeping our beloved beach safe and secure.

Chapter 1

THE LAST DRAWER of the cabinet, the one at floor level, slid out rough, like rust on rust, but the sight of the single-barrel whiskey bottle gave her an Easter-egg thrill.

She reached, then didn't, imagining the whiff if she opened the cap. She knew exactly how long it'd been. Five weeks and three days, and while she wouldn't embarrass herself at reciting the hours, she recalled the evening. A Tuesday, around nine.

Marie, the lone administrative staff, called from the front. "Chief Morgan?"

Police Chief Callie Jean Morgan shut the file drawer. Wasn't her liquor anyway, and it was too awkward to toss it now.

"Yes?" she hollered back. The station was small, and Callie talking to Marie was like being home and calling her eighteen-year-old son Jeb from his bedroom to supper. She opened another drawer. Surely the old chief had kept a personal log of some sort before he left for North Carolina, noting the people to watch, to avoid, to cater to in this town.

"We have a visitor who wishes to speak to you," Marie said.

Walking into the main open floorplan space of the Edisto PD station, Callie acknowledged Marie, a slightly frumpy, close-cropped blonde in her late-thirties, then approached the counter. "Yes, sir, how can I help you?"

Clad only in a red Speedo and sandals, the over-sunned Californian shook a citation in the air, loudly intent on having his *Constitutional say.* "This damn ticket is excessive, and I want it revoked. *Now.*"

Officer Francis Dickens had radioed her for confirmation before issuing the citation to a celebrity—for public nudity. The man had exited beach access twelve, flaunting his assets all the way back to his rental, prompting six complaints to 911. Callie'd heard the actor's name from television but feigned ignorance for no other reason than to irritate him. His series had come and gone over a decade ago anyway.

The visitor shifted to his other hip, and Callie wished his tiny stretch of spandex would pinch in a wrong place and send him on his way. If he'd kept the dang thing on he wouldn't be here. His obscenities flying, she let him fret until he pointed down at her badge from his ten-inch height advantage, snatching her to the present enough to lean back from his reach.

She walked around the counter into the lobby. Palms on her utility belt, she fought the instinct to pin the man's cheek against the wall, his bony hand twisted behind him. But this wasn't Boston, where she'd managed people like him with ease. This was her childhood beach home, a place in love with tourists where a show of force represented poor decorum.

It hadn't been an easy journey putting the badge back on. Admittedly, law was in her blood, and the mayor milked the opportunity to insert her diversity into his administration by offering her the chief's job. She was two years out of practice, but she had this. Hell, it was Edisto Beach, for God's sake. This loudmouth visitor was just a bum part of policing a tourist town, pun intended.

"I paid damn good money to rent on the water," the actor said, his spittle barely missing Callie's chin. "So much for your so-called *Southern hospitality*."

The two of them remained on the outside of the counter separating the discussion and whatever evolved from it, distant from Marie and the two empty desks that Callie's six officers shared on a rotational basis. The man hadn't fazed Marie, who pecked on her keyboard.

This guy lived on the higher end of the financial spectrum, and Edisto needed his wallet. Thank goodness, however, he represented an anomaly. Most of Edisto's visitors presented better manners.

The errant citizen shook himself, as if preparing to posture on stage. "Oh, why did I think a hick state like South Carolina would be progressive enough to accept the human body?"

"I'm sure I don't know, sir," Callie replied.

Mr. Speedo slid his ugly composure to one of congeniality, as if trying a new tactic. "So how will you deal with this?"

She smiled. "We're progressive enough to take American Express, sir."

His tanned complexion reddened. "Damn you! Maybe I ought to take this down to Wainwright Realty and demand *she* pay it. And refund my money for the whole damn vacation! I'll go home and tell everybody to avoid this place, and I *know* people."

Callie tried not to show her delight. Hell, she might escort him down to the real estate office herself to see his exchange with the former

Marine-turned-broker.

The radio crackled. "Dispatch, this is Francis. Marie, you there?"

"Dispatch here. What you got, Francis?"

Marie quit typing the monthly report summarizing the department's September accomplishments. Soon Callie would present her first report to town council, reciting the number of golf cart speeding violators and empty houses checked. Nerve-wracking stuff that she intended to love every minute of until she retired.

"Got a 10-50 at Scott Creek, just outside of town limits," Officer Francis Dickens relayed. "Single car and single occupant. Got a civilian on scene in the water attempting to assist. No doubt we'll need a wrecker, but nobody's underwater. Send an ambulance in case."

Callie glanced at the wall clock. Four thirty. Kind of early for someone to be that Bacardi'd up. Living within a stone's throw of the Atlantic, she learned to keep up with tides, and it was near to high. The water wasn't particularly deep at that spot, but deep enough. . . .

"Mike there?" Francis asked.

"He called in and took today off," Marie answered, glancing at Callie.

Officer Mike Seabrook's second need to skip a full day's work was highly unusual, leaving Callie to run the place without him. Ordinarily he served at her elbow, dropping subtle hints on how to approach different residents. Containing tourists equated to herding cats in her mind, but Seabrook had a science for that, too.

An ex-doctor turned cop, he often proved himself in that department, too. Callie felt over her healed ribs, recalling Seabrook's abilities after her run-in with the infamous Edisto Jinx six weeks ago.

A six-foot two-inch man who'd served six months as interim chief engendered more faith from the officers than a five-foot two-inch burned-out female detective not long out of a self-imposed sabbatical. Her experience still trumped anyone else's out here, though, and one by one she'd win these people over. She had to. She and her son had decided Edisto should be their forever home.

To aid the transition she even stopped dating Seabrook, postponing that inevitable ripple of whisper across the island. She missed their private conversations, the respectable kisses, and a man's arms around her.

The ticket almost touched her nose. "*Waiting*, Chief," the visitor said, almost vibrating with frustration.

Callie gestured toward the door and escorted Speedo man to the exit. "Sorry, I have an accident to tend to. The ticket sticks. You have thirty days to pay it."

"Bitch."

"So I've been told." She pushed the door.

"Humph." He marched past her outside to the parking lot and slung open the door to his Lexus.

Callie paused a second to ensure he left. "What a nuisance."

"You know who he is, right?" Marie asked.

"Yep, but can't let him know that." Callie lifted her cap from the hook on the wall. "I better check out that accident. I'll get with you on that report tomorrow. Aren't tourists supposed to be gone by September?"

"Not till the middle of October." Marie returned to her report. "I'll wait around a bit in case you get back before quitting time. Update me, if you don't mind."

Callie trotted to her cruiser. Things were better with Marie. The office manager had been leery when a woman stepped into the chief's position two weeks ago. Each of their conversations built another inch of trust, though. Marie had worked the desk since high school. Alienating her would alienate a third of Edisto.

Static sounded on her shoulder mic. "Callie? This is Thomas. You going to check on Francis?"

She waited for the "or not" on the end of that statement, grateful for its absence. She leaned in to her shoulder as she left the building. "On my way."

"Let me finish with this ticket, and I'll meet you there. Thomas out."

As she dropped into her cruiser's leather seat, the nakedness at the lack of a vest unnerved her yet again. None of the past chiefs had ever worn them, to include Seabrook. When in uniform in Boston, a vest was a second skin. This small community way of life took some getting used to, where the worst hazard was a teenager breaking and entering an empty rental for a television set. Or a dried up celebrity demanding special attention.

A Klaxon horn repeated itself at the fire station next door. She jumped, the old memory of her own fire in Boston rearing its head, then told herself to get moving. The narrow two-lane causeway onto Edisto Beach would soon bottleneck with first responders. Highway 174 was the only access across the water.

On a Wednesday afternoon, tourist movement was light. Callie drove her cruiser up Murray Street to Palmetto Boulevard where she allowed herself some speed. She waved as she passed Officer Thomas

Gage and a convertible of teenagers. A few houses later, she passed Seabrook's place, also on Palmetto. As the unofficial second-in-command, he maintained the fourth car in the fleet. It sat idle in his drive, his personal car gone, making her wonder what had been so urgent for him to call in last minute and take the day off. They'd become close enough to share such things, or so she thought.

They were overdue for a private dinner to air what was going on.

Three miles later she turned onto the highway and spotted Francis's vehicle, lights pulsing, but he was nowhere in sight. EMTs and maybe the short brush fire truck would appear in a minute. She eased up to the rear of the cruiser and slid her sunglasses on. Sunlight reflecting off saltwater blinded in autumn, as bad or worse than summer.

Her walk turned to a jog as recognition snapped her to attention. The trunk of the half-submerged car had popped open, one suitcase floating, another's contents strewn across the marsh. Sarah Rosewood's car. The full-time resident lived two houses down from Callie. The stuck vehicle rested maybe thirty yards off the road, having accelerated too fast judging by the distance. Not what she'd expect from Sarah. She was only in her sixties, not quite elderly enough to hit the wrong pedal or accelerate by accident.

"Help!" shouted a man Callie didn't recognize. Chest-deep in the water, he hollered, "The officer slipped under and he's caught! I can't get him out!"

Jesus!

Unbuckling her utility belt, Callie dropped it to the ground along with her phone, kicked off her shoes, and leaped off the road bank into the marsh. She swam to the driver's side and tried to stand, water almost up to her neck. Sarah huddled outside the car, a couple yards to the side, muddy and scared. Callie spit out a mouthful of the brown salty water. "Where's Francis?"

"Follow me." The civilian dove, Callie close behind.

She felt Francis floundering and pushing against the car before she saw him blurred in the stirred up muck. His legs had slid beneath the Volvo, probably as he tried to gain purchase, and the one-ton car had rocked back, entrapping him. Callie's feet sank into at least a foot or more of the sulphur-smelling pluff so renowned to the barrier islands. She and the civilian struggled to lift the car, finally finding the rhythm to function in tandem.

Air whooshing from her lungs with each exertion, she motioned a thumb up.

They hit the surface, and she shouted, "Deep breath and try again."

They dove together, more in sync. Again, they rushed to settle a stance in the uncertain marsh bottom, in a squat. Was that movement she felt? They shoved harder, each effort slowly swaying the car.

Her right heel slipped out from under her, then the left. Callie's feet slid in spite of her back-pedaling. The Volvo trapped her at an angle, up to her thighs beside Francis.

He wasn't moving.

And she couldn't either.

Panic rising, she shook him once, twice, needing him to help. Then she reached behind her to haul herself back out, but the stranger grabbed her left arm, disabling her attempt, not understanding her plan.

She yelled, "Stop," the bubbles reminding her she couldn't afford further loss of air.

The man said something incoherent under water, then yanked her with urgency. A jolt shot through her shoulder. She tried to pull loose, but he only heaved harder.

Her lungs burned.

Damn it, they had to quit fighting each other. Pushing into the muck, sinking deeper, she grappled, dug, reached for anything solid.

Spots formed across her vision. Could she breathe water?

Of course not.

But would they revive her if she did?

She squeezed her eyes shut. Though she held no air, her chest longed to explode, take in whatever the inhale contained.

Jeb! He'd lose another parent.

Another set of hands gripped her right arm, yanking it out from under her. The car moved. She slid free, heart pounding triple-time, and she dared to take a breath, only taking in water. Now she couldn't breathe at all. Choking, she glimpsed Thomas before he lifted her into someone else's grasp.

Like a baby, people passed her in an assembly line to the road where someone set her on a blanket, an EMT instantly rolling her to her side.

She gagged then threw up, salt water spewing from her lungs across the black sneakers of the squatting EMT.

"Slow down, Ms. Morgan. You're okay. Leave this on," he said, placing an oxygen mask over her nose and mouth.

"Francis," she said, voice scratchy and thick between coughs that couldn't reach the water still down deep. She snatched at the mask and struggled to rise.

"Oh no you don't," the paramedic said, his two-hundred-pound bulk easily holding her slim shoulders. "There are ten men out there right now, and you'd just be in the way."

The police chief . . . in the way.

Callie rounded from his grasp and pivoted on her butt to see the rescue.

In the short time she'd been trapped, Highway 174 had transformed into a circus. The ambulance beside her, a squad firetruck to her left. Cars backed up in both directions, tourists inconvenienced yet curious from the horde of two dozen people that continued to grow.

Two divers came up sputtering. "Still pinned," one managed to shout out. He swam to the hood, ordering as he splashed. "Everybody, lean into this side. On three, push."

The briny water's swirling pluff and sawgrass cared little about the urgency. Rescuers placed themselves, and three others jumped in from the road, one with a rope. A guy on the bank tied a loose end to a truck bumper. Others shouted that wouldn't work.

Too long. They're taking too long. Why did they pull her out first? He'd been under longer.

"One, two, three!" the lead man shouted again.

A firefighter waded in with a scuba tank, and Callie dared pray he could keep Francis breathing. Tears streamed down her face.

Her muscles clenched with those of the rescuers. *Not Francis. Not on my watch. Damn it, not on my watch.* Never before had she hated her small stature so much, logic dictating she let the brawny lead when every part of her being cried to help. And all she'd done, as the EMT put it, was get in the way.

A cry went out from the crowd. Two men slid under like she had, but they resurfaced, blowing and kicking to reposition. The eighties model silver Volvo barely rocked, suctioned in place, the slurping loud, the paper-mill odor of the marsh pungent.

Another firefighter prepared the ladder, but everyone sensed seconds fled too fast for a Plan B.

A winch hook from somewhere reached one man, and he positioned it in a quick yank. Then as the men lost their grips for the second time, he stood and punched the air. "Go!"

Onlookers backed up when the rope went taut, the cable stiffened, pulled by the firefighter at the truck. A few yards to the side, the four-wheel drive dug in, its engine growling, the odor of burning rubber drifting through the hint of white smoke rising into the wet Lowcountry afternoon.

Callie resisted a glance at her watch, her instincts screaming about the passing time.

The rescuers thrust their shoulders and backs into the task with new vigor, the cable holding their advances. Grunts and screams escaped from their bellies as the weight rolled enough for someone to grasp Francis and haul him out.

A line formed quickly. People passed his limp form through the water, and Callie ripped the mask from her face. They lowered Francis to the hard ground and began pumping water from his chest.

Hovering close by, reaching wide to keep others behind her, Callie felt each heave to Francis's chest in her own, her pulse frantic.

Francis was the first officer to greet her after Seabrook when she arrived on the beach so broken and lost. She found Francis naively charming, his youthful twenty-six years a constant contrast to his effort to wield authority. Eager. Sweet.

They pulled out the defibrillator. "Back!" one guy shouted. "It's wet here, everybody move back."

The circle widened.

"Clear!"

A flinch flew through Callie as Francis's body jolted. Another shock. And another.

Finally, the medics ceased effort. Each bystander seemed afraid to be the one to move first for fear of accepting Francis's death.

That's when Callie heard the silence.

She studied Francis's boots, needing to focus on something. Her heart felt ten times bigger in her chest, as if it might crack her ribs again. This couldn't be. It just couldn't be.

She searched for Thomas. He leaned against the ambulance, dripping, staring at the ground. Somewhere a woman sobbed. A man mumbled, "Oh, my dear lord."

Groups formed, searching each other for comfort.

An unknown gentleman asked her if she was okay. She waved him away.

This was not about her.

Once they lifted the body from the wet ground to a gurney, Callie pushed through. The medics gave her a moment.

Haltingly, she touched his still-warm face. "Oh, Francis," she whispered and wiped a grimy spot off his forehead. She stroked his cheek one time before straightening his collar. Resting her palm on his chest, she waited, praying to feel movement overlooked by the EMTs.

"We probably need to take him, ma'am," said one.

"Not yet you don't," she replied.

He moved aside, speaking in undertones to his partner.

Her hand roamed to another spot on Francis's chest. *Breathe, Francis. Please, for God's sake, breathe. We need you. I need you.*

But he didn't.

"Ma'am?" asked the medic again.

Finally, she stepped back. They loaded him in the ambulance and shut the doors with little wasted motion.

The fire chief blocked her line of vision. "They should take you in, too, Callie. You inhaled a lot of water."

Her "no" came in a raspy whisper. She cleared her throat and coughed. "No, I'm fine."

Of course she was. Her heart worked. Francis's didn't.

"At least get someone to look at you, ma'am," said her burly EMT. "Promise?"

Thank goodness he left her alone after a nod.

He entered the driver's side of the ambulance, and the engine fired up. The van inched forward, easing through the people, leaving Callie standing in an opening to herself.

Sarah sat in a messy collapse where they had treated her. After a brief moment of relief at being saved, she'd become the cause of Francis's death, embarrassed at the attention, turning emotionless at the sacrifice on her behalf. Judging from the scowls and murmured comments, much of the crowd appeared to somehow blame her too. Callie shoved her own similar instinctive thought aside. She'd check on Sarah—in a moment. Just not yet.

Thomas wandered over with Callie's utility belt, an observer slapping him on the back along the way. "You okay, Callie?"

She nodded, afraid words would break her. Then she silently accepted her belt.

Water dripped down his neck off black hair two weeks past a trim. His uniform clung to him, and Callie saw the outline of his T-shirt beneath. He peered down close so nobody heard. "You tried."

A heaving sigh from her roused another cough, and Thomas waited as she finished and spit. "Thanks, Thomas." She sniffled, digging deep in her gut for strength, second-guessing if he held it against her that she was saved first . . . or in the way.

He patted her shoulder and walked off. Cars backed up both ways. He moved toward those arriving from the mainland and, waving in animated fashion, ordered drivers to quit gawking and get on toward the beach. Then the officer turned to those on the other side, and in semaphore fashion, motioned them to move as well. Someone he obviously knew asked to help, and Thomas accepted, sending him to the other side of the catastrophe to aid traffic control.

A drop trickled below her ear, and Callie shivered in spite of the heat. Wiping her cheek, she turned in time to watch the ambulance taillights vanish, her officer's body disappearing around a slight bend down Highway 174. The ambulance driver didn't have to flip the lights on, but he did. Red flashers bounced off the dense oak, myrtle, and palmetto greenery, taking Francis to the coroner in Walterboro.

If she remembered right, Francis was from Walterboro. He was going home.

She realized the mayor cherry-picked her because of her gender and family's political reputation, but she'd accepted regardless the reason or conditions because she knew better than anyone on their radar how to run this department. She thought she had this.

Now Francis was dead . . . on her fledgling watch.

What if she hadn't been first to arrive? What if Thomas had been able to simply save Francis?

Her attention shifted to the muddied bank, and she moved further off the road so traffic would go on by unimpeded . . . and people would lose interest in her.

"Ms. Morgan? I think you lost these."

A firefighter passed her sunglasses to her. Then he tipped his head. "My condolences, ma'am."

With a forced smile she returned the gesture. He left, and she ran a finger under each eye, sniffled again, and donned the glasses.

Marsh to her left, marsh to her right. The Atlantic rolled and churned a few hundred yards behind her as if reminding her to turn around; that Edisto Beach was her home. She wondered if things would've been different if Seabrook had shown up to work . . . had remained acting police chief.

People began to move along the causeway. Callie, however, shifted attention to the catalyst of the evening's trauma. Sarah remained silent and placid on the road's edge.

Re-buckling her utility belt, Callie strode toward the woman, repeatedly reminding herself that her father's old mistress hadn't caused Francis's death.

Chapter 2

VEHICLES PASSED Callie both ways on the lone entrance to Edisto Beach, but even dank and sticky, she focused on Sarah Rosewood, the woman she'd come to call friend despite her old liaison with Callie's father. She walked to the woman seated in a puddle of salt water, damp hair matted around her cheeks and neck, and reached down to assist the sixty-five-year-old to her feet, sniffing for alcohol. None Callie could tell, and she was good at telling, but the stench of briny mud could've overpowered anyone's senses.

"Hey," Callie started. "How are you—?"

"Here's my card, Chief Morgan." A man wormed his way in, hand outstretched. "In case you need a statement."

His hair combed back, ruined loafers squeaking, a towel draped around his shoulders, the man who'd hauled Sarah out of the car appeared, a smartphone at the ready. "I'm so sorry for your loss," he said, as if remembering what his mother taught him to say.

His accent was South Carolinian but more Midlands than Lowcountry. Red hair, the curls showing themselves even through the mud. Slacks, as if meeting someone rather than beachcombing. Thirty maybe. Callie'd never seen him before, but that could mean he was only an Edisto guest.

Clothes wet, Callie inserted the card in the dry belt without reading. "Appreciate your assistance." She scanned the area. "Thomas?" She wanted to take Sarah's accounting of the incident. Thomas could deal with the hero. Anyone could manage traffic.

Thomas looked her way. "Yeah, Chief."

It was only the two of them today . . . without Francis. "Can you find someone to take your place so you can take a statement from this gentleman? Want me to call in Seabrook?"

Thomas returned a limp salute, sadness embedded in his manner. "No, I got this. Mike's probably in Charleston anyway."

The red-haired rescuer leaned in to Sarah. "Glad to see you're all right, ma'am. That door was rough."

"Yes, thank you," Sarah said in a wavering voice.

He twisted to speak privately to Callie. "Don't let the loss of a man send you back to the bottle. That was a fine effort you gave out there."

She jerked around. "Pardon me?"

He bobbed his head knowingly once and headed toward Thomas.

What the hell? Callie watched hapless as the guy slid into the melee, like a snake slipping under a rock. She retrieved the card. *Quincy Kinard, Associate Editor, The Middleton Post.*

A damn reporter.

Even in eighty-degree heat, Sarah's shivers increased. Callie needed to get her seated and hidden from everyone's scrutiny, comfortable enough to answer questions before answers escaped her, or her story had the chance to change.

Setting Sarah in the patrol car's backseat, Callie stooped beside the open door to a better level to speak, wincing once at the pain in her shoulder. She took a second to compartmentalize the afternoon's events to maintain some emotional stability and cough aside the thickness in her throat. "What happened?" Callie asked softly, tucking the emergency blanket inside so it wouldn't catch in the door. "This is hard, honey, and you're rattled, but better to tell me than a strange officer."

The accident took place barely outside Callie's jurisdiction, and being fresh in the position she might step on a few toes taking prompt charge of this case, but she didn't care if either the Highway Patrol or Colleton Sheriff's Department minded. Francis was her man, not theirs. Sarah her neighbor, a friend.

Sarah Rosewood scanned the people, the emergency lights, the interior of the police car, and fear reached her eyes. She took shallow, inconsistent gasps. Callie recognized panic and caught herself swallowing her own. She glanced to the side to avoid sympathizing with Sarah so much, willing the pumping in her chest to ease off. A police chief with an anxiety attack was unacceptable. To distract herself, she inhaled deeply and stood, moving around to the front seat to reach inside and grab a notepad from the console. She already had Marie call the Highway Patrol. They'd arrive soon.

Shaking, Sarah clutched the blanket around her. "A deer jumped in front of me. I should've hit it, but I couldn't. My foot stomped the brake to the floor. Nothing happened. Nothing! Just a sick feeling that I was out of control. Rather than cross the marsh and hit an oak, I turned into the water."

A deer in broad daylight on a road bordered by water? While deer were common in the marsh, they were too wild and wise to prance on that short stretch of road in such a confined area. Especially during deer season which started in August in this part of the state. "A deer on the causeway?"

"Yes, a deer," Sarah exclaimed, pointing toward her car. "A big doe."

"Anyone see you?"

"Don't remember any other cars, but I had things on my mind."

Callie wrote hard, using the shorthand language she'd developed over the years. "What kind of things?"

"It's personal."

Callie stopped writing and stared at the drenched and disheveled woman in her backseat. "Maybe if I understood, the accident would make more sense. You've lived here twenty-odd years without incident. Suddenly your clothes are scattered over Scott Creek, your car underwater, and my officer dead. I think I'm entitled to hear what the hell you were thinking, Sarah."

"Ask Ben."

"I'll certainly call your husband for you," Callie replied, going back to her notes.

"And ask your mother."

Her pen stopped. Her mother?

Sucking in, Sarah held it then let it loose, but her teeth chattered. "Anyway, next thing green water gushes up my windshield, coming through the cracks of my door. Have no idea what happened to the deer."

Callie wondered more about her mother than the damn deer. She reached up and pulled the blanket tighter around Sarah. "Have you been having brake problems?"

"No."

Callie figured Ben probably serviced the car. "Okay, then what happened?"

"Then suddenly that strange man's there," Sarah continued, "yelling at me to stay calm while he yanked at my door. The car moved . . . he . . . he . . . hauled me out the window . . . he . . ."

Bending over with a moan, emotion crackling into agony, Sarah touched forehead to her knees. Sobs tumbled out, dissolving the last of her strength. "I'm so sorry about Francis."

Callie dammed the buildup in her own throat.

Touching Sarah's back, kneading a fold of blanket material, Callie dialed the Rosewood house, hoping Ben would answer. He and his wife remained distant, processing the discovery of his wife's long-term affair with Lawton Cantrell. Callie had been processing her father's affair, too.

Callie tried phoning again. Surely Ben could garner enough loyalty from the dark depths of his pain to tend to his wife. Callie eyed the suitcase contents hung up in the reeds. Maybe he'd decided the time for understanding was over and kicked her out.

The phone rolled to voicemail again, and Callie left another message as she surveyed the scene. Bless him, Thomas stoically managed in wet clothes and drying mud to take Quincy Kinard's statement. The reporter spoke animated, hands gyrating. Drama personified.

Traffic seemed to run smoothly, making Callie search for whomever kept it flowing without Thomas. Her heart warmed at the welcome sight of Colleton Deputy Don Raysor waving at cars. The rotund, demanding officer had clashed with her when she first set foot on the beach, his stereotypical machismo causing him to suspect her as the culprit in a crime spree. After taking several bullets to his vest in the midst of the case, one nicking him, he'd been on a leave of absence from his co-op arrangement with Edisto PD. He picked the best and worst day to come back, poor Francis's death the keynote to what should have been a hearty welcome for Raysor at the station. She'd even welcome his derogatory woman-in-a-man's-job remarks.

She got up to head in the big man's direction. "Stay put, Sarah. I'll be right back."

But a force enveloped her from the side.

"Dear heavens, I was frightened into a tizzy seeing all this hoopla out here." Five inches taller than Callie, Beverly Cantrell squeezed her daughter again.

They almost never touched.

Beverly's longtime friend Promise Hollister stood at her side, her permanent fixture Tink peering out of the aqua straw tote over Promise's shoulder. The woman never went anywhere without that Yorkie. The dog owned more accessorized purses than Callie had in her entire life.

In her mid-seventies, the white-headed Miss Promise had become Beverly's ornament in her mayoral run in nearby Middleton. The biweekly friend over tea had evolved into a full-time advisor. As the widow of a beloved former South Carolina governor, Miss Promise not only made for great photo ops but also held a wealth of political knowledge.

Callie escaped the embrace. Her mother didn't know Francis,

understandably couldn't care less about Sarah, but Sarah's inference that Beverly Cantrell stirred enough trouble to cause this tragedy raised Callie's ire. Beverly rarely earned the benefit of anyone's doubt. "Sorry, but I can't do this right now, Mother."

Beverly reached to stroke her daughter's cheek when her concern melted, her sharp focus aiming past her daughter into the crowd. "Wait, what's *he* doing here?"

Callie turned. The reporter smiled wide in recognition then turned to answer one of Thomas's questions. "He saved Sarah's life," she said.

Wrinkling her nose, Beverly gave him her back. "He appears wherever I go. A snoop, a busybody."

Not unlike a politician to be concerned about the press. Callie studied Mr. Kinard acting bright-eyed, eager, and feigning empathy. Not to diminish his heroic behavior, she appreciated that as a journalist with a story dropped in his lap, he would welcome the attention, take names, and dig up information while he held the platform, and then go home and publish a story. Reporters . . . carpetbagging charlatans of the higher order.

If he lied in his zeal, she'd skin his hide. Thanks to her father's six-term tenure as mayor of Middleton, Callie still owned stock in influence.

And she was not a fan of paparazzi.

She turned back to her mother, having no time for soapbox drama, his or hers. "Just head home. We need to talk, but I don't have time this minute. This incident—"

"How's Sarah?" Beverly asked, stooping a little to peek in the car. "I actually came to talk to her."

In her mother's wake, Callie leaned in and checked on Sarah as well, who turned aside from them both. "Well, not going to happen today," Callie whispered, standing. "Since when do you talk to Daddy's old mistress anyway? What's going on between you two?"

Beverly straightened, ever vigilant about ears. "I thought we'd make amends."

There were no amends to make. The affair between Beverly's husband and Sarah Rosewood had been tolerated and that was that. At least that's how Beverly had presented the situation to Callie. No love lost, no hatred on reserve. Ben Rosewood held the only grudge, and rightfully so. Beverly's words rang too hollow.

"Sorry, but I have to go, Mother."

"Darling—"

Callie blew out hard. "I lost one of my officers. A good one. Only twenty-six years old."

The mild pout disappeared. "Oh, sorry, dear."

"Drive safe on the way back. Watch for deer."

With no adieu, Beverly and Miss Promise turned and picked their way through the horde.

Having neglected Sarah too long, and unable to reach Ben, Callie returned to the car with one more call to make. She'd speak to Raysor later.

But her call to Seabrook went to voicemail. Officer Mike Seabrook deserved to hear the news of Francis from her, not over the frequencies. "Mike? Call me. Please." She hesitated over how to word the message. "It's urgent." Sighing, she slid the phone in her pocket.

A vee of pelicans coasted overhead, studying the unusual collection of humans where there should be none. A breeze blew across the marsh with a moist, salty aroma. Cars crawled across the causeway, adding gas fumes to the mix. One Highway Patrol officer arrived; the investigative team would appear shortly.

Her cruiser idled, air flowing for her passenger. Callie opened the back door and welcomed the cool blast. "I think that's everything. Where do you want me to take you? Your house? A neighbor? Ms. Hanson's probably home. Ben's not answering."

"Take me home," Sarah replied.

Callie waved at Thomas that she was going, then leaned back in again. "Where's Ben to be so unobtainable?"

"Have no idea."

Callie hesitated at the clipped answer, then climbed in the driver's seat, the uniform sticky but no longer wet. "You sure you're okay? We promised the medics—"

"No," she said. "No doctor."

Callie studied her backseat passenger in the mirror. A quick whoop-whoop on the siren parted the people and cars. "The Highway Patrol will likely come by your place later."

Sarah stared out the side window.

Callie turned onto Jungle Road. More than two hours had passed since the accident, Francis's loss sinking in deeper. His death would devastate Edisto Beach. She blinked hard, knowing that eventually all the swallowing in the world wouldn't hold back the tears.

Damn. Marie. Alone in the station, no doubt the poor woman caught it on the radio. More than any of the other officers, Francis loved most joking with her.

Callie turned into the Rosewood's drive. "Need me to help you up the stairs?" she said, undoing her seatbelt.

"No, I'm fine. Let me out."

"You have a key?"

"They saved my purse and pulled my keys from the ignition. I have the house key."

Understandably, the woman was distraught, but clamming up seemed odd for someone normally sweet. Especially now they were alone without the gawkers. The trauma had her upset, or else something that happened beforehand consumed her attention . . . like Ben. Like Beverly.

While Beverly could spin facts and artfully twist her purpose, Callie saw no reason for her to fabricate a meeting with Sarah, yet the trunk's contents revealed Sarah had no intentions of keeping the appointment. "Where were you headed?"

Sarah's gaze darted to Callie then returned to the window. "Asheville."

"Family?"

"Um, yes."

But Callie knew of no family. Not that there wasn't a distant third cousin or great-aunt somewhere, but in their numerous get-to-know-each-other chats over iced tea, Callie heard no talk of kin. Sarah's niece Brea Jamison had died in front of Callie not long ago, killed at a beach house party gone bad. With her sister dead for years, Sarah spoke about how Brea had been her last relative. Callie couldn't swear to whether that meant the last relative she cared about or the last trace of DNA, but the message seemed clear at the time.

Sarah wasn't connecting glances. Callie's sixth sense said she ran away instead of toward someone, enough to make her lie about her plans. Callie peered hard at the rearview mirror. "What are you afraid of, Sarah?"

Sarah's eyes closed. "I want to go inside. I'm tired. I'm fine."

Callie exited the cruiser and opened Sarah's door. "No, you're not fine. With nobody home—"

"Damn it, Callie, back off!" the woman yelled, pushing Callie aside as she scurried faster than someone her age should up the required two dozen stairs that kept most Edisto beach homes above storm surge level.

Grabbing the car door, Callie righted herself, jolted at the animosity from someone she viewed as a gentle soul. Watching Sarah sort through a soggy purse, Callie dutifully waited until Sarah opened the front door and disappeared.

No judging, she told herself. The poor woman couldn't catch a break. She'd been a wreck since Callie's father died, then barely two months later lost Brea. Luck sure as hell wasn't cutting her any slack.

Only a mile and a half to the station, and Callie drove it slowly, wondering what she wasn't being told, what she was missing about Sarah. What Beverly was up to.

The sun began its descent, and the brightness of the day had reverted to blues, grays, and tans of evening. A musky aroma filled the car, clinging to Callie's uniform and the blanket Sarah left behind. Marie should have gone home, and Callie needed to change. But she bet the single lady hadn't left the station, hoping that somebody on the force remembered she waited patiently at HQ. It's what law enforcement did, administrative or otherwise. She deserved a moment of Callie's attention.

Beverly had probably called Jeb already, unable to contain herself with such news at her fingertips. Callie would have to sift through whatever drama her mother told her son and clarify the truth, not that the reality wasn't horrid enough.

But Beverly meeting with Sarah? Since when?

She needed to talk to both women and be blunt doing it. Callie continued replaying Sarah's conversation, trying to configure the cause and effect of the accident.

Unable to squeeze any more out of what she knew, she radioed Deputy Raysor. "Hey, Don."

"Yeah," he said, a heavy huff blowing into the mic.

"I know." She gave him a moment, taking one herself. "Need you to do something for me real quick while you're at the scene."

"Name it, doll," he said, mindlessly using his old derogatory name for her that had softened into a joke.

"When they haul that car out, check the brake lines for me."

"Seriously?"

The car was an old model. Sarah was overly secretive. Ben unavailable.

"For Francis, Don."

He sighed. "Damn straight, Callie."

Chapter 3

MARIE'S GOT-IT-TOGETHER persona dissolved into Callie's arms as soon as she entered the station. The phone rang unanswered. Gripping her clerk in a sound hug, Callie fought with everything in her to stifle her own trembling.

Visions of Francis underwater continued crowding her mind.

Tightening her embrace, she buried her face in Marie's shoulder. What she wouldn't give for someone to wrap themselves around her and tell her she did the right thing. Because at the moment she blamed herself for stealing precious seconds that could've been used to save her officer.

Callie's cell rang, a simple trill, no longer playing "Dixie" like it did in Boston where she loved to make heads turn. Seabrook calling. Finally.

"Hey, Mike," she answered, stroking Marie's hair once more as the clerk pulled back, wiped her makeup, and returned to her desk.

"What the hell happened, Callie? Francis?" he said, as close to yelling as Seabrook got.

So he heard about the catastrophe from someone else. Not what she'd hoped. Then out of all she wanted to say to him, "Where are you?" fell from her mouth first.

Shock had dissipated between the causeway and the station. Justice took its place, tinged with a desire for revenge. Why wasn't Seabrook at the scene and not on some flippant errand? Sarah wasn't at fault, but Callie wanted to make Francis somebody's fault. Somebody needed to pay.

"I'm in Florence," he said. "How are you? They say you almost drowned. You aspirated water?"

She stiffened. "You spoke to Thomas." The words came out flat.

"Yes, after he called fourteen times and left messages to call him first before I spoke to you. Did you have a doctor check you out, put you on antibiotics?" Then before she could answer, he replied, "Of course you didn't. Tell me you're at home."

"I'm at the office." She turned so the clerk couldn't hear. "Marie was here alone when it happened so I came here. I dropped Sarah at her house on the way." She changed the phone to the other hand, her shoulder aching from the underwater yanks and tugs. "She veered to avoid a deer."

A throbbing started in her neck. Tomorrow the pain would be worse.

"Maybe leave the deer part out when you call the family," he said. "No, let me do it. There's only a grandfather and a girlfriend in Cottageville. Tina, I believe. Francis thought he might propose come Christmas. He—"

"I'll call the family."

"You don't think it best that a person they feel familiar with—"

Absolutely not. "I'd be a schmuck delegating that task. Plus I was there." She coughed, her throat suddenly sore. Images flashed of Francis in the water, on the gurney. "I straightened his collar . . . was the last person to see him alive." *Underwater, his stare wide, crazy scared.*

Seabrook's voice came back firm but coaxing, much like the day she ran up the beach hunting for Jeb, weapon at the ready to defend him against an invisible pursuer. Seabrook talking her down from a panic attack. "Listen, honey," he said, "make the call if you like, but do it from the station. I'll head back. Don't go home, and don't stay by yourself. Besides, I want to check you out. That water—"

"You think I'll take a drink?" Not that she hadn't earned the right.

"I didn't say that."

She lowered her voice. "I'm not stupid, Mike."

Marie came around the counter, purse on her shoulder.

"Hold on a second," Callie said and muted the call. "Marie, you're more than welcome to stay home tomorrow."

Marie strode over and hugged her. "Thanks, Chief," she whispered, then left, meeting the mayor at the door. He held it open for Marie then came in.

Callie wearily held up a finger to Mayor Talbot. "Mike, the mayor just came in."

"Give me a couple hours."

She glanced at the clock. Seven forty-five. Ten wasn't too late. She hoped he drove fast.

She hung up to address her boss with a handshake when a chime indicated a text. Callie tried to subtly check her phone. This was how her schedule would be for days: soothing Edistonians who didn't see catastrophe on their beach. Tending to the bigwigs who'd expect her to carry on and maintain the tourist community as if nothing happened, when instead she wanted to make a monstrous announcement to the whole island, making everyone stop whatever the hell they were doing for ten damn minutes, at least, and respect mortality and the dedication of her man.

Are you ok, Mom? showed on her screen.

Damn, she should've called Jeb. Turning aside, she held up a finger. "Sorry, Mayor, my son just heard."

"By all means."

She typed, *Yes, I'm fine. Don't worry. We'll talk at home.*

When she accepted her position, she assured Jeb that police work on Edisto Beach was first grade compared to Boston, where he'd developed a hate for his parents' professions as a city detective and a Deputy U.S. Marshall. His father died because of one of his mother's cases. Of course he hated cops.

She prayed no one told him she almost drowned, though in all likelihood somebody took pictures. She hated smartphones as much as reporters.

Through the glass door, light waned outside. After eight p.m. She needed to go home. No, she wanted to go home, but somehow she didn't see that happening soon. Her main priority was calling Francis's grandfather before he heard via the grapevine. Walterboro wasn't that far, and the coroner might get to him first.

"How are you doing, Callie?" Mayor Talbot jumped into the conversation bombastic and in charge when she put aside her phone. A small comb-over dropped into his view, his words spilling in one long-winded sentence like he'd been holding it for far too long. "When should we honor Francis? After the funeral? I hate to wait too many days. Should we hold it on the beach? In one of the churches? That might be a dilemma depending on what denomination he was. How many—"

Callie held up her palm, hardly hearing him over the pulse in her ears. "Mayor. Please! Give me to tomorrow. Francis's family hasn't been contacted, and I'm still in wet clothes." Rubbing her temple, veins thrummed a current under her fingertips.

"Oh, yes. Quite understandable." He pulled at his Hawaiian shirt in embarrassment, the floral wardrobe his standard wear. "Tomorrow's fine." He turned to leave but held back when a familiar person entered the lobby, giving him unspoken permission to stay.

Brice LeGrand, a member of town council. These two men knew

her officer longer and deeper than she had. Why did that make her feel negligent?

Not surprisingly, Brice took over. He'd been the lone dissenting voice when Mayor Talbot proposed hiring Callie. She never understood why, hadn't had the inclination to ask. Since he'd been around Edisto since the dawn of time, she assumed it had something to do with her parents, hoping to hell it wasn't about her being a female cop, or their truce would blossom into war.

A belly softened by late middle-age and chamber parties hung a couple inches over the nautical web belt holding up his khaki shorts, a polo shirt snug in its grasp. Sun and liquor had given his nose a permanent bronze darker than the rest of his profile. His swagger silently coerced his acquaintances into following his lead. "This is devastating," he said, his tone smacking of accusation. "We've never lost a public servant."

Callie tightened her stomach, staving the assault. "The public servant had a name, and of course it's devastating."

Talbot launched into an oration about Francis's attributes, but Brice ignored him and focused on Callie, as if maintaining his stare would unnerve her.

It only served to stiffen her resolve. Entrenched in Edisto, this man was familiar with where the deepest of graves held which bodies. He was the last man to show weakness to.

The station door opened again, and September heat pushed into the room. Beverly and Miss Promise entered, the former striding, the latter in her baby-step mode.

"How are you holding up, dear?" her mother began, wading past the men as if her presence trumped theirs.

They'd already been down this road. Callie darted her gaze toward the others in hope her mother got the message the timing was wrong. Beverly's cologne wafted over the crowd.

"Doing the best I can, Mother."

Beverly glanced over at Miss Promise. "No matter how old they get, they need their mothers. Told you we needed to check on her."

Oh good heavens. Callie motioned toward the exit. "Go home, and I'll call tomorrow."

Miss Promise's glance seemed to measure how Beverly replied. "She had to check on you first, dear," Miss Promise said.

Funny how the men stopped speaking and froze reverently.

However, Callie knew Miss Promise's ways were far from innocent.

Often decked in soft colors to camouflage her approach, peach today, the governor's widow spoke her mind in short, conservative phrases, making people hush and listen to her rationed wisdom. She was a queen bee, accustomed to the days when politics crowned winners.

As the acting mayor of Middleton, Beverly addressed the man she would presume her equal. "Callie's well-being is what's most important, wouldn't you say, Mayor Talbot? She's already done so much for Edisto, and you don't want to lose this gem." She dabbed her lashes.

Every community had one of those older women who could throw her weight around and stifle the power base. Beverly was Middleton's, but the fact she'd owned a vacation home on Edisto for decades gave her a semi-status on Edisto as well.

When Callie told her mother to go home, she meant Middleton home, and she darn sure didn't mean the station. Talbot seemed stymied by drama Callie didn't need, but Brice appeared unfazed, redirecting his laser focus on her mother. There had to be a past there.

In a mental triage Callie chose to deal with the mayor first. No brainer. He hired her. Touching his elbow, she nodded him off to the side, but Brice retreated with them.

Brice started in on her. "This is horrible, Chief Morgan."

The mayor frowned and fell into a lobby chair. "Brice, stop it."

The ladies across the room pivoted, listening.

"No, that's okay, Mayor." Callie stared straight at the councilman. "I couldn't agree with you more, Brice. It's worse than horrible. I wish I could arrest someone for Francis's death, but it was an accident, a valiant effort to save Sarah Rosewood. He died a hero. This beach needs to heal, not fester over it."

He seemed to ponder his next words, animosity front and center.

"And don't blame Sarah," Callie said. "She's blaming herself enough as it is."

"The fire department should've taken over. He might've lived," the councilman flatly stated.

"Brice!" chided the mayor.

Callie was fast to step closer. On the tip of her tongue balanced the words for the councilman to bite her, go to hell, shut his fat mouth and leave her station, but she couldn't. Not without giving him ammunition to debate louder in front of these people and solve nothing. Instead, she released her words softly, to give him leeway to back down, too. "He would've drowned either way."

"Mayor," she then added, "I'll get with you tomorrow or the next day about what to—"

But Brice couldn't recede. "Talbot won't say it, but I will. The seconds they spent hauling your butt out could've been used saving Francis."

Callie sucked in to fire back, but the reality of the words out of someone else's mouth, words that had already set up shop in her head, struck her dumb. Beverly, however, appeared quickly and beat her to the punch. "Don't make me air your filthy laundry in here. We don't need your attitude amidst this tragedy, Brice."

"Nor your arrogance, Beverly," he replied.

Beverly's chin rose. "If not for your daddy, you wouldn't be on town council. You're nothing like him, and Edisto deserves better."

Brice bent at his rotund waist. "If not for your dead husband, you wouldn't be Middleton mayor . . . excuse me, *interim* mayor."

What the hell was this? Embarrassed, angry at whatever this *tete-a-tete* was, Callie'd had enough of it. "Mother? Go home."

"But—"

"Mr. LeGrand? You can take your disrespectful behavior outside my station."

Brice reddened.

She turned. "And Mayor? I suggest you be the one to contact Francis's family about a service, but not tonight. First, let me call them about his death. This"—she panned a gaze around the cluster of folks—"is not the way to cope."

Talbot's mouth mashed, accepting the dressing down.

"Agreed?" she asked, calmer.

The mayor suggested they wait to the morrow, like he was the voice of reason.

Miss Promise observed.

"Good night, then," Callie said, seeing they needed a catalyst to leave.

They almost bumped into each other to the exit, accommodating the women first. At the door, however, Brice hung a step behind. "The town will put this on you, Ms. Morgan."

She bristled, hot despite the air conditioned goose bumps under her damp clothes. She strode over and gripped the door, hinting at the idea he could leave, envisioning her black-sneakered shoe across his backside in assistance. "Life is precious, Mr. LeGrand."

"It's Brice."

She didn't give him permission to use *Callie*.

The mayor peered back in over Brice's shoulder. "I'm grateful you took the job, Callie. Thanks for all you do." A typical political afterthought.

She told herself not to take the mayor's reply personal though she couldn't say the same about Brice LeGrand.

Francis would've laughed at the temptation to kick the councilman's ass out the door. And would've enjoyed that she dressed down the powers of Edisto.

She locked up to avoid any more drop-ins. Alone, spent, and reluctant to perform this last task, Callie moved to her office, closed the door, and dialed Francis's grandfather.

Pushing composure into her tone, Callie spoke of Francis's valor, his commitment to the force, and the safety of its inhabitants and visitors. She admired his law enforcement skills and his congenial spirit, making him a popular personality people preferred to see in their time of need. She didn't want to stop, but the grandfather's attempt to remain strong quickly broke, ending in a slurry of tears, moans, and a congested "Thank you, Chief Morgan."

Someone banged on the door. She ignored them, head cradled in her hands, the noise in her head matched only by the beating in her chest. Anyone she needed to see would have a key. Anyone needing assistance could dial 911. Her son had her cell.

The drawer dragged more than she remembered, as if squealing a warning, but she didn't care. With a fell swoop, she opened the bottle, took a long, hard iced-tea-sorta chug, and recapped it, the dark liquor deliciously burning on its way down. Before she repeated the gesture, she shut the drawer, the evidence disappearing, no damage done.

Lights out, she left a sign on the door that said she went home and preferred not to be disturbed. Call 911.

The moon was almost new, leaving the night black as pitch. She paused in the tiny parking lot, half expecting Seabrook to slide in on the gravel apologetic, rushing to embrace her and lend his shoulder to cry into. But all that reached out to her in the dark was the surf's churning echoing up Murray Street from the beach, the crickets' song deafening from the wax myrtle thickets.

With a huge inhale, she welcomed the salt air. She loved this island, now as much as ever. Leaving Boston to come home to heal, she left a wake of arrests, solved cases, and a string of recognition and honors. Not that she hadn't brought the natural intuition with her. She only preferred it not be needed here.

She entered her cruiser and sat a second, the night coastal breezes shaking fronds in the palmettoes. Edisto was to be her simpler life. Damn it, she was sick of death. She'd seen more than her fair share but never so much as she'd experienced crammed in the four months since she'd moved here. Residents had no idea what she'd unearthed, solved, and made disappear on this island. The mayor and town council knew but weren't about to make that information public.

Brice LeGrand had lived on this beach longer than Callie'd been alive, and if he labeled her a magnet for disaster, then it wouldn't be long before he convinced the store owners and natives that she was bad for business. Her famous mayor daddy wasn't here to protect her anymore, and she wasn't sure her mother would know where to start despite her bluster. Seabrook could only do so much. She needed to stand on her own and lead this community through this ordeal, her head held high.

Rolling open the front seat windows, she took the cruiser down Murray Road to Palmetto Boulevard instead of turning left on Myrtle Street toward her home. Palmetto paralleled the water, and she yearned to more clearly hear rollers curling into themselves and melting back into the sea. Let that humid air fill her hair.

She turned off Palmetto to head to her own Chelsea Morning. Word was people arrived on this beach leaving the negative of their lives on the other side of the big bridge. Her job was to make them feel they'd succeeded.

Guess that didn't apply to the chief of police.

Chapter 4

CALLIE'S PHONE read almost 10:00 p.m. on a long-ass day. She thought Raysor would've called by now about the condition of Sarah's Volvo. Amazing how Raysor had crossed from adversary to ally in a couple of months. He'd memorized the Lowcountry region from each creek to every three-hundred-year-old oak, having traipsed the territory since a tyke.

Callie slowed in front of Sarah's house, hoping to find Ben's car. No luck. However, Beverly Cantrell's white BMW parked in Chelsea Morning's driveway two doors down. *Damn.*

The beach house once belonged to Callie's parents, but after she'd lived with them for an impossible year, they deeded it to her, a move she despised at the time. She'd changed the locks, but Beverly demanded a key, and Callie gave her one, sensing she'd regret it somewhere down the road.

Ten was rather late for her mother to be out considering she had a forty-five-minute drive back to Middleton. Without a bright moon, the highway lay pitch and desolate.

Her father had died on that road.

Callie strode inside, Beverly abruptly ceasing a chat with Miss Promise in the living room. Miss Promise had assumed a prim position in the recliner, leaving the footrest down.

"Is Jeb home?" Callie asked.

Her lanky, six-foot boy blindsided her in a hug that lifted her to her toes.

She returned the squeeze and pried him off. "I told you I was fine."

"So you say." Jeb held his phone inches from her view, flipping through pictures with his thumb. There Callie being passed to the shore, wearing the oxygen mask, tended by a medic, wet and dripping leaning over Francis.

A pang of distress penetrated to her core. "Put it away."

He did, but he also embraced her again. With events like this, he'd never go to college, having surmised recently that his place was at home, in his father's shoes, to protect her. Nice in theory; horrible for his future.

As Jeb released her, Beverly tried to take his place, but Callie dodged the trap and moved to the kitchen. "We need to talk, Mother."

"Why didn't you tell me you almost died?" her mother censured, following.

"Because I'm not into sensationalism."

Beverly drew snappy retorts out of Callie. This time, however, Callie tried to put herself in her mother's place. Difficult. Not only did mother and daughter not touch, but they rarely spoke the same language. Lawton served as their mediator, but since his death, they'd reached a truce of sorts. Stilted at best.

"Miss Promise, need something to drink?" Callie asked, peering back into the living room. Tink poised alert in Miss Promise's lap, his tote on the rug. No leash. Callie scanned the floor. "Has Tink been outside? It's rather late for Miss Promise, isn't it?"

Miss Promise crossed her legs at the ankle. "Dearie, I'm not in a home yet, so can the curfew talk."

Dearie. The old woman sounded like Beverly. Or did Beverly sound like her? Her mother had politically educated herself at the feet of this ex-first lady, so who could define where the habits began and ended.

Pouring herself a tonic and lime, her best effort to taste gin, Callie flopped on the sofa and tucked her feet under her. Her weariness bled into the cushion, and she allowed her head to fall back.

She enjoyed seclusion, having developed a shroud of it after John died. Tonight, however, she wasn't sure she wanted to be alone, but Beverly and Miss Promise weren't her idea of company. Seabrook was.

Holding her, using that doctor voice of his to soothe her. And as untimely as the thought was, she'd let him into her bed.

For the first time.

She checked the time on the cable box. His two hours had come and gone.

Stretching her legs out, feeling a bone pop, Callie wasn't phoning the man a dozen more times. While she wished he were here, he wasn't. She'd hoped to question Sarah before Beverly, but she couldn't.

Callie raised her head and went with the opportunity within reach. "Mother, when did you first arrive on Edisto today?"

"I don't recall exactly." She looked at Miss Promise. "One, two?"

In time to see Sarah before the accident. "And why were you here?"

Beverly's smile spread wide and saccharin. "To see you, honey. A mother's instinct . . ."

Callie shook her head. "Stop it. You saw Sarah. What was that about?"

"Oh," Beverly said, matter of fact. "Yes. Just social."

"You're full of crap. What generated the meeting?" Callie turned to Miss Promise. "Excuse my language, ma'am."

Miss Promise sighed and glanced up to the ceiling. "I wasn't born yesterday. I'm not a prude either. If you must curse, my dear, go for the fucking gold."

Callie re-swallowed a mouthful of tonic she almost sprayed.

Jeb's eyes widened the size of silver dollars. "And . . . on that note I'm going to bed."

Reaching out, Callie brushed his arm. "Good night, son."

Beverly scooted over, not to be outdone. "Night, sweet boy."

Switching over to give his grandmother a brief embrace, Jeb left the room chuckling. "Y'all have fun."

Beverly grinned until he left their sight, then gave a huff. "Thank goodness he's gone to bed. I don't like discussing this sort of business in front of him."

"I'll bet," Callie said.

"This running for your father's old office has proven a challenge. Against Hoyt Bishop, no less."

Callie knew of the businessman, a strong-willed and outspoken individual with financial ties to many of Middleton's activities. "What does that have to do with Sarah?"

Beverly readjusted her skirt in her seat. "Well, Sarah and I need to be on the same wavelength about your father."

Callie frowned. "You ordered her to keep the skeletons in the closet."

"She'll be on the record as a family friend," her mother explained. "I've already spoken to Ben Rosewood, and I needed to set Sarah straight."

Callie's mouth fell open. "You had the balls to meet with Ben? About Daddy's relationship with his wife? Geez, Mother, when was this?"

"Yes, she did," Miss Promise surprisingly stated. "Weeks back. At my recommendation. Mrs. Rosewood's dodged us up to now, but we're here to make sure she keeps her mouth shut about her affair and see that her husband doesn't ruin things."

We, like a force.

Sarah was rattled and secretive. Ben gone. Less of a mystery now.

Promise Hollister milked her reputation, with style and a hint of Machiavellian deceit. Her husband had been the most loved governor in the state's history, and she quite the revered first lady, but Callie suspected a devious streak had served up some serious damage in her day.

"Sarah doesn't want her life detailed in a newspaper any more than Mother does," Callie said. "Rightfully, Ben holds a grudge, but neither would talk about something so personal."

"Regardless, he's taken care of," Miss Promise said.

Callie leaned forward in her pretzel position. "Meaning . . .?"

The lady gently waved out, as if brushing crumbs.

Beverly took the cue. "Heavens, Callie, the woman had a thirty-year affair with your father. Ben was ready to serve her with papers."

"Why now? Why after so long, and especially since the other man is dead? It's none of your business, though. Let the poor man alone to cope."

With a sigh that could ripple curtains, Beverly shook her head in disbelief at her daughter's naiveté. "Legal papers might name your father. I couldn't have that."

"Oh my goodness, Mother," Callie said. "You're the victim. Wouldn't that just propel your popularity in the polls?"

"We don't do polls," Beverly replied. "But Hoyt Bishop . . . Brice LeGrand . . . they . . . anyway, I'll not be having Lawton's name dragged through the mud," she exclaimed after the momentary stutter.

"Humph," Miss Promise grumbled from her tufted seat.

Callie reared back on the sofa. "Maybe you should've thought of that years back when you agreed to an open marriage."

"Amen to that," Miss Promise added.

Callie recalled almost falling off the barstool in her kitchen when her mother raised the curtain on the Cantrell marriage. Beverly's beau had died after only a few years, but Lawton carried his affair to his grave.

Another thing . . . Miss Promise seemed to be holding the reins quite tightly on Beverly. Callie ordinarily couldn't see her mother needing a handler, but with Lawton gone, was Beverly running unchecked? Or insecure?

"Who expected your father would suddenly die?" Beverly continued, a bit of fluster in her tone. "If he were mayor, none of this would be a problem."

"Shame on Daddy, huh?"

Beverly narrowed her eyes. "I'm protecting your father's Middleton legacy as well as your name, ensuring his plans for the town continue under my administration. We can't let social mores interfere with community growth."

There was a reason Callie lived in a different town from her mother. "Why did Sarah pack suitcases and break the speed limit to leave after your meeting?"

Anxiousness crossed her mother's countenance. "Maybe she had a spat with Ben."

"You scared her," Callie said.

"No, I didn't, dear."

"You threatened her, and you were headed back to see her again."

Beverly gasped. "I did not threaten her."

"You're carrying Miss Promise around like a hood ornament, so I assume she's counseling you on how to take your political steps." Callie leaned toward Miss Promise. "You told her to control the Rosewoods. Only I think Mother's heavy-handedness probably made matters worse, and you came along to mend the damage. What did you threaten to do to them?"

"Nothing!" Beverly exclaimed. "We just talked."

Miss Promise, however, never flinched. "We've been meaning to speak to you as well, Callie."

Despite the woman being two generations older, Callie let her manners drop. "How dare you have the audacity to come in my house and attempt to groom me in how to behave? Especially today."

"Just keep a low profile and write your tickets," the little lady said, her aging voice cracking. "Protect the turtles and keep the beach safe and you'll be fine."

"I'll do what I damn well please, ma'am."

"You've always been a contrarian when it comes to politics, Callie," Miss Promise said from a sideways glance. "You forget how long I've known you, child."

Callie noticed her mother's uncharacteristic silence.

A shrug slid Beverly's necklace sideways, catching the pearl on a button.

"Don't shrug, Beverly," Miss Promise scolded. "And fix your pearls."

"Screw your pearls, Mother." Callie leaned forward, elbows on her knees. "I'll find out the rest of the story tomorrow from Sarah, and believe me, I'll get the facts. But since you're airing dirty laundry, what's the beef between you and Brice?"

"He holds different political views."

"Edisto is nonpartisan. Frankly, so is Middleton."

Her mother clammed up in a silent reply that the topic wasn't open for discussion.

Callie finished her drink and placed the glass on the coffee table. She couldn't help but see Sarah's wreck in the marsh as a metaphor, a sign of more mud-slinging things to come. What scared her was her mother's involvement. Callie so missed her father.

Beverly moved to Miss Promise, taking her barely touched tea glass from the end table. She returned to the kitchen to put both of their glasses in the sink. "But this brings us to why I'm here. I want you to do something about this reporter."

"He is becoming quite the nuisance," Miss Promise added.

Callie shook her head. "Mother, I'm not your bodyguard."

Beverly squinted. "Don't sass me. Don't you have ways to stop people from stalking other people? He's at every event I attend."

"You're a public official. Your events are public. You don't campaign in Edisto anyway, but what do you expect?"

"He was on Edisto, Callie." Beverly lowered herself back into her seat. "My trip to meet Sarah wasn't public information. Can you search my car and make sure there's no bug on it?"

Callie hollered, "Good *heavens*, Mother." She glanced at Miss Promise, halfway expecting a rebuke, not surprised to see the lady's lids finally closed. Callie lowered her voice. "He hasn't done anything for me to stop. Maybe he's a good tail. Maybe you talk too much. I don't really care."

Then Callie remembered Quincy Kinard's too-personal remark as he offered his card. *Don't let this send you back to the bottle.*

He'd arrived on Edisto before Beverly, seemingly the only witness to Sarah leaving the road. Had he arrived early enough to tail Lawton's ex-lover? If so, to what end? Seemed rather extreme activity to land a story.

Then Callie remembered Princess Diana.

"I'll check him out," she finally said, rising to end the conversation, not discarding the fact Beverly indeed spoke too much. Callie also wouldn't put it past Ben to use a reporter like this, a cowardly, back-door endeavor to strike back at his wife's dead lover and all that Lawton loved.

Beverly almost levitated to her feet, always attentive to her posture. "One more thing. I've asked Jeb to make a few appearances with me. He's so strikingly handsome on camera."

"What? No. Don't you dare involve him—" But Callie stopped herself. Jeb would be madder at her for speaking for him than he'd ever be at some silly request by his grandmother. He was eighteen and reminded Callie of it often. The child had money in the bank thanks to his father's and then his grandfather's deaths. She keenly hoped the autumn lull in his fishing charter business would entice him to enter college in the spring. Butting heads could only sabotage that hope.

"I could use you, too, dear," Beverly said. "A few campaign posters maybe?"

"No, Mother." Callie tilted her head toward Miss Promise, who'd slumped, her proper posture relinquishing to senior fatigue. Tink napped in her lap. "Take her home. Watch who you confide in, and for Pete's sake, be careful driving up that dark highway amongst those oaks."

Beverly touched Miss Promise, who sprang to attention, pretending she hadn't dozed.

Seeing her guests to the door, Callie sensed the mayoral election drove every molecule in Beverly's body, the exaggerated gusto a distorted way of honoring Lawton. No telling what she'd do in the interim until the title was hers. Especially having Miss Promise at the helm.

"Call me when you have a service set up for your deputy," Beverly said over her shoulder after settling Miss Promise in the front seat.

"Yes, ma'am." Callie waved once in good-bye. "And Francis was an officer, not a deputy," she added under her breath as she returned inside.

She hadn't eaten, wasn't sure she wanted to. With it after eleven, she could afford to wait till morning. Though exhausted, she worried today's event would jump in line with the slideshow of life experiences that haunted her each night. The Boston fire, the Russian hit man, even Stan.

Stan, her grizzly Boston boss she confided in. The man who'd had beers with her husband John and participated in much of what was the great life she once lived. The man who flew down in June to check on her mental well-being, urging her to shed the self-doubt and confront herself. The man she'd almost slept with, leaving them both uncertain about where their friendship stood.

Cop-to-cop, he would expect her to call after such a day as this, but Stan's wife wouldn't approve of such a late night call. She wouldn't approve of any call from Callie

Callie wouldn't think of Stan if Seabrook were here.

She caught herself thinking a lot of Seabrook these days.

Wandering to the screened porch, insides churning from the day, she parked her backside in her Adirondack chair where she did most of her thinking, unwinding, dissecting her lot in life, but she stood as soon as her back hit the wood. A drink of some sort was inherent to pondering on a beach porch.

Back in the kitchen, she stooped to study the refrigerator's contents. Tea and water. Some of Jeb's Cokes. Tonic. Her gaze strayed to the left of her fridge where the glasses stood like soldiers on an eye-level shelf. Though she couldn't see it, she knew what they guarded. A half-used bottle of her father's Maker's Mark, along with a short note from her son telling her not to touch it.

She pushed aside a glass. For this very reason, Seabrook had asked her not to go home. Yet where was he?

She gripped the bottle's neck, dripping with the signature red rubber. After a quick glance for Jeb, she poured one finger's worth into her dirty glass. Quickly she resealed the top, set the note in place, returned the low ball glasses to their vigil.

If Seabrook couldn't keep his promise, neither would she.

She lost an officer, almost died trying to save him. If that didn't warrant Seabrook's prompt return to Edisto, then what did?

Made her want to call Stan even more.

She downed the bourbon in one toss about the time her phone rang. "Hello?"

"It's Don," Deputy Raysor said, his words spoken hushed. "I figured you'd want me to call."

Callie stiffened. "You're right. Find anything?"

"Brake lines were cut. Suspect anybody?"

Ben? Quincy? Her own mother? She had no clue about Brice LeGrand's role.

"Not yet, Don, but give me a few days and I just might." A cold, familiar fear traveled along her spine, Don's message the proof of the foul play she sensed. "Keep this between us for the time being, okay?"

"I can't control the Highway Patrol's report, doll."

"No, but we don't have to spill it in advance, do we? This is our beach, not theirs."

Chapter 5

THREE REFILLS FROM her father's hidden bottle of Maker's Mark let Callie finally push the accident out of her head and drift to sleep in her Adirondack chair on the porch. She awoke with a crick in her neck around three. Before Francis could flash back into her semi-consciousness, she stumbled inside to the air-conditioning, ignoring how sticky she was from the nighttime humidity, stripped, and fell into bed. She wasn't ready to address the day. Not yet. Not . . . quite . . . yet.

She dozed, but as dawn penetrated her room, the white on her bedspread brightening against the chartreuse ferns, her mind turned over like a cold engine. Rolling to her back, a twinge in her shoulder, she stared at the ceiling fan slowly circling, a few tears rolling down her temples to soak into the pillow. Such an emptiness. Such a stupid loss of a young life. Slamming her fist into the bed, she choked on tears. *Goddamn it, Francis.*

And damn you, Seabrook. He'd never disappointed her so deeply. What was so damn hard about making a simple phone call? Or showing up? He had to realize how upset she was.

She pardoned herself from the run on the beach, a ritual she'd only managed to return to with her ribs healed. Then she changed her mind, not wanting Francis to be an excuse. Wiping the moisture off her cheek with a knuckle, she arose and freshened with a wet washcloth, trussed up her sneakers, and jogged down Chelsea Morning's steps. She veered left on Jungle Road, then right down Atlantic southward to the beach, feet and mind weighted by yesterday's events. By the time she reached the water's edge, however, she countered and pummeled the sand doing double-time, stretching out at a pace she wouldn't be able to keep long.

At a mile the sun cleared the horizon, turning scattered wisps of clouds lilac and creamsicle orange, allowing the surf to change from grey to its proper dark blue. Gulls glided and dove, targeting each other, more energetic than they would be in their laidback evening dance at dusk.

Having left her mp3 player at the house, she jogged to simply sort her priorities. Most of the day would be divided into two categories:

Sarah's accident and Francis's death. Finding answers and soothing nerves.

Sarah topped her to-do list. Ms. Rosewood ought to be stumbling over herself trying to aid the police, make sense of things . . . not hide. A man died for her.

Then there was Seabrook. What was more important than loss of life?

To heck with Beverly, though. For now. It wasn't like she was running for the presidency.

The roar of the surf made Callie's steps soundless, her thoughts louder. Two and a half weeks on the job, and she'd lost an officer. Edisto hadn't sacrificed an officer in its entire history, and the first female chief had to be the one to break the record.

She sniffled. Salty breezes began to clear her sinuses, but nothing could assuage the guilt clinging to her like the muggy air.

Sarah lived. Francis died. And somebody had to be disappointed at that freakish turn of events, because she suspected it was meant to be the other way around. Crime was for people who lived across the big bridge on the mainland. But whether the natives liked it or not, the brake lines were cut on Edisto. She didn't want to go down that path, but one of them might be a frustrated, unfulfilled killer.

She passed a tall, scrawny surf fisherman, white tee-shirt, cutoff jeans, bucket and cooler at his feet, sunglasses protecting him from the glare beginning to bounce off the undulating waves. A cigarette dangled from his lip as he cast his line with the slickness of someone raised on the coast. They didn't exchange greetings. She didn't know him. He probably knew her, though. Everybody seemed to know her, and if they didn't before, they would soon enough.

In one instant, that glorious high from accepting the shiny new badge had been engulfed into the pluff mud off the causeway.

Since the incident, the tide had gone out, come in, and presently worked its way out again, leaving her a good hard surface. Kicking her heels, she pushed her pace, shoving dark visions into some distant compartment, daring her body to give its personal best for the four miles, as if to do less was to shortchange her officer. She plunged out a harsh breath to make room for a deeper one. Everything would be about Francis in her mind for a while.

Like everything had been about John after he died.

Like everything had been about Papa Beach after his murder.

Her father after his car crumpled into a hundred-year-old oak on Highway 61.

Where the hell was her second wind? It felt like she had one lung.

Francis was an officer she'd met only four months earlier, broken bread with maybe five times. Not someone close. Three years into police service. Twenty-six years old. Loved vinegar-based barbecue sauce instead of Carolina mustard. Dated some little slip of a girl in Cottageville. Became a cop because his grandfather had been one in Walterboro.

Get your head on straight.

The world was about to beat on her door, and how the hell was she supposed to act? Show emotion because he worked for her? Not show emotion because she hadn't been there as long as anyone else? Be firm or release her feelings front and center for the public? Give comfort? Be comforted?

At the end of mile two, ragged gasps penance for the pace, she continued. It was in the high seventies, humidity low. She ought to be able to go on forever.

"Callie!"

Slowing to a jog, her legs trotted in place a few seconds then stopped. She stooped over with palms on her knees, then found herself coughing.

Dressed for work, Officer Seabrook caught up to her, blond hair blowing. His house on Palmetto Boulevard didn't front the ocean but instead sat across the road. An empty lot on the beach side gave him a clear shot of the Atlantic.

See you in the AM. You need your rest so I won't disturb you. Sorry I'm late.

After one stinking text in the middle of the night, he chose to wait and see if she jogged by this morning?

She let him come to her, acting like she worked to slow her heartrate. He rubbed her back, then reached around for her shoulder, making her turn to him. "Did you get my text?"

"Yes. Three hours later than when you promised to return."

"Yeah." He studied her. "I'm sorry."

She wanted to fall against his chest, be comforted, but damn him for abandoning her.

"I swear, I wish I'd been there, honey," he pleaded and drew her to him, running fingers over her sweaty hair. "I get what you're thinking. It doesn't matter whose watch it happened under; it wasn't your fault. Him being such a good kid makes it hurt more is all."

Shut up, she wanted to say, *you failed me*, but his fresh shower smell sank into her, a comfort she tried to resist. A moment later she drew back. Regardless of her disgruntlement with him, he was who she talked to. And he was always so damn understanding.

"I needed you, Mike. The first day you aren't there, and this happens. Somebody will want to blame someone. You understand how this plays out. I'm that someone."

Morning breezes whipped wisps into his eyes. His shades reflected the surf. "I doubt they blame you, Callie. We'll deal with it, and everyone will adjust. But for now it's about Francis for a week or two. All about him, to give everyone closure." He glanced at his watch. "Let me drive you home on my way in."

She stood in place, and he halted mid-turn at the resistance. *What the hell?* He hadn't given one bit of explanation.

"Where were you?" she asked.

"I figured we'd cover it over lunch."

She couldn't read him, and for a second she considered another woman. They hadn't known each other long enough to be exclusive, and goodness gracious, they had too much baggage between them to call theirs an easy relationship. But Seabrook seemed smitten with her, and she didn't find him uncomfortable at all. While this was not the time to ponder affairs of the heart, it pissed her off that he chose not to return to her side—either the girlfriend or the police chief side—when he was sorely needed.

It hurt way more than she expected.

Her fists found their way to her hips. "I'll take the explanation *now*, please."

He worked his mouth, teeth tight behind his lips. With a glance around for ears, he said, "I'm running leads on my wife's killer."

Callie almost doubted her hearing and fell a half-step back. He never spoke about the eight-year-old case that destroyed his life as a doctor and turned him into a cop. She never asked. Her raw spot about John could only be discussed at the right time, with the right person. Seabrook had heard some of that past. She'd been waiting so badly to be that person for him in return. This was new trust, a gateway to their future relationship.

"I've had feelers out for years," he said, "and a guy at county lockup contacted me a little over two weeks ago. One of their revolving door offenders gave him a three-month-old lead while jockeying for privileges."

She reached for his sleeve. "Oh my goodness, Mike. That's . . .

tremendous. Is there any substance to it? How well do you trust this correctional officer? More importantly, how can you trust this lead? You said it yourself, your snitch is a repeat offender."

He lifted the sunglasses and stared at her hard but with a spark of eagerness. "He gave enough detail to make it believable. I've been hunting him." No wonder Seabrook wanted to wait for another time. Every muscle in him tensed, like stiffening enabled him to speak. "The guy said his bunkmate claimed he stole one earring as a trophy, recalled what she wore."

Callie's pulse thumped in her neck. This they shared—loss of a spouse to murderous scum. His wife raped and strangled. Her husband shot and burned in their home. Late at night, when she had nothing else to hold her attention, Callie wondered if this was her connection with Seabrook, a link so incredibly strong, a random similarity so powerful that it diluted their interpretation of affection. A need for understanding each other's plight overwhelming love, an emotion they weren't sure they could recognize anymore. "What's his name?" she asked. "What'd you learn?"

He sandwiched her head, desperation in his gaze. "You understand why I didn't show yesterday, right? You of all people—"

But Francis died.

She placed her hands softly over his. "Of course, Mike. How could I not?"

Her touch seemed to give him the nudge to continue. "The guy only had a nickname, Pittstop."

"Surely they can identify—"

He nodded and gripped her fingers. "That's why I was so late. That's why I took off last Thursday. It's why I come in tired. Two weeks ago I visited the officer on his shift. In between his duties, he helped me connect dots and pull up information, dates, full name, and a rap sheet. Roman McGee. He's on parole, living in Florence. I've spoken with the parole officer, and I'm checking out his hangouts and learning his habits." His mouth flatlined. "I got your calls, but I was so far. I . . . guess I made a choice."

Yes, he did. But Callie saw him as the biggest of the officers, the only one medically trained, the one most able to save Francis.

Another day chasing his wife's killer wouldn't have mattered.

But he couldn't have predicted Francis, either.

"Come on," she said, resigned. They trudged up the dune toward the nearest beach access, his reach around her shoulder.

She'd have to get over this feeling that Francis may have died because Seabrook took a day off. Or was it he could have saved Francis when she couldn't?

Seabrook was the most responsible man she had. Finding a spouse's killer created urges no one could understand, until left horribly alone in that pain. The guy who killed John rotted in the ground. Or maybe his mob family cremated him. She didn't care other than he was dead as dirt.

"Let's get through today then do dinner tonight. My place," Seabrook said. "I'm excited to go over this in detail with you."

They peered both ways on Palmetto, traffic almost nonexistent. "Let the day play out, first," she said. "I need to fill you in about Sarah Rosewood's accident. It's unofficially attempted murder."

"Raysor phoned me. Cut brake lines? What is she saying about it?"

Thomas called him. Raysor called him. Callie called him, too, but he spoke to the others first. And second. Leaving her only a text.

"I'm speaking with her this morning," Callie said. "We found out about the brakes after I dropped her off at home last night." She let out a deep, cleansing sigh to right her head. "The mayor wants a recognition event for Francis. Brice LeGrand is trying to make me negligent in the accident." She peered up at him. "Is there a history between him and my mother? You know him better than I do."

"No idea."

They walked to his drive where the patrol car waited. "Nothing adversarial?" she asked.

Seabrook shrugged.

"Anyway, Raysor's coming in today, but you probably already heard that," she said. "He was there last night. He looks good."

Seabrook opened his passenger door, missing the tiny barb. "It'll be great to have him back." He allowed a smile. "They ought to charge admission to watching how you two will function, you being his superior and all."

"I think more people are wondering how you and I will function, Doc."

"I have no aspiration to be in your shoes, m'lady," he said, holding the door. "But Raysor? There's more stubbornness there, if you get my message."

Regardless of the bluster, she didn't expect the middle-aged, puffy-cheeked deputy to give her much trouble. Both had almost died by the same man, the Russian she'd killed the second week she was on Edisto. They had an unspoken camaraderie.

She reached up and around Seabrook's neck, pulling him to her for a kiss. "I missed you last night. Was sort of hoping you'd stay."

He hesitated at the invitation then kissed her back. "And I should've been there. Won't happen again."

He closed her door and walked around the patrol car to get in. A mile later, he dropped her off at Chelsea Morning.

"Go on to the office." She leaned down, hands on the door and the roof. "I'm taking a shower then heading to Sarah's." Callie wanted to speak to Ben as well, sift through Beverly's mixture of fact and fiction. "Make a copy of the causeway cam footage before the Highway Patrol asks for it, please. And if Brice LeGrand shows himself, tell him nothing."

"No problem."

"Yeah," she said. "He might use this as a political move to disgrace me, and I'm not sure I have the balls it takes to beat him if he wages war."

With a humorous frown, Seabrook shook his head. "You have me, the mayor, and a lot more people than you think behind you, Callie. You're what this beach needs, in a big way. See you at the station."

The patrol car headed west on Jungle Road, allowing her gaze to slide from Seabrook's taillights to the Rosewood drive. The drive remained empty.

Callie scooted up her steps for a rushed shower. Somebody booby-trapped Sarah's car, and friend or no friend, affair or no affair, there was a crime involved, and that crime had killed an officer.

It was time to step on toes.

Chapter 6

CLIMBING THE STAIRS to Shore Thing, otherwise known as Ben and Sarah Rosewood's place, Callie halfway expected no one to answer. But Sarah opened her front door in khaki capris and a tiered, ruffled top inadvertently accenting tanned plump arms, dressed as if yesterday never happened. The smell of coffee escaped from inside.

But the missing makeup and swollen, red eyes said differently. Sarah had tried to meet the day but not quite made it.

She hadn't called Callie. Most people would want an explanation why their car quit working, crashed, and killed another person.

Wearing jeans and tank top, a light cotton button-up covering her old burn scar, Callie feared wearing a uniform might put Sarah on the defensive. She scanned for signs of Mr. Rosewood as she entered the foyer. "How're you doing?"

No suitcases in the hall. No ruined belongings hanging around to dry.

"I ought to be asking you," Sarah replied. "They didn't have to give *me* oxygen." She stepped back with a pained smile. "I can throw some muffins in the microwave, courtesy of Ms. Hanson."

A deep pile cream runner accented the hall. This was no rental, not by anyone's standard. The house flaunted rich, polished woods, leather, and dull brass and glass fixtures, byproducts of Ben's success as an attorney. Sarah pretended hard, had for a long time, but Callie fully understood how sad this house really was.

"Sit," Sarah said, motioning to the kitchen table. With all the opulence in the living room, Sarah seemed to prefer the more low-key setting whenever Callie came over. "Iced tea? Or have you had your coffee yet?"

"Iced tea's perfect." Voice catching on a word, Callie cleared her throat. She hadn't dreamed about Francis last night . . . just the water. Swallowing water. Waking with a sore throat.

Ice clinked from the freezer. Silence filled the rooms as each lady's presence seemed to remind the other of the previous day. Sarah set two glasses on mats and sat at the table's end, catty-cornered from her guest.

"Where's Ben?" Callie asked.

Sarah twisted her glass. "I'm not sure."

She wasn't sure? "The Volvo," Callie said. "You said the brakes gave out. The Highway Patrol has the car, by the way, not us. I thought Ben would tell me who last serviced the brakes or did any work on it."

"Oh. He left on a business trip, but I'm not sure which client."

The man was an attorney, his clients littering the Eastern seaboard, but otherwise he worked from his upstairs study, the only place Callie'd ever seen him come and go. She'd bet a week's pay he kept a bed and bath up there. Sarah confided to her months ago that they hadn't slept together in eons.

Beverly had mentioned a Rosewood divorce. Sarah pined for Lawton but told Callie she owed Ben, but then Ben had means, and she had none that Callie knew of. He harbored a strange love-hate dependency that kept him affixed to the marriage, however, an oddity Callie never grasped. A divorce would not surprise her.

"When my mother harassed you, what exactly did she say?"

Color drained from the woman's face, her posture pressing her into the back of her chair as if Callie would leap.

"I gave that reporter nothing," she said, voice tremoring. "Tell her. I don't want to. Your mother scares me sometimes." Trembling, she reached behind her as if seeking stability. "No, don't tell her she scares me. She might not like that. Wait, are you here to check for her? Oh Jesus!" she cried and huddled into herself. "Just go. Please go."

What the ever-loving hell was this? Beverly wasn't volatile, more irritating than threatening. With a seething annoyance for her mother, Callie reached for the shaky woman. "Sarah, what the hell did my mother do?"

Sarah shook her head silently.

Callie almost touched her, then drew back. Any wrong move and she'd be considered in cahoots with Beverly Cantrell, accused of battery.

"Sarah?" she asked gently. "I don't understand, but I want to set this straight. You hear me?"

The mid-sixtyish woman peered up like a child.

Retreating, Callie put a few more inches' distance between them. "Please, let's chat about this."

Callie strode to the refrigerator and refilled the half-full tea glass, brought it back, and set it down with a muffin. "Tell me exactly what Beverly said."

The injured wife had finally challenged the other woman. Guilt atop a soft personality made Sarah perfect fodder for Beverly whose temperament cut through bone like a Ginsu knife.

"She came over last week," Sarah said through a watery gaze. "Asked for documents, gifts, emails, or photos that would incriminate Lawton and me. I refused to give her anything. Then she warned me in a nasty huff she better not be blindsided, and she left. Yesterday she showed up at lunch a whole different person, but she asked where Ben was. I told her I had to go and Ben wasn't here, and she said she'd be back later. I didn't want to stick around. I didn't want to discuss Ben, or Lawton, or anything with her."

Callie listened, imagining Beverly's audacity in this house, picturing the intimidation she threw around which she could distribute in spades.

A memory hit Callie like a block of ice. Dinner at the Cantrells, Callie in tenth grade. Lawton running for his second term. Beverly threatening to do terrible things to the opposition because his wife had embarrassed her at a soiree meant to honor Lawton. Something about his house at night, once they were asleep.

Beverly was all talk, though. She never followed through, but this time she'd divided and tried to conquer the Rosewoods. Callie could see Beverly meeting with Ben, playing the victim card, allying as the two tolerant, sacrificing spouses. If that was the case Sarah had every reason to feel browbeaten.

Sarah tucked arms beneath her breasts then rested them on the table, drawing up small, her weak voice imploring. "Ben had already left. She told me to avoid a reporter who's been snooping around. Said I couldn't miss the red hair." Fear welled again. "Gracious, I wouldn't talk to a reporter, Callie. She didn't have to come into my house and badger me. I wouldn't do that to Lawton's memory."

No. Beverly worried more about her own reputation. "What else?" Callie asked, dying for a pad to take notes, but she couldn't risk losing the momentum. "Did she . . . threaten you? I mean, with specifics?" Callie hesitated at what might merit dragging her mother into the station.

Sarah started to speak, then halted. "It wasn't what she said. It's how she said it."

"Was she alone?"

"Yes, the first time. The second time she had an old lady with her."

Miss Promise.

Damn it, Mother. You're no saint, but this is beneath you.

Callie held back, nodding in agreement with Sarah's description of the confrontation. She chewed her lip once or twice, historic events with her mother sliding past her mind's eye. Beverly hinting at what a younger Callie should do . . . and Callie afraid not to listen. At least until she reached high school when hormones, teenage angst, and a bellyful of small-town aristocratic haughtiness caused a rebellious rebound that continued to this day. Sort of like Scout in *To Kill a Mockingbird*, only Beverly was no Atticus Finch.

Callie's phone rang. The 843 area code meant anywhere in the Low-country. She refused the call. Press would pester her today, and she wasn't in the right mindset to juggle words to their questions twisted to elicit wrong responses. With her jinx case, she'd learned how people read headlines and tweets, assumed the story, and ran with gossip and lies.

Seabrook didn't mind the press, though. Callie might delegate these calls to him. No, she couldn't do that. Not being the first lady chief. They'd think she couldn't manage the pressure.

Damn journalists.

"Callie?"

Callie brought herself back to the present. "I'll speak to my mother, but what's the deal with Ben? I'm betting I'll find a calendar upstairs with his client schedule that tells us where he is." She started to rise from her seat.

Abruptly, Sarah stood and pushed ahead of her to the stairs. Stroking the banister, she seemed to take a moment before facing her inquisitor. "He left four days ago. No note. The bank accounts haven't been touched, but then he kept cash on him most of the time. Carries one credit card. No activity showing online."

Resting back in her chair, Callie waited. She had assumed Sarah fell into the category of those who enjoyed the successes of their men over scripting their own. Both Ben and Lawton fit the stereotype. She was somewhat happy to see Sarah take some control. "Did you call any of his clients?"

"No. Afraid of hurting his reputation . . . in case I'm overreacting."

"Fight?" Callie asked.

"No," Sarah replied.

"Abuse?"

Sarah rubbed up and down the polished dark oak railing. "Just cold shoulders and sarcasm."

Callie put her glass in the sink and strolled toward the door. "We can do this all day, me asking questions and you half-answering them. Or you can tell me what the heck is going on. If you'll lie to me about Ben, you'll lie to me about my moth . . . Beverly."

Sarah snatched her head around, and a medley of expressions flashed until she seemed to settle on one of tired detachment. "I think Ben left me."

"Why not say so?" Callie asked.

"Because I haven't wrapped my head around it yet."

"Okay, then why were you so anxious to leave Edisto?"

Sarah drew in an angry sigh and blew it out. "To get out of the damn house. To escape your mother's hostility. To avoid some stalking reporter she spoke of. Is that so mysterious?"

"Not when you spill it instead of making me lasso and drag it out of you. That only raises suspicion, Sarah."

A pout came and went as understanding set in. "Fine," she said and pushed off the banister. "What else do you need?"

"Who would want to cut your brake lines and kill you?"

Sarah backed up. "Kill me? Ben would never kill me, if that's what you think." Then with fazed perplexity Sarah took a defensive stand. "Would your mother? Oh my, would she go to that length to make sure I didn't talk?"

"No," Callie said, appalled at the thought. "Needle you, yes, but physically harm? Never."

Stunned, Sarah slowly reached out, as if blind, seeking her bearings. "I don't have a car," she mumbled. Then she spoke louder as she grabbed a chair. "Callie, I don't have a car! What if someone tries again? I can't even escape."

"Are you sure it's not Ben?" Callie asked.

"Are you sure it's not your mother?"

Callie sensed Sarah was as sure about her answer as Callie was about hers.

"Stay inside with your doors locked," Callie ordered. "Call me about anything amiss or if you hear from Ben. Keep trying him. I'll check a few things and be in touch. When the Highway Patrol calls, phone me. I'd like to be there when they speak with you, if you don't mind."

Sarah slid closer. "You're scaring me."

Callie left the kitchen. "Yesterday should've scared you. I can see where my mother might've scared you. Not knowing where Ben is ought to scare you." She opened the front door, unlocked as were most homes on the beach. "I'm the last person, place, or thing on this beach that ought to scare you, Sarah. And the first person you ought to call." She tested the deadbolt; no telling how long since it had been operated. "And keep this door locked."

Hesitating on the porch, Callie waited to hear the latch, then tromped down the stairs. Once she checked in with the station and updated Seabrook with this strange turn of events, she might find her way to Middleton this afternoon. Beverly's connection to this accident suddenly wasn't to be ignored.

The Highway Patrol would be all over this case, their investigation holding the potential to ruin Beverly's run for office simply because the accident drifted off Edisto Beach, barely outside the city limits.

Beverly didn't know what brake lines were. Did she?

Would she?

Gripping the railing, Callie wheeled around and marched toward home. Damn it, she yearned to wring every bone in Beverly's neck. She didn't want to see a connection between her mother's stupid approach to Sarah and the Volvo's brakes, but any half-brained law enforcement officer would sit up and take notice, with the Lawton Cantrell affair making for a grand headline reaching way further than Middleton. And if she was innocent, her mother-the-mayor was consuming too much of Callie's time—time that ought to be spent finding a wannabe killer.

"Yoo-hoo, Callie, wait up." Footsteps lighter than most flitted down stairs.

"Crap."

Between Chelsea Morning and Shore Thing sat Hatha Heaven, its owner the first friend Callie made on Edisto. This most remarkable lady, about five years Callie's senior, felt it her duty to collect every snippet of data, intelligence, and gossip on the island. Each native at one time or another had attended her yoga classes in the back of a beachfront bar. She'd seen to it with a mission to teach everyone inner peace and flexibility. It also put each and every one on her radar.

Since Callie'd become chief, she'd seen less of Sophie Bianchi. Not that she didn't like the yoga mistress. In reality, Callie found her comical, lighthearted, a tiny lady who enticed anyone to rear back and laugh, something Callie found herself needing more than a few times. A good soul with charisma in buckets. What their conversations had begun to lack in quantity thanks to Callie's new job, Sophie learned to make up for in an enriched, denser style of banter as she pumped her law enforcement friend for forbidden details of Edisto's residents. Callie's tight lips only challenged Sophie to poke more, using antics that often made those tight lips crack a smile. However, Callie always came away with more info than she gave. Truth was, Sophie made for a good source.

Sophie nimbly approached, followed by a lady Beverly's age who wasn't so quick to glide down the steps, her muscles and broadness too unforgiving for fast moves.

"Hey, girl, what's going on?" Sophie asked, her cohort still tackling the steps. Then before Callie could respond, added, "Did they really have to drag you out of Scott Creek and resuscitate you?"

"No, Sophie, I—"

"Uh oh." The frosted pixie shag bobbed, Sophie's finger rising up and down, pointing at Callie. "You're not wearing your outfit." She leaned in close. "They didn't fire you already, did they?"

Callie had given up making Sophie call her police garb a uniform. Military, police, even hunters, in Sophie's opinion, wore *outfits.* They moved further from the road near the huge hawthorn bushes that divided the properties. "No, not fired yet," Callie said. "As a matter of fact, I was about to go up and change. How are you?"

A waning September had reduced daytime temps to the mid-eighties, but a beach sun dazzled twelve months of the year, and Sophie's assortment of bangles glinted. Even as lithe and stealthy as she was from thirty years of yoga, her signature bracelets, rings, and long dangly earrings announced her arrival. She only took them off for yoga, and even then she wore a dainty anklet that accented an om Sanskrit tattoo.

Sophie snatched a glance over her shoulder. "Call me later. We need to talk. And I mean *talk*."

The friend caught up, a tad winded, and smiled. Callie smiled in return.

Sophie flashed a grin at her cohort until a genuine concern took its place. "I'm so sorry about Francis. He had good energy."

Callie squeezed her arm. "Thanks, I'll tell the staff."

"For real," Sophie said, shaking her friend hard once, bracelets jangling. "They said you almost drowned."

How many more people would bring that up? Each time made her throat hurt, her stomach roil. So she turned and reached out to the friend. "Hey, I'm Callie Morgan. Don't believe we've met."

"You just don't remember," she said, taking the grip with only her fingers.

Callie squinted from behind her sunglasses. Seabrook hadn't introduced her to this woman, so she wasn't a business owner or in politics. Nor a preacher. "My apologies for not recognizing you. Enlighten me, please."

Looking from face to face, Sophie's mouth formed an *O*, her thick lashes wide. Miss Yoga had been gossiping, and the hair on Callie's neck told her she'd been the subject. Yes, they would have to talk later.

The stranger who wasn't a stranger paused for effect, tucking a stray curl back under a floral silk hairband struggling to contain the rest of her dyed-red hair. She didn't wear the brass and gold that Sophie did, but she darn sure sported the diamonds. "I'm Aberdeen, honey."

Callie pondered the name, having heard it but unable to place it.

"LeGrand," Sophie said in a whisper.

"Brice's wife?" Callie asked. "Oh, nice to meet you."

No wonder Sophie asked if she'd been fired. Aberdeen lived with the man most eager to sign the pink slip.

Aberdeen donned a thin, orange-smeared half grin, delivering a silent message. "Tell your twit of a mother hello for me. She'll understand."

The metaphorical bitch slap took Callie aback, but she let the inciting remark remain untouched and deemed this conversation at an end. "See you, Sophie. I need to report in."

However, each step back to Chelsea Morning raised a fire in her belly. Beverly feuding with Brice in her office. Sarah afraid of Beverly's threat. Now Aberdeen's dark opinion of Beverly. Her mother excelled in verbal abrasion, but Callie never expected it to spill into Callie's career and into an investigation. Without even trying, Beverly interfered.

But Sarah's safety worried her more. Sarah was docile, pleasant. But there was always her affair with Lawton . . . which continually brought Callie's suspicions back around to Beverly.

Chapter 7

CLIMBING CHELSEA Morning's front steps, Callie fumbled her house keys, fighting against instincts screaming to interview her mother. She dug deep for logic to rule that out and couldn't find any. A gull landed on the railing at the end of her porch, flying off as Callie's feet hit the landing.

She unlocked her front door eagerly, and leaving the keys on the credenza, she entered her bedroom, retrieved her *outfit*, as Sophie would call it, and laid out the summer uniform on her comforter, absorbing its authority, letting her finger rest on the rank insignia on the collar.

While her mother disagreed with Callie's choice of career, leading to many a late-night head-butting over the years, Callie sensed Beverly accepted the calling this time. She'd stood front and center at the swearing-in ceremony, maybe even shed a tear.

Yet now Callie had to use that job to confront her.

Training told her she was not the person for this task. One could argue that the entire six-man PD had a conflict of interest under Callie's oversight. Colleton County or SLED, the State Law Enforcement Agency, were more suited, but relinquishing control meant relying on strangers to pursue Francis's death . . . and dear old Mother.

No. Not yet. She'd dig deeper first before passing the baton. That could not be undone.

Before the sun set, she'd cruise to Middleton . . . before someone realized Beverly was a suspect.

Beverly had guts, but Lawton wasn't but three months dead. Unfortunately, or fortunately depending on how one looked at it, she'd chosen a mayoral run to step back into the limelight. Zero to sixty in a blink with Lawton's legacy hopefully the wind beneath her wings. The man of her dreams. But of Sarah's as well.

A combination of facts that could make for serious criminal motive.

She could almost feel Stan's huge paw of a hand pulling her aside, ordering her to find someone else to interview this woman ASAP. His advice had never failed her, and for a moment, she pondered whether to call him.

Instead, her phone rang. Seabrook.

"Calls are pouring in for you."

"I'm coming," she said, shedding her jeans, phone on her shoulder. "How's it going? Two guys in the field, right? You in the office. Raysor come in?"

"Thomas and LaRoache are on duty around the beach. Raysor will be any moment. And Marie said to tell you she couldn't stay home."

Good people staffed Edisto PD. They understood a man down meant digging in deeper and covering for a few weeks, because asking to fill the job this soon seemed downright rude.

She tucked in her summer shirt with the short sleeves, revealing her scar. Eight inches long. Somewhat ragged, the wound remained a permanent reminder of when John died. But scars fit uniforms like stripes on a sleeve.

Moving to her dresser, she opened a drawer, the wrong drawer. Or was it the right one? Bonnie's blanket sat in its tissue paper, the only item inside. A memorial to the baby girl lost to SIDS six months before John died. After opening the tissue for a soft sniff, she gently refolded the paper and shut the drawer.

It was like the two reached out to her, understanding she needed the touch. She was stalling and couldn't explain why.

Yes, she did. Today she'd walk in the station without Francis, without him breezing in with a white-toothed grin and a dorky joke. And while she'd concentrate on Sarah's case, her deceased officer's memory was vivid. His frantic eyes underwater . . .

She donned her utility belt, made one sweep around the house touching each of five cams, and set the alarm to leave. If one counted the cams positioned outside Chelsea Morning, she'd installed way more security than any other house on the beach. Good thing Edisto had so much sand, because residents stuck their heads in it on a regular basis, pretending crime didn't happen. Her job, and that of her department, was to allow them to feel comfortable doing it.

She ran down the steps, then under her house where her cruiser waited. The houses existed twelve and fourteen feet off the ground for water protection, which made for fantastic carports.

Fingering her car fob, she approached the rear of her vehicle, only to stop. *Son of a biscuit.* A flat tire.

She pulled out her phone, walking up to study the tire closely. "Marie, send whatever service we use to fix my flat tire. I'll drive my Escape to the station."

"We use J&J for stuff with the cars, but the guys usually change their own tires, Chief."

Callie could change a tire, but today wasn't the day for it. She continued around the vehicle, out of habit . . . and stopped. Another tire flat. She backed up to study the other to her right. Flat. "I'm not believing this."

Drifting to her sidearm, she scanned the carport area, under and around the grown-up hawthorns she'd planned to cut back. No sign of strange vehicles, no out-of-place straggler trying too hard to seem normal. No notes on her windshield like a couple months ago when a killer ran loose.

That case erased any respect she held for journalists, because social media had splashed Chelsea Morning's picture and address for the world to see. And this was the precise type of thing that could happen as a result.

She went back and circled the vehicle. "All four tires are slit."

"What?" Marie exclaimed. Then in the background, she repeated the news to Seabrook.

He took the phone. "Can you tell anything?"

"Had to be after eleven last night, but give me a chance to check my cams."

Moving carefully outward, she studied the ground. Seashells and gravel made for poor tracking. No prints on the carport pavement. Nothing out of place.

A honk from Jungle Road caught her attention. Quincy Kinard waved. What was he doing back here? Middleton's beat didn't extend to Edisto. Walking toward the road, she watched where he might be headed only to see taillights as he turned into the Rosewood drive. If he were a gentleman, he might be checking on Sarah after her ordeal. But in Callie's experience, a reporter didn't drive forty-five miles during a workday to check on a stranger. Not unless he expected a story in return.

Unfortunately, Quincy was the hero. How could Sarah not let him in and hear him out?

"Callie? What're you doing?" Seabrook asked.

She continued watching Quincy. "Hunting for clues. About the car?"

"We'd have to pull the spare tire from every car in the fleet to accommodate yours. Like Marie said—"

"Guess the garage needs to send a rollback truck this time. See you in a minute."

Still staring down the road, she hung up blindly. Sarah shouldn't welcome anyone inside after someone tried to kill her. Inviting Quincy in was like asking an alligator for tea and him promising not to bite while he's there. But Callie chose to wait and see if Sarah called her.

Callie ran back inside, disabled her alarm, and then opened her laptop, pulling up cam footage from the evening, through the night, and into the early morning. The only people who knew of her cam obsession also knew better than to make fun of it. Holding the forward down, more, more, stop. Back up. There. Two views. From the front and from the rear of the parking area.

Two forty in the morning. With the streetlight two houses down, the lighting made for bad shadows with no moon, but no doubt a body entered the back of her driveway from Jungle Shores Road.

He wore jeans, couldn't really see the shoes. Hair must be short because she saw none escaping the simple ball cap. A dark long-sleeved shirt made him more generic, meaning in this heat he had clandestine intentions. Probably one of the most nondescript individuals one could have for a crime. Could've even been female.

He disappeared behind the car against the house, came out, and made his way to the side in view of the cams. An easy job taking him two minutes tops.

Inserting a flash drive, she noted the length, start, and end, then copied the footage, studying it again for details while she waited. Wait, did she see that correctly?

The recording ended, and she played it again from the flash device, freezing it at the 1:14 mark. For balance, the intruder rested his knuckles on the pavement, avoiding prints on the car, fingers splayed. At least the ones he had. The culprit was missing above the top knuckle of his left middle finger.

Someone who worked with machinery, possibly. Farmer, construction worker, industrial labor . . . mechanic. Someone maybe also educated in cutting brake lines.

Her call to Jeb rolled to voicemail. "Hey. Someone flattened my tires so I'm taking the Escape to the station. A wrecker's coming for the patrol car. Probably a prankster, but you know me and you know the drill. After work, stick with Zeus and Sprite. Be careful and aware of your surroundings. I don't want you alone. I may have to drive to Middleton to see your grandmother, and there's no telling how late I'll be back, but I'll keep you apprised. Go back to doing the text check-ins. Yeah, I hear your groan, but humor me, son. I'm not changing, and you're the only kid I've got. Hourly. Don't forget. Love you." She barely got it all in.

Jeb would gladly remain in the company of Sophie's two children. When he wasn't working the fishing charter business, he spent every waking moment with Sprite, Sophie's daughter, a voluptuous young lady with long spiral raven curls who'd be graduating from high school this year. Callie prayed Miss Bianchi chose to attend the college in Charleston a year from now, drawing Jeb to enter his freshman year alongside her.

Though Callie lived a mile and a half from the station, it took fifteen minutes to reach work with the golf carts, bikers, and residents waving, one beckoning her over to mention Francis.

She held up the flash drive as she entered the station. "Got the bastard on my cam."

Raysor and Seabrook looked up from their attentive work over a computer. "Know him?" Raysor asked, his gruffness always challenging.

Callie shook her head. "But he's missing part of a finger. This one," she said, showing a familiar gesture.

Seabrook didn't react, but Raysor sneered. "About time you showed some damn balls."

She retreated the demonstration, making a fist. "He's between five foot seven and five foot ten. Thirties, maybe late twenties from how slick he moved. Ball cap."

"Know exactly who he is." Raysor hefted his almost-fifty backside onto the corner of the desk.

Callie slowed. "Seriously?"

The deputy snorted. "Only guy missing a digit in these parts is old man Garrison over on Oak Island Road. Lost it getting his sleeve caught in an auger hooked to his tractor. Bone of that finger hung up the mechanism to keep it from ripping his arm off. Not that particular digit, though."

"Well, it's something." She liked Raysor better than before, but he wouldn't be cutting her slack anytime soon. And she wouldn't confide in him about Beverly's involvement anytime soon, either. Walking behind the counter, Callie checked with her office manager. "Marie?"

"Yeah, Callie."

Warming at Marie's first mention of her by name, Callie grinned. "You okay?"

"Ten-eight, Callie."

Callie caught Seabrook's flicker of a smile as he recognized the bonding moment, too. "Today might get busy, but if you get a second, can you pull a photo from this footage and give us something to show people and hopefully identify this idiot?"

Marie took the flash drive and winked. "You got it."

Callie relaxed at the first bright point in her day, short of Seabrook's news about his wife's killer. Like that could ever be cheery.

"Hey, is Pittstop missing a digit?" she asked.

Seabrook shed the smile. He looked tired. Callie guessed he slept little chasing clues. Once upon a time, she had been electrical, antsy, and impatient at anything in her way chasing her husband's murderer . . . and it screwed up her career. Seabrook's level-headedness, however, would surely not allow such excessive firebrand maneuvers. Not after having ruined one other career before.

He shook his head. "Fingerprint card in his record showed ten fingers."

"Never mind," she said. "You saw him in Florence until, what, eleven? I doubt—"

"You think I led him here?" Concern creased his crow's feet deep.

"Chill, Mike," she said. "I'm winnowing out possibilities."

"Besides, can't see him coming here," Raysor said.

Callie turned to her deputy-on-loan. "You knew about him and I didn't?"

He gave her an attempt at an innocent shrug. "Talk to Seabrook."

But Seabrook seemed hung up on the seed Callie inadvertently planted. "Stop and think. If he senses I'm watching him, he could learn about you. If he killed Gracie, he could—"

"Stop it, Mike. You're reaching ridiculously far with this. Like another universe reaching." She hadn't realized he'd wound himself up so tight.

Her worry for him rose a few levels.

Indeed, Pittstop could easily trace where she lived. "It's probably someone with a grudge, probably pulled over or hassled by any one of you. He got even messing with the chief. Goodness knows my name is out there more than y'all's."

Seabrook nodded.

Raysor moved back toward the computer they were hovering over when she walked in. "We have the highway cam footage from yesterday. That's what we were watching when you came in," he said with a weight to his words that shot trepidation through her.

Walking in no hurry over to Raysor, Callie leaned toward the screen, her tiny form wedged between the tall blond officer and the bulky, middle-aged deputy, the latter at least twice her weight. The former a foot taller. Seabrook's hand rested on her shoulder blade as he hit play.

Highway 174 seemed almost desolate, a car crossing the marshy creek every minute or two, a lot less activity than a couple weeks ago, more than would be by Halloween. Tensing for the moment, Callie noticed the deer but only because she knew to hunt for it. Sarah's Volvo appeared with a late model copper-brown Jeep Wrangler trailing two car lengths behind. Then as deer did, the doe jumped from behind an oleander into the road. Sarah's taillights instantly shone, went off, came back on, then flashed, flashed, flashed as she pumped dead brakes. The deer actually stopped once the action passed it by, as the vehicle swerved left with no change in speed. Then as if changing its mind, the car veered right, momentum taking it airborne off the highway and into the marsh. They could only see the back end of the car as it settled into the water at high tide, the depth Callie intimately remembered around four and a half feet.

The Wrangler parked on the roadside, a man leaping out. He dove into the water and vanished from view.

"That's Quincy Kinard," Callie said. "A reporter from Middleton."

Raysor harrumphed. "Not many would dive in like that."

Seabrook turned around to her. "You know him?"

She glanced away from the screen. "Because he's from Middleton? No, but Mother probably does. Thomas interviewed him," she said, being loose with her facts. But at the mention of her other officer, she recalled how shaken her backup had been. Her rescuer. She owed him dinner, an award, something.

An "oh" escaped her when she returned to the recording. By this time, Callie's cruiser parked behind the reporter's Jeep with no sign of her.

Instinctively, she sucked in a breath.

Thomas arrived on the scene. EMTs. Men lined up, reaching.

Though Seabrook and Raysor had already witnessed the recording, their gazes remained affixed. Though Callie lived the moment, she couldn't stop watching. She started craving all over again the air she couldn't get.

Hand over hand, volunteers passed her from the water to medics. She appeared helpless.

Pressure kneaded her shoulders from behind. "Breathe, Callie," Seabrook whispered.

She hadn't realized she wasn't. With a gulp she took in an overabundance of air and a drop of spittle raised a cough. She coughed again, her lungs too easily recalling the moment she smelled the oxygen mask.

"You okay?" Raysor asked, out of character for him.

She nodded. "I—"

Nausea rolled through her. She gulped it down. One grip on the desk, the other embroiled in the back of Seabrook's shirt, she watched with apprehension as they extracted Francis's body.

"Can't—" Callie bolted toward the back door of the station, into the common hall that joined the PD, fire department, and administrative offices. Shouldering the women's room door as if bursting upon a crime in progress, she barely reached the first stall before losing her breakfast. Again, and again, until the spasms heaved nothing more.

A cool, wet cloth draped across the back of her neck.

"One or two more of these panic attacks might sneak up on you, Callie. It's been less than three months since you had the last one, and this job might prompt them anew. Not that you won't overcome it."

She rocked back and plopped on the floor, reached around and retrieved the cloth to wipe her face. "This is the ladies' room," she finally said as her stomach no longer protested. Seabrook reached, and she let him lift her to her feet.

He gave her a cold Coke. "Just saying you should've seen a doctor. You can catch bacterial pneumonia from that water."

Callie refolded the used cloth. "You sound like somebody's grandmother."

Her cell rang, echoing in the acoustics off the tiled walls. Callie ceded the cloth to Seabrook and retrieved the phone. She showed him caller ID and gave Seabrook a puzzled scowl as she answered. "Hey, Sarah. Hear from Ben?"

"No," her neighbor said, voice shaky. "But please do something about this reporter."

"The one who saved you?" Callie asked, to make sure Sarah understood she was targeting a hero in the minds of most of Edisto.

"The one who finagled his way into my home only to come off sounding like he worked for your mother. Whether you do it in the name of Police Chief or Beverly Cantrell's daughter, get this damn man out of my house."

"Hold on a minute," Callie said as if they spoke over drinks at Whaley's, talking down Sarah's fear.

Sarah's *hmph* came out hard. "He says he has secret information about my past."

"Did he try to bribe you?" Callie asked, then put the phone on speaker.

"He's like your mother. He did but he didn't. It's how sleazy he said it. I tell you, he's working for her."

Dropping her head back, Callie exhaled hard. "Did he say that?" He should have opposite motives from Beverly.

"Quit trying to protect her." Sarah's harsh whisper took Callie aback.

Seabrook frowned at the accusation, attempting to read the gist of the conversation.

"Are you hiding?" Callie asked, recognizing the hushed tone.

"I'm in my bathroom," Sarah replied low. "He's in my kitchen."

"Is it unsafe?"

"How do I know?"

"Stay there, and hold on a sec." She quickly muted the call and nudged Seabrook toward the bathroom door. "We need to go."

He pulled up short as a clerk from the mayor's office met them in the exit. Callie ran into his back. Shocked, the clerk pressed against the doorframe, grinning as the two pushed past.

"Excuse us," Seabrook said.

"Great, she'll have that spread by dark," Callie said, hustling to the hall entrance to the PD office. "Get Raysor. He can recognize Quincy Kinard." They reentered the station. "The two of you pick up that damn reporter and bring his butt back here." She unmuted the call. "Sarah? Someone's on their way. Is he still there?"

"I'm not going out to check. Can I talk to you until they get here?"

"Sure, hon," Callie said, glad to hear Sarah closer to normal.

Raysor and Seabrook left for their car. Callie ignored her stomach's final churn and sat at the desk where the screen showed the highway cam footage. She hit stop. The movie had reached its final act anyway. The ambulance was already gone.

Chapter 8

COOL AND SWEET, the Coke helped quell Callie's stomach. Waiting at the station while Seabrook and Raysor headed to the Rosewood house, she glanced at her cell. A text vibrated Jeb's hourly safety notice, with a taste of sarcasm. She returned the device to her ear, keeping her promise to keep Sarah company.

"I'm sorry I let him in," Sarah said for the third time. "Sorry I didn't listen to you."

Callie wiped her mouth on her shoulder. "Quit being sorry and start being careful until we figure this out, okay? I'll come by this afternoon."

We need a chat, Mr. Kinard.

"Hope you're doing okay," Sarah said, as if hunting for topics to fill in the time.

Callie hadn't felt ill before the accident, but today? Not so good. Missing Francis wouldn't let her mind settle, either, scrambling her attempted focus to identify the unknown saboteur of both the Volvo and now her patrol car. That old sense of someone watching, hovering, waiting in the shadows crawled over her.

"They're here," Sarah said.

The phone crackled and muffled, then Seabrook came on the line. "Hey, Kinard must've taken off."

"Drive around. That Jeep is easy to spot. He might not be off the beach yet."

"Will do."

She hung up and finished the cola. She couldn't wait to chat with that cocky SOB journalist. He had no right to capitalize on Sarah's trust.

Per the video, he tailed her across Scott Creek, making himself awful convenient to *rescue* her. Who says he didn't cut the brake lines to create an opportune situation? A stretch, but except for rare exceptions, reporters whored their morality. If Quincy Kinard caused this accident, she'd go after him with every letter of the law.

But what was so important? What information was worth that sort of risk?

Her day was sliding away, and that was with Marie catching the incessant calls. Callie needed to interrogate Quincy, re-interview Sarah, and shoot to Middleton.

Marie stood, purse on her shoulder. "McConkey's has a soup and sandwich special. Feel like lunch?"

Callie glanced at the wall clock. Noon. Hungry but afraid to eat. Plus she wanted to be primed when Raysor and Seabrook escorted Quincy through the door.

"I'll nurse this instead." She held up the bottle. "Thanks. And . . . sorry for the episode." Callie hated showing weakness this early on the job.

A soft smile showed understanding. "If you think that's embarrassing, ask Raysor about Ms. Hanson's cookie date with him. Get Thomas to tell his story about upchucking his lunch on a man he pulled over for speeding. Francis once had . . ." Her cheeks flushed, a pain flickering in her darting look. "Oh, I—"

"Tell you what, Marie," Callie said, rising. She hugged the clerk and patted her back. "A sandwich would be great. Nothing spicy. You pick." Reaching in her pocket, she tugged out a twenty and tucked it in Marie's half-gaped purse. "That should cover both of us."

Once Marie left, the phones rang with fervor as every other Edistonian offered condolences, asked for Seabrook, some bittersweet as they welcomed Callie and issued solace in the same sentence. Marie made it seem so easy.

Callie felt the vacuum of the opening door first. She looked up, hoping her uniforms would walk in only to see Mayor Talbot in an oversized navy and tan floral Hawaiian shirt. With the punch of a button, she rolled the calls to voicemail. Tensing, she shook hands with him at the counter and invited him in to have a seat, but as she lowered herself to hers, a flustered Brice blew in. The mayor stared with venom as the councilman rolled a chair next to his.

How often had they checked in on Seabrook like this? Or the previous chief?

"What's the deal with Francis?" Brice asked, ignoring that Talbot had arrived first.

"The *deal*," Callie said, bolding the word, "is that Francis's grandfather wants a small service in Walterboro next Saturday."

"We'll be there," Talbot said. "But does he mind that we hold a ceremony here?"

Callie gave a gentle shake of her head. "The man's in his late seventies. He might not be up to two services, but I say we proceed regardless." Her past experience on the island was for family vacations, leaving her foreign to the routines. "Where do we normally hold such events?"

"There's nothing normal about *any* of this," Brice said in a mean undertone.

Callie started to speak, but the mayor leaned both hands on his knees and glared to his right. "Damn, man, be congenial for once. This boy deserves civility from us to honor his memory."

You go, Mayor.

"You didn't want Ms. Morgan chief of police," he continued, then gave a wide sweep of his arm. "Heaven knows we get that. But she's qualified. She proved herself. She took care of some nasty business we didn't."

No doubt this pair lived on opposite sides of the fence. "Back to Francis," she said.

Talbot glowered. "Exactly, Ms. Morgan."

"Mayor," Callie said. "About the memorial service—"

"You old jackass, you're nothing but a figurehead," Brice said, ignoring Callie.

The mayor's shoulders drew back. "I hired her as chief of police, you moron—"

"She's a has-been!"

Callie perked up. "I'm right here, Brice. And I wear the badge regardless of how that makes you feel. Try to stick to Francis, if you don't mind."

Brice moved to the edge of his seat, speaking across Talbot at her. "Oh, the lady who came here to lean on Mommy and Daddy can talk. Well, Daddy's not here, and Mommy's gone off her rocker pretending to be political material."

Bristling, Callie stood. "Meeting's over, Councilman. Get the hell out."

Talbot actually seemed to relax and enjoy the moment the way he slid backward in his seat.

"I approve your paycheck," Brice said, eyes narrowing.

"So fire me," she said.

Talbot harnessed a chuckle.

"Maybe I will." Brice slung the counter door back to leave. When it clicked back in place, he turned. "People choose sides quickly on Edisto, Ms. Morgan." He exited and tried to slam the glass door in his wake only for the pneumatic mechanism to stifle his effort and slowly ease shut.

"Amen and amen," Talbot said.

Brice's animosity made no sense to Callie. "What's his problem, Mr. Talbot?"

He studied her and seemed to make a mental decision. "Long story. Nothing you need worry about. Man wears a short fuse."

"So how does he remain in office?"

His grin came across fatherly. "People like being cozy with people with the power, and until he embarrassingly screws up, his family name carries weight."

Seabrook came in the door, Quincy behind him, and Raysor bringing up the rear.

"Just passed Brice steaming like a bull," Quincy said. Wearing a deadpan expression, he glanced up to his right, then to his left, at the two uniforms that braced him. "Seems the Edisto PD has grave questions for me." He waggled his brow like a cartoon character. "Serious business . . . this police work on the beach. I would expect more of a hero's welcome."

Raysor moved close with a swagger of his own, his voice deep. "Not before Francis gets one first."

Well said, Don.

But there would be no hero's welcome for this guy under her watch. Not yet. Neither Talbot nor the beach community could afford celebrating a man who might be using everyone for a scoop. "Mayor," Callie said. "I'm open to whatever the administration wants to arrange for Francis, but right now Mr. Kinard and I have business."

Talbot lifted a silent hand, stood and left.

At Callie's direction, Quincy sauntered around the counter, but as Seabrook and Raysor tried to trail along, Callie stepped in their path. "Let me play this, if you guys don't mind."

Raysor studied her, then he shrugged, as if recalling the difference in rank. Seabrook, however, clouded up. "Don't you need a witness?"

"I have a recorder, Mike." She patted his toned bicep. "I've done this before."

"Not crazy about the idea—"

"You weren't there yesterday," she said and shut the door before she showed remorse for the words. "I know what to ask." Besides, she might say something she didn't want him to hear yet.

Quincy chose the seat nearest the exit, like she would do. In a smooth routine, she sat, pulled herself closer to her desk, then nonchalantly hit record on the phone placed to her right.

"Go ahead, record me," he said and set his own phone on record as well.

She readjusted her phone to sit beside his. "Your name is Quincy Kinard, a journalist with the *Middleton Post.* An associate editor," she said, laying his card on the desk. "Is that correct?"

"Yes, ma'am."

He acted comfortable. Good. She needed him that way.

"Yesterday, September 27, you saw Sarah Rosewood's Volvo leave Highway 174 at the Scott Creek causeway, parked your car, and entered the water to see to her safety."

"Yes, exactly."

Callie nodded. Usually she kept a list of questions with possible follow-up, but she hadn't expected Quincy on the island today. It felt good winging an interview. "Why did you visit Sarah Rosewood at her home today?"

A hint of concern in his expression, but he seemed to dash it aside. "To see how she was after the accident."

Callie waited, because she knew he knew she knew more. She tilted her head to prod him.

"You already spoke with Ms. Rosewood," he said.

"I did," she said.

He wobbled his head like a bobblehead doll, an unbecoming habit, she'd noticed. "Okay, okay. I questioned her about her current and past relationships. Specifically . . . *surprise* . . . your parents."

No surprise. She'd already put two and two together and come up with an arrogant reporter who'd connected her parents and Sarah. Made him more a suspect. He called Brice by first name, too.

She wanted to peg him for the causeway situation but contained herself. They had no evidence.

"Who are you working for?" she asked.

"The paper," he said.

She pushed harder. "Specifically. A name."

He appeared flummoxed. "My editor?"

"Were you chasing Ms. Rosewood?"

"Um, what do you mean chasing?"

"Let's say following then. Were you intentionally *following* her as she left the beach?"

"Um, I might have been. I missed her at her house, so I thought I'd see where she was going and catch her there."

A clear and *obvious* suspect. She didn't ask him about the brake line;

he'd only say he didn't do it and then use the intel in a story. "What information did you need from her that warranted you tailing her? Where she was headed?"

His forehead creased. "How would I know?"

"And this information you needed couldn't be obtained by a phone call?" she asked.

He scoffed through his nose. "Doubtful."

"And this information was about the Cantrells' relationship with the Rosewoods?"

He crossed his arms. "Not sure I want to say any more about that. Especially with you."

After a second of pause, Callie leaned on her desk. "Mr. Kinard, we've had two complaints." She exhaled slow and obvious and decided to drop a hint. "Somebody sabotaged the car you were tailing."

His tanned complexion paled white around his mouth. "What the hell?"

"That's called attempted murder."

He jumped to his feet, the chair on rollers sliding back. "Wait a damn minute."

Callie withdrew her phone from his reach. Quincy stopped short with the curse, his expression morphing from quizzical to analytical. "Do I need an attorney?"

"Have you done anything to need an attorney?"

His changing expressions told her he pondered the idea, but paparazzi couldn't pass up opportunity for material.

Thus far he probably told the truth. Sarah saw no one tail her. Right after the accident, she addressed Quincy like a stranger. That didn't mean he didn't do it, though.

"Take your seat," she said.

Reaching around, he rolled the chair back under him.

"You appear to know where Ms. Cantrell always is, to include her nonpublic appearances." She dragged out the words before snapping, "Your desire for press appears rather predatory."

In Boston, ever wanting to follow the regs, Stan would've given her the eye. This question didn't apply to Sarah's case, but Quincy had interest in the Cantrells, and Callie wondered why. Stan also used to give her enough rope, and she'd never hanged herself.

Quincy didn't react to the predatory reference. Maybe because he was accustomed to it?

"Mr. Kinard, I have little regard for your profession; however, I must draw a line when your actions endanger those within my jurisdiction. You're a stalker."

He shook his head. "I haven't endangered anybody."

"Sarah Rosewood locked herself in her bathroom."

His chin went up a degree. "She overreacted. I was no threat whatsoever."

"Did she ask you to leave?"

"No. She went to the bathroom and never came out."

"And you didn't wonder why?"

He shrugged. "People go to the bathroom."

"But you left. Why not at least tell her you had other obligations?"

The silence was palpable. His stare on Callie moved to different items in the room, for once a retort not ready.

"Her car crashed, Quincy," she said, seizing upon his uncomfortable moment. "With you on her bumper."

"And thank goodness I was there to pull her out." He tipped his head toward the recording phones. "I'd like to ask you a question, if you don't mind."

Callie remained static and silent.

"What's your mother's connection with Sarah Rosewood?" he asked.

With a grin, she replied, "Funny, I was going to ask you the same question."

"How many affairs were there, Ms. Morgan?" Not Chief, but Ms, taking her authority down a notch. "The secrets lead to Edisto Beach. It's rumored Mr. Benjamin Rosewood is filing for divorce. Witnesses recall seeing the oh-so-noble Lawton Cantrell in public with Mrs. Rosewood. Beverly Cantrell has the most motive to kill Sarah Rosewood, I'd say."

Callie's heart flipped at the derogatory remarks, most of them true, but she willed it to settle. Lifting the business card, she squinted. "Oh, I forgot you work for the *Middleton Post*, not *Star Magazine*."

But he must've smelled her deflection.

His mouth screwed funny then slid into a half-smile. "Is Mama how you got the job? You were pretty damn washed up when you arrived here. Two years out of uniform. Suddenly you solve a ghost story and you're chief."

Pulse kicking in, Callie prayed the flush she felt wasn't obvious.

"Sir . . . Mr. Kinard," she enunciated to remind him of the recording. "You walk a fine line between journalism and breaking the law. Another word from either of these two ladies, and you'll be our guest in the Colleton County jail."

"I have rights." He got up again, straightening his web belt. "And I've got your number. I can add you to my story. Your drinking, the way you enticed that Russian to come down here so you could slit his throat. Your affair with your subordinate officer."

The guy spoke like he'd stolen her diary, twisting the facts until they were almost unrecognizable. The public didn't know how she killed the Russian . . . or that he would've killed both her and Jeb if she hadn't.

She came around the desk and positioned her nose six inches from his. "Yes, you do have rights," she said, teeth tight. *And it's those rights that keep me from smashing your cranium against that concrete block wall.*

As acting chief, Seabrook had refused to confirm facts about the Russian to the public.

And sure, they'd dated prior to her accepting the role.

Her drinking was controllable.

Quincy must have seen the recanting thoughts darting through her mind, because he stupidly pushed harder. The familiar queasiness returned to her gut.

"Like mother like daughter, right?" he added. "With the affairs, I mean. Maybe the drinking, too. She hasn't murdered anyone . . . or has she?"

Fire bloomed in her chest, a fast beat pounding. If this tabloid idiot spread these rumors, Jeb would be stunned at some, embarrassed by others, his charter business possibly damaged. Mayor Talbot would be disconcerted at her becoming so controversial in such a short time. Brice LeGrand would run with the accusations. Beverly would lose her election.

Quincy grinned, and her blood raced faster. The recording was still live.

"These complainants have rights, too," she said, grinding out the words. "I'm letting you off with a warning." She stepped back and glanced at the clock. "This recording is concluded at one thirty p.m. on September 28." She turned off Quincy's phone but held the device. She raised hers, however, and snapped Quincy's picture. "You're now one of my special projects."

As if his soul were captured on film, he reared back. "Wait, what did you do that for?"

Callie held the picture out as if bringing it into focus. Smiling, she clicked the phone off. "Every officer will have a picture of you and a description of your car."

"You can't do that."

"Just did. Why would you want to remain clandestine?"

Frustration showed in his rippling jaw muscle.

Callie stretched to her fullest height, wishing it were five inches more. "And in recognition of your heroism, whenever you come to Edisto, I'll have an officer escort you to ensure you have a pleasant stay. It's the least we can do."

He snatched his phone when she offered it. "I notice this so-called recognition isn't recorded."

"Good gracious, Mr. Kinard, of course not." She studied her phone like it had special powers. "We don't put it on record. We don't have enough officers to offer that service to everyone. You're special."

"Only more material for an expose, Ms. Morgan." He blew a sigh that could thaw ice, spun, and left.

Rubbing her midsection, Callie exited her office in time to see him blow past Seabrook as if scorched. Marie glanced up, then went back to her computer.

"You look flustered," Seabrook said. "But not as much as he does. I take it went well?"

"He's a pain."

"So he's remaining on our radar?" he asked.

Most definitely. But she feared she'd just fueled his hunger for a special edition.

"Not in that car and not in those clothes, I suspect," she said. "But he's not giving up on his story."

"So what's he after?"

"A smear piece on my mother," Callie said. "And I'm completely perplexed about who's funding his mission. The Middleton newspaper editor wouldn't be that keen on debasing a Cantrell."

Marie motioned toward a white wrapped package on the desk. "Your grilled cheese. Might need to nuke it if you want it warm."

Absentmindedly, Callie unwrapped the sandwich by feel, her gaze on the glass door though Quincy was gone. She took a bite, thinking, hopping up on the edge of the desk, her feet dangling.

Politics, reporters, and attempted murder. What a cliché. "What if Quincy tampered with the brakes to become Sarah's white knight?" she said.

"And he didn't know what he was doing, so he didn't predict where the brakes would fail," Seabrook added.

"It was an older model car—" Callie spit a mouthful of sandwich into the trash, bile rising like a thermometer in her throat.

Throwing the sandwich on the desk, she returned to the bathroom, trying not to trot. The lunch came up into the toilet before the bathroom door had a chance to fully close. Heat flushed up her neck, and she puked again. Then the ordeal quickly ended.

Ripping toilet paper out of the dispenser, she sat on the floor and wiped her mouth, her nose running.

"Callie?" This time Marie called from outside the stall.

"I'm good," Callie replied. "Give me a sec."

"Gotcha. I'll keep Seabrook occupied, but you understand I gotta ask."

Callie frowned in confusion then spread her eyes wide in understanding. Head on her knees, Callie released a sigh. "No, I'm not pregnant, Marie."

"Text if you need me," she replied and exited.

Thank goodness. Privacy.

Staring at the tiled floor, trying to avoid thinking of what might be embedded in the grout, she ran the interview through her head again. Quincy wouldn't know Beverly likewise sought damaging evidence about Sarah, making the Rosewood mistress flighty and nervous when Quincy repeated the same request. Not that he wouldn't love that information, too—the widow leaning on the mistress.

Leaning against the stall, she stood, judged her stability, and exited. She wet a paper towel, and sinking her face into it, recalled the guy with the missing digit who slit her tires.

She and Sarah could be targets of the same individual, which would rule out Beverly. If the same man, he targeted Sarah one day and Callie the next. Unless he made a mistake coming to see Sarah, or vice versa.

If it was Pittstop, why choose Sarah by day and Callie by night? That made no sense.

Or maybe someone just hated cops. Goodness knows that had become a trend across the country.

Quincy had all his fingers, but how easy was it to pay someone down on his luck to do two simple tasks? But what would Quincy have against her? Another dead end.

Sarah already saw Beverly as a would-be killer, but killing for the mayor's slot? Beverly wasn't helping her own credibility in that regard, and the Cantrells had enough money to make almost anything happen without such off-color tactics, but Callie wasn't ready to believe it.

And Ben was the loosest dangling string of them all. He held a grudge against every party involved.

A headache grew behind her lids. She tried to push the questions aside, to chill. Her mind used to be clearer than this. Rewetting the towel, she covered her face again.

She didn't have time to feel like hell.

Chapter 9

CALLIE PAUSED before exiting the bathroom, collecting herself. Fact was she was clueless who cut the Volvo's brake lines. So many people were transient on this beach. She yanked the bathroom door open, eager to reach Sarah and seek answers.

"Let's take you to Charleston to get checked out," Seabrook said, leaning against the wall.

"Nerves, Mike." She passed him and entered the office, him on her heels. "Just nerves." If not for three years of abstinence, she *would* consider herself pregnant.

Geez, had it been that long?

He touched her forehead with his palm. She let him, enjoying the touch and concern. "I'm fine."

At Marie's desk, Callie straightened the pens in a red Wainwright Realty cup, pondering her two remaining fire-missions for the afternoon. "I'm headed to Sarah Rosewood's in my car, then to Middleton. They say when my cruiser would be ready?"

Marie clicked into a calendar on her screen. "They'll pick it up by two today and returning it tomorrow morning. J&J said he'd get the tires from Charleston. He does good work."

"I'm good for keeping business on Edisto. I need to go—"

Seabrook held out another Coke. "Here. Why don't I drive you?"

She accepted the unwanted third bottle and walked twenty feet over to the front lobby to avoid Marie's ears, noting for Seabrook to follow. "Hey, I understand you're concerned," she said.

"You almost died."

Like she needed to be reminded. "Yes, well, you're needed on Edisto. I don't have to remind you we're down a man."

He wiped his chin. "No, you don't."

She leaned in. "Mike, listen. No doubt your guilt is as big as mine about Francis."

With a sigh, he lowered his gaze to his feet, acknowledging the fact.

She closed the space between. "It is what it is." She kissed his cheek.

"Don't smother me to compensate for any regret. Makes me look bad and aggravates the rumor we're dating."

His forehead creased. "We aren't?"

She wasn't sure how to answer, so she put a Band-Aid on her reply. "We haven't been since I took over, but we will. It's been too long for me, too."

"So you're foregoing our dinner tonight."

She'd forgotten about the morning's offer on the beach. Here they stood at the crossroad of work and social, where she undoubtedly had to choose work when she yearned for him to take her in an embrace. They discussed how these moments of work versus feelings would be frequent. Even joked about it the day she accepted the position.

"Let me go talk to Sarah, then Mother, and if I can get back in time, we'll grab a bite. If not, tomorrow night. I'll call you. We have one, maybe two idiots running loose out there, and I cannot fathom who or why."

His kiss surprised her, both her hands on the bottle wedged against her stomach, while both of his cradled her face. Finally, he parted from her. "You're even hotter in uniform, Chief. Stay in contact."

The unexpected humor drew a quick snicker before she could catch it. Yes, it *had* been too long.

Marie smiled at her computer. Nope, no secrets in this department.

With the warmth still on her lips, Callie left with lifted spirits. Seabrook was a sweet, sweet man, with the strength and charm that made tourists love him. None of the overbearing cop machismo but enough to earn instant trust. Just as he'd won hers.

Most of Edisto wouldn't care if she dated Mike Seabrook, but she had to figure out the ones who would, then come up with a game plan from there.

The passing of John and then her father left her financially comfortable, and Chelsea Morning was paid for. However, no relationship would force her out of this job. Her previous absence from law enforcement left her restless, floundering, and the mysteries she'd solved had rejuvenated her into a whole person with a passion she'd forgotten she owned.

She wished she could tell naysayers to jump off a pier and leave her personal life alone. But that wasn't how small towns operated.

She headed east and soon pulled into Sarah's drive. Parking to the side, Callie ambled to where Sarah normally stationed her Volvo, studying the ground. She stooped in one area, then another, touching gravel, sniffing her fingers.

Ten minutes later, she found the spot. Brake fluid was clear or slightly amber in color so not readily seen, but its castor oil odor was unmistakable. She never would've been able to identify the scent if not for a case Stan used to train her years back . . . way back.

She needed to call him with an update. Get his feed on this.

Sarah's would-be murderer had stood here, forecasting a catastrophe. She wished she'd realized enough to scan the spectators at the marsh, but nobody expected the wreck to be deliberate.

This time when she knocked on Sarah's door, the lady of the house had to unlock it. Good girl.

"Is it safe to sit on the porch?" Sarah asked, peering out. "I so need air, and with you here that reporter won't catch me alone again."

Residents lived on Edisto for the nature. Nobody locked themselves up when the surf was a stone's throw from the front door. Callie understood and assumed a place in a wicker rocker, Sarah on a two-seater. Policing on Edisto came with its perks.

"Heard from the Highway Patrol?" Callie asked, crossing a foot over a knee, rocking her other foot so the chair moved.

"They took my statement over the phone," Sarah replied then caught herself with a gasp. "Oh, I was supposed to call you."

"No, you're fine," Callie said, disappointed at HP's intrusion on her turf without notice. But without forensics, without Sarah directing them to a suspect, neither she nor they had anything. HP would deliver their findings to SLED, the state law enforcement agency, or Colleton County Sheriff's Office. Jurisdictional formality because the accident happened a tenth of a mile from the town line. She needed to introduce herself ASAP and officially insert herself in the case. "Heard from Ben?"

Sarah seemed to reflect on a swarm of waxwings in two palmetto trees, fronds draped and in need of pruning, unmoving except for the birds. "He hasn't called and I haven't tried."

The day was waning. "Tell me how everything really happened, in the right order."

The temperature was moderate, but Sarah's complexion flushed as if ten degrees higher. "You won't like it."

Callie stopped her chair. "I'm not paid to like a case. I'm paid to solve the crime."

Sarah winced, skeptical. "Is this really a crime, Callie? Can't brake lines leak or something? The car was old."

"Your wreck was deliberate. I can't let that behavior run free. Tell me what you know, and I'll decide what's criminal and what's not. Also, the more you hold back about Ben, the more I suspect him."

Jumping up, Sarah reached the railing and hugged the post.

"Sarah," Callie said, no longer willing to coddle her father's mistress. "You had an affair. Accept the consequences."

Sarah flipped around, her back against the wood. "It's not just about me, Callie. It's about Ben, your mother, Lawton's name. Even you."

Callie lifted a notepad from her pocket. "If it is, it is."

"I'm a bit concerned about you. You've never—"

"Tried to be a cop in front of you?" Callie tightened her mouth. "Well, this is me on duty."

Callie hated to turn on her friend, but sympathy made the woman moodier and less cooperative, the total opposite of Beverly, which made Callie question what attracted Lawton to Sarah in the first place. But feelings of the heart, while often unexplainable, held a long, ancient history of instigating crime.

As if accepting her plight, Sarah's shoulders dropped. "Your mother and Ben met a week ago."

Callie wrote. "Were you there?"

"No, I was at one of Sophie's yoga classes."

Figures Sophie finally coaxed her to a class. Sophie felt she could cure anyone's ills with yoga, and Sarah had been solemn for some time.

Sarah returned and sat, slow and uncertain like an old person. "Ben and I have fought relentlessly since Lawton died."

Callie scribbled Sarah's words along with a few questions to ask.

"I called Beverly," Sarah said, then waited for recoil from Callie.

Callie gave her none.

"I apologized, said I was guilty but without much regret because I loved Lawton Cantrell. We had a long conversation."

Glancing up, Callie blew out, irritated. "Why would you do that, Sarah? Why not leave well enough alone?"

Sarah suddenly played with her cuticles. "She was cordial, Callie, unbelievably empathetic. Ben had mentioned divorce, but she suggested we move forward and make something of our marriage. As the wronged widow, she requested I give her all the proof of mine and Lawton's relationship, saying its presence would damage our effort to renew our vows."

Callie held a snort. Beverly held no compassion for Ben and Sarah. She sought to rid the earth of evidence damaging to her political aspirations. She thought she would appear weak allowing her husband to carry on an affair, and even weaker having endorsed it. Callie might not agree with Beverly, but she darn sure understood her.

"She asked if we would consider leaving Edisto," Sarah continued.

Callie dug into the paper. She couldn't imagine her father's reaction to that level of Beverly's hubris.

Then Sarah's soft voice hardened. "But she warned Ben that if we opened our mouths about Lawton, she'd make us sorry, beginning with Ben's legal profession. He asked what that meant, but she refused to specify."

Callie quit writing. "Was Beverly by herself? No Miss Promise?"

Sarah gave short jerky shakes no. "Not that I saw. And there's more."

Of course there was. "Go ahead."

"She bragged that you'd make our lives miserable and frame us for some crime. Said you could make an angel appear guilty."

Callie's head throbbed. No doubt she had to remove that tool from Beverly's arsenal. Callie definitely would head to Middleton at the conclusion of this chat.

She fought to stay on topic. "One more time . . . where's Ben?"

Tears slid down Sarah's cheeks. "He told me this then packed and left four days ago, like I said. But Ben's important to me. If he files for divorce, he's entitled. If he stays, I'll stand with him, but this disappearance, and the way he left. . . . We have a past, Callie." Her chin quivered. "We have a past."

"So where were you headed if you're so devoted to him?"

"Nowhere."

"With luggage?"

She twisted her nose in a sniffle. "I wasn't sure where."

She'd said Asheville yesterday, but that was obviously a lie. The woman's shoulders shuttered with a small sob, but Callie didn't believe her and didn't pause for sympathy. "What did Beverly say? And when?"

Sarah brushed at tears. "The day of the accident, Beverly came by."

"Alone?"

"Yes, alone. Ben was gone, remember?"

"I meant did she come alone, but go on."

"She . . . she asked for my letters from Lawton. Wanted my hard drive. Demanded pictures . . . and other things." Sarah's makeup had smeared.

Callie flipped a page, fighting not to show her ire, surprised Beverly knew what a hard drive was. "Did she threaten you?"

"No, but she reiterated about keeping quiet."

"Did you give her what she wanted?"

"No. Absolutely not."

Callie was glad to hear it. "Have you heard from her since the accident?"

"She called once, but I didn't answer when I saw caller ID."

Callie closed her notepad, slid it back in her pocket, and stood. She had enough for the moment.

"I'm so sorry, Callie." The woman's apologies were growing tiresome. So was her mother's behavior.

"I asked for the truth. Hopefully that's what you gave me." Callie turned to leave. "Give me a call if you leave town. Okay?" Without waiting for a response, she took the stairs to her car, with one turn back to wave.

Her phone rang. Sophie.

Callie started not to answer, but on instinct she turned toward Sophie's house only to see the leotard-clad woman hanging over her porch railing, phone to her ear, a neon green tunic fluttering.

"What?" Callie answered. "I'm in a rush, Sophie."

"Well, I didn't want to yell out that I needed to see you," she said, covering her phone as if keeping the world from eavesdropping. "Give me five minutes."

Hanging up without good-bye, Callie walked the three dozen yards to Sophie's stairs. Sophie motioned her inside.

Callie sniffed, noting Sophie had already burned her sage in preparation for the message. "Rough news if you're already smudging."

Sophie swished, her sleeveless top taking air then settling. "Aberdeen hates your guts."

"Oh, Sophie, I have no time for gossip."

"Hey." Sophie lifted the smoking sage stick, waving it under Callie's chin. "I don't invite negative conversation under my roof, so you could at least appreciate my concern. Heavens, Aberdeen LeGrand is worse than your mother."

I doubt that. But Callie recognized the yoga teacher had stepped outside her comfort zone. "I can't sit, just tell me."

Sophie set down the sage. "Brice wants you gone."

Callie scoffed. "Tell me something I don't know."

"He says your mother is crooked, she lies, and she cheats."

The instinctive urge to defend her mother ebbed quickly. She couldn't discount anyone's opinions about Beverly after the dreck heaped on her plate today. "Why do you entertain this Aberdeen woman in your house, Sophie? From the short moment I met her, she seems way negative for your taste. And your news is old hat."

Sophie lightly touched Callie's sleeves, her movements always so smooth. "Oh, honey, I've messed with that woman for years. I realize you're in a hurry—"

"Yes, I am."

"But you have to hear this."

Callie waited, in case Aberdeen had inadvertently enlightened Sophie as to something that might help explain . . . anything.

"I met Brice before Aberdeen, at Whaley's, back when I moved here. We talked over a drink at the bar, not that we were interested in each other, but—"

Callie sighed.

"Anyway," Sophie continued, like a hummingbird that never stops, "people thought we were dating. One day Aberdeen caught up with me in the Piggly Wiggly, before it was BiLo, which is why we call it the Pig-Lo now . . . and I explained I wasn't interested in Brice. Honey, I like my men way more fit than that, and amazingly we ended up laughing. She's liked me ever since."

"Sophie, really?"

Surprised at the lack of response, Sophie let out a *humph*. "You said you didn't understand about Aberdeen. Anyway, Brice told Aberdeen that you were like your mother. That you'd use your position to take advantage of people. With your family stock and your ruthlessness, as well as you having killed someone, you were a time bomb."

"I'm going to single-handedly destroy Edisto?"

"Aberdeen said you would."

Blowing out hard, Callie turned to leave. "Guess time will tell. Thanks for looking out for me."

Sophie followed as though tied to Callie's belt. "Aberdeen says Brice's mission is to take you down."

Holding the doorknob, Callie glanced back. "Where does this drama come from? Did she say?"

Sophie shrugged. "No, but she kept referring to your mother like she was Satan Incarnate." She ran back and grabbed the sage.

"Why does she hate Mother?" Callie yelled behind her.

"Don't know." Sophie returned and raised her sage like the Statue of Liberty.

"And what did you say once she polluted your house with accusations?"

No taller than Callie, Sophie puffed up and tossed her shag, the earrings rocking almost to her chin. "I told her she and Brice best watch their backs, because you were a force to be reckoned with."

Great. Just what Edisto needed—a civil war, and Sophie reinforcing the LeGrands' thoughts and repeating what Beverly was spreading around.

"Thanks, Soph," Callie replied and opened the door. "But let me take it from here."

Sophie leaned on the frame. "But what if she wants to talk again?"

"Then be my CI, my cooperating individual. Inform me, just don't inflame it."

"Ooh." Sophie shimmied. "I'm your snitch?"

"Unless it makes you uncomfortable," Callie said and headed down the stairs.

Sophie moved to the porch. "Where you headed?"

"Middleton. Beverly and I need a talk in the worst kind of way."

"Oh, honey, I'll be praying for you."

Callie cranked up the Escape. Easing onto Jungle Road, she soon reached Highway 174 and drove as fast as she dared. God help her, if she had a siren and blue light, she'd burn them out the whole forty-five miles to her mother's door, as if seconds meant years off her life.

The sun flitted in staccato flashes through the limbs of oaks and pines, and in no time she reached Adams Run. She turned north and sped up again, her anger rising with each mile.

Aberdeen was simply a mouthpiece for Brice, and on tiny Edisto, mouthpieces were a dime a dozen. No telling what Beverly'd done in her past to keep that fire stoked.

Today, however, she'd inserted herself too deeply into Rosewood business and served coy threats, calling Callie's name.

She reached Highway 162, stopped, and gunned the engine back up to speed.

Beverly's ugliness usually filtered through smiles and deft passive aggression. After thirty years of political two-stepping, this in-your-face business wasn't her form. Had Lawton's death altered her personality that much?

As much as Callie didn't want to agree with a damn reporter, Quincy was right. Beverly had more grudge than anyone against Sarah Rosewood, and ample means to act on it.

Chapter 10

MIDDLETON TRAFFIC seemed eager for rush hour, nothing like it was when Callie lived there as a child, and it only served to raise her irritation. She disliked passing the outskirts where strip malls and anchor box hardware stores drew most of the town's business. These newer structures lacked old Middleton's soul, decorated with its multitudes of azaleas, dogwoods, and camellias bowing to hundred-plus-year-old homes.

The newer residents had no clue how to appreciate that history. Her mother seemed about to fall into those ranks the way she was destroying the Cantrell name.

She had to hear her mother say it: *I did not try to have Sarah killed.* Even then she wasn't sure Beverly would tell the truth. How the hell was she related to this woman?

Driving into the old section, Callie headed down Rikard Street where she knew wisteria smothered the old oaks and pines each spring and the town hall stood tall. There it was, her mother's white BMW in the mayor's parking slot. Good. Callie could lock horns with her mother without Miss Promise's interference.

A text pinged in, Jeb, which made her check the clock again. Almost four thirty . . . about the time all hell broke loose on the causeway yesterday. Reaching under her seatbelt, she rubbed her chest, massaging, telling the ache to leave. Ever since Thomas hauled her out of Scott Creek, stress had nagged her from a headache to nausea to pressure in her chest. The sore throat. To do her job she needed a grip . . . but her body refused to cooperate.

There would be no slipping back into her earlier days when stress literally took her down . . . or into a bottle.

Her date with Seabrook had fizzled with her decision to come to Middleton, provoking her even more about Beverly.

A small zing of panic came and went.

Beverly couldn't stand not getting her way and had been heard making light threats under the Cantrell roof. White lies that should mean nothing. Callie recalled her mother's words: *I wish she'd have an accident.* A line said more than once about people in her way.

Francis floated back to the forefront. Her officer directing traffic, stopping bikini-clad girls on a speeding golf cart. Lying in a freezer under a draped sheet. His grandfather sobbing. Francis struggling beside her underwater.

Instinctively, she rubbed her chest again. She parked down the street at a meter. After feeding the machine, she rotated her shoulders once, the wrenched one biting in protest. Time to find Beverly. She inhaled to gain full control.

The back of a red-headed man disappeared into town hall way ahead of her. Surely not. Hopefully not. There had to be more than one ginger in all the souls doing business with Middleton. Callie had no desire for Quincy Kinard and Beverly Cantrell in the same evening.

She collected herself and entered the building. People nodded as Callie made her way to the inner sanctum. Anyone who'd lived in Middleton long recognized Lawton and Beverly's only child. The receptionist almost stood at attention when Callie asked if her mother was in.

"I'm not sure I can interrupt her, Ms. . . . um . . . Chief Morgan. She's in a meeting."

Callie'd hated this treatment as long as she could remember. A staffer genuflecting at the royalty's progeny.

"Don't bother her," Callie said, noticing a cane and a dog bed in the corner of the outer office. Geez, the old woman was even sitting in on town business. "Thanks. Ask her to call me when she gets out. I appreciate it."

Her shoes making tiny squeaks on the tiled floor as she exited, she wondered what she'd do for the next hour or two. She should've called in advance, but the surprise was meant to shake facts loose. Advance notice usually gave a suspect the upper hand.

In the lobby, she speed-dialed her favorite officer, not wanting to send a text of regret like he'd done to her.

"Hey," Seabrook answered. "Everything good?"

"You seem to think something's wrong whenever I call," she said, but didn't discount his concern. She enjoyed that concern.

"Instinct, I guess. Maybe habit with you," he said. "Catch up with your mother?"

Callie moved against the wall when two men ran into each other and opened a conversation about permits. "She's in a meeting, so I'm waiting."

"Hmm," he said. "No making it back to Edisto, then."

"Tomorrow, I promise," she said. She'd barely seen her son, either, but she had to pursue Sarah's open case before SLED or Colleton County took it from her.

"I hear your wheels turning, Callie. We'll leave our date open. Something wrong with your mother? You never said why you ran down there."

She hadn't brought herself to tell him about Beverly and Sarah's run in, and that struck a guilty nerve. It had to seem odd she checked on her mother amidst Francis's death and Sarah's case. Her officers were her team, and there weren't many left. Six, counting her. "I don't want to explain on the phone," she started.

"I've got two calls holding for me anyway," Seabrook said. "Call me when you head back."

She was relieved he had to disconnect first.

He deserved more from her, both professionally and socially, and maybe it was time she gave the guy a chance. Two weeks she'd been chief. Two weeks of pretending they hadn't dated. Time to just throw off the cloak and admit to being Seabrook's lady regardless of what Brice or the mayor thought. Seabrook deserved it, she deserved it, and half the beach already knew it.

Wow that felt pretty good. Screw gossip.

She slid the phone into her pocket as another uniform entered the building, the thick, sizeable body behind the badge familiar. "Chief Warren. How are you?" She hadn't seen him since her father's funeral.

He held out for a shake. "Callie Morgan. Chief, so I heard. Congratulations." His grip engulfed her tinier hand like it was no more than a marshmallow. "I'm so sorry to hear about your officer. You've had a tough time here lately, gal."

"Yes, sir." Her smile went somber at memories of her daddy's funeral.

"Here to check on your mother?"

"Affirmative. How's she doing, if you don't mind my asking?"

Warren was a good barometer for how well Beverly fared. He'd been a loyal lieutenant under Lawton's regime, meaning, hopefully, a continued supporter for the widow. Add that to his and Callie's common bond in law enforcement, and he just might shoot straight.

His brief scan for ears showed he understood discretion. "She runs a little fast, Callie, but she's trying."

"I see."

His skin darkened a bit. "She's not your father, but this town has operated under your father's style for, what, thirty years? Of course she's a contrast."

Spit it out. Was Beverly a loose cannon or just a little off base?

Stooping the one-foot difference in height, Warren leaned in. "Desperate is not the right word, but . . . she tries too hard to pretend she's Lawton."

Suspicion validated.

His big lungs pushed out a sigh, regaining his stature. "Your daddy's previous supporters are concerned. The guy running against her is a veteran with medals and a Middleton native. He's raking in the donations."

Callie'd heard of the man several times as a child, a teen, adulthood as the man's business savvy took hold. African American with a go-getter attitude to make Middleton great. Beverly braced a worthy adversary.

She patted his shoulder. "Thanks, Chief. Keep me in the loop, would you?"

"Will do. Feel good being back in the saddle?"

"It does," she said, taking notice down the hall to her left as the familiar head of red hair exited an office and moved her way.

I could take aim right now, and . . .

"Enjoyed seeing you. Tell Seabrook hey." Warren disappeared at a trot toward a man peering out a doorway, waving him down, passing Quincy Kinard on the way.

See? Even Chief Warren saw her closeness with Seabrook.

"Callie Morgan," Quincy called, his voice weak without echo, absorbed into the late-nineteenth century walls.

"You caught me," she said, taking fists to her waist.

His Cheshire cat grin held no trust. "You're in my town this time."

"Which was mine long before it was yours, but how about that."

"I'd love to be your escort, offer the same hospitality you did me on Edisto."

"Knock yourself out trying," she said, turning toward the exit.

He skittered along beside her. "My editor says your treatment of me was borderline harassment."

"Funny how borderlines work." The man had no idea what harassment was. Callie had Marie running background checks across five states on this idiot, which is how she knew he wasn't a Lowcountry native. Atlanta, to be more precise. Practically a foreigner.

She hated him way more than she could justify other than he scared

Sarah, which was enough for serious dislike but not the roiling feeling she carried. Her gut guiding her. If she had to name suspects, he was on the list, but he hadn't the animosity of Beverly. . . or even Ben. But still.

Slowly she took the stone stairs toward the sidewalk, having rushed here only to have time on her hands and a red-headed shadow. Time that could've been spent with Seabrook.

Quincy made another comment about family secrets, but Callie ignored him like he pedaled cheap goods on the street. He followed, heckling, asking questions she tuned out. Her car was parked across the street and one block down. Heading toward it, she studied the familiar venues on both sides and down Ashley Avenue to her right. Attorneys, insurance, the types that would encircle a town hall and courthouse with one exception: Grayson's Pharmacy.

Her stomach rumbled.

"I've uncovered some juicy stuff," Quincy said. "Want to hear?"

She gave him her back and chose the pharmacy. Built in the late 1800s, Grayson's had meant cherry orangeades atop a vinyl-covered barstool to Callie rather than prescriptions. A cooler near the counter refrigerated a wide assortment of chocolates. At the entrance, black and white ceramic tiles accented the tiny stoop, old-fashioned gold filigree lettering in the bay window.

She entered and saddled up to her old barstool, the one to the left of the chilled chocolates, and propped against the coolness like so many times as a kid.

"What can I get you, ma'am?" asked a guy in his early twenties, young enough not to know who she was.

She expected Quincy to speak up, but he stood in the doorway texting.

"Can you make a cherry orangeade?" Callie asked.

The clerk nodded. "Coming right up."

She watched the young guy press the oranges in a tall green squeezer contraption, then confident he understood the age-old recipe, she glanced back at the reporter. Still texting. Sarah was right. This dude was creepy in a stupid sort of way.

Her gaze continued around the store. The dark mahogany warmed her to good memories, and if not for Quincy's presence, she'd relax. Subtly, she ran her fingers under the counter on the unfinished wood . . . and smiled. CJC. Her initials, engraved in eighth grade. Took her three trips with a nail file to leave her mark for what she convinced herself was posterity engraved by a famous mayor's daughter. Her father caught her doing it in an unexpected appearance after a cancelled meeting. Then he etched his own beside hers.

"What's under there?" Quincy asked, leaning down.

"Nothing," Callie said, trying to shoulder him aside.

He stooped, using his phone to light the underside. "Would you look at that! What a cool special interest piece for the paper. Deceased mayor and his police chief daughter defaced the pharmacy in their Camelot days."

The clerk delivered the drink to her with one motion, sliding a straw in it with another. A cherry floated on the foam. Callie forced a pained grin, still smarting from her private secret exposed by the man at her elbow. Something so deeply personal, but too trivial to explode over.

"What'd you order?" Quincy asked.

"Arsenic," she replied. "So I can escape you."

She took the first sip, sugary and citrusy with a squirt of cherry juice to sooth her temper and her throat. With concerted effort, she closed her eyes and made the reporter disappear. Another sip, and she tried to recall the last time she'd sat here with her father. Too many years ago. In her disgruntlement with Beverly, she'd allowed time to speed by too fast in Boston, with too few trips home.

"Hey, kid," Quincy said, a grating edge to his nosiness. "How about another one for me?"

Callie stirred the drink, watching the pink cherry juice turn the orange to peach, fighting for the old feelings.

"What can I say to get you to talk to me?"

Her pulse rising, she gave up. The backlit clock on the wall with a shaving cream logo on it read five thirty.

Using a straw, Quincy poked her forearm, on the scar, hitting a nerve. "Hey, Chief."

She whirled and barely caught the glass before it hit the counter, sloshing half her drink. "Son of a bitch, Quincy. Do they train journalists to be obnoxious, or is that your specialty?"

The reporter snickered. "Got your attention."

"Next time my attention might break one of your bones," she said.

"Why are you in Middleton?" he asked. "To clear Mommy Dearest from the Sarah Rosewood incident? I saw her at the scene, remember. Awful coincidental."

The bell over the entrance jingled as a half dozen middle-schoolers rushed in, bookbacks shed on the floor.

The clerk cleaned up the spill. "I'll get you another," he said.

"No, that's okay." Callie lifted her glass to let him wipe beneath it, then finished the remnants in a big mouthful.

"I'm not letting up about Beverly Cantrell."

Callie laser-stared at the off-center mole between Quincy's brows.

"Bet there's a story behind that scar on your arm, too," he said.

"There's a story behind every scar," she replied, sliding off her stool. "And if you follow me this time, I'll give you one of your own. Back off."

"How does it feel to be stalked, Chief? Like you did me on Edisto," he said to her back. Then louder he proclaimed, "You're a lawsuit waiting to happen, and I'll be there to record it. On top of your father's affair and your mother's twisted involvement."

The two drugstore employees froze. The middle-schoolers stared at each other quizzically.

Tense, posture at attention, Callie exited and stood on the pharmacy stoop, huffing, wishing Quincy to come outside and give her some sort of reason to haul him to Chief Warren's jail.

Across the street, more middle-schoolers chased each other like leaves in a wind. Hard to believe any adult was ever that innocent. Well, maybe Sophie.

Beverly's parking space was empty. Callie slid on her sunglasses. Beverly hadn't called, because Beverly waited to *be* called, or called upon.

She walked toward the corner, hearing Quincy a few yards behind her. A man emerged from around the corner of the pharmacy. "Hello, Chief. You about ready for dinner?"

Seabrook grinned down on her from behind his own shades, still in uniform.

This was a surprise she could live with. "About time," she said and turned to Quincy. "Afraid you're not invited to dine with us, Mr. Paparazzi."

Holding up his phone, he snapped a couple pictures. "Like I said, an affair with the subordinate."

Seabrook took Callie's hand and inserted it through the crook of his arm. "Paint it what you will, reporter, but I call it a date." Then he escorted her toward his two-door Cadillac coupe, leaning over and speaking low. "Left the patrol car back on the island, Chief. Wouldn't want to break any regs and get in trouble with the boss."

Quincy started to follow. Both uniforms turned.

"Don't even think about it," Seabrook said.

"Chief Warren's on my speed dial, reporter," Callie replied.

The double-team effort sent Quincy back to the corner, then he crossed the street toward town hall without a glance back.

"Where to?" Seabrook asked when they reached his vehicle. He held her door.

"Anna Belle's?" she replied. "I'm in love with their crab omelet."

"I aim to please," he said, shut her door, and came around.

One of Middleton's most popular eateries, Anna Belle's sat only three blocks from the town square, but in that small distance, Callie's burning, aching chest settled into a normal heartbeat. Finally, an evening with her officer. Even better out of the scrutiny of Edisto. The only downside no alcohol, not in uniform.

Smart moves indeed, Mr. Seabrook.

They assumed a corner booth, both preferring to watch the door than have their backs to it. Orders placed, Seabrook took a drink of water. "I need to explain my behavior of late, Callie. Couldn't wait another day."

"Mike," she said, reaching for the hand encircling his glass on the table. "Think about who you're talking to."

"I know it, and I'm afraid of taking advantage."

She smiled and shook her head mockingly. "It's about time you took advantage, wouldn't you say?"

He didn't reciprocate the humor, and she retracted the coyness.

"When I learned of Pittstop," he said, "every piece of information became a hellacious fix. I wanted more, never satisfied. I thought I had overcome the obsession after a year of it . . . after losing Gracie. I'd let it replace my grieving for her."

"We aren't the types to let time heal us," she said. "We're proactive, reactive, with an emphasis on *active*. When I left Boston, bringing Jeb to South Carolina to more or less convalesce, the inability to investigate crushed me. That's when—" and she caught herself. He always overreacted in his opinion of her drinking issue. "That's when the panic attacks got bad."

"Leaving medicine for law enforcement fed the fix enough to keep me out of trouble, but now . . . this . . . it's busted wide open again, and I can't get enough." He lifted the water glass again, her hand losing its place on his.

"Mike," she said and leaned back in the booth. "Call me when you need to talk about it instead of making these impromptu runs to Florence. Let me give you some perspective."

"Like you're supposed to do with me about your drinking?"

His words stung. His mantra was: *Call me before you drink alone.* Of course she never did.

She sniffed, smelling the hollandaise sauce before the waitress reached the table. Her crab omelet was as light and decadent as Callie remembered, but at the sight of Seabrook's shrimp and grits, she almost regretted her choice. After filching a spoonful of the grits along with one of his six shrimp, she moaned with approval then dove into her own, grateful to shift their attentions.

But she made it halfway through the omelet and had to quit, her enthusiasm dampened by a protesting stomach.

Seabrook halted and lowered his spoon. "You just changed color, Callie. I swear, if you don't go see a doctor, I'm dragging you home and giving you a physical of my own."

"Wow," she said, smiling through another stomach flip. "That's some threat."

But his glower only worsened. "I'm not kidding. Almost drowning is nothing to play with. What are your plans tonight?"

She glanced at her watch. "Oh, crap. It's after seven." She snatched the napkin from her lap and dropped it beside her plate. "I haven't even met with Mother yet. She'll go to bed before ten."

He snared two huge quick bites and wiped his mouth, waving at the waitress for the check. "Wait, you haven't seen her?"

"No, she was in a meeting, remember?"

The waitress hustled over, fumbling with the ticket. Seabrook glanced at the tab and pulled out two twenties and a ten, pushing them to the girl with his hurried thanks.

"Can't it wait? It's not like you don't have a full agenda. Come on. We can talk on the way back to your car."

She didn't wait for the chivalry, jumping in and buckling up before he could show his manners. He started up the engine, arm over the seatback as he backed out of the parking slot. "So what's the deal with the illustrious Ms. Cantrell?"

"I'm not sure we have time for this, Mike."

"Give me the wiki version, then."

Her thoughts took them two blocks closer to her car.

"Mother seems to be too conveniently involved in Sarah," she said.

"Meaning?" He pulled up next to Callie's Escape and parked, car running.

"Mike—" Suddenly she worried telling him too much. While he was too steady a person to jump to conclusions, conflict of interest was plain common sense, and he'd call her out on it.

"I think I get it," he said, a sideways glance almost taunting in its delivery. "Hey, come here." He reached around her neck and pulled her to him. The long, warm kiss snaked deeper and lower than she expected after such an abrupt change in subject.

When they parted, he touched his forehead to hers. "Not my best idea for a date, but we broke the ice. Tell me about your mom tomorrow, okay? No secrets."

"Um, are you listening to yourself?"

"Yes, I am," he said and gently let her go. "I understand it's a two-way street."

She wasn't sure he did. That magnetic draw to solve a cold case had a magical, tempting appeal that sucked a person in.

The same way that a desire to protect a family member from an attempted murder charge had of keeping information close to one's chest.

She exited his Cadillac and hopped quickly into her SUV. The house wasn't far, but she needed to hustle nonetheless. So little time to coax Beverly to talk straight.

Cantrells had never played the underdog nor been forced to vie for power. Callie bet Beverly worried little about opposition, or that the reporter was more than a nuisance. She'd functioned in the Cantrell bubble most of her life.

However, the average voter would snicker all the way to the polls if Quincy reported a story of love pacts and middle-aged affairs. But Callie preferred that story to one of her mother attempting to murder her husband's mistress.

It would be a long night in Middleton as Callie attempted to convince her mother that her small town royal blood would in no way insulate her from charges and cuffs.

Chapter 11

CALLIE TURNED ONTO her old street. A long night lay ahead; it was past seven thirty.

The Cantrell home rested in the heart of old residential Middleton, built by Callie's grandfather during his second term as mayor. Architecturally dated with its Tudor style, the huge square footage stood ostentatious for the fifties, the two-story's majesty landscaped to the hilt. Not a centipede tendril over the sidewalk, the azaleas draped perfectly. What began as a march up the sidewalk slowed to a stroll as Callie brushed the limbs she'd pruned as a teen. Formosas and George Tabors mostly, old-school Indica hybrids. Beverly made her learn.

Now it was Callie's turn to teach her, and the lesson wouldn't be easy for either of them.

Beverly strode into Sarah's life as if she were untouchable, and Callie had to take her mother down a notch.

Beverly's behavior made her a suspect. Quincy and Ben remained on her list as well. Callie prayed whoever it was operated alone, but proving any of them would be no easy feat.

Fear belly-crawled through her at the thought that as police chief, she could destroy the Cantrell family. Relationships her father fought hard to preserve. He wouldn't be there to shout "Enough!" this time when this argument reached its boiling point.

Maybe it was time the gloves finally came off.

Quincy tailed her, had watched her turn on her mother's street, even followed to the driveway. Maybe sensing he wouldn't get through the Cantrell door like he had at the Rosewoods', however, he sped off.

Twenty steps from the drive to the front door in two-foot measures. As a child, Beverly reminded Callie not to stride like a farmer. She always wondered what was so bad about farmers. She rang the bell knowing Beverly preferred it, then knocked out of spite.

Jeb texted he was okay, literally *I am okay.* Over an hour late this time.

The walnut door swung open. "Dear! Why didn't you say you were coming? Inside, inside." The Cantrell matriarch swept Callie in. "We're finishing up dinner."

We?

"Your secretary didn't talk to you?" Callie asked, waiting for Beverly to shut the door. Callie laid her keys on the entry table on an embroidered runner, in a bronze dish supposed to be used as a card receiver for guests, an old Victorian etiquette rule Beverly loved to emulate. These days, people threw their mail in one, or their keys. This one held a couple of Miss Promise's notecards, of course, befitting a woman insulted by computers.

Beverly usually remained dressed for success until bedtime. Just in case. The only exception being silver lame slippers slid behind the bar for after dinner, ordered only from Belks. She tsked and lapped Callie toward the dining room, short heels clicking the hall tile. "Why, of course she told me you were in town. Just thought you headed back to Edisto when I never heard from you."

Callie smelled fried chicken before she reached the table, the striped bucket on a trivet between Miss Promise's and Beverly's places.

Crap. Did Promise ever go home? This was a game changer.

"Wow," Callie said. "The Colonel dining at the Cantrells. A tailgate special at that." Beverly had indeed expected her to appear, only not this late.

"Oh hush," Beverly said, taking her seat. "You can sit there."

"I remember where to sit," Callie said, acknowledging the chair she'd occupied for decades, except when company relocated her to the other end. "Hey, Miss Promise."

"Callie."

Conversation ceased with only Miss Promise's tiny smacking noises and Beverly's coos to spoon second helpings of the sides. Callie missed Tink until she caught Miss Promise discretely lower her arm toward the floor, a small piece of chicken skin disappearing in the process.

The grease would do little for Callie's stomach, so she pinched off of a biscuit. Wondered when Promise would go home . . . how she would go home. Would asking to take her be in poor taste.

Beverly remained unusually quiet. So not like her, as if the company made her sit taller, mind her manners, speak only when spoken to.

Miss Promise clung hard to Beverly these days, or was it vice versa? Maybe the old lady had prompted the showdown with Sarah: prodding the dominant mayor to overpower the guilty mistress into submission.

The old lady laid her paper napkin beside her plate and shuffled to the living room without a word, triggering Beverly and Callie to clear the table. Tossing empty containers into the trash, Callie sucked in a deep breath before turning to rest her backside against the kitchen counter. "We need to talk, Mother."

"What about, dear?" Beverly lit a lemon-scented candle to rid the air of dinner smells, then wiped at the granite though nothing had been cooked.

"Sarah."

Beverly kept wiping beside the range.

"You threatened her . . . and Ben," Callie said.

"I don't threaten," her mother replied, without looking up. "Sarah and I are fine."

"You said I'd use my power as chief of police against them."

"Surely they misunderstood."

Callie's eyes narrowed at the lie. Beverly should fly off melodramatic and hand-on-her-bosom shocked at any sort of misrepresentation. Instead, she wiped countertops.

Beverly shifted to the end of the island and Callie followed. "You're better off to admit you were the jilted wife than haranguing Sarah for old evidence that means nothing."

The wiping stopped. "Nobody debases your father."

"Except you."

Beverly clutched the dishtowel to her chest. "I would never."

"Hell, you're all but doing it by the way you're acting," Callie said, contrary at this irresponsible side.

"I have no idea what you mean," Beverly replied coyly. "And watch your voice. Promise might hear you."

"Mother, shut up with the whole Steel Magnolias pretense."

Beverly righted herself, draping the towel across the sink edge. "Listen to how you speak to me."

Tested, Callie pushed off the counter and verged into her parent's personal space. "Be glad I don't haul you into an interrogation room and turn you over to a SLED agent. Right now you're a suspect regarding Sarah's attempted murder."

Beverly spun, one of her pumps coming off her heel. "Attempted murder? A deer caused her wreck."

"No, ma'am. Someone messed with her car. You were the last person to visit her, and damn it, Mother, you have motive. Especially since you threatened her and Ben, so answer my questions and quit farting around!"

"Hush," Beverly said, finger over her mouth.

Damn it, the woman cared more about etiquette than murder. "I don't give a rat's ass what Miss Promise hears . . . or thinks. You probably took her with you every time you screwed with Sarah and Ben."

Beverly inhaled, held it, then let it out. "I expect you not to sass me, or corner me like a perpetrator."

The offensive counter shot didn't escape Callie, but the confrontation had her heart pounding beneath the uniform she was trying to represent. "You left Sarah's place in the morning, then came back to meet her, which happened to be about the time the car crashed. That appears like you returned to see if your plan worked."

"Sakes alive, I didn't do it," Beverly exclaimed. "You profess to be such a good detective. Find the bad guy and quit wasting time with me."

Callie searched her mother for telltale signs of half-truths, seeing no signs of a cold lie. "Mother, I want to believe you, but thanks to your supercilious airs, you've drawn attention to yourself as a likely suspect."

Beverly waved as if seeking the right words, the movements uncertain, her voice pitchy. "Then . . . fix this! Don't police have ways to make things disappear?"

Callie recognized the slipping refinement, but couldn't believe her ears. "Don't you ever . . ." she said, finger stiff and critical, "ask me to abuse my position. Or use me for your personal gain. I'll ruin your campaign myself." Then she added a definitive strike on the end. "Daddy would be appalled."

Flushed, Beverly poked Callie in the stomach. "I forbid you to use your father against me."

Fire flew through Callie, her instinct to put anyone who touched her against the wall. Her hands twitched at the restraint, a disappointing pain throughout her being. "Then don't give me reason to."

Something was indeed different with Beverly. A secret, a sense of dodging reality. A flustered lady falling off the edge of her ivory pedestal.

Beverly's chin rose, a sign of her ego centering itself. "Anything else?"

Damn this woman. Callie moved to the other side of the island. "What time did you see Sarah yesterday morning?"

Taken aback by the switch, Beverly read her watch as if it recalled appointments. "I don't remember exactly."

Callie flicked her shield. "You can speak to this badge now or one you don't know later."

Beverly remained attentive to the watch. "After eleven. Not quite time for lunch."

"So you had no appointment?"

"I called once I was on the island. She'd contacted me a few days prior, the conversation somewhat . . . atoning. I happened to be coming to Edisto so . . ."

"You meant to catch her off guard." Callie gave a small moan of impatience. "Was Sarah's car in her drive?"

"I suppose so."

No yes or no answers, but Beverly always addressed confrontation with pretty words and nuances.

"Did you touch it?"

Confusion drove her mother's response. "Touch?"

Callie raised her voice. "Did you or anyone with you do anything to Sarah Rosewood's Volvo?"

"No," her mother shouted in a heavy whisper. "Oh, how asinine," she added as if the word *no* was blue collar. Beverly nudged around Callie to the refrigerator. "Miss Promise needs a fresh glass of tea."

"Miss Promise can wait. Damn, Mother, this is coloring way outside the lines even for you. Why did you return that afternoon?"

"To see if she'd changed her mind about giving me those letters and photos." Her gaze traveled to the hallway, toward where Promise sat in the living room.

Lawton lived under an hour away and owned a house two doors down from his lover. What clandestine couple recorded gobs of physical evidence that could be easily used against them if found? Especially when one was a politician.

"Not to see if by chance the cut brake lines worked?" Callie asked.

Beverly's mouth dropped open. "Callie!"

Callie winced at the chastisement, then ran fingers through her hair. *Crap, this isn't working.*

Beverly harrumphed and gently pushed Callie apart from the refrigerator. As she turned with the tea pitcher, Callie took it from her. Snatching a glass out of the cupboard, she poured a glass full and held it toward Beverly. "Take this to your sidekick in there. I need to talk to her, too."

"Don't you lecture that poor woman." Beverly left, spinning on her heel.

With three deep inhales, Callie counted, wondering why the hell she was here without Seabrook. She even had him in town! Emotion distorted her questions and Beverly's answers. Why did she think tackling her mother on Cantrell turf could result in anything but a Beverly win?

Callie followed the clipping heels to the living room. Tink lifted to a sitting position in an eighteen-inch stuffed circle bed, his mistress awakening from a doze in the Queen Anne chair next to him.

The dog had a bed in the Cantrell house?

"Why didn't you come see me yesterday, Miss Promise?" Callie asked. "Before the accident. I can't imagine the both of you visiting my beach and not dropping by. I'd have taken you to lunch."

"Here you go, Promise," Beverly cooed. "Ignore her." Moving to the mahogany wet bar, she donned the slippers, held up a martini glass toward Callie, and started to speak only to have the grandfather clock in the hall gong nine. Each of them remained poised, waiting. As the last gong accented the huge emptiness of the house, Beverly spoke. "I assume you still enjoy these?"

Of course Callie did, and her mother didn't wait for a response. Soon an extra dirty martini sat before her on a tiled coaster, a pitcher behind it on a china trivet. French gin.

Beverly's means of fawning to Miss Promise and diluting Callie's behavior.

Beverly sipped. Callie would guess a double. Quincy was right about one thing: her taste for gin was inherited.

Miss Promise sat ankles crossed, a napkin under the base of her cold glass so as not to dampen her soft blue skirt. "I thought we agreed you'd stay on Edisto."

Prim, proper, but a continual pissant.

Callie wanted to gulp the damn drink in one swoop. "No, ma'am. We agreed I'd do my job and stay out of politics. Seems y'all screwed that up yesterday. Did you speak to Sarah or was that all Mother?"

"I just tag along," she said. "I'm an old woman, entertained by your mother's enthusiasm, grateful for her graciousness in letting me accompany her in her campaigning."

"So you did see Sarah?"

The lady smiled and gave a tight shrug, lifting her glass. "Just going wherever—"

"Ma'am," Callie said, smirking. "There is no *just* in anything you do. But tell you what . . . let me offer some advice."

Miss Promise gave another tiny, charitable grin.

"Back off from the Rosewoods and stay in Middleton," Callie said.

Beverly fluffed up. "I demand manners under my roof, young lady."

Unbuckling her utility belt, Callie leaned forward on the sofa to remove it. "Mother, please." She grimaced as her shoulder pained her at the reach around. She gently laid the belt on the cherry coffee table, afraid of a smudge on the embroidered sofa. Drinking meant she spent the night. The house had one generic guest bedroom plus specific rooms for Jeb and Callie, and she was sure she'd find a toothbrush somewhere.

Fifteen years drawing confessions out of the most abominable hoodlums in Boston, and she had succumbed to a woman in Dior who mixed a damn fine martini.

She could try again. Maybe with more strong-arm this time. Or scream and throw her friggin' glass against the imported wallpaper and protest. But fact was this interrogation went as badly as one could go, and she'd been a fool coming to Middleton.

She reclined deep into the sofa, enjoying the gin she'd denied herself for weeks. Call it change of tactic. They might even loosen up and talk.

She sent Seabrook and Jeb texts about her staying the night, told Jeb he could stop texting when he was in for good. She dropped the phone on the sofa and fished out an olive from her drink. "Your problem is that you can't slide into the mayor's job on Daddy's coattails like you'd hoped."

Beverly twisted in her seat, legs together, never crossing. "That reporter is trying to sabotage me. I hate the way those people search for dirty stories instead of the truth."

A hypocrite to the end. "That's priceless. Your problem is he might find the truth."

Miss Promise stiffened. "That's cruel, child."

"No, ma'am," Callie answered, the gin making her no longer reserved about the hierarchy in the room. "That's reality, and if you don't see that, you're doing Mother no service." She moved her attention solely to Beverly. "If Daddy's fling is the only chink in your armor, then get in front of it. Hey, look at Hillary Clinton. Instead talk issues. What *are* the issues, by the way? What's your platform?"

Beverly eyed Miss Promise whose head tipped up ever so slightly.

"I asked you, not her, Mother," Callie snapped. Where the heck was Beverly's head? Surely she absorbed more political savvy than this from Lawton. Had Promise Hollister harnessed Beverly so tightly she couldn't think for herself?

"When your father was in office, he thought . . ."

"This isn't about Daddy," Callie said.

Beverly flinched at the interruption.

Callie tossed back her second martini, her tongue suddenly dry, and reached for the pitcher. She might pay for it later, but she needed it now. "Want to honor Daddy's legacy? Then serve Middleton."

Miss Promise eased out of the chair. "Says the girl who abandoned her hometown. I think I'll turn in, ladies. Beverly, quit with the drinks and get to bed. Alcohol ages your complexion." She baby-stepped her way to the hall, then to the guestroom at the end. Tink tippy-toed behind her.

Callie waited until the door shut. "She's staying here? How long's that been going on?"

"Since I decided to run for office. She offered, and she's been such a grand friend over the years. So knowledgeable from her days in the Statehouse. I feel honored." Beverly finished her third drink and headed back to the bar, leaving the pitcher with an inch at the bottom.

Callie started to polish it off, but her stomach burned. "Mind if I stay?"

"Of course not," Beverly almost slurred, but it was a depressing slur, not the normal kind from a great evening of good drinks. "There are clean sheets . . ."

"I know, Mother." Callie stood, putting her dry glass in the pitcher. "Seriously, this situation with Sarah is not good. What makes it worse is that an officer died in the process. I almost died. Someone's vendetta crossed the line."

Beverly addressed the mirror, her back to Callie, silent.

"While I hope not, someone might try again," Callie said.

Still no response.

"Fact is, any suspect who contacts Sarah tilts the scales toward themselves as the guilty party. Are you hearing me, Mother? Answer, please."

"I hear you."

"Good. See you early tomorrow, at which time we can talk about Brice LeGrand."

"Don't think so. 'Night, dear."

Always fighting for control. "Oh no, you don't get off that easy. Brice LeGrand wishes me fired for some who-knows-what reason related to you. His wife Aberdeen all but spat on me."

The senior woman spoke into her drink. "He wouldn't dare."

Callie walked closer. "Then enlighten me, so I know what I'm dealing with."

"I've already said good night. Now go to bed."

Callie decided not to challenge through a haze of gin. Instead, she set the pitcher in the kitchen sink and headed to the stairs.

Ten till ten on the grandfather clock. Her bed called for her from the second door on the right upstairs. Suddenly her body dragged from the days' stress, the drink, and this damnable bug she couldn't shake.

A gold goose down comforter covered a four-poster bed. A white fluffy area rug lay beside it on oak floors. Her awards and ribbons, posters and photographs had disappeared somewhere, maybe the top of the closet, sanitizing the room like a *Better Homes and Gardens* photo. Chocolates beside a bottle of water. Her mother had hoped she'd spend the night. She ate the chocolates and tossed the wrappers on the dresser to give the room reality.

Callie had failed so badly tonight. No doubt Seabrook should take it from here. She dialed his number, but it went to voicemail. "Hey, we've got to talk," she said. "I haven't told you everything about the Sarah Rosewood accident. Call me."

Or should Raysor take lead? Seabrook's head was rather preoccupied.

And Brice puzzled her even more now. His intense animosity coupled with Beverly's too quick dismissal meant a history. While not at the top of her to-do list, the Brice and Beverly story needed to be peeled back.

Callie unbuttoned her uniform, laying it carefully across a settee to avoid wrinkles. A hint of stomach trouble, but the buzz made her not care. At least not barfing. Stripping down to her underwear, she brushed her teeth and slid under the satin. She tired of the Cantrell pretense, but as sleep took her, she highly appreciated their quality thread count sheets.

The air conditioner hummed. Sheets slid lusciously over Callie's legs, but something woke her from the deep repose. Eyes shut she listened, her instincts sensing the space in the room.

Tink barked. More like a yip. An irritating little noise.

The grandfather clock downstairs chimed once. Two thirty? Three thirty? Wait. She shouldn't be hearing the gong that clearly. Her bedroom door was open. She'd shut it.

Slitting her lids, she remained fixed, half expecting Beverly to be doing something motherly like leaving new towels. There. A rustle. A dark movement at the dresser. Not Beverly.

In a quick reach under her pillow, she retrieved the Glock and jerked up, aiming at the man at the mirror. "Freeze!"

He bolted out of the bedroom, and she heard him hit the stairs.

Entrapped under goose down, Callie snatched at the satin, kicking at covers for freedom. Scooting to the edge of the bed, her foot caught in a sheet tucked tight under the mattress, taking her to the floor.

Jumping upright, she raced to the stairs, taking them four at a time, schooled at skipping them in practice as a child.

The front door agape, a night breeze sent chills racing across her exposed skin. She hugged the wall, eased to the stoop and peered outside, listening. She turned her head to the side and listened again.

"Callie? What are you doing outside in only your panties?"

Callie whispered, "Mother, run get me a phone, please. And stay inside until I come back."

"You can't go outside like that!" Beverly clutched a silk robe, the silver lame slippers on her feet. "Oh my, is that your gun? Is there an intruder?"

"Get me a phone!" Why did her mother have to return to her old chatty self at such an inopportune moment?

Callie moved to the driveway, leading with her weapon. No smell. No sound. No out-of-place vehicle. Goose bumps prickled her arms and legs and across her bare breasts from the coolness of a humid, early fall night.

She walked tentatively around her car. All four tires slashed on her Escape.

Once she canvassed the house's periphery, she returned to the front door where Beverly held out a wireless. With no place to put her weapon, Callie left-handedly dialed 911, relayed the pertinent information, then gave the phone to her mother.

"Oh my, what is going on?" Miss Promise exclaimed from the hall, wrapped up in a quilted robe that dragged the rug, Tink clutched against her. "Oh," she added as Callie turned in her nude glory.

"We had a break-in, Miss Promise. Go back to your room."

Callie shut the door with a hip to avoid touching the knob. She planted Beverly, still connected to 911, on the living room sofa while she ran up to her room to throw something on. The Cantrell address would attract Middleton PD en masse.

Entering the bedroom, she flipped on the light and gave the space a once-over, scanning for anything that sent the intruder to her room, or anything he could've left behind. Of the bedrooms to enter, hers held the least value and the most risk. If he randomly entered this house, his luck stank, choosing the one with the Glock and without valuables.

But if this break-in wasn't random, then what was its purpose?

On the dresser. That wasn't there before. She ventured closer to find an envelope . . . with Seabrook's name on it.

This wasn't a damn bit random. Not at all.

Chapter 12

AS A RESULT OF the impromptu sleepover at her mother's, Callie had only her uniform to wear, and no way would she display herself to fellow officers without it worn properly. So at three thirty in the morning she was up for the day. Cops would swarm the house and not leave until business hours, when she'd need to be back on Edisto. She barely had her shoes laced before Middleton PD arrived at the Cantrell mini-mansion.

"Callie?" Beverly hollered up the stairs. "The police are here."

"Be right there," she yelled back, the effort escalating a dull headache. After drinking the entire bottle of water, she hit speed dial on her cell.

Time to bring Seabrook into the mix, not only because of the envelope but to change places with him regarding investigating Beverly. Maybe hook him up with Chief Warren. Time to rein in his trips to Florence and direct his attention back to Edisto. She felt like Stan back in Boston, when he pinned her ears back due to misguided focus.

Hopefully their short dinner date had turned some of his attention back around.

Seabrook answered, surprisingly alert. "Callie? What's up?"

She cocked her ear at the *What's up* line rather than the standard *What's wrong*? "There was a break-in at Mother's," she said, raspy, then cleared her throat. "I awoke with him in my bedroom. My tires are slashed."

"You okay? Your mother okay?"

A door slammed in Seabrook's background. Where was he? "Yeah, but the perp got away. Listen, I have no way back to Edisto, plus we need to finish our talk. How quick can you be here?"

"Not for a few hours. After I left last night, since you weren't coming back to Edisto . . ."

What the hell was this? Her bet was another Florence trip. She so did not have time for this. "Want me to call Raysor?"

"Yeah," he replied, his voice low as if he didn't want someone to hear.

"Taking the day off?" she asked, guessing the answer.

"Might be late. Can't really talk. I'll explain once I get there. You'll understand."

Would she?

And this was so not the time to quickly say *By the way, the burglar left an envelope for you in my bedroom.* News best delivered in person.

"Fine," she said, trying for benign and unemotional. "Got to go. Middleton PD is waiting."

"Understood," he said then hung up.

She held the dead phone, a bit taken aback at him hanging up first. Hell no, he didn't understand because she didn't explain.

She damped down the disappointment and called Raysor. Contrary to Seabrook, Raysor answered like someone woken from a drunken stupor. "Hey, it's Callie," she said. "You awake enough to talk?"

Snorts and movement on the phone spoke that he fought to awaken. She discarded visions of him scratching.

"Better be good to wake me from *that* dream," he said.

She relayed the news and her inability to drive back. Raysor lived in Walterboro, a half hour distant. Better than calling Thomas on Edisto. And she preferred the senior deputy's experience.

"Keep your pants on," he groused. "I'm coming."

"Callie?" her mother called again.

"Coming."

Callie hadn't touched or opened the envelope lying innocent on the dresser. She didn't care to drag Middleton PD into Edisto business any more than she wanted the Highway Patrol investigating Sarah's case. But what the hell was she supposed to do with it? Turning the envelope over to Middleton, she'd lose control with it retained as evidence in probably the wrong case.

Plus the name Seabrook on the envelope had nothing to do with Beverly or Sarah . . . and everything to do with Callie.

How many damn cases did she have?

Using a pen, she flipped the short envelope, the block letters spelling *Seabrook*, over to hide the writing and pushed it to the side next to the chocolate wrappers, water bottle, and Hummel figurines to be part of assorted stuff instead of an anomaly. Something small and irregular inside. A chill raised her suspicion as to its identity.

But she had to great Chief Warren's guys. She ran downstairs into a circle of three officers caught with Beverly in an arm-waving recant of the crime she knew nothing about.

"I awoke with him in my room," Callie interrupted. "Want to start there first?"

"Yes, ma'am," they said, eager to escape Beverly's drama.

As expected, they did a once-over, checking windows for signs of ingress, and returned downstairs.

A couple of techs shortly arrived to take prints. Chief Warren appeared around four forty-five.

"Callie?" Beverly caught her daughter in the hallway before Callie exited and reached the chief. "They're leaving a mess on my doors," she complained, pointing at the fingerprint technician.

Yes, let's worry about smudges and ignore the crime. "No other option, Mother. They'll take your prints as well, to rule them out of the ones they find. Just do as they ask. And can you bring me about three aspirin?"

Beverly held up her hands, flipping them over to analyze her nails.

"Jesus, Mother, they aren't here to inspect your manicure."

Beverly snatched her fingers closed. "I know that."

"And I want that explanation about Brice," Callie whispered in her mother's ear.

Miss Promise shuffled out of her bedroom, fully dressed with pearls, Tink cuddled close.

"You might explain the fingerprints to her, too," Callie said and walked over to greet Warren in the living room, who chatted with a uniform in his twenties. "Thanks for coming, Chief," she said.

Though early, he stood alert and in charge and gave her an empathetic grin. "I take it he was unidentifiable?"

She shook her head. "Dark clothes. Dark hair. No light. He bolted when I yelled and brandished a weapon."

"Gloves?" Warren asked.

"I assume so," she said. "But I'm not missing anything. Mother either. Miss Promise is visiting, so I doubt she had much more than the rings on her, but you might check on that. She's lived here a few . . . days." Or was it weeks?

Callie crossed her arms. "But why tonight when Mother has two visitors? The guy couldn't have worse luck choosing my bedroom, either."

"He's lucky enough," Warren said. "He picked the locks, so my bet's on gloves. Nobody can identify him, and your mother didn't use her alarm system. Said Miss Promise sets it off when she takes the dog out. Sounds like he's scot free even after taking the time to flatten your tires."

Callie sighed hard, noting to double check the alarm whenever she stayed. "Maybe she'll use her system now. There's no telling her a damn thing."

"She's mayor. I'm chief of police. Tell me something I don't know," he mumbled.

The copper-colored Jeep caught her eye as it passed under a street-light, taking the corner fast. Quincy didn't live far, because as he rolled into reach of the Cantrell front spots, his wipers cleared dew from the windshield. He parked and officers ignored his presence, parting like oil dropped on water when he crossed the damp lawn.

"How does he show up like that?" Callie asked Warren.

"You met him?" the other chief asked. "He's not a bad guy, he's—"

"Involved in that accident that took my officer," she finished. "And he birddogs my mother in some supernatural way." *And now apparently me.*

Quincy trotted up as if late to the opera. "Hey, Chief . . . and Chief. What has Middleton's finest at the mayor's house? And Edisto's PD in Middleton?"

"An amateur break-in," Callie replied, not giving Warren the chance, then left the conversation, noting that Raysor had pulled up and waited in his car at the curb.

"Sorry to drag you from a good sleep," she said.

He passed her a coffee. "It may not be what Mommy-dearest serves, but thought you wouldn't be picky this time of morning. It's black."

"That works, thanks." She took the cup, blowing through the sip-ping hole to cool it.

"What happened?" he grumbled, remaining in the cruiser.

What happened indeed. The perp had intel about her, was familiar with Seabrook, clearly targeted Callie in her mother's house, but she explained only the facts while Raysor's gaze traveled around the yard, landing on Quincy. "What's that little bastard doing here?"

"Good question," she said, leaning on his door. "How'd he know to come? Police radios are encrypted, or at least they were in Boston."

"He must connect with somebody." They each watched the activi-ties a moment. "So," he said long and slow. "Where's Mike? Surely I'm not your number one on speed dial when you need a ride."

"You tell me," she said. "Said he was busy and unavailable."

"Hmmm." Raysor stared off, his mouth moving slightly.

"We're a small outfit, Don. I need to understand how fanatical he is in this quest."

"He's in Florence," he said. "Left me a text."

But not her?

An officer seemed to be hunting for her. Callie rose from her place against the car. "You need me?" she called.

"No, ma'am. Only wondering where you were. We're good. Wanted to say we'll try not to be too much longer."

Callie repositioned. As soon as these guys were done, she needed to leave. The Brice and Beverly conversation would wait. "How long has Seabrook been going over there?"

"He's always hunt-and-peck investigated over the years—he has to have told you that—but the effort intensified the week before you came on the job. The fact you were taking over fired him up even more. Never saw a man so ready to pass over the reins. Sometimes he drives in from Florence after an all-night vigil."

"What the hell does he expect to do with the man when he meets up with him?"

Raysor gave a quick gravely morning cough. "Hell, he has no plan."

She needed to schedule another meet with Seabrook pronto and redirect it into a deep discussion on priorities . . . and common sense. And the envelope. And maybe them.

Why was that one always last?

An officer climbed in his car and left. The techs appeared to be packing up. A neighbor stood on his step across the street, drinking his coffee.

But Quincy had corralled Beverly. Callie almost jumped up to intercede then talked herself out of it. Neither knew they were fellow suspects. The two deserved each other.

"Mike can't keep up that pace," she said. "And what's he expect to accomplish? Talk the man into a confession after all these years?"

"Hate to say pot calling the kettle black, but why did *you* do it, doll?"

She started to say her case was different. She had jurisdiction. She had the force of Boston PD behind her. Her guy was part of the Russian mob which meant Boston had background on the players. She had backup.

Seabrook, however, freelanced, with no rhyme as to what he'd do if he cornered Pittstop, Roman, or whatever his name was. Not only was that not Seabrook's style, but he hadn't the experience. He'd watch, stalk, maybe speak to people in Pittstop's wake as he went to work, ate out, dated. Hunt, watch, ponder the moment time after time after time how he'd kill the guy. Yeah, she knew.

Beverly gestured wildly, pissed at Quincy, pointing at an officer to serve as her bodyguard and dismiss the reporter, which only made Quincy pepper the uniform with questions. Indefatigable, the journalist owned gumption.

Warren waved her over, and she yielded her half-empty cup to Raysor.

"We'll run prints, knock on a few neighbors' doors, but not sure we'll accomplish anything, Callie. I'll send someone to change her locks, but you need to make her use that alarm system."

She reached for a handshake. "Thanks, Warren. Have a patrol come by the house regularly?"

"Absolutely," he said.

She turned to go inside only to almost bump into Quincy. "I need to speak to you," she said. "Don't leave."

Ogling and pretending to shiver, he laughed. "Ooh, intriguing."

It was five thirty, and the horizon lightened a bit, the indigo navy easing into shades of blue, the sun not quite ready to appear. Lights began to pop on in the surrounding homes, the residents suddenly aware of an incident as they retrieved morning papers. By six, clouds showed dark on one side, but illuminated on the other as oranges and purples announced the coming day.

In a holding pattern, Callie waited for Middleton to finish its thing. And she pondered the people, places, and incidents that swirled in a tornado with no place to land, none of them much linked to the other. Quincy being a nuisance. Seabrook off his game. A B&E, attempted murder, and accidental drowning connecting them all, but not really.

The chief's car was the last to leave, except for the Jeep. Callie lectured Beverly about the security system, even running through the steps in case it had been too long for her to remember. Then Callie exited, listening to hear Beverly set the alarm behind her.

Quincy waited on the steps, he and Raysor staring each other down. When Quincy started to rise, she sat beside him. "I need your help, newspaperman."

At first he was leery and tilted his body back, disbelieving. But when she remained somber, he tossed the cheeky mien.

Pausing, she rethought her decision, but then proceeded. This could kill two birds with one throw. "Need you to check on a guy for me. Name's Roman McGee, with a nickname of Pittstop."

"Is this about your mother?"

"No."

"Sarah Rosewood? The car wreck?"

"No."

His chuckle rang sarcastic. "You're sending me on a goose chase."

Yes, but it was a goose worthy of the chase. "Shut up and listen," she said. "You recall that case in Charleston eight years ago where the guy killed the doctor's wife? They never caught him."

"The doc went nuts or something," Quincy added. "What's this got to do with me?"

"I think a guy named Roman McGee might have done it."

"So pick him up."

She blew out as much for her own exasperation as she did for show for him. "Can't. He's in Florence and there's no evidence. He just got out of jail, serving a short time for another charge." Pittstop would eventually recognize Seabrook whereas Quincy snooped from an entirely different angle. A short red-headed journalist didn't stick out as much as a cop, and Quincy could pursue info online and make calls as a nuisance reporter and not be deemed a threat. Pittstop would be less threatened by Quincy, assuming their paths ever crossed. "Sometimes reporters can go places, talk to people, and uncover details that uniforms can't. I'd like you to use your resources to see if he's bragged to anyone or dropped clues. I doubt anything you're writing beats this story."

Raysor started to exit his vehicle, and Callie motioned for him to stay . . . and not hear. "I gotta go, but can you do this?"

Skeptical, Quincy stood. "You don't give a damn about me, so what's in it for you?"

"You recall Officer Seabrook?"

"Oh yeah," Quincy said. "He and your ogre over there in the car brought me to your office to be harassed."

"That's right. He's the doctor."

The reporter's mouth fell open. "You're shitting me! The officer you're dating is this doc?"

"Will you help me or not?"

"Give me the info again," he said, grabbing his phone to take notes.

She repeated the information, Quincy leery but curious enough. "I'm on it," he said.

"Keep me up to speed?" she asked.

"Remove me as a suspect on the Rosewood deal?" he replied.

She scoffed. "That's whatever it turns out to be, Quincy. If you're innocent, you have nothing to worry about."

He did his head wobble. "How many times have you seen that logic backfire on cop shows, Chief?"

He was right, but she didn't care. She'd continue to investigate him, though she suspected him less and less. No real motive. "Tell me something before I have to leave," she added.

"Depends."

"How did you learn to come here this morning? Who called you?"

He removed his foot and took the stairs to the sidewalk to leave. "Nope, not revealing my sources, Ms. Morgan. You know how that works." He turned and strode across the dew-laden grass, Raysor studying him all the way to the Jeep.

Warren had spoken kindly about the reporter, so maybe Quincy had an understanding with the department. Or he had a friend on the force, or in dispatch. Still too much like a friggin' snake, in her opinion.

Callie watched Quincy leave then plopped in Raysor's Colleton County cruiser. They headed toward Edisto Island, the decision being to pick up her patrol car with its four new tires at J&J's. Chief Warren had promised to have Callie's Escape towed to a Middleton garage to have its four tires installed.

Traffic moved, not thick. Raysor reached the rural two-lane in easy minutes.

"How much detail do you have about what Mike's doing?" she asked, almost wishing she'd stayed on Edisto to have that dinner. Whoever broke in wouldn't have entered the Cantrell house, or so she assumed. Seabrook might've explained everything, not gone to Florence, and she could have talked more sense into him.

"Not much more than you," Raysor answered. "He'll be all right, though."

"No," she mumbled. "He won't." Callie started to explain but didn't, that gut sensation rising when she remembered nabbing her first gold-plated clue from a two-bit hood on the street she'd leveraged for the information. Like crack to an addict, she fell into a habit where the tiniest of connection made her hungry to slip off from her work cases to chase John's. Until Stan called her in.

He coddled her at first, placing her back on track, assigning her deadlines like a rookie, accounting straight to him, but it wasn't too long, three or four months, that he had to call her in again, lashing her with a word scolding that almost left marks. Good for a couple more months.

That's when she learned to turn in enough work for them to consider her recuperating, only not at full speed, buying enough latitude to pursue Russians. Until the Russians told Stan.

She came to South Carolina on leave to visit her parents. Jeb thrived. She didn't, but one of them improving was enough to justify leaving the Boston force for good and losing all identity except for that of Jeb's mom and the Cantrell daughter. Until she reached Edisto.

John's situation took its toll on her. Gracie's was doing the same to Seabrook.

"He'll escalate," she said, admiring a small whitewashed house go by, an American flag flying from an anchor in a pine tree. "He can't get the scent out of his nose. He's had eight years to think about how this day would feel."

"Seabrook will keep his act together, Callie. Takes discipline to be a doc."

"Don, he quit being a doc because he couldn't keep his act together."

They rode along, finally crossing the McKinley Bridge.

"Has that car been following us?" she asked, watching the side mirror. A nondescript gray sports car seemed too familiar for too long.

"Yeah, for a while. But we're sharing the only road to the beach."

Callie returned to the issue on her mind and slid out the envelope from inside her shirt. She contained it in a paper bag to preserve it from contamination, sealed plastic often causing more damage than good to DNA. Holding it lightly in her lap, she wondered what to say about taking evidence.

Raysor glanced over.

"The intruder left this on my dresser," she said. "Saw no need to leave it in Middleton's hands."

"They see it?" he asked, raising his brows when she held up the side with Seabrook's name on it.

She shook her head.

"You call Mike about it?"

She shook her head again. "Didn't want to in the two minutes we had on the phone."

His nod barely perceptible, he asked, "Open it?"

She kneaded the bag from her mother's cupboard. Her fingers moved over the outline. "No, but I have a feeling what it is."

"Some guy breaks in to your mother's house and leaves a gift for Seabrook?" he asked, passing the Serpentarium. "So, what is it?"

Suddenly she realized she'd never even seen a picture of Seabrook's wife. He'd never seen a picture of her John, as if their light conversations of past memories were enough. A shared experience without the need for tangibles. Keeping the item hidden behind paper seemed to preserve a cherished memory, as if opening the seal would release a dark chapter. "It's an earring."

Raysor snapped another look, the car dipping as he had to slow for the car ahead. "What the hell?"

"Yeah." She hated to leap to conclusions. It might not be *the* earring, the one never found after the murder. It might be *an* earring, symbolic. Regardless, someone connected to Seabrook's target had just visited Middleton and left a statement.

"Shit," Raysor grumbled.

They pulled up at J&J's garage where Callie's cruiser sat waiting to the side. Neither of them was ready to get out of Raysor's vehicle. She pondered what to do with the evidence, and what it meant to Seabrook, but mostly, she had a creepy, uneasy sensation that she was someone's conduit to him.

She studied out her window at her patrol car. Was its slashed tires the object of a guy after Sarah, Seabrook's hunted target, or just someone who hated Callie . . . even cops in general. A tourist? The Speedo-clad television actor came to mind, but he had all his fingers.

"Okay, I have to say it: Seabrook's getting too stoked about his guy," Raysor said.

Tapping a fingernail on a tooth, Callie kept staring at her car. "That obsessive-compulsive crap rarely works." She turned to him. "By any chance was that guy on my cam footage Roman? Did Seabrook recognize him? The guy may have fingerprinted with all his fingers, but who's to say he didn't lose a knuckle in the interim?"

Raysor reared back deeper in his seat. "Mike didn't say, and I would think he'd tell me." He nodded at the envelope. "You're gonna have to tell him, Callie. Not sure you should've taken it from the crime scene, either."

A guy from the garage noticed and waved, walking toward them.

"Middleton, Edisto, and now Florence. Already dealing with Colleton County and the State Highway Patrol on Sarah's accident. I'll need a spreadsheet to keep up with these shared investigations." *And who to keep secrets from.* She opened her car door.

"I might be able to take care of one of those troubles for you," he said. "Colleton County told me after you left yesterday that they're bowing to Edisto PD with this Rosewood case. Highway Patrol will forward their investigative results to you. SLED don't want to get involved. Francis was your man, and I'm the liaison. The case is yours."

She blew through pursed lips and smiled. "Thanks, Don."

Awesome. An opportunity to hold her mother's involvement secret a little longer until she could decipher the mess.

But the odds of Seabrook's situation going ballistic grew with each of his trips to Florence, and she wasn't sure if she could do anything to steer him to reason, much less convince him to stop.

Nobody convinced her to stop until she'd almost lost it all.

Chapter 13

TRULY A SHADE tree mechanic sort of place, J&J's managed to provide much of the automotive needs of the island, and Callie drove off with her patrol car 10-8.

She admired a gorgeous sun glistening off the rising tide in the marsh, rust and honey golds of bowing reeds in the water, and then noticed the same gray vehicle hanging six to eight car lengths back. Maybe a Camaro, distance keeping the driver indistinguishable. This seemed like old times when she learned to channel a heightened awareness. Control oozed through her, and she recalled her days on the street. *Sweet.*

It beat worrying about Sarah and Seabrook and her ridiculous mother. Quincy.

Attention forward and back, she resigned herself to return mentally to Sarah's case. Her primary focus as chief of Edisto PD. Brakes tampered. Quincy conveniently there to haul out the person he chased about a scandal. Beverly conveniently present when the car went into the marsh. Sarah's disgruntled, I-want-a-divorce husband nowhere to be found.

Some badges would try to connect the brakes, slashed tires, and break-in to one culprit, but instinct warned her to maintain an objectivity. Like with this guy behind her.

Someone tailed her to Middleton, broke into the Cantrell house. She wasn't quite ready to place a fifty-dollar bet on Mr. Camaro being last night's intruder, even if she'd watched him in her mirror for the past twenty miles. Like Raysor said, Highway 174 was a one-way highway to the beach.

Since their brief chat at three a.m., her calls to Seabrook rolled to voicemail. She tried again. Same result. "Where are you? Don't make me have to pull out the employee manual on you." She hesitated, picturing him shot or wrecked in a ditch. "Be careful."

She hung up. *At least text.*

The driver remained so far back now she lost sight of him. No, there he was.

Think about the case, Callie. A car sabotaged. Then hers. Then hers again. Three cars with her being the common denominator. Well, sort of. She knew Sarah. Sarah dated her father.

She seemed like the connection.

A zing of foreshadowing finger danced across her shoulders. She had a past. It had followed her to Edisto before, but if she was the epicenter of recent events, why involve Sarah? Which swung her back to Ben.

The envelope threw her for a loop. No doubt the earring message was personal for Seabrook, with Callie the delivery girl, but why?

Unless Seabrook had stirred up too much trouble, and this was a warning.

The gray car came closer. Snaring a right turn just past Atwood Real Estate, she let the driver pass, waited a few seconds, then returned to the highway and sped up. Glancing down every path and drive, she passed two dirt roads, then Edistonian general store, slowing at State Cabin Road. He must've pulled off and dished her own move back at her.

Enough cat and mouse. Marie would call soon needing her ETA. Callie headed back to the beach, one eye on her rearview mirror, the other glancing down roads en route. At Scott Creek, she ignored the thump against her ribs at the muddy bank and turned right onto Jungle Road. She needed a shower, change of uniform, and a check-in with Jeb, but first she called Marie.

Callie pulled the car to a stop beneath Chelsea Morning. "You aren't familiar with a gray Camaro around here, are you?"

"Nope," Marie said, "but I can ask around. Seabrook called, by the way. He's on his way in."

"Does that mean on his way in two hours or on his way in two minutes?"

"The former. What's your ETA, Chief?"

Callie'd kill for a nap. "Depends on whether I'm allowed a shower, why?" Then realizing how soap-opera that sounded with Seabrook also late, Callie added, "My mother's house was broken into last night, so I just got back from Middleton. Been up since three. Raysor took me to get my patrol car at J&J's."

"He only got here," Marie said. "Thomas has been on his own and staying busy."

So much for the shower. "I hear you. Let me at least change clothes."

She exited the vehicle. Each stair to her landing accented the weariness in her bones. Damn Beverly and her martinis. Damn the pre-dawn break-in. And Seabrook coming in late . . . again.

But Callie had aided and abetted most of it. She should've made Beverly come to Edisto for the interview . . . and passed her off to Seabrook. Might've solved everything.

As she set foot inside her doorway, she wanted to melt into her throw rug, curl up, and sleep. Her dull head had grown into a full-blown skull splitter. Beverly never brought her those aspirins. She praised herself for drinking less than Beverly, but this sharper headache poking the backsides of her eyes had nothing to do with alcohol. She and that particular headache were intimate. This was different.

"Grandma can call me about someone breaking in her house, but you can't?" Jeb approached and peered harder. "You look like hell, Mom."

Callie gave Jeb a weak grin. "Thanks, sweetheart. Love you, too. Guess I figured your grandmother had all bases covered. Why haven't you texted this morning?" She rubbed her forehead. "I need to know you're okay, son."

"That works both ways. Anyway, Zeus took a guy from Atlanta out fishing solo today. Sprite's school has some kind of work day, so I'm about to head over to her place." Ducking down from his six-foot height, he peered at his mother. "Seriously, you seem like you don't feel good. You ought to get your boyfriend to give you a physical or something."

"Funny."

"Not what I meant." Traipsing to the kitchen, he grabbed grapes out of the fridge. "I do like Officer Seabrook, though. Why haven't you two hooked up?"

She wasn't sure of the term or her son's meaning of it. "Pardon me?"

He popped a grape in his mouth, then two. "The term is strategically ambiguous," he said. "Hooking up—meaning a date, but also meaning sex if it works out all right."

"We are so not having this conversation," she said.

Her discomfort only raised his humor, and he ran around in front of her. "The guy's cool. Guess I'm saying you have my blessing to get it on with him. Bring him by. You can even kiss in front of me."

Blushing, she realized her mouth hung slightly agape and closed it, saying, "Wow."

His laughter told her he also strategically pushed her buttons.

"Funny, kid," she said. "I need to get to work." But a certain degree of comfort blossomed from his approval, then a bit of a thrill. Jeb was the center of her universe. If he seemed pleased with Seabrook, there really were no other obstacles that mattered.

"By the way," he said, "do I still have to text in? Really?" His new name for checking in by text.

"Yes. We remain on alert." She wanted to kick her shoes off so badly and shed the belt even more.

Reminding her of John, Jeb cracked a teasing half-grin. "What, we have alert statuses now?"

"You heard me." She pushed her bedroom door shut, choosing not to remind Jeb of a certain criminal who'd kidnapped him only three months ago because they lowered their defenses. She'd rather think of him like now . . . approving her potential beau.

Which made her look in the mirror, the reflection that of an older woman. Miss Promise's remark came to mind, the one telling Beverly about alcohol aging one's skin. But this drag-ass feeling had to be from the crunch of Francis and the list of items needing her attention, growing with each passing hour. She was not rebounding like she used to do. She craved a shower, picturing her palms on the shower wall, hot water running, streams diverting across her curves to the drain.

"Jeb?" she hollered. "Can you put on some coffee? Make it strong."

No response. He must be gone. She lifted her weight from where she'd sat on the foot of her bed and started to the kitchen. Then she stopped. They had coffee at the station. Besides, it was time to powwow with Seabrook and Raysor on the history between Sarah and Beverly and her doubts about Quincy. The break-in. This evening, she'd make time for Seabrook.

She owed him the fact that she sic'd Quincy on Pittstop. She didn't expect that news to go over well.

"Callie? Yoo-hoo! You decent?"

Callie peered around the corner to the front door. "Sophie?"

The yoga lady had slipped in, naturally light on her feet. "Hey, your son told me you were under the weather."

"Late night and early day," Callie said. "Sorry, can't socialize. I'm late."

Dressed in aquamarine yoga pants and a tight, tie-dyed long-sleeve T-shirt, Sophie held up an ice-tea glass etched with seashells. "Brought you some carrot juice."

Callie grimaced as she took the glass. She pushed aside the celery stick and sniffed. "Why's it green, and what the hell's floating in it?"

"Spinach, silly. Chia seeds. Stir it with the celery, like a Bloody Mary, oh, sorry, didn't mean to say that. And I chopped up a piece of a mango I had in the refrigerator."

Callie sipped once, then downed a third of it, her stomach way past empty. She smacked her tongue to the unsweet taste. "Not my favorite way to start a morning, but I appreciate it. Toss me that aspirin bottle from over there on the counter, and I'll really be Wonder Woman for the day."

Sophie opened the container and poured two tablets in Callie's hand. Callie motioned for two more then took them with the carrot juice.

"You okay?" Sophie asked.

"Just work, Soph." But damn her head hurt, body ached. Her chest felt like it carried a twenty-pound weight.

Studying Callie's worn uniform, Sophie peered in the bedroom. "Hmmm, where'd you lay *your* head last night? Yesterday's clothes, puffy eyes. Tell me something good. I've been so waiting for this . . ." and she flopped on the sofa, legs bent under her in a contortion only Sophie could do.

"My mother's." Callie sat at the kitchen bar and tried another sip of the juice.

Sophie sat up. "Wait, you stayed in Middleton the whole night? Thought it was just dinner. She's not ill or anything?"

"She got busy at the office, then we talked until it was too late to drive back." She skipped the mini-date info. The martinis. The rest was crime-related, and Sophie had no business hearing about the martinis, so Callie changed the subject. "Why aren't you jingling?" Sophie's earrings were unusually simple today. Thin wire loops.

Sophie held out her left arm, the bracelets hugging her sleeves, then reached up to her ears. "Oh." She smiled. "That's my music, isn't it?" She giggled. "I can most certainly change that. What's your music?"

"Anything Neil Diamond."

"I mean you. Your brand."

"I have no idea what you're saying, Sophie."

Grasping a couch pillow, Sophie hugged it. "Your music's internal. Honey, you need to learn to share yourself more so others can hear it, too. Mike, for instance. Or Seabrook, as you call him, as if the formality puts distance between you. He's just waiting for you to say the word. The whole beach thinks you two bang like rabbits, but I believe y'all haven't crossed that threshold."

Callie swirled the carrot juice, watching the seeds. "Yep, my music's internal."

"Aberdeen says—"

Callie pointed at her friend with the glass. "Not interested in what Aberdeen thinks."

"Okay," Sophie said, tracing her finger over the pillow's seam. "Can I ask you something?"

"Make it quick." Callie rose and finished the drink out of kindness.

"I was thinking I could take Sarah to lunch, but didn't want to if it compromised your police stuff. I don't understand the rules. I don't wish to give Aberdeen and Brice ammunition against you."

"Ain't that the damn truth," Callie said, in the dark about the *why* of that couple's boggle.

Sophie stood and took the empty glass. "Sarah's had so much negativity around her of late, and she could use someone's support since it's quite apparent her husband isn't around." She then eyed Callie as if waiting for confirmation. "Everyone's talking about him being gone, you know."

Escorting Sophie to the door, Callie noticed the mirror in passing. Definitely a need for heavier mascara and lipstick. "I can't tell you anything about the case, Sophie. Or about Sarah, but nothing stops you from taking someone to lunch. Knock yourself out. It's a sweet gesture, frankly." She turned from the mirror to Sophie. "Just don't rattle the poor woman with questions about how scary it was or if she saw the afterlife. Promise?"

"Promise." Sophie stepped to the porch at Callie's coaxing. "But . . ."

Callie set the alarm and stepped out with her, locking the doors. The uniform change would wait. "But what?"

"If she tells me anything, you want me to tell you, right?"

If Callie said no, she'd be lying. If she said yes, Sophie would consider herself undercover, armed and primed. "All right, yes, but think of it like this: If they put you on the witness stand and asked if you initiated the conversation or she volunteered it, what would you testify to with your hand on a Bible?"

Her cute little forehead creased. "Oh."

She'd taken some of the wind out of Sophie's sails but just enough to keep her out of trouble. "So, there you go. Thanks for the breakfast."

"Honey, I'm only keeping you from passing out." Sophie hugged her friend. "And you need to let that gorgeous man invite you for a sleepover, girl. He won't wait for you forever." With a flutter of her fingers, she danced down the stairs. "See ya."

Callie took in a cleansing breath, pushing Sophie out and prepping for her next conversation. She needed advice from someone who understood managing cops and cases and fighting too many questions without answers. He niggled her brain too often of late, which told her she needed the feedback.

She had seven people on speed dial: Jeb, Beverly, and still Lawton, Seabrook, Sophie, Marie . . . and Stan.

Stan Waltham had been number three on her speed dial for fifteen years.

Callie could not imagine her life without Stan a phone call away. Her mentor instilled her detective skills, his shoulder and discipline ever ready. Fair but firm. After she lost John and sacrificed her career, she found herself missing Stan terribly. But he found her. During her worst times, he nurtured her long distance, reminding her she had worth.

He came to Edisto when her daddy died, tending her through a drunken binge, almost accepting Callie's green light, her misinterpreting his warm presence as sexual energy. Not that the fifty-year-old man wasn't handsome. Not that they hadn't felt a mild attraction over the years. He had been two weeks' separated. Not one of her finest moments.

They reconnected by phone when she accepted chief of police, accepting his congratulations with relish, her old boss patting her on the head again. The night they almost slipped left unsaid.

She took a seat in the rattan chair he'd sat in the morning they'd watched the dawn, unsettled about what they'd almost done.

"Well, well," said the deep bass voice. "How's the job, Chicklet?"

"Why I'm calling, Stan."

"Let me postpone my ten o'clock," he said. "Hold on a minute."

"Wait," she said, but he'd muted her. She didn't have enough time for more than one or two questions. She just didn't want to see Seabrook without some sort of advice mantra in her head.

But this was like Stan. He'd never shirked her, accepting her call every single time.

"Okay, done," he said. "First, how are you?"

"Fighting a damn cold, but I need your smarts. Maybe this stuff will make more sense to you. I've dealt with worse, but . . ."

"Start chronologically, Chicklet. Begin at the beginning."

She didn't want to start at the beginning. She only wanted his thoughts about Seabrook's behavior. But that's how easy it was to talk with Stan. Telling him about almost drowning was the hardest part, but she did, in fits and stops, a hitch threatening when she got to the part about Francis.

"Oh, Jesus," he said, a groan added at the end, then another. "Losing a man . . . there just aren't words to make that better, sweetheart. You sure you're okay?"

"Yeah." She bowed her head. The rush of those visions again, partnered with doubts she'd been pushing aside. "Why did they save me first, Stan? That hurts the worst."

"You were easier, closer. He was stronger, deeper in the mud. Maybe too far gone already. Second-guessing will send you to an asylum. Don't do it," he ordered. "I lost a man, too. Stupid, dumb mishap. He didn't wait for his partner . . . you feel responsible because they're yours, but you can't let it eat at you. They died doing the job they chose, what they wanted their lives to represent."

She wiped a tear. "Your life wasn't substituted for his."

"And neither was yours, so stop it. What are the leads? Get your head on straight."

She paced the porch, halting at the east end, noticing her palmettos in bad need of pruning, the dried fronds hanging. She explained the reporter, then Ben . . . "and then there's my mother. I just got back from Middleton trying to interview her, and—"

"I don't have to explain why that was inappropriate, do I?" His gruffness so familiar.

Conflict of interest. Yeah, she got that. "It went badly."

"Where's your man Seabrook?" he asked.

She waved the air. Damn, the mosquitoes were bad in the fall, even worse in the shade. "That's another problem."

"Hmmm."

She glanced at her watch and trotted to the stairs. Damn. She was supposed to have been back over a half hour ago. "I'm sorry, but I really have to go, Stan."

"Drive and talk on speaker."

She preferred Stan at his desk, her seated in the hot chair. Just to get it over with because afterwards he'd tell her what to do or reprimand her for what she did. But the break-in would take too long, and no doubt he'd ream her over the envelope.

"What envelope?" he asked.

"What?" She cranked the engine.

"You said *envelope*."

Glancing at the locked glove box containing the paper bag, she chose to keep that information quiet. Regardless of how close Stan was, he needed plausible deniability. She'd probably taken evidence on an unsolved SLED-level case. After they'd so graciously stepped aside and given her the Rosewood case.

She sighed. "Sorry, juggling too many balls." She dove into a Cliffs-Notes version of Seabrook, Roman McGee, and Florence.

"Yeah, I had to kick your ass for going off half-cocked like that," he said, "and maybe you need to kick his, but you'd lost your spouse and carried a bigger load with a child to raise and two dozen cases on your desk. He's had eight years to grieve, and he's done well by Edisto, hasn't he? Cut him some slack."

"I remember you being harder than this, Stan."

His chuckle had a bitter tinge to it. "Lot of good it did. Sorry, but if I'd been successful dealing with you, you'd still be working for me."

"You were my only thread to sanity."

Turning into the gravel parking area, she scouted for Seabrook's car. Not at work yet. Raysor was, though. Grump though he was, she welcomed his reliability, especially of late.

Parked under the oak, in her designated spot, she remained in the car. "I don't want Seabrook to be me all broken and obsessed. He's too good a soul. He's—"

"Special. You care about him. I hear it in your voice, but I think you're missing the bigger picture. Here we'd separate the two of you, but there . . . be careful. I've said for a long time you needed someone, but your staff has to rely on both of you. The minute you let emotion override the department's need, somebody gets hurt. You, him, another officer, a civilian."

Just when she'd decided to give romance a chance. She fought the defensive irritation rising to the surface. "So one of us should find other employment. Is that what you're saying?"

"I was only your boss, Callie. You, however, are also his romantic concern and a person who relates to his past."

She laughed with a skeptic edge. "Which means what?"

"It means he'll listen to you. Sit down with him ASAP. Set the rules before anything gets out of control. I'm not saying work apart. Just work smart."

Callie scratched at a seam on her steering wheel. "But what do I tell him? How do I say it? As his boss? As a girlfriend?"

"Your call. You of all people understand the hazards of him not thinking straight in our type of environment."

She glanced at the radio. After eleven. Edisto would soon consider *her* AWOL. She coughed at a tickle in her throat, then launched into a coughing fit that took her a moment. "Sorry, Stan."

"Callie? What kind of cold is that?"

"Not sure, but I'm about to go talk to an ex-doctor, so don't worry about it."

"Wish I could help more, Chicklet. You know where I am."

A bittersweet twinge poked her heart. "That I do." In an afterthought, she stopped herself from inquiring about his wife.

Hanging up, she checked her phone. Jeb's check in text had come through along with Marie's saying Raysor came in, Seabrook hadn't, and people were asking for the chief. Sophie left one stating Sarah accepted her invitation to Finn's at eleven thirty.

Callie sighed hard and exited her car. Stan had tried hard fixing her in Boston, but in hindsight not hard enough. They might not have dated, but he'd let his personal affection interfere. He should've kicked her ass harder, even fired her. Instead, she crashed and burned on her own.

Seabrook was on his way in, and she had no idea how to treat him when he arrived. However she did it, though, there was no denying some part of their relationship would get hurt.

Chapter 14

BRICE LEGRAND MET Callie inside the glass door of the police department as Marie's warning text about him came through. The councilman's wife Aberdeen scowled in tandem at his elbow. The midday sun burned off the first sign of fall coolness outside, but there was no denying the heat indoors.

"Where the hell is the Edisto force?" Brice wasn't one to talk with movement, but his cheeks reddened enough to take their place. "Not two days since our officer dies, and our three most seasoned police take off on personal business. What would we have done about another accident?"

"Or a death," Aberdeen added, her carrot-hued tresses tied up in an asparagus green turban affair to augment her jungle tunic. A cartoon if there ever was one.

Callie pushed past the couple and went behind the counter, not inviting them to follow. Raysor came in the back door that led to the other administrative units of the government center. "I heard your voice all the way out back, Brice."

"And the entire beach will hear it before I'm done," the councilman bellowed, reaching for all available ears.

"Who said we were on personal business?" Callie asked, then leaned over to Marie and said low, "Please find something that needs my immediate attention."

"Sorry, Chief," Marie mumbled. "Nothing since Mr. LeGrand called earlier."

"What call?"

But Marie shook her head, unwilling to say much in front of the guests.

Brice braced palms on the counter, elbows stiff. "Word has it you were in Middleton last night," he said. "Visiting family when we're short-handed here at the beach. What kind of outfit do you run? This morning I asked for you, then Mike, then Don . . . everybody late coming in. Three out of a seven-member force with one of them dead, another off duty, and the other having already worked night shift . . . according to Marie."

Marie grimaced a little, but Callie held nothing against the office manager who'd been intimidated by one of Edisto's legacies.

Aberdeen's silver bracelets clanked as she stiffened in defense of her husband. "Yes, thank heaven Thomas Gage was on duty, poor guy."

Poor guy because he had to come to work? More like the one stuck dealing with these people. "Was there a problem?" Callie asked, wondering who notified Brice about her trip to Middleton. Of course . . . Aberdeen.

Of course she was. Sophie's new BFF made sense now. Damn it, if Sophie was going to befriend everyone, foe and friend alike, in the name of whatever it was she practiced, the pixie lady had to judge when to keep her mouth shut. Apparently, Brice sicced his middle-aged birddog spouse on Sophie, a friend who championed Callie and adored Seabrook. Who wouldn't talk about the ones she loves if baited properly?

Brice riveted his stare. "We had a domestic in a condo on Dock Site Road, but we diffused it."

"We?" Callie asked, picking up several pieces of mail Marie slid across the desk to emphasize that the day's business beckoned.

Brice stared down his nose. "Thomas showed up, and I stood by in case he needed assistance."

No, Brice lived on Dock Site Road and butted in. Callie flipped one envelope on the desk and opened another. "Then it was covered, no?"

"What if it had escalated?"

"So you want two officers for each call?" she asked. "Will you introduce that budget request for me? The one for twice our personnel so we can have extra help *just in case*?" She dropped the mail. "Brice, there's some sort of scab you keep picking at that I don't understand. I seriously want to invite you over for drinks and shrimp so that we can have a conversation without this public posturing."

"Not interested," Aberdeen spouted at the same time Brice said, "You're on." Aberdeen cocked a no-you-didn't look at her husband as he puffed up even madder.

The phone rang. "Chief?" Marie said after a listen. "Better take this one in your office."

"We done here?" Callie asked of the couple.

"No," Brice replied. "I need a status update on Sarah Rosewood's incident. Highway Patrol says it's not their case anymore. SLED doesn't have it either."

Callie suddenly lost her appetite for frivolous banter. "You're calling about my cases?"

"The phone, Chief?" Marie reminded.

Trying not to stomp back to her office, Callie entered and shut her door in a façade of control. Raysor sat in the same chair Quincy shared not two days before, the black in his uniform unable to slim his paunch, one boot propped on a knee. "There's no call," he said. "Stay back here and see if he cools off and leaves. His only goal is to push your buttons, and he's real close to doing it."

She fell into her chair. "I don't even know the man, Don."

He rocked the chair a little, his bulk causing a creak. "It's what he does. He thinks he's his daddy."

"Did he treat Seabrook this way? Not trying to play any sort of minority card, but damn, he's got a real bellyache about my presence."

The chunky deputy got a steady motion going with the chair, like he needed a drink in his hand on some deck facing the Atlantic which made Callie rear back in hers as well. "Have to admit he leans on you harder," Raysor said. "Might be a female thing. Might be your parents. Don't let it be your problem."

Raysor oriented her quite well when Seabrook wasn't around. "What is *that* story with my parents?" she asked. "My mother dodged me when I asked."

Raysor shrugged. "Have to ask someone their age. Or ask your yoga lady. She keeps her ear to the ground."

Hmmm, maybe she would.

Five minutes went by while Callie sorted ideas, Raysor appearing to doze. She broke the silence first. "Seabrook ought to be here in another half hour or so."

He peered out of one open eye then closed it. "Yep."

"I'm sure the Highway Patrol didn't tell Brice anything, at least I would hope not," she said, "but you, me, and Seabrook are dissecting the Rosewood case the second he arrives."

"Yeah, I figured."

The phone rang, and she answered. "Hey, Marie. Is Brice gone—what?"

Marie spoke low but urgent. "Sarah Rosewood says there's a break-in at her house and the door's open. She thinks the person's still in there."

Callie jumped up from her seat. "Tell her we'll head over."

Raysor leaped up with somewhat more effort, primed for a directive.

"Follow me in your car," Callie said. "Break-in at Sarah Rosewood's house."

Callie exited, Raysor in tow, and paused a split-second at seeing the LeGrands in a holding pattern in the lobby, but she had neither the time nor patience to offer apologies for the wait or the brush off. Outside, Raysor slid into his vehicle, Callie into hers with the new tires.

Lamenting her luck, she watched Brice and Aberdeen hustle to their Mercedes, no doubt eager to scout the call . . . and scrutinize Callie's ability to handle it.

Without lights or siren, Raysor close behind, Callie drove to Shore Thing, the Rosewood residence, and parked along the street one house back. Sophie waved over her head from her house, and she and Sarah scooted down into rattan chairs on Hatha Heaven's front porch, shielded behind the banister. Callie pointed for her to remain there. Sophie nodded and ducked lower.

Brice and Aberdeen had enough prudence to remain in their car parked in a drive across the street, but Callie bet they took notes if not pictures, heck, video.

She motioned Raysor to take the back entrance. Against the railing, Callie advanced, firearm drawn, shoes silently taking each stair ball to toe. On the porch, she hugged the wall to the left of the door that hung six inches open, giving Raysor a full minute to get into place.

Sliding the door open just enough to enter, she sent up a grateful blessing Sprite, Zeus, and Jeb weren't there. She halted, listening, again grateful she recalled the Rosewood house well enough to traverse it intelligently. A sound came from the master bedroom, like a drawer closing with a controlled, gentle *whump*.

Callie moved to the end of the hall enough to see Raysor at the back door. *Locked*, he mouthed, pointing down.

She held up a finger telling him to wait. The bedroom was ten feet to her left, the back door over twice as far from her in the opposite direction. Inching right to the deputy, she justified to herself the need for backup and a stupid desire not to damage Sarah's home.

She moved toward the back while glancing at the bedroom.

A form moved past the door, too vague and quick to identify. Callie froze. Hangers moved in the closet.

There was no car in the drive. Ben? Would he slip into his own house and not inform his wife? Park someplace else?

Eye on the door, Callie eased toward Raysor again.

The bedroom door flew open.

Callie spun and aimed.

Raysor kicked the back open.

And Beverly screamed.

Fists quivering beside her scrunched up mouth, Callie's mother screamed in bursts like a blue-light alarm in a department store sale.

She wore gloves. Not black, not rubber, not anything that one would find on a thief, but almond-colored, matte satin ones extending barely over the wrist . . . from her inauguration days. The rest of her appeared ready for a luncheon in black ponte knit slacks, camisole, and stand-up collared jacket.

Callie holstered her weapon. "What the hell do you think you're doing? How did you get in here?"

Raysor scratched his neck and holstered his Glock. "Well, she's paying for a damn door."

Two fingers on her collarbone, Beverly panted, her mouth moving like a fish gasping for air. She reached into her pocket and extracted a lone key. "Your father had his own access to the house. Callie, oh my lord, you frightened me."

"Where's your car? How'd you get here?"

Beverly pointed behind her. "I parked in a rental drive three doors down on Jungle Shores."

Her mother started to pocket the key, and Callie held out for her to pass it over. "Callie," her mother started, "this isn't what you think . . ."

"Don't," Callie said harshly, then let the weight of the command settle on the room. Beverly puffed more softly, and she raised her hands in the air. Callie pointed to a red leather recliner. "Lower your arms and sit."

"Dear, I—"

"No," Callie said, the word scratching her already raw throat. "You don't get to speak. As a matter of fact I am formally required to advise you not to speak, and that you have the right to remain silent. If you do say anything, it can be used against you in a court of law. You have the right to have a lawyer present during any questioning."

The heavily mascaraed lashes widened. "Callie, dear, I don't think—"

"Let me finish," Callie continued. "If you cannot afford a lawyer, one will be appointed for you if you so desire. Do you understand these rights as I have explained them to you?"

"I'll go tell Ms. Rosewood it's okay," Raysor said and stepped over a busted piece of framing to exit the undamaged front.

Beverly quit speaking and remained stationary as ordered. But Callie's anger roiled to the point she could see herself cuffing the woman and almost shoving her down the stairs . . . except she remembered her mother falling down Chelsea Morning's front steps a few months ago, making Beverly appear older than Callie cared to accept.

Pain flooded through her, a deep agony squeezing her guts at the sight of this woman who'd raised her stoop to breaking and entering. And for what? Some ridiculous proof that Lawton had an affair. Love letters or some such.

"Sarah will understand," Beverly said, having regained a loose level of control. "Just ask her."

"She made the 911 call to us, so I'm not so sure of that."

Beverly wrinkled her nose. "Yes, she will. Because it's me. She—"

"You're under arrest, Mother."

"Oh, Callie. Sarah will—"

"Beverly Cantrell, I said you are under arrest."

"Oh, this is primo," Aberdeen said from the entrance. "Brice, are you seeing this?"

"Deputy Raysor!" Callie hollered. "Get these people out of here."

Brice ignored the order and entered the living room. "Beverly, honey, whatever has forced you to stoop to robbery?"

"Get out," Beverly said through her teeth. "You don't understand. You never understood anything that didn't raise your egotistical sense of self, you old bastard."

"Says the woman who thinks the sun rises and sets on her image," he replied.

Beverly jumped up, fists clenched. "Don't make me smack you."

"Like you could in those Sunday go-to-meeting gloves." A low laughter bubbled under his words.

Callie stepped toward her. "Sit down, Mother." She turned to the man. "Brice—"

Aberdeen shoved past. "Queen Bee finally getting her comeuppance that she and her smug *dead* husband have been long overdue."

No, this stupid exchange from the past was not happening. This bitch had crossed a line. Callie snared Aberdeen's upper arm. "Get out of my crime scene."

Brice rushed over and grabbed Callie's forearm in turn. "Let go of her, or I'll—"

"Or you'll what? Get your hand off me or you'll lose it. Is that clear?" A voice she'd used many a time in Boston. Though the tiniest person in the room, Callie had to dilute this anger in spite of her desire to take each one out in cuffs to throw them to the sharks. Every damn one of them.

Brice let go.

Callie walked Aberdeen backwards, Brice following close, then she released the wife with a snap. "Trespassing, interference with an officer, assault of an officer, I can continue, if you'd like."

She wanted to arrest them, heaven knows she did, but doing so would make bad matters worse. "Both of you get out. Raysor!" she yelled again.

Heavy boots clomped up the steps, others skittering with him. "What?" he said, winded.

Clamoring to be the sanest person present, Callie spoke with a challenged calm. "Escort these two people to their car, and I mean put them inside it. Stand there until they leave, and if they aren't out of your sight in thirty seconds, arrest them."

"You could try," Aberdeen said, standing her ground.

"Don't push it, Ms. LeGrand," Raysor said. "Come with me."

Brice pointed, his finger jabbing the air. "You are done, missy. Not only are your days as chief over, but I'll see you off this beach, this island, this state if I can."

"Threatening an officer?" Callie asked. "Deputy, pull out your cuffs."

"I mean it," Brice yelled, scooting out in front of Raysor.

Callie turned back to her mother. "Thank you . . . for *all* of this," she said, sweeping her arms wide. "What did I tell you last night? Stay in Middleton. Simple. And what else did I say? The next person who appears at Sarah's door is the most likely suspect in her attempted murder. What about that did you *not* understand?"

A teenage voice spoke meekly from the entryway. "Mom? I heard Grandma was in trouble."

Oh good gracious. "Get home, Jeb."

"Hey, this involves my family. Don't you think—"

"I said go. This isn't the time." She tried to lower her tone because this child was innocent in the whole damn affair.

Almost petulant, he pointed toward the door. "People are showing up outside, and I want to stand by my grandmother."

Versus standing by his mother? "Trust me, this isn't your business."

"But I want—"

"Sweetheart," Beverly said low. "Let us manage this. Having you here only makes things more difficult."

Jeb tried to push through, but Callie moved between them and held a palm against his chest. "No, Grandma," he said, casting an irritating stare at his mother. "I want to be here for you."

"Listen to her, Jeb," Callie said.

"No, Mom. Grandma's had it rough losing Grandpa. No way will I—"

"What the hell!" Callie pushed Jeb back a step. "Why is everyone waiting for me to blow a gasket to make myself heard? Jeb, go home. Mother, sit back down and don't move."

Beverly nodded at a flustered Jeb, and he moved a couple more steps back, reluctant to turn around to leave.

Sarah peered around Jeb, by this time, a bit pale at this side of Callie Jean Morgan. "What about me?" Sophie peeked out as well, wrapped around Sarah.

"You can stay, Sarah. Sophie can go. Take Jeb with you, Soph."

Bodies shuffled until only Callie, Sarah, and Beverly remained. In spite of the autumn breeze wafting up the hallway and the sound of gulls enjoying no responsibilities in their dips and dives overhead, the atmosphere in the Rosewood house hung thick, tense, and too warm for a gentle fall afternoon.

Callie would have appreciated Seabrook assisting with his composed demeanor, and the fact he'd been off in Florence again only fueled her frustration. Nobody could've predicted this abrupt, deranged state of affairs, but this was the second emergency he'd been too distracted to attend.

And since when was a daughter expected to arrest her mother? Brice and Aberdeen's witness only added to Callie's burden to run this case by the book. She'd have Raysor take her mother in. Seabrook would interview Sarah. And Callie would . . . go write traffic tickets along Palmetto Boulevard. Walk the beach and lecture those with unleashed dogs.

She scratched her head. "Mother, where's Miss Promise?"

"At home," Beverly replied, falling back into her socialite-speak. "She wanted to come, but I told her she didn't need to be involved in this. At her age, I didn't feel it wise."

Callie laughed once. *Fabulous.* The ex-first lady had dabbled in the plan, too . . . but would let Beverly take the fall alone.

"Beverly," Sarah said softly. "We need to tell her."

Beverly frowned. "Hush, Sarah."

Sensing more than a squabble over love poems, Callie cocked her head. "What's going on?"

Raysor's heavy steps sounded, and Sarah walked to the entry way. "Don, do you think you could give us a moment here?"

Callie nodded an okay. The Sarah-versus-Beverly feud might finally come out, embarrassing letters exchanged, or both sides could admit defeat and accept the need to put the past behind them. "Shut the door and wait on the porch if you don't mind, Don. I'm thinking it's best you take Mother in when we're done."

The big deputy saluted two fingers and pulled the door shut.

"Okay," Callie said. "Sarah, you sit on the sofa across from Mother. I'll stand here. In low-key, sane, and civilized voices, the two of you settle whatever this is."

Instead, Sarah walked to Callie, one arm around her waist. "No, dear. You sit. We already know the truth."

Chapter 15

STANDING IN THE middle of the Rosewood living room, Callie restrained her frustration at Sarah's gentle command. "No," Callie replied. "I will not sit. Speak what's on your mind, then I handle this break-in by the book. I cannot afford to let my mother off the hook because she's related. Frankly, Raysor ought to be a witness to this conversation." She turned to the door.

"No," Beverly and Sarah said together in a rush. Callie halted, puzzled at the unexpected collaboration.

Sarah lowered herself to the sofa. Raysor waited outside on the porch, at their request. Silly because Raysor would learn all the dirt anyway. Her mother had cast her private business into a public announcement by breaking in and getting arrested, backing Callie into a corner. An arrest meant papers, files . . . and public records.

"You two have been the cause and effect of so much soap opera drama and don't even recognize what it's doing to this community, your neighbors, your family . . . and Jeb, in case you forgot." Callie pointed back and forth to them, pressure rising in her chest, her neck, the headache pounding. "Mother, get over yourself. You loved a man before Daddy, then continued to see him after you married. Sarah loved Daddy, and he loved her back. You and Daddy stayed married in spite of all this. You said we were all adults about the deal. If I can accept it, you can. So why isn't everyone moving on, for Pete's sake?"

The last sentence reverberated in the silence, the two women gazing upon Callie with . . . what, sympathy?

Enough of this. "Raysor!" Callie yelled. "You can come on back in."

"Beverly," Sarah pleaded, reaching for the other woman. "You need to tell her. I never liked keeping this secret. You know I'm right."

"The hell you are," came the matriarch's reply, her dignified upturned nose belied by the wariness in her eyes.

Raysor pushed the door open. "So, what's the verdict?" He walked in, cuffs at the ready, prepared to begin his bad cop routine.

Heart beginning to race at the decision, Callie directed an open palm toward Beverly. "Take her in. Book her."

Sarah jumped up. "No."

This fiasco needed to move to the station. People noticed police cars in private drives. "Ride with me, Sarah," Callie said. "Raysor can deliver Mother."

"No, this isn't right," Sarah protested as Raysor assisted Beverly to her feet.

Fighting the urge to look away, Callie watched Raysor hold her mother's arm like any other perp, maybe with a slighter touch. Beverly stared off, distancing herself.

He visually queried Callie, asking how she wanted to play this out.

Admittedly, this was no place to play bad cop to the hilt. "No cuffs. Come on, Sarah. Lock up the front. Mother will pay for your back door."

Raysor assisted Beverly to his cruiser as Sarah and Callie paused on the porch. If word got out, her mother's run for mayor was quashed, especially being arrested by one's own daughter, but she'd given Callie no choice. She was lucky to be caught empty-handed. Beverly kept her head down, studying her feet, and a sharp jab penetrated Callie's heart.

The woman never tackled life in any mode but driven, chin high, whether in the grocery store or approaching a dais to deliver a fundraiser address. Never, ever had she acquiesced. An irritation to adversaries and naysayers, but suddenly a respectable trait to Callie—a trait she'd just crushed.

Sarah tapped Callie's elbow. "This is a mistake," she whispered, because at least a dozen people waited in front of Sophie's house and the residence across the street, to include an anguished Sophie hugging Jeb. Was he trembling? Sophie's daughter Sprite shot nasty stares. Callie broke eye contact, escorted Sarah to her patrol car, and headed for the station, a radio message going to Marie they were on their way and to hold all calls.

"And when Seabrook shows up," she said, "tie him to a desk."

Seabrook still wasn't at the station when they arrived. A couple of the firemen hung at the open bay of the firehouse . . . Brice wedged between them no doubt narrating the day's event.

Callie held the door for Sarah to enter the lobby. "Have a seat here, and we'll call you back in a moment."

Sarah grasped Callie's wrist as she tried to walk off. "Don't do this to your mother. I refuse to press charges."

"Sarah."

"And mention this. If she won't tell the truth, I will."

Easing herself from Sarah's grasp, Callie went to her office where Raysor had promptly disposed of Lady Cantrell. A melancholy swell came over Callie as she shut the door.

She assumed her place behind her desk. Raysor had rolled a chair in the back corner to witness but remain out of direct fire to give Callie latitude. Any of them could reach out and almost touch the other in the small space.

Callie pulled out her recorder and set it on the desk in front of Beverly. "Before I turn this on, Sarah said she won't press charges if you're honest. She also said if you don't tell the truth, she will. Since I caught you red-handed, her testimony isn't all that important, though." She cut herself short of saying *Mother.*

Callie clicked on the recorder and spoke into it to establish the time, date, and persons present.

"That's not what she meant," Beverly said. "Turn off the recorder."

"Ms. Cantrell," Callie said for the record. "This recorder protects both you and the department so that there is no doubt as to what is said."

Beverly frowned up at the formal addressment. "I have something to say, sweetheart, but only if you turn off that machine."

At the use of *sweetheart* Callie reached out slowly and clicked off. That rarely used endearment spoke volumes, clearly telling her that whatever the message, it was best delivered privately. Callie suddenly sensed she might be the only one in the dark. The strange reaction to this statement might just be her own.

Soft-spoken and wilted, Beverly studied her gloves and said, "Bring Sarah in here."

"That's not quite appropriate, ma'am," Raysor said.

For the first time since Raysor escorted her out of the house, Beverly laid a deliberate stare on her daughter. There was a depth to her aged, wrinkled face Callie had not seen even at Lawton's funeral. Suddenly touched, Callie noticed a deflation in her mother, with a sense of no return to it.

"Dear," Beverly said. "Do as I request or I say nothing." She turned to Raysor. "Are you two not witness to anything I say? Of course you are. Do it, or else lock me up." The air thickened at the dejection in her command.

Callie sighed. "Go get Sarah, Don."

He gave her a slight nod, as if to say, *hold it together.*

Beverly peered only at her lap. Callie thought a tear fell onto the gloves. "Mother?"

But her mother shook her head.

A tightness formed in Callie's throat. These two worlds of hers were not meant to collide.

"I wish we had Miss Promise in here to be accountable as well," was all Callie could bring herself to say while they waited. "I suspect her talent in the middle of all this."

"Don't hate her," Beverly said with a softness Callie never heard. "She's all I have since your father died."

Callie felt like an ogre. "But *we're* here. Edisto isn't that far. It beats Boston, don't you think?" Her police chief role struggled to remain front and center. "And you have so many friends in Middleton. You belong to every civic and ladies' group. Remember that lady who offered to buy you a new turntable when the last one busted on my front steps?"

"There was no lady," Beverly said, picking at her gloves.

Stunned, Callie replayed those couple of days in her head. She had no doubt about what happened and what was said.

Beverly ceased her nervous motions and cupped one hand in the other to regain composure. "Miss Promise was the first real person to come see me after your daddy died . . . and really talk. Some brought casseroles, some ran errands. Many paid condolences and never called back. You'd be amazed at how few cared to see me cry."

Pressure and guilt filled Callie. She pictured her mother a stone mountain of dignity and aplomb, in control of her actions and emotions.

True, she never saw her mother cry before or after the funeral. She assumed Beverly preferred someone more her age, someone closer . . . though Callie couldn't put a name on who that someone would be.

They'd fought the day of the funeral . . . Beverly ordering her out of the house, proclaiming an ability to function without her daughter, sending Callie back to Edisto.

Sarah entered, Raysor behind her. The deputy edged around and moved his chair beside Beverly and motioned for Sarah to sit. He backed into the corner, though his bulk filling the dark uniform was anything but discreet in the tiny room.

"So," Callie said, not quite sure where to start but desperately wanting to get it over with. "Mother, you asked for Sarah. Sarah, you gave Mother an ultimatum to be honest or else. Here we are. Who goes first?"

Sarah reached over and took Beverly's hand. Nervous at the gesture, Callie waited to hear their secret, noticing Raysor's puzzled reaction at the ladies' union, too.

Oh my dear lord, are they gay?

"Want me to say it?" Sarah murmured.

Amazing how strong this meek woman had become in a time of need . . . assuming that's what this was. Callie wanted to say *spit it out*, but she'd been raised better than that.

Beverly nodded. Sarah patted the gloved hand and turned toward Callie.

"Okay." Sarah inhaled. "You're aware I cared for your father, Callie."

She nodded, like a child being told about her parents' divorce and how the split wasn't her fault.

"You're also aware of some of the circumstances. Your mother had a lover and gave Lawton the go-ahead to have his own. Beverly's relationship . . . ended, but Lawton and I continued ours for a while longer."

"A while," Callie interrupted. "I thought it was to the end, like for thirty years."

Holding up a gentle hand, Sarah requested more room to speak. Callie hushed.

"We've spoken enough across my kitchen table for me to grasp how you viewed your parents' situation," she said. "It wasn't all correct, but I didn't feel it my place to edit."

A sigh escaped Beverly, her gaze down.

Pulse galloping, Callie's curiosity crescendoed. She held her father in high esteem and wanted to continue to do so, but these women had danced down some Peyton Place road and wanted to, what, clarify? For what, salvation and sympathy? Hunting for advice from Raysor, Callie caught only a speculative frown.

"Callie," Sarah said with a tone of consummation, "Beverly's relationship ended sooner than she stated, and mine went on . . . different than you've been told. Her lover didn't die. She ended it to choose your father."

"What?" Leery, Callie said, "Why'd you lie about that?" But Beverly gave no response. "Wait," Callie said and gave a gasp. "The day in my house when you first told me about the affairs, you told me Daddy was still my father."

Beverly peered up. "I know, dear. I wasn't completely honest with you that day."

"Mama!" Callie exclaimed, her professional demeanor cracking wide open. She examined hard each woman's expression. What pieces were missing that had such power to dilute Beverly's patrician airs and infuse backbone into Sarah?

Righting herself, Beverly sat up tall. "I left Brice LeGrand, choosing a monogamous life with your father right before his run for Middleton town council. But Sarah was already pregnant with you."

Callie gasped, but no air entered her lungs, as though obstructed . . . like in the marsh. She grasped the edge of her desk as she'd grabbed for the metal of Sarah's car, anything to drag her to safety.

Brice? Sarah . . . pregnant with her?

In an instant, everything she'd embraced of her family disintegrated into a tawdry tale for the likes of Quincy and a dollar grocery store tabloid. Everyone lied. For the sake of . . . what?

Her brains banged like a drum against bone, even the roots of her hair taking her headache to a new level. Tears ran down her cheeks though she hadn't thought of crying.

"Callie?"

Her fist balled as she snapped around. "What?"

"It's me," Raysor said. "Why don't we take a break." He turned her chair around so she could stand, but she gripped the desk again to stop him.

Both women wore matching pale expressions, like sisters.

The other woman . . . was her mother? And her mother was . . . not?

"Why," Callie said, muscles taut from her neck down. "You . . . I . . ." She pounded her chest with one fist then couldn't finish her thought. Sarah started to say something, but Callie couldn't help but run over her attempt. "Why?"

Beverly lowered her head in her gloves. Were her shoulders shaking, because Callie couldn't tell for her own quivers. This was so utterly out of this world that she couldn't think straight. She liked Sarah better when she wasn't her mother and Beverly when she was.

"Beverly was seeking your birth certificate," Sarah answered. "I didn't want Ben to use it against me, um, us. Any of us."

Callie let the information settle, groping for logic. She instinctively turned to who raised her. "It's on public record, Mother." The emotional connection of the name seemed . . . broken. "I used a birth certificate for elementary school, my driver's license, college. Your name was on it as well as Daddy's—" She clenched muscles at the revelation. *Oh good lord.* "Daddy paid people off."

"Not paid," Beverly said, like the facts of the issue sobered her.

"Your father never paid for favors."

"I kept a copy of the original before it was altered," Sarah said. "When it had my name on it. For posterity's sake."

Beverly added, "Keep in mind that forty years ago nothing was computerized, and everything was negotiable."

Callie coverd her mouth in disbelief. This surreal moment hung over her, through her, suffocating her. It was as if they spoke of a litter's pedigree and how to get the most for the pups. Then she spoke to this would-be mother. "Why did you give me up?"

Her own tears streaming, Sarah's eyes searched Callie. "Because I trusted Lawton to raise you properly. He was a beautiful person, and I wanted you to love him up close, not on weekends. I wanted you to have a full-time family with all that the Cantrell name would offer." Wiping her cheeks, she sniffled. "I lived on Edisto, not terribly far from where you were. When you were ten, they bought Chelsea Morning so I could see more of you. He . . . they," she corrected, reaching for Beverly again, "did a marvelous job." She patted Beverly's knee with their joined hands. "We ended the affair, Callie," she said. "Right after you were born. We only met to talk about you. How well you were doing."

This wasn't happening.

Callie exploded out of her chair and exited her office craving distance, miles, oceans between her and these women.

Seabrook sat at the desk opposite Marie. Callie paused just long enough to notice, then headed out.

"Callie?" he called, running after her. "What's wrong?"

Jeb pushed off from his post at the hundred-year-old oak outside by the parking lot. "How long are you going to rake Grandma over the coals, Mom? She doesn't deserve this. She's family, and if Miss Sarah doesn't want to press charges like Miss Sophie said, then let her loose. No matter what she did, this isn't right."

Callie couldn't explain this to Jeb, not in her state of mind. She reached her car and beeped it open. Someone touched her from behind.

"Don't," she yelled, flinching. Seabrook stepped back, Jeb surprised behind him.

"Chief," Raysor called from the doorway. "We need to make a decision."

"I don't give a *damn* what you do with them," she hollered back and got in her vehicle.

With a heavy foot and spit of gravel, she left down Murray Street so they wouldn't see whether she turned left or right at Palmetto. She went left with no idea where to go.

Giving up a child because you're destitute. Giving up a child because you have a terminal disease. But turning a baby girl over because she could be a politician's daughter? Politics! One of the most despised parts of her childhood.

God help her, she couldn't put herself in their heads. Never would she give up a child. She'd kill to not have lost her baby girl to SIDS. She *had* killed to save Jeb. What sick level of insanity came up with this scheme? And worse, why had they waited so long to tell her?

She brushed off the tears. At forty, she ought to weather the news with adult skills. Listen, digest, and in judging them, do so maturely. It wasn't the apocalypse.

But a sob escaped anyway. Her daddy had lied to her, too. No wonder Lawton gave her the deed to the beach house, to keep her closer to Sarah.

She sped up and around a creeping car, the female passenger watching the ocean, the driver studying beach houses for sale.

There was another innocent party here, too. Heaven help her, but she felt sorry for Ben. In his shoes, Callie might have cut Sarah's brake lines, too.

Chapter 16

CALLIE DROVE FROM the beach, across the marsh, running on adrenaline. Edisto Island held an innumerable quantity of waterways, marshes, and dirt trails for the person who wanted to disappear. Sixty square miles of island veined with creeks and marsh to hide everyone but her, because wearing a uniform and driving a car decorated with a logo and blue lights made obscurity impossible.

So she just drove. Down to the public boat landing on Edisto State Park where two people trailering a boat waved, then back to 174. Down Peters Point Road, then back to 174. Past the Presbyterian Church, dredging up images of Sophie's kidnapping at the mausoleum.

Though childish, eating up highway and kicking up dirt on the detours kept her mind occupied. Driving and naming who lived where, recalling the landmarks Seabrook taught her, reciting who owned what business. Mental exercises, because if her brain slowed she'd fall apart.

The mother she knew wasn't her mother, and her father's girlfriend was. Lies. Forty years of lies. The life she knew had dead-ended like one of these island roads, with no place to go but over the edge into the brine.

Jeb hadn't heard about the affairs, much less the results. He loved his grandmother. She was there for him when they stayed a year in Middleton—when Callie was too far into a bottle to fully be there for him. He didn't recognize Sarah except by name.

After first learning of the affairs, Callie kept her unusual feelings for Sarah away from him.

Callie thought Lawton hung the moon. Ever present in a superhero way, he understood Callie. Beverly never did, which made more sense now . . . or should. Ever since Callie learned of the affair, she'd been drawn to Sarah. Was it maternal . . . or was Sarah simply the last vestige of a loving connection to Callie's deceased father?

Her phone rang. Seabrook. She declined the call and threw the device on the seat. She didn't have time for his excuses and personal issues. Plus reception sucked out here.

Her radio hissed on her shoulder. "Callie, you headed back to Boston or what?"

Reception wasn't the excuse now. She ignored him again.

"Don't make me talk to you on the airway for others to hear."

She snatched at her mic to give him an order to bug off when her phone rang. "What," she said.

"Pull over," Seabrook said with calm authority.

Glancing in her rearview mirror, she spied him six lengths back in his patrol car.

"Don't have time for you right now, Mike."

The big bridge spanned a few miles ahead, but for some deep reason, she didn't want to leave the island, as if crossing the Intracoastal Waterway would release her new genealogy to the world for scrutiny. That's where the Quincys of the world resided.

Veering left, she took the closest, most desolate road she knew, Pine Landing. The jostle of the unpaved road warned her the route would only deteriorate. She liked the bumps and took them hard. The car fishtailed several times yet she sped up, daring anyone and anything to touch her. Anger throbbed in the pulse of her neck.

After a mile and a half, she stopped. Water met the far end of this road, but she halted far before that. Water and road equaled people. There was no pulling over on such a narrow road, no traffic to pull over for. Seabrook soon did the same.

Woods encroached them from both sides. Jungle and an undisturbed nothing.

She exited the car and motioned with a jab for him to remain inside his. He obliged.

She paced first, the loop of the stationhouse conversation playing and playing in her head. Forty damn years! She so wanted to hit something and break every bone doing it.

You don't want an anxiety attack.

No, she didn't. Damn them, these women would not make her backslide into the disturbed, broken-down being that arrived on Edisto. Callie had rebuilt herself. How dare they erode the progress. *How dare they!*

Breathe.

Flopping her backside against the hood, she closed her eyes, counting. In for ten. Out for ten. Then her head tilted back. Deep, like the doc taught her in Boston. Deep, deep breaths. Listen for those things outside herself.

A squirrel chirped angrily up high to her right. Leaves falling. A small branch smacking the rotting forest floor. No cars. No people. No family.

She heard the car door open and turned as his steps reached her.

"I'm sorry, Callie."

"About what, Mike? There are just so many damn things to be sorry about these days, and you seem to be absent for all of them."

Nasty. She almost rued the words, because as mad as she was, she missed him when he wasn't available for these crises. His sun-bleached blond hair, kept longer than a regular officer, and his shoulders. He filled his uniform better than any cop she'd ever known, his biceps leaving little room around his sleeves. Probably thanks to the doctor in him, he always smelled clean.

Seabrook gnawed the inside of his cheek a second. "I guess it seems that way."

"No, it is that way."

He leaned against the front quarter panel of her car. "But this time I'm here. Luckily without Jeb and Raysor, but they agreed to give you some space. Talk to me. What happened back there?"

Callie threw a short, sarcastic laugh at him. "Which time? Which situation? Which disaster?"

"Callie, I—"

"You dropped this job on me, Mike." Dumping on him felt good in spite of it not being the immediate issue. "Once I accepted the position, you gave up and took off on your own personal chase. *Callie can manage it. She wears the badge now.* And here I am playing the fool."

He scowled. "Nobody thinks you're a fool."

"How the hell would you even know?"

Arms out, in a crucifix stance, he said, "Fine. Take your shots. I'm telling you I let Florence overwhelm me. I'm sorry. Talk to me. Forget Florence."

The man never failed to temper a situation, the king of calming people down. Even now, guilty as hell, he disarmed the anger right out of her.

"I can't forget Florence," she said, twisting to him. "Because I've been sucked into it."

He shook his head. "No, you haven't. My wife's case has nothing to do with anything on Edisto. I'll rein it in. So it doesn't interfere anymore with—"

"Shut up and listen!"

Off balance by the backlash, he hushed and waited.

"Sarah's attempted murder led me to suspect Mother, like that was fun. She'd had words with Sarah the day of the incident. I went to Middleton to interview her because you weren't up to doing it so I could avoid a conflict of interest." She tipped her head at him. "Thank you so very much for that."

He retained his cool.

"Anyway, I spent the night, because—" and she caught herself. Seabrook had been the first outside of Jeb to bring attention to her drinking. No point mentioning to him the three martinis. "Anyway, someone broke in."

Seabrook nodded, waiting for more pieces. She was losing her momentum.

"The guy who broke in didn't take anything. Instead, he left an envelope on my dresser . . . addressed to you."

"Wait, what? To me?" he asked, rising off the car.

She took a second. "Yes, it had your name on it." Excitement ebbing, her body lagged though it hadn't reached 4:00 p.m., like she'd worked a forty-eight-hour shift with no meals.

"Where is it? What was in it?" His eagerness blasted through his previous attempt to be there just for her.

"I haven't opened it," she said, then broke into a cough. The spell lasted longer than normal, each hack deeper than the last, pushing the perpetual headache against her temples. Finally, she reached inward for a small taste of air.

Seabrook cupped her shoulder, waiting. "Callie, I don't like the sound of that."

She inhaled again, regaining her bearings. "It's a cold, and I have no time for sick leave. Not with being a man down and another not showing up for work."

Quietly he took the shot.

"The envelope is stashed at home," she lied, the evidence maybe six feet from them in her glovebox. "I hid it from Middleton PD. For you."

He reached and drew her against him. "Oh, Callie. I wish I'd . . . never mind. Come here."

Like a cliché, she melted at the warmth of him, at his concern. She resisted only a second, soon encircling his waist, allowing his chin atop her head, his breath in her hair, and for several minutes they stood alone on that damp dirt road. She let the forest speak to her, her nostrils filled with a mix of autumn and Seabrook's musk. The vitriol Callie'd held against him softened. It always did when he came close.

She missed him. Stupid of her to let personal entangle professional, but it was what it was.

She needed him. Not only as a cop, but as a friend. As support. She'd be an idiot not to.

Finally, he let her loose. "But this isn't why you rushed from the station. Marie said you had your mother and Sarah in your office. I didn't have time to question Don."

Blowing out in an effort to put the moment into words, she fingered a button on his shirt before she could collect the words to explain. "Mother broke into Sarah's house. We caught her in the act . . . with gloves, no less."

Seabrook's brows went up. "Sarah filing charges?"

Staring up at him, she noticed the dark shadows under his eyes. Callie wasn't sure if he had any more stamina than she did with his lack of sleep. "No, but I left all that up to Raysor." With her temper gone, tears threatened, and she caught herself blinking to avoid showing the weakness. "I could have used you for this, Mike. They said . . ."

"They said what?"

She squeezed his arms, massaging, avoiding the phrasing that made her new lineage reality. "I need a drink."

"Whatever it is, you can weather it sober."

She retracted. "Damn it, I said one drink. Don't piss me off."

"Not trying to. Come on," he said and took her hand. "Go home, change clothes, and come over. I'll cook. Or pick up something on the way. Let's talk without anyone around." A breeze whipped up the road with a coolness that sent goose bumps up Callie's back. Seabrook saw her shiver and opened her door. "Wait, want to drive straight to my place? You might have family waiting at yours. Regardless of what you think of them right now, they'll want to see that you're okay. At least text them." He scoffed. "At least so they don't pester me."

She jumped at the offer to talk elsewhere. She wasn't ready to say the words out loud. Not yet. One drink. Just an ounce. Then it might be easier. "Need to park this car other than at your place, and mine is in the shop," she said and coughed to clear her throat.

"I'll follow you, and we'll take it from there."

She got in her cruiser, and he shut the door, leaving her with an encouraging smile.

They headed back toward the beach, him in the lead. So many loose ends. No order. And she'd have to settle on some sort of new normal.

With a night to think about it, maybe two, she could cope. But how would she tell Jeb?

TWENTY MINUTES later, she parked and ventured into her house expecting Jeb's interrogation. She found a note from him on the credenza instead.

Mom, why did you have to run off like that? I'm at Grandma's. Text me when you get this. Love, Jeb.

She set the note down like a feather, as if he could read her presence by her touching the paper. Why was her life always a burden on her son? Though he thought of himself as nurturing her, she tired of his play-acting the parent. She ought to be chiding him for staying out late, drinking underage, and not cleaning his room . . . not that his room was all that unclean at the moment.

Why wasn't he resenting the hell out of her?

Then a fear rippled through her. What if Beverly beat her to the punch, explaining the bloodline, to make it sound as proper as the stupid sordid affair could sound? Callie wanted to be the one to break the news to him.

She should've thought of that before she bolted.

A noise sounded from the kitchen. "I'm in here," came the voice.

She ran from the hallway and around the bar, tackling her son as he closed the refrigerator door, hurting as she hugged her child. A child undeserving of what the adults around him had done.

"I was about to leave, Mom, but I couldn't." Her eighteen-year-old leaned back and studied her, obviously trying to take in what wasn't being said. "Back at the station, Mr. Seabrook stopped me from following you. He said give you space. I stalled Grandma when she asked me to come home with her. Left her at Finn's with Miss Sophie with an excuse I had to do something first. I was hoping you'd come by. What's going on?"

So Raysor had cut her mother loose. As much as she despised Beverly at the moment, Callie frankly didn't want the grief of dealing with the arrest.

Cheek still pressed against Jeb's shirt, Callie spotted the low-ball glasses moved on the shelf beside the refrigerator, a couple glasses on the counter. The Maker's Mark sat on the counter as well, like she'd caught him in the act of taking it. Or hiding it from her.

Jeb smothered her again when she didn't answer his question. "I had to see your head was in the right place, Mom. It can't be that bad.

Not after what we've been through with Dad."

The voice of reason, from a body so young.

"Sit down, Jeb." She shadowed him to the kitchen table, and they sat at their accustomed places, on the end and to one side, her gun and equipment banging against the chair. Holding his hand seemed dramatic. While she contemplated where to place her own hands, she interpreted the discomfort as nothing more than facing the pure reality of spitting out the facts.

He dipped his head down and peered at her. "Just say it."

"Right. Yes," she said and reached for a placemat anyway, more afraid of opening this discussion than drawing down on a drug-addled murderer. She blew out once. "Your grandmother is not your grandmother," she started.

He let go. "I don't understand."

"Of course that makes her not my mother, either. She raised me, but she didn't birth me."

He sucked through his teeth a little before speaking. "And Grandpa?"

She appreciated how that reality remained true. "He's still my father and your grandfather."

With a squint he sorted her words, then his came out harder than she expected. "Is this what you just found out?"

"Yes," she replied, meeker than planned. "I'm . . . digesting it."

Memories slid into her head. Holidays with Beverly and missed with Sarah. First dates, proms, braces, report cards good and bad. Beverly pretending her DNA influenced it all. Sarah in the background, accepting periodic news from Lawton about how Callie failed her first driving test or recovered from a broken arm on the playground. None of the Middleton scenes seemed real anymore. Ping-pong rationalization had her afraid of deciphering what she missed from Sarah or would have missed from Beverly if things had gone differently.

Jeb's fist on the table jerked her to the present. "How dare he?" he grumbled.

Stunned, she repeated his pronoun. "He?"

"Grandpa. He couldn't keep it in his pants. Figures that he would die first. He doesn't have to confront this, and us. Poor Grandma." He flashed her sympathy. "And you."

"No," Callie replied, her synapses trying to snap fast enough to keep up. "I'm not letting you rest this crap completely on your grandfather. He wouldn't have gone to Sarah if your grandmother hadn't already—"

"Wait." He reared back. "Ms. Rosewood is . . . my grandmother? I don't even know her."

"And I was just beginning to," she said.

"So you *did* know."

Callie vigorously shook her head. "No, Jeb. I knew she'd . . . been with your grandfather but had no idea she was my mother."

He leaped from his chair. "Geez, Mom! You knew my grandfather had an affair and can honestly say I don't have the right to hate him?"

Jumping up, she pursued him out of the kitchen to the living room. "I learned about it after your grandmother fell down the front steps back in June. I learned the whole truth today."

"My grandfather cheated on my grandmother?"

"Oh no you don't," Callie scolded, her defenses rising. "You do not get to lay all this on him. He was a good man. A wonderful man. He's your flesh and blood. Your smile, your chin, and your beautiful presence are proof positive he was. But you need to hear the whole story."

Jeb pushed past her to his bedroom. "I think I've heard enough."

"Son, turn around," she ordered to his back. He disappeared, noises of items slinging, shuffling. This was not how she'd hoped he would react. He was young but not immature, inexperienced but malleable. Open-minded, she thought.

"Your grandfather wouldn't have met Sarah, and you or I wouldn't have been born if none of this had occurred . . ." She allowed herself some air. "If your grandmother hadn't cheated to start with. If you want to blame people, then you need to be an equal opportunity blamer."

There, she'd said it.

Keys in his grip, he reappeared, backpack over one shoulder. "I'm taking Grandma back to Middleton. She's in no condition to drive. Her car's at your station."

"Did you not hear me?"

"I heard, and I'm hearing the other side before I pass judgment."

"Jeb, I'll go with you." Callie headed toward her bedroom. "Let me change clothes, and we'll sort this out." She'd have to explain to Seabrook, who waited patiently downstairs.

But Jeb ignored her and opened the front door. "Mom, I love you, and there's no way this isn't a shock for you, but Grandma spent her life raising you. She's the victim here. There's no denying that she sacrificed herself to bring you up, and therefore me. We have to be there for her. Grandpa's gone in my mind."

Callie spun and quickly covered the distance. "Young man, you don't have the right to make a statement like that. Without her past, none of this might've happened."

"So she pushed him to do it, right?"

Callie paused at the simplistic, short sentence. "In a way, yes."

In the doorway, Jeb hesitated. "Maybe it's best I spend the night with Grandma, Mom, because you and I don't see this shit the same way. You've always butted heads with her anyway. You might even be glad she'd not your real mom."

"That's not it, Jeb, but she's not innocent."

"She's not like you say, either," he said and left.

"Don't go yet," she shouted as he trotted fast down the stairs. "I didn't explain this right."

"Grandma will," he yelled then disappeared under the house, his Jeep parked in the back.

Running, she leaped off the final three steps and bolted past Seabrook's car. Jeb got in his vehicle and started the engine. "Jeb!" she hollered.

He looked down to his lap taking a moment, set something in his seat, then put the Jeep into drive. Then with a limp wave and a benign expression Callie couldn't read, he turned right up Jungle Shores toward the commercial area, where Beverly waited at Finn's.

Lump filling her throat, she turned back toward her front steps, legs like stone. Seabrook met her halfway. "What's wrong?"

"He learned what happened," she said, exhaustion sinking her deeper into the gravel drive. At the steps she sat and pushed hair two days past a shower behind her ear.

Seabrook didn't ask for the facts, instead focusing on Callie's emotional need. "That's not like that boy, Callie. If whatever was said is a shock to you, then it might be more so to him. He's a kid."

Dropping her head into her hands, she agreed. But therein lay the problem. She could tell Jeb the *what* but not the *why* in the decisions of these people.

No, she couldn't stomach Jeb hating Lawton Cantrell. But she couldn't deny his point. Before and after the news, she loved Lawton and wrestled with Beverly. That had not changed. Lawton was just as guilty, only not available beyond the grave.

Tears wet her palms. Damn it to hell, if Beverly twisted this Grimm's fairy tale romance into anything more than the facts, and her son came home ignorant of the truth, she'd plant a Wainwright Realty for sale sign in Chelsea Morning's front yard.

But Jeb wouldn't leave. He'd remain steadfast beside his grandmother.

"I can't do this anymore," she said, slowly peering up at Seabrook. "Seriously, I'm done."

But she couldn't define what that meant other than leave all this behind.

Chapter 17

SEABROOK REACHED to lift her from her seat on the front steps. "Hey, you just want to stay here? I'll order out." He glanced at his watch. "It's after five. I'll call Buck's for pizza."

But witnessing Jeb leave her for Beverly, listening to him blame his grandfather, realizing that Chelsea Morning represented anything but the simple safe haven she professed it to be, Callie shook her head. "No." She dusted ever-present sand off the seat of her pants. "Let me grab some things. The last place I want to be is here."

Clomping up the two dozen stairs, she reached for her phone to call Jeb, then stopped when she saw the screen. A text from him read, *Still love you, Mom. Please don't drink.*

Her heart thumped at the message. But he'd chosen his grandmother over her, over Lawton. A knife to her heart.

Gazing down past Sophie's house to Sarah's, Callie contemplated a warning call to her mother not to influence Jeb against Sarah. Beverly would champion Lawton, so that wasn't an issue, but . . . wait a minute. Callie changed her mind. It might even be best to let Beverly confront her grandson's questions. Let Jeb hear it up close and personal from the mouth of the woman who'd lied to him his entire life. Then as the scene played out mentally, she shook her head once and realized her mother probably wouldn't have the guts, because to do so would be to slight her father. No doubt that they loved each other, strange as the scenario was.

Feeling incapacitated smothered her where she stood. Cops were fixers. Parents were fixers. She was both and couldn't find a damn solution to fix what was busted in what had rapidly turned into a dysfunctional family of the highest order.

Callie ran to her bedroom and grabbed her most comfortable sweater and jammed it in a small gym bag. She couldn't stand thinking these personal thoughts in her uniform, especially one she'd worn two days without a shower.

Jeb was a good kid, she reminded herself. Rational. He'd be okay. She was the one on the cusp of insanity.

Adding jeans, socks, and sneakers in the bag, Callie halted at the idea of a toothbrush. Was this overnight or not? She considered Chelsea Morning uninhabitable, at least for a few days, or was she making an excuse to stay at a certain other beach house?

Suddenly Seabrook was such a small issue.

Her emotions churned, and as long as she remained in this place, they would rule her through the night and into the next morning . . . or ruin her dreams. The toothbrush and hairbrush went into the bag.

House alarm set, she ran downstairs and slid into Seabrook's car, leaving hers parked under the house. But she wasn't naïve enough not to see she was leaving one stressful situation for another. Seabrook's spill about his business with Pittstop was long overdue and was on the agenda. She wasn't sure she was up to this.

She had no idea what he'd been up to other than he felt he'd identified his wife's killer. That topic needed serious discussion, and not just from his angle. From hers as well. The police chief in her had to lean on him for shirking his time on Edisto and then do an abrupt shift, informing him about Quincy's insertion in the Pittstop situation.

A frickin' maze. Complicated. And timing sucked.

Like either one of them was straight enough to counsel the other right now.

"You okay?" Seabrook asked as they pulled onto Jungle Road. "Jeb texted me."

"He's with his grandmother. I left a . . . what the hell? Stop." A gray Camaro sat parked in the Rosewood drive. "Pull over here."

He did as ordered. Her mind snapping back to the Rosewood case, she exited the patrol car, curious and anxious to pursue. She'd never seen the Camaro before this morning when it followed her and Raysor up to and across the big bridge, then followed her after she picked up her patrol car. All of which made her wonder even more why it sat in this particular drive.

Strolling around the car, she recognized it as a rental. Sarah's vehicle wasn't returned yet, and this wasn't Ben's.

"Wait." Seabrook got out, shouting over the roof of the car. "I'm in the dark, Callie. What are we doing?"

"Checking out that car," she replied, marching across the lawn toward the stairs. "I think it followed me earlier. Back me up on this."

With his long-legged stride he caught up quickly. "Followed you?"

She climbed the stairs to Shore Thing. "Mike, there's too much info to bring you up to speed now. Roll with me." She knocked on the door, piqued feelings standing on alert.

Ben Rosewood answered. "When's my car being returned?" he asked, the challenging mood clear. His hair was slightly disheveled, but otherwise, his display seemed normal in slacks and a white button-up shirt, collar open and tie discarded.

"It's at a garage in West Ashley," Callie said, referencing the Edisto side of Charleston. "Feel free to pick it up. We're done with it in our investigation, but I doubt it's drivable."

His sardonic grin sought to draw her out.

Clicking into professional mode, she said, "We need to talk."

"I have nothing to say." He started to close the door.

She stiff-armed it open. "Yes, you do. Where have you been?"

"My business." He pushed harder.

Seabrook stepped up. "Let us in, Ben. Or we can take you to the station."

Ben pivoted and walked to the living room. "Don't bother having a seat," he said. "If it's longer than sixty seconds, I'm calling my lawyer."

Callie entered, Seabrook closing the door. "Why would you need an attorney?" she asked. "And you didn't answer my question. Where were you when your wife was almost killed?"

He snatched his glass, half-empty of scotch from an end table. "Drop the melodrama. She dodged a damn deer."

"The brake lines were cut," Callie said. "And you might be the last person to have touched the car."

Glass dangling between two fingers, his mind appeared to struggle to assimilate the news. "Don't think I swallow the brake story, Ms. Morgan. Not out here."

Deliberate non-reference to her rank. Frowning, she stepped closer. "No fear for your wife's life? No demand for investigation? No wish for action taken against whoever did this to Sarah?"

He shrugged, a comical skepticism in his movement. "What are the odds? People don't cut brake lines. You can't even do it on current models."

"Precisely," she said. "Someone understood it could be done only on an old car. You have the vehicles serviced, so why not you?"

An inebriated "hah" left his mouth. "So I'm the culprit you seek?" Then he chuckled. "Aren't we feeling high and mighty with our new badge? Are you formally accusing me of attempted murder, Chief?"

"Not sure yet." She wandered farther in. The bedroom door was shut. If Jeb was already gone with Beverly, then Sarah ought to be . . .

"And what about my damn back door that your officer kicked in after your mother broke into my house!" He waved, the drink sloshing. He'd had a nip or two, maybe something else priming his temper before they arrived.

Seabrook cast a questioning glance at Callie. Her glance told him to trust her.

"She's replacing it," Callie replied, certain Sarah hadn't pressed charges since Beverly went home.

With an oily smirk, Ben reached into his pocket. "Was the illustrious Mrs. Cantrell hunting for this?" The paper had been folded four ways, and he shook it open one-handed. "Just call me *Dad*."

A flash of heat flew through Callie, and she moved to snatch the document, but he lifted it out of reach, like a high school kid on the elementary playground. "You're not my father," she said, jaw tight.

"Oh, excuse me," he said, cramming the document back into his pocket like a used napkin. "*Step*-Daddy. It's a copy anyway. Sarah can't find the original. I made a copy, no, several copies, for . . . posterity, let's say. Further back than she knows. Kept waiting for her to spill the truth, but no, Beverly and her friend told me first, which is really sad." He took another drink. "And who says I don't have the original birth certificate stashed someplace for insurance?"

And therein lay the abrasive spousal relationship.

Embarrassed at Seabrook hearing the news of her heritage in such a juvenile banter, Callie slammed her previous question back at Ben. "You can shove that paper up your—"

Seabrook touched her elbow.

"Answer my question, Ben," she continued. "Where were you two days ago when Sarah fought to keep from drowning in the marsh? When someone else did!"

Ben took another sip.

"Answer me!" she yelled.

"Myrtle Beach," he slurred. "I have receipts."

Over three hours away. Close enough to go back and forth, regardless of the receipts.

She'd pegged that Camaro around eight thirty this morning. Nothing saying he hadn't followed her from Middleton, either. "Where were you around three a.m.?"

He laughed. "Asleep like any sane person." Leaning forward, he added, "In Myrtle Beach."

Seabrook remained quiet, absorbing the news, holding his questions. Bless him for the professionalism. Most of this information was foreign to him, and Callie'd have to fill in the holes later.

The bedroom door handle sounded, metal retracting, and Sarah peered out. "Callie?"

She wasn't harmed physically, but the discomfort spoke clearly in her eyes. The timidity Callie'd come to expect in the woman had returned, the strength exhibited at the station gone.

The idea that this man intimidated any woman to this degree triggered a white-hot fury in Callie. After the long day and too many surprises, she was too tired, too impatient, and too pissed to maintain a decent composure and dispassionate distance. Stiffening, she entered Ben's personal space that smelled of peanuts and booze.

"You son of a bitch," she said, almost growling. "My officer died. You will prove you didn't do it, or I'll assume you did."

"Callie."

Seabrook's mild mention of her name tempered her a bit, but not much.

Ben groped back for his leather recliner, felt for the armrest, and almost fell into the seat. "That's not the way it works, Chief. Innocent until proven guilty, honey. Besides, Sarah knew where I was."

Callie twisted toward Sarah, disappointed at this evolution of the conversation. "You said you had no idea."

"I didn't that day, but I did the next," Sarah said, her submission painful to watch. "His call's on my phone if you want to check."

But Sarah hadn't told Callie. Why did that sting so much? "You followed me this morning," she said, preferring to harass Ben.

"I was only coming home," he replied.

Sarah moved to Callie's side, only for her new daughter to sidestep the closeness. "He wouldn't do this, Callie. You have to remember; he's been through a lot."

"*He's* been through a lot!" Callie exclaimed, surprised at the level of her own tone. She refused to allow Sarah to play mother.

Callie shouldn't let her involvement cloud the issue. But how could she not?

"Where's your other car, Ben?" Seabrook asked, his hand brushing the back of Callie's to let him take over, a notepad in the other.

"Garage in Myrtle Beach. Some sort of engine trouble."

Seabrook wrote as he spoke. "And they gave you a Camaro to drive in the interim?"

The man chuckled. "Never owned one, so I felt I might as well enjoy something different. No law against that. No law against coming onto the island behind Chief Morgan." He leaned forward and winked at her. "I saw you try to dodge me."

"Sarah?" Seabrook asked. "Are you okay?"

Her warm smile appeared, the one she gave every time she answered the door or greeted someone in Bi-Lo. The one Callie knew was well practiced and anything but genuine. "Of course I'm okay, Mike. Why wouldn't I be?"

He put his notepad back in his pocket. "Then we'll be on our way. Ben? We might be back in touch for a statement once you're sober. Do not leave the beach."

Ben held up his glass. "You guys can find your way out."

Callie turned at the threshold. She wanted to say something but couldn't decide what. A mixed bag of feelings carried her from hating Sarah for decades of lies to pitying her for accepting such a screwed up life. Nothing had changed other than Callie learning she shared genes with a different woman. Or so she told herself.

"Time to go," Seabrook said under his breath.

Sarah stood alone on the white wool carpet in the foyer, hugging her body. Searching for some sort of invitation to remain, Callie hung back. Sarah sadly mouthed *It's okay* as Seabrook closed the door.

In the car, Callie spun toward Seabrook. "I want to haul his ass in. We couldn't find him for days, and who's to say he won't disappear again?"

Seabrook silently started the car and eased out of the drive.

"Did you see how he treated her?" she said, jerking at her seatbelt. "He had motive to cut those brakes. Their history is toxic. Go back. We'll bring him in and see just how deep he's involved."

Seabrook turned left on Portia Street, headed toward the water.

"Mike," she said. "Listen to me."

"No, you listen to me," he said at the stop sign. He watched both ways then took a right. "He's too drunk, you're too distraught over personal baggage, and there wasn't a damn bit of evidence to connect him to the mishap. I take it a lot went down today, but let's eat dinner, let you settle down, then have a long discussion."

She huffed out once, choosing to ignore his latter comment. "We might build a case on circumstantial evidence against him."

"This isn't a case we can solve, Callie. Not without a confession or eye-witness."

"Then we'll get a confession out of him."

The old Sarah behaved more the victim, a woman who fell in love with the noble Lawton Cantrell. Callie understood that. The new Sarah, however, discarded her child and lied. Made Callie even madder that Francis died trying to save the woman. Where was the right in all this?

Windswept, Seabrook's beach house, came into view a block down, not a car in sight on the road. "No confessions from Ben today, and probably ever," he said. "And if you weren't so overwrought you'd see that."

"Damn son of a bitch," she uttered, her temper bottled with no release. Tears welled. *What the hell?* She whisked them away.

This place, these people. They never believed her. How was she to police this beach if they only wanted to think happy, pink, fluffy thoughts about each other? Damn this place. She'd almost rather be the Confederate back in Boston again, in its worst back alleys, chasing the scum, listening to people yelling at her for not doing enough. There she could try harder and nail dealers, murderers, and rapists and go home at the end of the day having made some sort of difference for somebody.

Seabrook remained silent the last couple hundred feet to his drive. When he parked, he remained stationary, except to glance at his rider. Callie's gym bag wadded against her in a crunched up grip, her gaze fixed on the oleander bushes in his back yard, her mind choosing to remain on Boston streets.

"You're flushed. You're mad. And I bet you haven't eaten," he said.

She turned to him, her frustration distilled down to a sullen, cold rage. "You have no idea what's going on in my head."

"I'm simply stating what I see." He reached for his handle. "You're a damn mess."

He exited the car, and she remained seated, clutching her bag tighter. Two weeks on the job, in a Lowcountry town an hour from civilization, and she'd let the job get to her. A cop was supposed to be able to compartmentalize, especially when family got involved.

Seabrook didn't get it. Nobody got it. She'd lost control of her life again, and that wasn't something she felt like sharing.

Four years ago she had this beautiful family. Her daughter just born, her father and husband still alive. Soaring at the peak of a stellar career.

Today . . . hell, how would she describe what she'd turned into today?

Yeah, she felt sorry for herself. The remaining good things left in her life weren't even good. Son refusing college because of her drinking. A mother she didn't like versus the mother she didn't know. The new job helped, thrilled her even, but she felt like she'd killed Francis. She couldn't keep a grip on Seabrook.

She hung her head. "Just take me home," she mumbled as Seabrook came around the car and opened her door.

Studying her, he leaned against the window. "You're tired and have a hell of a lot on your plate. Just come on in," he said.

"Don't think so," she said. "This is more than a hard day. Anyone around me seems to pay some sort of price. The kind with no turning back attached to it. Take me home, Mike."

He walked back to his side of the car and slid in but didn't turn the engine.

She stared again at the oleander—didn't care how long he stared at her. This was a sleepy coastal town, a factor in taking the job. The task shouldn't be this difficult, but somehow she'd made it so.

The clouds had brought in a stiffer breeze than earlier, and the oleander's lanky limbs dipped and danced, long overdue for pruning but hanging onto a few fuchsia blooms even this late in the season. She tried to use them to settle her attitude.

From her viewpoint, she had two options, and the one most appealling was to compose her resignation.

Chapter 18

CALLIE TRIED NOT to cut a glance toward Seabrook slouched in the driver's seat of his cruiser, his fingers slowly massaging the steering wheel. He'd rolled his window down while they sat parked in his beach house drive. It was going on six o'clock, which meant a dip into the upper sixties, the heavy heat of summer gone.

Windswept wasn't on the water but on the inland side of Palmetto Boulevard. While the houses on the water side used their back porches to enjoy the view, Seabrook's did the same from the front because two lots remained undeveloped, leaving his vista exquisite. The day had started sunny, but clouds moved in. No threat of rain, but the overcast changed the waves' color from navy to steel gray, giving the white caps a more ominous contrast.

Callie's thoughts tangled like a damn can of fishing worms. Brice LeGrand waging war. The whole dual mother issue. Losing an officer. It was like Edisto Beach had baited her to come with its mellow, undemanding ambience only to smack her in jest, shouting, "Gotcha."

Her place in this world made less sense than when she arrived in June.

"I contributed to this," Seabrook said. "Not being there. Maybe even pushing you into the job since I didn't want it. Maybe because my craving to chase Pittstop dominated everything else."

She softly snorted once, relishing the retort. In spite of his good guy image, she wanted to lash out at him so badly the curse words backed up like a full-moon wave holding back, holding back, its energy poised before doing its worst damage on the shore.

She was mad. If she mentioned her mother problem he'd interpret her entire emotional moment as personal, when it wasn't. At least not totally so.

"I'm not exactly cut out for police work," Seabrook said. "Not like you."

Wonderful. Now it was about him.

"I don't know how you do it, Callie. You can step into an investigation and sort every facet in this proper, precise manner. You sift out the sand and find the nuggets. Even with your world in what you think is shambles, you remain focused."

Focused?

"You're somebody everyone can rely on."

On what planet had he been hiding? Oh, wait. It was called Florence. He had this so backwards. She'd seen the crowds part when he approached, the people hanging on his every word, the office running smoothly under his command. "You're a frickin' idiot, Mike."

"Maybe. About some things. Including you."

"This beach loves you," she said, ignoring his come-on. "You could take it over again in a heartbeat if I left."

"Since when are you leaving?"

Shit, she didn't mean to say that.

"There is no going back, Callie."

Her head snapped around. "*You're* telling *me* that?" Says the man who can't get through the day without finagling a way to investigate his wife's case.

"Hey," he said, his tone authoritarian and a hint too loud. "I moved on. You dug a hole and hid."

"Oh, Florence is moving on?"

"Doing nothing is hiding, Callie. *Damn*!" His mouth flat and tight, he pointed at her. "You're being a child."

The bitter pill of his truth only made her want to leave all the more, and she opened her door.

He got out as well, rushing around the car. If she took her job seriously, she'd take this indoors, but she couldn't define seriously anymore, and just about didn't care.

Palm out to keep him at bay, she slung her bag on her shoulder. "You need this job more than I do, Mike. This damn beach has been the bane of my existence. So . . ." She hesitated before saying the thought aloud. "Have a great life chasing rumors and hiding in empty houses," she said, referencing the time she found him camped out in a rental, using some unconventional method to catch a thief.

A neighbor across the street and over one house did a double take and waved. Seabrook waved back. Callie glanced up at what had his attention and did the same. He smiled. She tried.

The neighbor brightened and hustled to the curb, scanned both ways for traffic, and ran across the street. "Mike," she said, gasping when she reached the other side. "I wanted to say how sorry I was about

Francis. Oh my, he was such a sweet man."

The agony of the condolences going to Seabrook, who wasn't even at the scene, collected heavy in Callie's chest. This was the ultimate slap and the final push to confirm she didn't belong here.

"Ms. Anderson, have you met our new police chief?" Seabrook said, and Callie had to steel herself. This nice woman didn't deserve to be dragged into this storm.

Hand over her mouth, the woman inhaled in astonishment. "This is Callie Morgan?"

"Yes, ma'am," Seabrook said and gave her a complimentary smile.

"Ooh," Ms. Anderson said, offering a middle-aged jiggle and giggle of glee. "You were all we talked about at Bunko two nights ago." She patted Callie's shoulder. "Just imagine, a woman police chief." Fluttering fingers, she added, "Nothing against you, Officer Seabrook. Everyone knows you're sure easy on an old lady's eyes, but this . . . a woman . . . it's nice."

Callie envisioned her telling a different story at next week's party, chatting up how the woman police chief up and left Edisto high and dry. Brice might even be blamed, especially if Aberdeen ran her mouth—but the two would bask at her being gone nonetheless.

Politely, Ms. Anderson smiled and paused to give Callie a chance to speak.

"Um, just doing my job," Callie said. The routine phrase crept back as natural as tying her shoes, but she felt like a fraud saying it.

What would Stan think of her?

"No," the neighbor said, "you do so much more than the job. Maybe—"

"Nice seeing you again, Ms. Anderson," Seabrook said, interrupting. "We were about to chill after a long day."

"Ooh, what happened?" she asked.

"Nothing serious," he replied, "just a lot of everything, plus Francis's death took its toll on us."

"Oh, yes," she replied solemnly, hands together. "You poor dears, don't let me keep you. It is an honor to meet you, Ms. Morgan. Wait until I tell my group." And she trotted back across Palmetto, phone to her ear before she reached the other side.

Callie fell back against the car, the syrupy thank-you having snuffed the ire out of her, making her think about how her resignation would be perceived. That and she was too damn tired to walk anywhere. Pushing fingertips into her temples, she let the beach fill her head with surf noises, a gull screaming to another to get off his turf.

Where would she go if she left? Boston, Middleton or Edisto: the only places she'd lived. She pictured herself alone in a house, maybe an apartment. No responsibility.

No friends.

No family.

Maybe a dachshund.

The car door closed, and she jumped. Seabrook walked around and shut the other, locking the vehicle. "You're welcome to come in," he said and headed to his porch. "Don't want to be accused of forcing you to do anything."

His low-key way of challenging her.

She shouldn't care about his treks to Florence, not if she was giving in. Nor about Sarah, either, but then a shot pierced her as she realized she was running away from Francis. That dropped her stomach to her knees.

Seabrook deserved to know about Quincy. Or did he? Diverting Quincy's attentions off Beverly and onto Pittstop was . . . for Beverly? Or Seabrook. Both, really. The reporter could dredge up information Seabrook might not find. Pittstop had recognized Mike, so a new strategy was in order anyway. Feeling her shirt, she ran her palm over the lump that denoted the envelope. He deserved to have that, too.

The mothers were *her* problem.

He reached the top of the stairs and was unlocking the house. She was off work, nobody home, her frustration fast surrendering to the need of a friend.

Callie had been to Seabrook's place only once, in a quick meet-up to head to a cook-out sponsored by one of the real estate firms. He'd been late getting off, she wasn't the chief yet, and she recalled waiting out front as he finished changing out of his uniform.

Seabrook left the door open.

She followed him in.

The living room wasn't freshly decorated but wasn't worn out, either. The décor seemed to come from off-island, but the deep blue upholstery on light oak suited the beach well enough. Soft gray distressed hardwood flooring and a woven area rug of grays, blues, greens, and beige. The white kitchen accented with federal blue tile. Gray plantation shutters on the windows. Simple upkeep. Simple privacy.

This was the first time she realized that she liked houses suiting the island. The Rosewood place was an anomaly out here, and she'd never felt right crossing that threshold with its teak, white, and gold. But then, the décor might not be what fed that sensation.

Seabrook removed his weapon, undid his utility belt, and pulled out the tail of his shirt in quick easy motions. She did the same, setting her items on the same buffet. There was something comfortable about the parallel.

"Shrimp work for you?" he asked, opening the top freezer in his kitchen. Every native kept shrimp or crab at the ready. "A baked potato with it?"

"Sure." She picked her gym bag back up. "Guest shower?"

"Two doors down the hall," he said. "Take your time."

She found it easy enough and locked the bathroom door behind her, instantly questioning her need for precaution. Her stomach knotted, then it rumbled. All she'd had that day was coffee, her last meal being her short date in Middleton, then bites of one of the colonel's biscuits at the Cantrell homestead. No wonder she was shaky.

She turned on the water and shed the uniform, hanging the pieces on a generic wall hook most likely from the small local hardware store. The seashell shower curtain showed some effort at embracing the ocean, the blue and green towels as well. Not that Seabrook had the time or access to a feminine taste for domestic attention.

The envelope in its paper bag fell on the floor. She tucked it more securely in the pants pocket.

Did she want to stay on the beach or not? Did she want the job or not? This behavior was so not her, or wasn't her of late. Was this fussy, negative, juvenile behavior she'd just exploded all over Seabrook's car a replacement for the panic attacks from months back? Her fear of dusk?

If she left, her days in any sort of law enforcement were done. Authorities like Chief Warren or Stan in Boston would see her inability to cope on tiny Edisto Beach as the ultimate end to her career in blue.

Her father would make her take a step back and weigh the pros and cons, if he were alive.

She changed her mind about any sort of conversation with Seabrook about Pittstop. It was rather psychotic on her part to mention resignation then bring up the office and expect civil, believable discourse.

Steam filled the tiny room. Wiping moisture off the mirror, she froze as the reflection took her aback. Her features drawn, she seemed ten years older. Felt older than that.

For a second she thought her ears were ringing but wrote it off as fatigue, maybe echo from the plumbing as the water got hot. Stepping under the stream, she assumed her shower pose, palms on the wall, the water raining on her drooped head, neck, and back. Something about that position undermined tension, loosened her, and as drops cascaded through her hair to her cheeks, she fixated on the drain. If she were covered in mud or blood, that's where it would go. So that's where she envisioned dramatics and emotional dander, too, draining in rivulets off her and down some six-inch PVC pipe to a sewer where it belonged.

It's also how she'd sobered herself so, so many times in her past.

Soaked to the bone, her tongue went dry in memory of gin, with a splash of tonic, lime . . .

"Callie?" Two knocks sounded on the door. "You all right in there? Dinner's almost ready."

"Coming." She spun around and found shower gel, never used. The relief he hadn't recently entertained a guest caught her by surprise . . . then she reminded herself that any sort of female *guest* would use his shower. Snatching the bottle, she popped the seal, soaped up, and rinsed off quickly.

But the shower meant to put her back to right only served to exacerbate her exhaustion. Too much down the drain.

As she exited the bathroom, hair towel-dried and makeup forgotten back at the house, she caught a whiff of the bay leaf and shrimp.

"Ready," Seabrook said, holding up plates. He walked out the front door. Apparently they were eating their dinner on the porch. Still daylight, but waning, a golden haze coated everything. Sunsets periodically gave her pause, instilling the memory of the flames devouring her home in Boston and licking the evening sky, and she questioned the weakness of her mental defenses after this hell of a day. She thanked the angels the sun set behind them and not over the water.

On one of Seabrook's exits, she opened the refrigerator and stole a beer. One hand cupped over the other, she stifled the pop top then drank like she'd spent two days in the desert.

"Come on out," he hollered.

"Coming," she replied, then finished the beer, retrieved another, and headed out.

She exited in sock feet, jeans, and the old sweater worn smooth on the elbows over the years, sleeves pushed up to hide the fact. Here she could display her scar. After taking her prepared plate from Seabrook, she bypassed the small table set up between two chairs and carried her meal to the wide porch swing with red cushions. She set her beer on the railing.

"This works, too," he said, dropping a bucket for the shrimp peels on the floor in front of them. He took his place beside her and let her control the motion of the swing.

While the natives recognized Seabrook's house, few of them were out and about. No tourist events on the beach's agenda, only the occasional contractor's truck rolled by, and three or four cars. Pelicans drifted overhead, a few gulls swerving and dodging, vying for whatever creature ventured to the top of the surf, grabbing dinner before roosting for the night. Two brave gray-headed souls tackled a beach walk, dressed in cardigans and rolled up long pants.

While Callie harbored a laundry list of discussions to hold with Seabrook, the roar of the waves and placid in-between temperature of summer and fall lulled her from a day of snapping, sparking nerves. Here was an evening where she could put her mind to rest, at least for the length of a meal. She contemplated taking her behavior back to Chelsea Morning afterward.

"Thought you'd rake me over the coals for the beer," she said, deftly separating meat from shell, popping the first shrimp in her mouth.

"Would've just made you madder," he said without judgment, shelling his even faster. He drank water.

She reached over and held her can up, then took another generous swig. "You could have one and make me feel better."

"And what kind of example would that make?" Nonchalant with a hint of defiance. Choosing his battles.

But after a half dozen shrimp and two bites of potato, her appetite disappeared, a hint of warning that her stomach wasn't in tune with the meal, but somehow it still craved the beer. Or was the stomach issue *because* of the beer? "I'm done," she said, bending over to set her plate on the floor.

"You sure didn't eat much," he said and reached down and swiped up the half dozen shrimp she left behind.

A light breeze swooped in off the water, shaking a navy and soft blue windsock hanging at the other end of the porch. Her toe pushed the swing again. She went to take another drink only to suck on a dry can. "Need a refill."

Seabrook took the can from her and replaced it with his barely touched glass of water. "Drink that."

"Mike . . ."

"Sit." He placed his plate on the floor as well and took her sleeve. "Tell me about your mother."

He said it easy, like asking how the ballgame went. Ben's stepfather comments surely hadn't escaped him, maybe confused him for a minute, but Seabrook was smart. The way his tone contradicted the seriousness of such a personal topic muddled her a second, though, which instantly lowered her guard.

"Which mother?" she asked.

"Whichever," he said as if everyone had two moms, and he ate another shrimp.

"I learned today that Beverly Cantrell is not my biological mother and Sarah Rosewood is."

"Hmm. And?"

He ceased moving but paid attention, and then she understood what he was doing. "And I learned I'd been duped my entire life," she said. "After someone broke into my bedroom, after my fake mother threatened my real mother, after someone slashed the tires on two of my cars. After I tried to save my officer and he died." There, she'd said enough.

Like a hurricane pushing a wave at high tide, pressure built inside her, only this time she hadn't the strength to quell it and hide the distress. She cleared her throat and studied the ocean.

"Come here," he said, and without her okay, reached over and lifted her into his lap. He swung his legs gently so that he was seated lengthwise in the swing. Then he rocked her.

Which made the tears come. She cried quietly into his shirt, almost ashamed, equally relieved. No conversation, but a communication nonetheless.

He rubbed her sleeve, even touching the scar, in a slow rhythm so gentle Callie almost thought she heard him hum, melting her deeper into him. For almost an hour, she relinquished to his long arms, his understanding and patience so tender. With her emotion finally ebbed, she explained the day, from Beverly's break-in to Jeb turning his back, and her parents' history in between.

He squeezed her. "Sorry, honey."

Two words, but they soothed her more than anything she'd felt in ages. She shrugged and shifted to lay her head on his shoulder. "Guess it is what it is." She blew out a sigh as if ending her emotional moment.

"Oh, Callie," he whispered against her head. "Let me be there for you. We could be good for each other."

She reached around his neck and pulled his mouth to hers.

Pressing hard, she inserted her tongue, her body mashing against his, wanting no space between them. They'd nuzzled each other's necks before saying goodnight at her door, but this ardor was a whole different animal. It had been a long time coming.

Erotic pain shot down and through her. Ten, fifteen, maybe twenty minutes passed, and she held onto him, mouths together this way, then that, tighter, softer . . . and he equally returned the heat. Their exposure to whomever happened to drive by a distant concern in her mind.

Finally, she pulled back, touched his forehead, and smiled, a cough or two escaping. "You might catch my cold."

He nudged her back, his embrace wrapped tight. "So worth it, lady. You don't know how long I've waited for this. Guess that's a yes?"

"A yes?"

He ran his palm over her hair. "That we could be good for each other."

She smiled. "That question was like a half hour ago, but yes, Mike, I think the whole island knows that."

With a quick swing around, he planted feet on the plank floor and hefted her into his arms. "I think fall has arrived, Chief. It's getting a little chilly out here."

She held onto his neck. "So find a way to warm us up, Officer."

There was no sweeping of settings off the table or a tangle of legs on the floor, not that their hearts weren't racing enough to break glass or collapse a table or two. Instead, Mike carried her inside Windswept, awkwardly locked the door, even setting the alarm, then deposited her on his bed. It wasn't quite eight, but when he closed the plantation shutters, it might as well have been midnight.

Even with the house secure, the muffled sound of the surf made its way in. So much louder than at Chelsea Morning three blocks inland. Not that she listened long, but she loved it being there.

She undressed quickly on her knees from the center of the bed as he did the same standing three feet away, their gazes locked, each wanting to see the other disrobe but not wasting time doing it. He beat her in the race but when his knees pushed down on the bed, and he moved toward her, she stopped. Stripped down only to her jeans, she laid her palms on his bare chest and took a second to take in his warmth, his clean smell, though she was sure he hadn't showered. She wanted to appreciate what she'd imagined for the last two months.

But then her breath hitched. It had been years . . . since John.

"It's okay," he whispered, nuzzling down her neck.

"Yes," she said, covering her concern, and they came together in a kiss, Callie easing to her back on the spread. Seabrook slipped her unzipped jeans off neatly and quickly but left her panties. While their lips tasted, with his finger he outlined the lacy elastic below her navel, teasing.

"Oh, God, you're horrible," she said with a quick gasp, her back already arching.

"Don't beat me there," he replied with a husky chuckle and slid the nylon down to her knees where she aided the panties off one leg at a time.

For a second she started to compare this man to the one she married twenty years ago, but all it took was Seabrook suckling her breast for her to return to the present. He pulled back and looked softly down on her. "Callie, I've thought of this so—"

"Hush," she said, the word escaping her with a moan, the rhythm in her already rocking beneath him. "Goodness I wanted to be subtler than this—" and she gasped and he began to move in sync with her, tempting with a smile.

He laughed. She loved his laugh and sniggered back.

"Now? Or shall we . . . wait?" he said, sliding his toned, beach-tanned body over her, his mouth eating up every inch of her breasts, her belly, then down the inside of one leg and back up the other until he moved up and poised over her. More winded than he, she flushed as embarrassment flew over her at how horny she must appear.

"Now." Her voice cracked. She repeated, "Now."

His fingertips traced her hip bone. "You sure?"

She swept a hand down and encircled him. "I think we both are." Then as she reached both arms around his neck and dug in her fingers, she slid her legs apart on the quilted spread. He entered her with the fervor they both wanted and had denied themselves for so many reasons that made absolutely no sense now.

Chapter 19

IF CALLIE WASN'T exhausted before, she was after twice enjoying Seabrook's affections and would have gone for a third, but her body caved to sleep.

The dream chases that ravaged most of her nights gave way to a new experience. She found herself jogging on the sand, the heat blistering, almost unbearable for that time of morning. Tourists sat on their porches, watching, as though waiting for a break in the swelter. They flashed surprise that she weathered such an overbearing sun when shade made much more sense.

Sophie waved enthusiastically from one house then contained herself, withdrawing like she'd done something wrong. Stan and John stood on the steps of another, Jeb a few stairs below them. Where was her father . . . or either mother? Everyone grimaced, but though she was thrilled to see her loved ones, the miles of sand called for her. She had someplace to be . . . before temperatures climbed too high. Sweat ran in her eyes. As quickly as she wiped the stinging drops, more ran in until she teared and couldn't tell which moisture dripped from her chin.

A man jogged toward her too far down the beach to recognize yet, maybe a quarter mile. Wiping her temple twice, she shielded her view but couldn't make him out. Then panic zipped through her as she recalled her first week this summer living on Edisto and how Mason *conveniently* stumbled across her, then again, and then again days later.

"Callie," Seabrook said, suddenly running at her elbow. "You're too hot."

"I have to finish," she huffed, digging for air. Where was her second wind?

"You're too hot," he said. "Stop."

"Can't," she tried to say, but couldn't.

"Look at me. You hear?" His firmness jarred her attention. Why was he so blurry? Blinking, she fought to remember . . . where she was . . . oh, gracious. She shut her lids. Her head was splitting to its center.

"Callie, you with me yet?" Seabrook sat on the edge of the mattress in sweatpants and T-shirt, feeling her forehead. "I need you to sit up a minute."

She tried to rise only for her entire torso to quiver at the effort. "Mike?" A cough racked her, and it shot pain through her chest.

He helped her sit up. Holding onto him, she waited for the bed to cease its spin. "What's happening?" she whispered.

"You're sick as hell is what's happening, and my guess it's from almost drowning three days ago. I told you to get checked out. Here." He offered her a glass of water. "Can you hold it?"

"Of course . . ." But she found herself having to make her muscles work to do so. She was weak as a kitten.

"Open up."

As instructed she opened her mouth. The bitter taste of aspirin, and something else that held an equally horrid twang, registered on her tongue. But she relished the cool water which went down easy enough, the pills catching but finishing their journey with a second attempt.

"Drink all of it," he said. "We've got to get your fever down and fluids in you."

She did, then he propped her up with three pillows, leaving just the sheet over her body. "I feel like crap." Her head lolled back on a pillow.

"Yeah, I can tell. I woke up with heat radiating off you like a furnace."

She shook her head only once, the pounding almost causing her to upchuck the water. "Give me half a day in bed. Tell Marie—"

"Your temperature was a hundred and two. I already talked to Marie. I feel like a heel coming onto you last night."

She remembered. "It was so damn worth it, though."

The smile appeared forced, his medical side conflicting with the boyfriend he'd become.

"What time is it?" she asked, a chill swooping over her. Seabrook covered her with the bedspread.

"Seven," he said. "You don't feel like eating, do you?"

Shaking her head, she sank into the pillow.

He left and soon returned. "Here's a glass of ginger ale. You want me to stay with you today?"

"Absolutely not." She took a sip and moaned, enjoying every inch it traveled down her throat. "I need you to run the station and stay on the island."

"Try to chase me off it. I'm worried about you."

Good. She sank into the covers, aching like she'd been beaten. Her illness would keep him on island, an unexpected side effect of whatever this crap was she caught. His itch to hunt Pittstop maybe quelled for at least a day. So her brain could rest. Good. It hurt to think.

She'd not yet explained the envelope. That conversation required her sharp, and if she couldn't discuss the envelope with him, she could stall about Quincy, too. Surely Seabrook would understand.

The crazy headache still shouting, she withdrew inside herself for a bit, Seabrook's hand on her ankle, worried.

Heat coursed through her again, and she shoved the spread off. Geez, she wished she could go comatose for a week. "Do something for me, Seabrook."

"Sure, what is it?" he said from his perch on the end of the bed.

"You don't have the resources to investigate Pittstop." She omitted saying *or the experience.* "Seriously, pass it on to SLED."

"We're discussing this now?"

She gave a cough. "I'd prefer to think we're putting an end to this lone wolf quest you've got going on. I'd sure rest easier."

He rubbed her lower leg. "We got sidetracked last night, and we were supposed to discuss what I've been doing and what I've found. You were supposed to talk more about what happened at your mother's."

"Yeah." Her chest burned, brain drumming to its own irritating heavy-metal song. "Can you turn the light off?" she asked, covering her eyes. Unexpectedly, tears leaked through, not from emotion but from simply feeling so damn bad.

His cool lips rested on the side of her head. "I'm sorry, honey. This is not the time. You're too sick for all this. Let me get a shower, then we'll check your fever again. We might head to the hospital."

She lowered her arm. "No, I'm not as sick as that. We've lost Francis and I'm . . . it's just . . . Brice is all over my butt about my inability to juggle manpower and tend to Edisto. But he trusts you."

"I said don't worry." He touched her cheek. "I won't be long."

Last evening seemed an eternity ago. Her petulance outside at the car, the headaches and cough that should have warned her she was ill. Ashamed, she recalled her looping thoughts about resigning and retreating across the big bridge to big civilization. Edisto was all she had and forgave her for all she had once been, though they didn't understand the half of it. This was home.

Plus Seabrook was here.

He didn't have anyone else either.

She dozed what felt like only a moment before she awoke to the scent of soap and the form of Seabrook in uniform leaning over her. "Callie? Your temp's down to under a hundred. I've put your phone here on the nightstand along with a bottle of water. More antibiotic and aspirin, but I'll check on you later when it's time for that. Call if you get worse, you hear me?"

"Gotcha," she said with exerted bravado, faded once she heard his key turn in the lock. But sleep eluded her. The pills might be kicking in, but she wasn't planning a run for a while. The more she drank, the quicker she'd feel better, and she'd finished off her ginger ale.

She eased her feet onto the floor and tested her stability. Not great, but she wouldn't fall down. That's when she realized she wore one of Seabrook's T-shirts. When had she put that on?

All she had left of John was a dress shirt she often wore to bed. She wore it less these days, saving its lifespan, his scent having long left the material. The past disappearing with the onset of the present, a concept she knew Seabrook fought hard to avoid. Even having lost his wife so many years ago, he held ridiculously tight to the vendetta. In some ways Callie'd graduated emotionally past this stage, with only three years since John's passing. Jeb might claim differently though.

Discovering she clutched the T-shirt, she let go and smoothed out the wrinkles. She liked wearing Seabrook's clothes.

Glass in one hand, phone in the other, she took a slow walk to the kitchen for a refill. Gaped open, a paper bag lay on the counter, something white beside it. She put down the glass and reached for the bag.

No. The white envelope labeled *Seabrook* had been opened, a knife slit down one of the short sides. No sign of the earring.

Oh good gracious, why? Seabrook understood evidence handling, and this damn sure wasn't in the lesson book. It would be impossible to explain this in court and make the evidence stick. Not that she'd made it any easier confiscating it from Middleton and hiding it in her clothes.

And to think they were supposed to be cops.

She activated her phone and speed dialed the office, coughing while it rang.

"Edisto PD."

"Marie," she said. "Put Raysor on the phone."

"Callie?" Marie responded. "You sound horrible."

"You have no idea. Is Raysor there?"

"Yeah, Mike's here too. Do you need him? He said you might call."

"No, I'm not worse, just tired. Get Don, please. And don't tell

Seabrook."

Marie stalled. "Um, okay."

Callie coughed, phone against her chest. Even with the cell muffled against her, she heard Raysor answer in his deep bass tone. "What's up?"

"Don, give me a few hours to rest and kick this, whatever it is, and I'll drag myself to the station. Mike's technically in charge, but do me a favor, will you?"

"Sure, doll," he said lower.

"Keep an eye on him. He's still fixated on Florence. Way more than I thought. I'm pretty sure as long as I'm sick he'll stick around, but . . ."

"I hear you. Don't worry."

She tried to exhale in relief and about choked.

"You sound really bad, gal. Need me to do anything for you?"

"Just what I said," she said, and her voice trailed into an unintelligible croak.

"I'll let you go. Get some sleep."

She hung up as it hit her she was in Seabrook's house, in Seabrook's bed, and nobody knew where she was. Her car at her house. For the moment she was Seabrook's property and sole responsibility, and she couldn't walk ten feet. The room tried to spin, and she lowered herself along the dishwasher to the floor. She was glad nobody could find her.

The rush of an enthusiastic tide crescendoed outside. A spring tide, if she recalled right, meaning waves at their most active in a moon's cycle. Still seated on the kitchen floor, elbows tucked against her chest, knees bent, she let the background noise soothe her. Feathery thoughts flitted from fear for Seabrook to Beverly's lies, from Sarah to Jeb, until she let the clutched phone slide down her cheek to her chest. Darkness fell over her like an eclipse, the churning and clawing at the sand filling her ears until she fell so deep she heard nothing.

Thumping dragged her out of her sleep.

She raised her head, unable to collect herself.

"Callie! Come to the door."

Her phone vibrated from the depths of the T-shirt, the ringer muted. A chill shivered up into her core from her naked butt on the linoleum floor.

What time was it? With a squint, she found the microwave and realized she'd been asleep against the dishwasher for over two hours. It was almost noon. Oh, good gracious, Seabrook would have a fit finding her on the floor.

"Callie, it's Sophie," came another yell. "Are you in there?"

The phone vibrated again. Callie untangled the cell. "Hello?" Then she repeated, because she wasn't sure she even heard herself, the word woefully cracked and weak.

"Where are you?" Sophie said in dramatic exasperation. "Why weren't you answering your phone? I need to talk to you. Three people saw you and Seabrook swapping spit on this front porch yesterday, so the whole beach figures where you spent the night. Are you in there?"

"Hold on," Callie managed, and she heaved herself to her feet like an arthritic cripple, a grip on cabinetry. Once standing, she made her way to her yoga friend on the front porch.

"Hurry, now. Let me in! You've got trouble, and we don't have time to screw around—" Sophie gasped. "Holy cow, you're a disaster."

Callie waved her friend in. "Lock the door," was all she felt like saying as she made her way to the bed and crawled against the pillows.

"Girl," Sophie said, flitting up to Callie's side of the bed studying. "You can't be sick. Not now. Aberdeen is gloating about Brice stirring crap about you, and we have to fight back."

Arm over her face, Callie said, "Let them stir."

"Callie?" came Seabrook's voice as the front door closed. "Did I see Sophie come in?"

Sophie winked at Callie. "You sure did, you sweet hunk of a man. We're in here." Easing onto the bed, Sophie crossed her legs in a lotus position inches from Callie's side. "I was checking to see if she wanted to eat."

He appeared and made his way to the bed, hand instantly cupping the side of her head. "Warm. When's the last time you had any aspirin?" he asked, already making his way to the bathroom.

"When you left," she replied.

Sophie mouthed, *I need to talk to you*, then pointed to the bathroom. *Tell him or wait?*

Wait, Callie mouthed in return.

Leaving the bathroom, he approached her nightstand and gave her more pills. "Where's your glass? I told you to stay in bed, Callie."

Crap, she'd left the glass in the kitchen, before she passed out on the floor. "I had to go to the bathroom, then I got thirsty," she said, clearing her speech. "Got a drink in the kitchen then came back to bed."

He returned with two glasses, a ginger ale and water, and ordered her to take the pills.

"I could've done that," Sophie said. "You're fussy."

"No, I'm a doctor," he corrected. "How about you staying with her the rest of the afternoon? I'll owe you a dinner at Finn's."

"With or without . . . *her*?" she said, tossing a shake of her head toward Callie in jest.

He winked. "Depends on how fast you get her well."

Stooping, he kissed Callie full on the mouth. "Sleep the whole day, you hear?"

"Guess doctors don't think they can catch bugs from their patients," Sophie said, a smirk showing her satisfaction.

"Trust me, I've already been exposed." And he kissed her quickly again, pulled up the spread over her, and headed to the door. "Sophie, I'm counting on you."

The front door closed . . . and locked.

"Oh my goodness!" Sophie squealed. "You finally did it. I'm proud of you!"

Callie sat up and twisted a pillow around. "Timing sucked, though."

But then Sophie went serious. "You couldn't be more right. Brice has gone off his rocker. He's trying to turn the whole beach against you."

"Well, I can't do a lot about that from here, can I?"

Dismayed, Sophie inched her cross-legged posture closer until she touched Callie's hip. "You don't understand. Brice is calling for an emergency council meeting to discuss letting you go because of Francis."

Aww, damn. "Well, nothing I can do except show up when the time comes." Then she rethought the karma of hot and cold decisions about remaining chief.

Sophie touched Callie's arm. "You're warm. No, not good at all. Look at me, honey."

"I'm not delirious, Sophie. Just say it."

"The council meeting is tonight," Sophie said. "At seven o'clock."

Callie stared. "What?"

While they couldn't fire her tonight, the meeting would set the stage and plant the seed for some later official forum where they'd debate, maybe call for remarks from the community. A certain amount of pride reared its head from beneath the weakness and ague.

Did she want to remain chief or not?

A knock sounded on the door. Sophie hopped up and ran out of the bedroom. Callie sat up. Anybody hunting Seabrook would go to the station.

Surely once the council heard she was ill they'd postpone. But being found in Seabrook's bed might taint the sympathy. Fraternizing with a subordinate. Of course nobody would recall she and Seabrook were sort of an item before she landed this job.

Who cared about that stuff anymore anyway?

Sophie's teachings weaseled into her head. If not rude of her, she might call this council meeting penance for Francis, especially with her too ill to fight the succession of events.

Sophie peered around the doorframe and whispered, "It's the mayor."

With a swoop, Callie yanked the tangled covers over her as far up her chest as it would go.

"Callie?" the mayor called from the entry hall.

"Seriously, Mayor?" she said, irritation tinging her answer.

"I'm sorry to, um, interrupt you," he said, voice raised. "But it's important . . ."

Callie tucked deeper in bed in embarrassment though nobody could see.

No telling how many people knew where she spent the night now. "Mayor Talbot, what is it?" Her throat protested at the level she had to speak to be heard out of the bedroom and down the small hall to the door.

"Brice LeGrand," he shouted.

"Sophie told me, sir. Not sure I can make a meeting tonight."

He cleared his throat. "I can't stop him."

"Ask him to give me a week," she said. "Flu, pneumonia, bronchitis, whatever this is won't exactly cooperate with Brice's agenda."

"Doesn't matter," he said loudly. "You don't have to be there."

"Ugh," she moaned and fell back into the pillows. "Then why bother me," she muttered to herself.

Sophie glanced at the mayor then back around the bedroom door. "Everyone likes you, sweetheart. They'll expect you to fight this."

"Oh, Sophie, Brice has generations of clout." Callie tried to speak louder. "Where do you stand, Mayor?" A coughing spell quickly followed. Why hadn't he picked up a damn phone?

"I'm the one who got you hired, young lady. I'm a man of principle, not one to back down when the going gets tough."

She weakly grinned at his support, in spite of his clichés.

"Today we canvas the beach for residents to appear tonight in your defense," he said. "The Maxwells, Ms. Hanson, Sarah Rosewood, anyone you've helped. Possibly Janet Wainwright. Haven't worked on her yet. But these people need to see you out and about today, if that's at all possible."

Callie had support, even in the few weeks of her tenure, but the mayor was wrong about Sarah. She wouldn't defend her, and Callie wouldn't expect her to. It would be like Brice to bring up the affairs in the Cantrell family, since it would be like Ben to inform Brice out of spite. Secrets. Didn't matter what kind they were, they disturbed voters, and the councilman would use that angle to his advantage to sway council members and residents alike.

"Callie, did you hear me?"

"Sorry, Mayor. My ears are ringing."

"I said the residents of Edisto Beach expect to see you tonight. Can I count on you? We can't let Brice win. I fought to bring you here. This is the time we—"

"Yes," Callie said. "I'll be there."

"Good," he said, then shouted again, "Good."

Callie heard the door creak open. He was obviously eager to leave. "I'll be in touch."

Sophie disappeared to show him out.

Her energy in short supply, Callie left the bed once Talbot was gone. She wandered out into the living area and found her uniform folded on the dinette on the other side of the kitchen bar, her jeans and sweater the same. Seabrook's attempt to tend to her clothing had revealed the envelope, and who would blame him for opening it? But he should have addressed it with her, not behind her back.

And she should've discussed it by phone with him the morning it was delivered.

Now it was . . . messy.

She slid the uniform, her weapon, and her utility belt into the gym bag, and not wanting to walk more than necessary, she shed the T-shirt on the spot and began putting on the clothes she wore last night. Slowly she slid the sweater over her head.

Sophie scurried in. "What can I do?"

Bag passed over to her friend, Callie pulled out a chair and sat. "Would you put my shoes on my feet? Then drive me home so I can shower and grab a fresh uniform. Probably need to dress the part of police chief when I knock on doors."

Sophie snatched the sneaker shoelaces like she would a child, tight and neat. "There. Want me to call Mike?"

Callie shook her head, grateful for the deep dull brain throb replacing the piercing stab from earlier. "Let's go home. What time is it? How much time do we have left?"

"It's almost two."

They eased down to Sophie's vintage powder blue Mercedes, Callie happy to see the top up on the convertible. The grayness from last evening had graduated into dark clouds. The surf churned, kicking three-foot waves to more like six. Not a soul would put a toe in that angry water. Up and down the boulevard, oleander, palmettos, and hawthorns jumped and danced in warning.

"Hop in," Sophie said. "We're about to get some rain tonight. Hopefully that'll keep people home from this stupid meeting."

Yeah, Callie thought. Maybe they'd cancel.

Sophie pulled onto Palmetto. Though they were less than a mile from Callie's home, in a blink Sophie announced they were in Chelsea Morning's drive, Callie having dozed off enroute.

"I could've walked over from your house next door," Callie said, doubting her words as she said them.

Sophie took the gym bag from her at the base of the stairs. "Ha, whatever."

Going down Seabrook's two dozen stairs proved much easier than climbing Callie's, but she did it, only to freeze two steps from the top.

Quincy waited in one of her rattan settees, his nose cut, cheeks bruised, and a brow open in bad need of stitches.

Chapter 20

"WHAT ARE YOU doing—?" Callie's words fell short at her deep cough, urged by her climb to Chelsea Morning's porch where Quincy waited. His cuts were semi-fresh, the dried blood not yet crusted on the bridge of his nose and bottom lip. One cheek puffed fatter than the other.

The mayor might have to wait an extra hour for her to shower, dress and assist the campaign to get the Morgan supporters to tonight's council meeting. No way was she shooing Quincy off. She had to hear the story behind those cuts.

Callie immediately rued having fed him anything about Pittstop, assuming her decision led to those bruises. She could almost write an incident report from the signs. Quincy had overstepped, spoke too sassy, and suffered at the end of someone's fists.

"You and your locks," Sophie said, inserting herself between them, her attention on Quincy's damage. "Open the door so I can get this poor man some ice. We don't want his skin to scar."

Poor man indeed. "I don't do stitches," Callie said, unlocking the door, "but we'll let you clean up." The closest she could come to feeling sorry for him until she heard the details.

She shut off the alarm and gestured for him to sit in her living room, each of her steps shaky. Sophie would sage the house within an inch of its life once she heard the man's background, and Callie suspected ulterior motive out of this guy, but the wounds added some credibility to his words. Sophie scampered to the kitchen while Callie continued to the bathroom.

Her lungs heavy and thick, once hidden in her bathroom she rested against the counter for a moment. *Damn it.* Seabrook was probably right about the aspirated water causing pneumonia. Each ache and cough worsened, bit by bit, fast bits at that, ever since Sarah's event. But she could continue to hurt, a small price to pay considering Francis. She hated it when she forgot to remember him.

She fished the first aid kit from under the sink then entering the living room, set the kit and a makeup mirror on the coffee table. "Use that." Easing into the recliner, she decompressed. "So, what happened to you?"

"I fucked up is what happened to me," Quincy said. "Your Roman McGee guy was none too happy to see me. Happy?"

From his stalking skills against Beverly, Callie thought Quincy shrewd enough to investigate and be discreet, smart enough to research the guy without actually confronting him. She'd overestimated his abilities.

"You're walking like a geriatric," he said. "What's with you?"

"Woke up sick." She hacked again. "Tell me what you did."

"What *I* did?" he said, twisting his mouth with indignation, flinching as the pain of a cut reminded him not to. He opened the first-aid box and fiddled around the contents, found what he needed, then moved the mirror on its stand to inspect his cuts up close.

Sophie set a glass of tea before each of them and presented Quincy a plastic bag of ice wrapped in a kitchen towel. "Need me to do that?" she asked, reaching for the alcohol.

Quincy smiled and shifted over. "Aren't you a sweet one." His leer at Sophie morphed to a sneer at Callie. "Unlike other people."

Sophie didn't need to be in the middle of this. "Soph, don't you need to make some calls about tonight's meeting? This gentleman is consuming more time than we can afford."

"This won't take a moment," Sophie replied and sat.

"You aggravated Pittstop," Callie said. "I didn't say get in the guy's space, Quincy. Calls and emails would have worked fine. Did you find out anything for your trouble? Or are those bruises from somebody totally different?"

"He did them, all right," he replied, letting Sophie dab his lip.

Callie sighed. "And?"

He stared at her in lieu of his reflection. "All I did was sit outside his place for an hour. Asked his neighbors some things." With a hint of guilt, his gaze slid back to the mirror. "I might have gone inside his place."

"You broke in?" she said. "Is that what you do for your stories . . . break in? Wait, so, how many times have you broken into Sarah Rosewood's place? Or maybe mine?"

"Damn, you sound bad."

"Answer me," she said.

He cleared his throat, as if her hoarseness had infected him. "I don't do that. This was the exception. I was working for you."

"I can't give you that kind of permission. I asked for intel and whatever story you could gather. Have you not covered any criminal cases before?"

He winced and patted Sophie on the knee. "That's enough, sweetheart."

Sophie flashed surprise at the touch and retracted, gathering up the used materials.

"I've done a few," he said to Callie.

"Not enough, apparently," she said. "Anything you discovered in Pittstop's place while in the midst of your illegal entry might be worthless to us. Especially if you tout that you worked for the police. A cold-blooded killer could walk because you freelanced, you idiot. You weren't supposed to talk to him," she repeated. So stupid!

"Whatever," he said, touching fingertips to the finished bandages. Then he stopped, a serious, stone-cold expression replacing his lackadaisical air. "You better watch yourself, though. He recognizes who Seabrook is, says he's familiar with you. Thanks for telling me to check him out after he was already riled about what y'all have already done."

Y'all hadn't done anything. However, she also had no idea what Seabrook did during his clandestine trips to Florence. Whatever it was, he'd left enough crumbs for Pittstop. But Mike damn sure wouldn't tell Pittstop about her. "How did he learn who I am, Quincy?"

He gave a sarcastic shrug. "He asked who sent me."

Eyelids narrowed, her temper climbed like her fever. "And you told him?"

"He drew out a knife. I didn't want that thing against my neck! He's certifiable."

She savored a few more inhalations, shallow though they were. Quincy's gung-ho, cinematic effort to play secret agent may have triggered the bad-ass side of Pittstop.

"Did he recognize me?" she asked. "I mean, when you said my name?"

His head tilted, analytically. "What do you mean?"

Impatient, she tried to reword. "Did you say the Edisto Police Chief sent you or Callie Morgan?"

"Both," he said. "Edisto Police Chief Callie Morgan. Trust me, I wanted the cop part in there."

Fabulous. "Was he surprised?" she asked.

He thought. "No, not really."

"Did he recognize the name?"

Rolling his gaze to the ceiling, he gave a flamboyant shrug. "I honestly have no idea what was in the man's head. I was too busy paying attention to the knife."

"Idiot," was all she could find the strength to say, and she couldn't say that very loud.

Sophie balled up her legs to her chest atop the barstool, mouth buried into her knees. Callie wished her friend hadn't heard all this.

The envelope had been a message. Callie was sure of it. In spite of him entering her mother's house, Callie never felt in danger when he had every opportunity to do more than he had. The only way to interpret the act was *"Here is proof who I am. Leave me alone or I will get you where you live."*

He hadn't confronted Seabrook, to her knowledge. Or slashed *his* car tires during one of his late night treks. Or since the culprit liked knives, slit her throat some night in retaliation to Seabrook's obstinacy.

So she had him pegged as wanting to be ignored. Quincy, however, labeled him as a powder keg. What made him change other than Quincy's appearance?

"Was he missing part of a finger?" she asked.

"Huh?"

"Part of his middle finger, above the top knuckle," she added.

"Can't say definitely no, but then I wasn't studying his anatomy."

"Never mind," she said. "Did he mention Sarah?" That accident remained unsolved, and the two car incidents might be connected.

"No, was I supposed to ask? You sure didn't give me much idea what to say if you needed all these answers."

"I didn't tell you to strike up a conversation with the man, but since you did, I need to note what was said."

Loose ends all over the place. Her edge gone, thoughts muddled. Head hurting so damn bad.

All Pittstop had to do was write on Seabrook's window, send some flunky to leave a note under his wiper blade. But he supposedly drove to Middleton, maybe came to Edisto. What was she missing?

She hadn't even seen the guy's picture. Mental note to self: *get pic from Seabrook.*

"Did he specifically mention Edisto?" She was frustrated at her physical and mental inability to be hundred percent cop. "Seems it would be quicker to just recant what he said, Quincy."

He gave her a sympathetic look.

"I can't read your mind," she shouted. "Tell me what he said."

"He said he thought you should've gotten the message, and since you didn't, he needed to deliver a new one in person, where you live.

Said you might understand it better that way."

"Wait," she said, pushing up in the chair. "He's coming . . . here? When?"

"Didn't say."

What was there for her to understand? Steer clear? Leave him alone? She was just figuring that out, damn it.

But if he appeared on her island, she'd haul him in for questioning, but what could they hold him for? Seabrook mishandled the earring and all but stalked the man. Quincy broke into his place. Pittstop would deny any admission made in jail, and the only witness to that was a guy doing time. At this rate Pittstop would have to fall to his knees and confess in front of a herd of people to do anything to him.

Seabrook would go nuts watching the man who killed his wife walk free.

Now Pittstop's sights were set on those who wouldn't give him peace.

She needed more info on this guy. "Where's he live? Specifically?" She could at least start there.

Leaning to the side, Quincy extracted an off-white card from his back pocket folded in half, making it four layers thick. He'd scribbled across the back, and unfolding it, across the front of it, too.

"Thought you kept everything on your smartphone," she asked, recalling the accident, the station interview. Almost every time she saw him he texted, recorded, and took notes.

"Had to be quiet, and it was dark at the time, so I grabbed the first paper within reach. Give me a break."

Callie reached out for the card, and Quincy held it to his shirt. "Sorry, can't let you have it."

"Oh, for Pete's sake."

Flipping the card over, he read, "4475 Cheetum Street. C-h-e-e-t-u-m. Not the best neighborhood."

She bet his gold Jeep stood out like a dime in a bowl of wooden nickels there, too. No wonder he got caught.

She beckoned to Sophie. "Can you please get my phone?" They needed SLED more than ever. They'd take serious issue with Seabrook's personal vendetta, Quincy's break-in, and Callie's mismanagement of evidence, but that was nothing compared to someone getting hurt . . . or killed.

As Sophie rummaged through the gym bag, the doorbell rang. Cell retrieved, she halted midstep and pivoted. "It's your mother!"

Sharp raps on the glass reminded them of Cantrell impatience. "Callie? Why are you making me wait out here?"

Callie rubbed a circle into her temple. "Let her in, Sophie. It's not like she'll leave. She has a key. The knock is so she can make an entrance."

Sophie unlocked and opened the door.

"Why, hello, dear." Block heels echoed on the hardwood floor. "We've come to talk," Beverly said before she rounded the corner. "It's time I spoke with my daught—what's *he* doing here? And oh my goodness, what happened to him?"

Miss Promise hugged Beverly's side with a squint-eyed scowl at the man, Tink peeking out of his cream and turquoise tote bag. "You! Hah, somebody else had their fill of you. Good."

"How do you always find me?" Beverly exclaimed. "Everywhere I go, you're there. Sir, I've had *my* fill of you."

Beverly's words smacked Callie, a reminder that Quincy followed her mother like a shadow, often appearing before she arrived. Suddenly Callie wasn't sure she believed a word out of his mouth about his presence on her stoop being because of Pittstop.

The word was bound to leak out from yesterday . . . about how Beverly Cantrell hadn't birthed Callie and Sarah had. That could be his ultimate motive for arriving, confirmation of that news, and he might've used Pittstop as a way to gain sympathy, enter Callie's house, and blindside her mother.

Would he seriously lie and go this far for an election smear story? Cut and beat himself to fake a mugging?

Callie dropped her forehead to her hand, unable to think straight. What was truth and what wasn't?

Sophie darted to the recliner. "You okay, honey?"

Callie lifted her head and moved to the edge of her seat, taking the phone, pointing it at Quincy. "Tell me—"

With a rush across the room, Beverly stopped smack dab in the way. "What's wrong with you?" She cradled Callie's cheeks. "Dear, you don't feel well at all, do you?" She touched a cheek here, then there. "No, you are definitely under the weather." Her purse looped over her left elbow, she dug into it for her phone. "I'm getting Lawrence to work you in this afternoon." She glanced over her shoulder at Miss Promise. "He's seen Callie since she was born."

Awesome. Probably the doctor Lawton paid to alter the birth certificate.

"Out of the way, Mother, please." Trying to see around Beverly, Callie noted Quincy had honed in on Miss Promise. The old woman's mouth had soured into crinkles while the reporter peppered her with queries only she could hear. Tink joined their chat with little growls.

The phone vibrated, and she glanced at the screen. Five missed calls and six texts from the mayor.

Frickin' great. "Sophie, would you call Mayor Talbot for me? If I could get all these people out of here—"

"Let me do that, mayor to mayor, dear," Beverly said, trying to peer over to read the texts.

Wouldn't that be a wonderful discussion? "No, Mother, just get Quincy's attention for me," Callie said between a wheeze and a cough.

"Gladly," she said and walked over to Quincy. "Little man, stop badgering this lady and pay attention to my daughter. She's ill. Treat her with courtesy, or I'm sure she'll *haul you in*."

Callie let her head rock back in embarrassment.

Quincy came around the sofa to the recliner and chortled. "I just love your mother."

"About Pittstop . . ."

Humor draining, he turned somber. "Not sure what more I can tell you," he muttered. "He's a scary dude, and I'm done with him. You have his address, his name—"

She snared his shirt, drawing him close. "Did you make all this Pittstop stuff up? Yet again, you show up when my mother does. Your typical MO. Who told you she was going to be here?"

He tried to pry her off. "Would I beat myself up? Are you even in your right mind?"

Callie wasn't sure. The room behind him tilted oddly. She clenched hands to fists to focus, shaking at the work it took out of her. "I'm sick of your deception. I almost believed you about going to Florence." Her chest heaved and spasmed as she fought to hold the cough.

"Callie? What's going on?" her mother called, worry in her voice.

"Not now," Callie replied and drew closer to Quincy, a moldy stench of sweat filling her nose from his dank shirt. "You play sleazy journalism games for your stories. I tell you to research a man, giving you some credit for research skills, and you come back here and lay a threat in my lap. I'm back to believing you sabotaged Sarah's car for a headline."

But believed Pittstop could've done so, too. She and Sarah lived close on the same road. Which could explain why he, they, someone slashed Callie's tires the next day, getting it right.

Hand encircling her wrist, Quincy snatched her loose from his shirt, but he retained a hold, remaining close. "I admit I have my ways to gather information, but they are none of your business. Yeah, I was excited about Pittstop. Aroused, even." He released her and propped himself on the chair's arm. "But I came here to warn you. I had no idea your mother would be here. You gave me a lead. I followed it. This" —he pointed at his nose—"is the result."

Then he whispered. "You're not thinking straight, my friend. I can see the fever in your cheeks. You better get Seabrook here, because you're in no shape to manage this."

Beverly appeared at his side. "You better not have put a bug on me, you little twit. I'm taking out a restraining order as soon as I can get back to Middleton." She shook her finger at him. "And don't think I won't be meeting with your editor."

Her mother continued with a highbrow tongue-lashing while Miss Promise cast a perpetual glower from her proper position against the end of the couch.

Having returned to her bar perch, Sophie's attention flitted from person to person. "Can I fix anyone something to drink?"

Miss Promise nodded, and Sophie leaped off the stool toward the kitchen.

Bone-weary, Callie slumped back in the chair, watching the old lady expect to be waited on.

The old first lady felt damage control in order after the whole guess-who-my-mother-is fiasco the day before. *Settle Callie down,* she probably told her mother. *Get your story straight with Sarah. We can't afford this story to leak before the election. We'll cover it after the inauguration. Don't wear that color. Pick another lipstick.* What had they poured into Jeb's head? Oh, good gracious, where *was* Jeb?

"Callie? I called Seabrook," Sophie said.

Where had she come from?

"Honey, you just passed out on us."

Opening lids she hadn't realized she'd closed, Callie touched her forehead, heat rising. Where was Quincy? He was gone, and Sarah stood in the room. Beverly kneeled beside the chair. She'd run her hose if she wasn't careful. No decent older woman ever went without hose.

"I was concentrating," Callie said, straightening. "Too many people in the room." She pushed herself to her feet, retrieved her empty tea glass, and stared at the kitchen to create an imaginary line to follow and not stumble. She never saw them approach her chair, and the lapse of consciousness scared her.

She played stories and players in her head as she refilled her glass, staying busy, focused . . . conscious.

"That miserable little man did this," she heard Beverly say. "I'll file charges."

"Oh, dear lord, Mother," Callie said between gulps of fluid she expected Seabrook would order, along with four aspirin. "If you want to complain, go to the station and put it in writing. I don't feel like hearing it."

"I don't think so," Beverly replied. "I'll save my complaints for Chief Warren."

Callie weakly scoffed at her mother choosing which police department to deposit her business. "Oh, just email it in, why don't you?"

"Email is vulgar," Miss Promise said from her roost.

The headache escalated, sending jabs into Callie's hair roots, each follicle screaming for relief. "I've heard enough social etiquette bullshit, Mother." *From the both of you.*

Straighten your pearls. Watch your posture. Keep your makeup fresh and don't cross your legs. Damn, Callie was glad she left those days for Boston. Maybe Beverly ought to file a police report on Miss Promise's stationery, in calligraphy. Black ink, of course.

Callie groaned as she returned to her chair, staring at Miss Promise en route . . . who stared back in some sort of defiance.

Chelsea Morning was barely a mile and a half from the government complex where Callie worked, and suddenly she heard Seabrook's siren. Tucking her legs under her in a semblance of leisure, Callie attempted to give the appearance that the room was little more than a social event. She didn't want him freaking out when he arrived.

"Sophie, what did you tell Seabrook?" she asked.

She gasped like a fish. "Just how sick you were and that you passed out."

"I did not."

The siren cut silent a couple houses down. Soon his feet skipping steps up the stairs announced his arrival. "How the hell did she get here from my place, and why's she not in bed?" Seabrook strode in long steps to the recliner and felt her head. "Jesus, honey, I've got to take you in."

"I took four aspirin. I'm glad you came. Quincy just left. He said—"

"Sophie, pack her a bag," he ordered, "because she's not coming back, at least not tonight, probably not for two or three."

Sophie bolted toward the bedroom.

"Mike, stop it," Callie said. She'd kill for everyone to leave. "The mayor needs me."

"Screw the mayor," he said.

She sort of agreed with him. The council meeting was a distant crisis to that of Pittstop and Quincy. But she'd promised the man, and he'd gotten her the job.

Returning, Sophie held out the bag. "I threw a few things in on top of whatever else was in there, Callie."

Seabrook swooped her up from the chair, angst embedded in the wrinkles around his mouth. "Damn it, why didn't you call me? I never should've left you alone."

"This is embarrassing. I'm not that bad off," she said. "Put me down."

"No." He swung around. "Out of my way."

"I'm coming with you," Beverly said.

"Can you fit the both of us in your car?" Sarah asked.

He paused and glared hard at them both. "No damn way."

"At least tell us where you're taking her," Sarah demanded.

"Roper Hospital," he said, readjusting Callie in his hold.

Door left open in Seabrook's wake, they all turned as heavy footsteps hit the stairs then the porch. "What can I do?" Raysor said, huffing, a cool moist wind coming up with him. "I heard Marie on the radio say something about an emergency here."

"I got this, Don," Seabrook replied.

"Wait!" shouted someone from the drive.

Everyone moved to the porch. Quincy clamored from halfway up the stairs, waving his phone. "Just got a text from Pittstop. He's coming," he yelled, fear etched in his face. "He's on his way to Edisto."

Chapter 21

CRADLED IN SEABROOK'S arms, her strength ebbing, Callie twisted her head toward the reporter and cursed.

Waving his cell phone, Quincy reached the top of the stairs. "The son-of-a-bitch wants to meet me *here*." He puffed a few times, scanning the three women spilling out of the front door, Miss Promise left behind, perched on the sofa. "What do I do?" he cried.

"Which son-of-a-bitch would you be referring to?" Raysor asked, not the least ruffled at Quincy's drama. "As for what you can do, I've got a few suggestions . . ."

"Pittstop." Quincy placed an edgy, tenor emphasis on the name. "Who else would I be talking about?"

Seabrook halted, as if struck. His grip tightened under Callie legs and back in reflex. "What did you say?"

"Wait—" and Callie's words were cut short by a cough. She fought to get a grip. When she finished, Seabrook stared at her with more than concern.

"Set me down," she whispered, patting his shoulder. He had no idea what Quincy had been up to, and Callie wasn't sure she wanted to be in his arms when he learned. Guilt rode a huge wave of regret as her feet hit the porch. She should've confided in Mike from the start. She'd owned the right to find her husband's killer, and Mike would feel the same about his.

Wilting fast, her mind scrambled to think this out.

Usually late September air blew warm, but a storm dropped the temperature. Low sixties. A weak shiver rolled through her, fast robbing her energy. For the first time, she worried about herself.

Like he sensed her thoughts, Seabrook readjusted his strong grip around her waist.

Quincy shoved his phone at Callie, but Seabrook snatched it instead. "Look for yourself."

Callie peered around, attempting to read the texts. "I'm sorry, Mike. I asked him to unearth some information on Pittstop, and instead he went to Florence and pissed the man off. Or so he says."

Meet me in a half hour on the first road past the big Edisto bridge.

Then, *Do not tell anyone. Do not bring anyone.*

Seabrook scrolled, finding nothing else from some number that wouldn't surprise Callie to be a burner. "And this is supposed to be Roman McGee . . . Pittstop?"

Pointing to his facial scrapes, Quincy gave a full-blown sigh. "Who do you think did this?"

Seabrook let her loose, jaw tight and working.

"Let's just go to Charleston," Callie said and rubbed once across his lower back. But now she worried their afternoon was not that easily determined.

"Come here," he said brusquely and led her further from the group, toward the porch's corner. Leaning down to her height, he said, "What the hell did you do behind my back?"

"Helped you," she said. "Admittedly, a knee-jerk decision at Mother's after the break-in. You were unavailable, so I couldn't discuss it . . . I wanted to use his skillset to aid your effort and get you to back off."

"Maybe get him off your mother's back?" he said, tone curt and fingers tight on her arm.

"That, too, but—"

"So this is your fault." He released her, and she rested against the railing as he leaned in closer. "You found me that shortsighted, did you? Damn it, Callie."

"You've been distracted, Mike."

He slung a wave toward Quincy. "And that was your answer?"

She chose not to speak. He was right. She was tired. Words weren't worth the energy.

He blew out a fast sigh and drew her to him. "I'm sorry. You're in no shape for this. Forget your motive. Let's say he's right and Pittstop is coming."

"I'd rather not. The man can't be trusted."

"Yet you involved him," he said softly.

For you, she thought, but didn't want to argue.

He glanced back at Raysor, which made her do the same. The deputy gave Seabrook a supportive nod. Though having no idea of what was going down, Raysor was willing to back Seabrook, a relationship Callie'd come to respect.

Seabrook refocused on her. "If we had any idea of capitalizing on this, SLED would be two hours arriving. The sheriff's office is an hour distant. It's up to us—"

"No." An alarm pinged inside her at his urge to engage. "It is *not* up to us. Quincy made this bed. Keep in mind he makes stuff up, Mike."

He studied her, mouth taut. "You made a bad choice when you were well. Who knows what you'll do this sick."

Stung, she hesitated then touched his back again, patting once softly to calm and focus him . . . to feel his warmth on her palm. "Nothing has happened here to act upon."

"Don't you blow me off!" An edge laced Quincy's words. "We'll see how that plays out in the papers if you don't help," he shouted, spittle flying. "And I need my phone back."

Seabrook gave Quincy a snap-to response over his shoulder. "Your journalism shit has crossed into *my* case, on my beach, after all I've done to keep it discreet." He scrolled the phone's screen again, as if more text might appear, and in his frustration shook the phone. "You led him here, you idiot."

Quincy pointed to Callie. "It's her fault."

Callie could argue, but the moron was half right. Seabrook's dour expression showed he agreed. "We don't know that he led anyone anywhere," she reminded Mike.

He slid the phone in his chest pocket. "Why would he text *you*, Quincy?"

"Hey, you can't do that." Quincy strode toward them, hand outstretched for his cell.

Seabrook's stare stopped his move. "Answer me, Kinard," he said, the curt use of the reporter's last name giving a scary side of the former chief.

Quincy withdrew and rubbed his unruly red hairline. "Because I gave him my card."

Raysor laughed once. "So if you don't show up, he goes to Middleton." He snorted. "Hey, problem solved."

"No," Quincy cried. "He asked who sent me and if I knew Dr. Seabrook."

Raysor sobered.

Seabrook's complexion darkened. "You confirmed my name . . . and Callie's name?"

"Had to!"

A gust blew through them, the palmetto fronds clacking three feet off the porch. Sarah, Beverly, and Sophie remained frozen in the doorway, unsure of the predicament.

Quincy stepped closer to Callie, causing Seabrook to turn his body as a buffer. "I'm doing you guys a favor. I shook him loose for you to catch."

"Hey," Sophie said, to be a part of the fray. "You're such horrible, negative energy." Her nose pointed toward the porch ceiling. "And I don't say that very often."

After a sarcastic glance at her, the reporter turned to Raysor, then back to Seabrook. "If I don't answer, he'll come after me."

"He has no beef with you," Callie said. "You act like ignoring his texts equates to nuclear detonation, and I'm not buying it." She coughed as much for relief as to draw attention to their plan to go to the hospital.

Quincy's thumb deeply massaged the other palm, his gaze darting. Fear of Pittstop, maybe? Some unspoken threat or blackmail meaning they had half the story? Or a quick search for an excuse to get them on his side, but for what end? A creepy, crawling aversion for the man slithered up Callie's back.

His performance transformed to one resembling remorse. "Pittstop said I caused him to flip. He could see that Dr. Seabrook wouldn't stop. He said he was coming to Edisto to bring the confrontation to the doc, to let him see how it feels to be stalked. And if Seabrook didn't take him seriously, he'd do something to make sure he did." Quincy scratched his ear in twitchy movements. "Um, he wanted me to remind you how easy it was to reach Callie in Middleton."

Callie tried to shove the man in the chest, stumbled, and Seabrook caught her. "You idiot! Why didn't you say this in the house earlier?"

"Because he hadn't acted on it with texts!" he yelled.

Seabrook elbowed Quincy aside and handed Callie to Raysor.

"Wait, no, Mike." Callie fought the exchange, but Raysor was no small man. "You are not a one-man army," she said. "Pittstop will leave when Quincy doesn't show."

Waving toward the surf, Seabrook turned on her. "I can't take the chance of him retaliating in our absence." He settled a pointed finger on Sarah. "Maybe he already made his initial mark on her brakes."

"That makes no sense whatsoever," Callie said. "If the man wanted to play mind games, he'd choose someone other than her."

"Like you?" he said.

"Maybe, but see how you aren't putting things together?"

She loved the man's devotion to Edisto, but police work didn't come natural to him. Missteps and miscalculations didn't matter with traffic and tourists overheated in the summer, but he was out of his realm when it came to murder. He never recognized the Russian's intent until he found Callie covered in the man's blood. He didn't believe her about the jinx until the culprit almost killed her friends. Both times she'd taken serious risk but mastered the situation, saving a life other than her own. Seabrook would connect the dots, eventually, but cops couldn't play such slow catch up without ultimately paying a price.

Even through the wheezes, the realization gobsmacked her. Seabrook attempted to make up for his shortcomings, but he was not getting this right, and she was in no shape to stop him.

Pushing off Raysor, Callie straightened her sweater. She'd try to go with Mike. She couldn't be his muscle, but she could try to be his common sense. That and she was a much better shot. "You are not going alone."

But Seabrook ignored her. "The text said meet in thirty minutes. And it was sent fifteen minutes ago. We'll barely make it."

Callie went pale. "No." She saw what this was . . . opportunity for Seabrook to confront his adversary, avenge his wife, and make up for the past.

Pittstop had brought the fight, and Seabrook was accepting the challenge.

She held windblown hair to the side, aching from sickness and the memory that she'd spent the night with a man she could seriously come to love. Who also thought she sabotaged him. "Listen to me, Mike. I've been where you are. It's stupid to go this alone."

But Seabrook went to Raysor. "Roper Hospital, Don. I'll catch up later."

Raysor reached to support her.

"No, I'm coming," she said. "So is Raysor. We'll show a sign of force and talk sense into him."

"You can hardly stand," Seabrook said, his hard-boiled attitude showing no sign of his bedside manner. The cop instead of the doctor for a change. And little sign of the boyfriend.

"At least take Raysor," she said, tugging his shirt. "Sophie can drive me to Charleston."

Raysor muttered, "She's right, Mike."

"So what's going on?" Quincy fretted. "A cop's going instead of me, right?"

Appalled at Quincy's cowardice, Callie held disgust at herself for involving the reporter in the first place, pained Seabrook held her at fault . . . because he was right.

Seabrook launched Quincy toward the steps. "I *am* going," he said. "But you're driving."

"Again, don't," Callie pleaded. "At least go get a vest," she said, reaching for anything to delay, maybe make Seabrook too late for it to matter.

Seabrook ignored her plea and escorted the reporter down to the drive, fat sprinkles leaving spots on the back of his uniform.

Raysor's beefy reach hugged Callie to his side before gently easing her onto a floral rattan settee. "You're not changing his mind, doll. I'll take care of him." Then he rushed in a clumsy hip-hop to the cars.

This was the wrong damn time for Mike to decide to be proactive . . . reactive . . . male.

"I have your bag packed," Sophie reminded, appearing at her side.

At the base of the stairs, fingerlike branches of her twenty-year-old sago palm swirled crazily without rhythm, a protest to the winds of an incoming storm from the beach, the opposite of the norm that blew in from across the mainland.

None of this would've happened if not for her being impatient. Now Mike was going crazy with revenge because of her giving Quincy this damn bone.

In Boston she dreamed of pulling a trigger, watching her husband's killer's soul seeping out and straight to hell. Her past urges scared her shitless now. How would Mike react if Pittstop indeed showed?

Wearing a petrified mask, Quincy got in the driver's side of the Jeep, Seabrook on the other. Raysor leaned in the door for a moment of discussion and waved them on. Once at his car, he glanced up at Callie and the three other ladies, and for some reason, felt the need to wave.

Quincy turned left on Jungle Road toward 174. Raysor did the same after allowing them some distance. His easy-to-ID cruiser couldn't be affiliated with the Jeep.

Feeling impotent, Callie cupped her mouth, heart bruised from mix of adrenaline and rejection. She'd wanted to help Seabrook through his past, like he'd helped her through hers. But this was not the way.

Fate was screwing with them all.

"Come on, honey," Sophie said, touching her elbow. "I don't like the color in your cheeks."

Callie nodded, pushed hard against the chair to rise, and then descended the stairs with her friend. Beverly stood in place, hesitating. In that moment, Beverly was her go-to mother and Jeb's forever grandmother. "Where's Jeb? Can you—"

"Go on, dear," Beverly said, waving as if shooing children into the yard. "Call us, please."

Callie wanly smiled back.

With care, Sophie tucked her friend safely in the blue Mercedes, cranked the engine, and pulled onto Jungle Road. A light rain came down, the dampness smelling of dead grass and brine.

A gray pallor settled over the small coastal town. A socked-in type cool front would drive everyone inside, put less traffic on the road. Almost 7:00 p.m. when the council meeting started. The mayor would be disappointed . . . Brice getting his way.

Sophie stopped at the end of the road and checked both ways.

"Hey," then Callie broke into another deep cough that stole her words.

Sophie mashed the gas and took off after a slight skid under her too-quick foot.

"Don't . . . sound's worse than it is." Callie tried to smile.

"I'm not taking chances, girlfriend," Sophie said, her grip white-knuckled.

After crossing the marsh causeway, they entered the tunnel of trees and island jungle that walled both sides of the highway. "Slow down," Callie said. Oaks and pines were unforgiving to errant drivers. Then turning to the window, Callie closed her lids. "We need to talk, Soph."

Her hands at ten and two on the wheel, Sophie kept glancing at her mirrors. "You'll cover for me if I get pulled over, right?"

"Please, don't make me use more words more than I have to," Callie whispered, the cough climbing up her throat with imaginary claws, making barb-like pricks in her chest. But she swallowed and held it together. "I think they're meeting on Jehossee Road. The text said the first road on the right after the bridge, which means the McKinley Bridge."

"The boat ramp is the first road. So? We're not stopping."

Too winded to argue, Callie sought a strategy. The day was aging. Why did all the shit in her life happen at dusk? "There's an old farm road just past that. We're going there."

"Un-unh," Sophie said and shook her frosted pixie. Her earrings slung, silver beads tinkling. "We're hightailing it to Charleston."

Callie leaned the seat back and prayed harder that Quincy's plan was bogus.

They passed The Old Post Office Restaurant, the parking lot almost empty with the weather. One third of the way to the bridge.

Quincy and Seabrook wouldn't be in place yet.

"Mike thinks he knows what he's doing," Callie said, hoping Sophie understood. "When you're toe-to-toe with the person who killed your spouse, you do not grasp reality."

"Aww." Sophie started to reach out, then re-gripped the wheel. "Honey, I'm so sorry for what you've been through."

She wasn't getting it.

The exhaustion accompanying what Callie deemed pneumonia made each sentence more taxing than the last, but the angst for Seabrook's safety carried her through it.

Raysor would drive on, keep in touch with Seabrook, then when opportune, turn around and park at the road's entrance, not only as safety backup but also containment. These island roads were one way—no side streets or alternate exits. All Seabrook had to do was travel deep enough until he identified Pittstop, call Raysor to meet them, and they'd apprehend.

But she worried Seabrook wouldn't settle for a move that simple. He would contact Raysor . . . but at a time of his choosing. Once he'd had a chance to deal with his wife's killer.

She tried to logically label all this a pretense, but she couldn't. "We're going to help them," Callie said. "Let's check the boat ramp then each road coming back toward the beach."

"You can't help them, and I don't know how," Sophie said. "We're only two tiny women. They're strapping men. They were made to deal with this."

"I'm the damn police chief, for crying out loud, Sophie!" A shiver rolled through her, and Callie folded into herself. The headache was back, along with fluctuations of heat and cold. Heart hammering, she recognized the limited time before she was incapacitated . . . but damn it, once they crossed the bridge they left Seabrook with a dumb-ass reporter and a feeble plan to meet a man who'd gotten away with murder.

Again assuming Quincy wasn't playing to a headline. But could she risk those odds?

She could see him setting the stage for the cops, building tension for the story. Then when it fell flat, he'd write a piece about Seabrook and his heart-wrenching eight-year vigil for his wife and the sad disappointment at the culprit not showing. She'd be surprised if Quincy didn't have a cam in his Jeep.

She hoped this was a joke that made a fool out of them all.

They crossed Russell Creek.

Raysor would wait at the head of whichever road they felt was the right one. There was no way to travel down any of them in an SO patrol car and not be seen, but he didn't need to be.

Sophie's back no longer touched the seat, elbows bent, her chest forward barely a foot from the wheel.

But Callie was more intense about two officers on a crazed, uncalculated mission. Her instinct told her to stay on the island. The closest other help was Thomas, barely a year older than Francis was. No. No way would she risk another young officer.

"Callie?"

She opened eyes she hadn't realized she shut. "What?"

"Am I supposed to keep you awake or something?"

That was for concussions, but Callie didn't want to nap. "Yes, keep me awake," she said and dug into her gym bag for her phone.

"Okay, I will. By the way, I threw your nightgown on top of the stuff you had in there from Seabrook's, and—"

"Hush a moment, please, Sophie." Shaky, it took Callie twice to unlock the phone and dial. "Don, update me."

"Go to the hospital, doll." But he continued muttering, "Son-of-a-bitch. I'll kill that little bastard."

The SO cruiser made a thump through the phone, like it hit a pothole. "Where are you?" she asked. "I mean, exactly. I'm not crossing this damn bridge without an update."

"I lost them," he said. "Damn it, I lost them."

Chapter 22

"RAYSOR? STILL THERE?" Callie needed their bearings. Raysor was Seabrook's backup and rolling blind. No damn way she was crossing the big bridge to the mainland and leaving her officers in this predicament. Regardless of how sick she was.

Raysor cursed between cell reception static. Callie hugged the phone to her left ear, leaning her head against the cool passenger door glass. The low, gray cloud ceiling promising a long visit, a drizzle set in as did the darkness.

"Where are you?" she asked. "Come back to me. The first road to the right after the bridge, right? That's what the texts said. Confirm, please."

Sophie barreled the two women down Highway 174. Callie'd have to stop her, but she needed Raysor to answer first. "Don! Which road did y'all agree it was supposed to be? The boat ramp, the farm road, or Jehossee?"

"Jehossee," Raysor finally said, his gravelly voice deep, concerned. "I kept their taillights in sight, hanging back, but a damn deer ran across the road when the rain started. I swerved, almost went in a ditch near that big horse farm, but by the time I regained control, they were gone. I assume they reached Jehossee before I could catch up."

Callie leaned over to Sophie. "Slow down. No, pull over."

"No," Sophie answered. "Mike said . . ."

"Pull the damn car over, Soph!"

The Mercedes eased into a flat dirt drive, Sophie's pout evident at the order.

It didn't make sense for a murderer to incorporate a reporter he'd never met into a scheme to confront his adversary. Seabrook had jumped too easily to meet Pittstop, especially in the middle of nowhere. This plan had so many missing pieces and no assurances.

"We were keeping in touch," Raysor said. "Then suddenly he's not answering his cell or his radio." He grumbled. "I'm at the end of the road. He's not here. You were right to not want to do this, Callie."

Rain now drummed the convertible's canvas.

Callie didn't care to be right.

"I'm parked at the beginning of Jehossee," she said. "We'll take the farm road a quarter mile down. You come back up to the highway and go check the boat ramp road. Stay on the phone."

Mouth puckered, Sophie glowered. "We are not supposed—"

"Should I get out and walk?" Callie pointed a stiff finger toward the highway. "Help me or I'll call Beverly. Then afterwards you can listen to her blister you over dumping her daughter. And I'll have her do it at your house, tossing all sort of bad energy under your roof."

"Thought she wasn't your mother . . ."

"Drive!" Callie shouted, instinctively reaching up to the side of her head as the word shot a ripple of a headache. "Sophie, please, just help me instead of arguing."

But Sophie stayed put. "You're always telling me to stand up for myself. Well, this is me . . . standing up for what is right. This is not our issue, and you need to let the men—"

Callie smacked the dash. "Finding them most certainly *is* the issue! So help me if we don't find Mike I'll get out and run down Pittstop myself in the damn rain. You hear what I'm saying? Do you? We don't have time to chat over the pros and cons here."

Her explosion about took her down, the car's interior trying to spin. But Seabrook was the first man she'd loved since John. Yes, she dared think the word. She hadn't until this berserk, impossible moment, but reality told her she could not lose another loved one to some crazed scum she didn't catch in time.

They crossed another creek, two herons stiff-legged and frozen not far off the pavement as headlights hit them. In passing Jehossee, Callie stretched her neck, scanning down the road, not spotting Raysor coming back yet. No sign of Quincy's Jeep. Seconds later, they reached the farm road.

"Turn here," Callie said.

Sophie did, maintaining silence, her usual calm, smooth complexion now wrinkled in a knot.

They cruised down the silt road, and Sophie turned on headlights. Callie sent up a thank-you that it hadn't rained long enough to slick up the tracks or fill the ditches. It wouldn't take more than another half-hour to do it, though. By then she prayed all this to be done and over, with the lot of them feeling stupid at the silliness.

An urgency zapped through Callie like a current. She willed herself straighter in the seat.

"There were no recent tracks on this road but mine," Raysor said.

"Don't waste your time then," Callie said, keeping the conversation going. She was thinking, analyzing. Why would Pittstop use Quincy as his mouthpiece unless he wanted a story about himself? Why else trust a scuzzy journalist?

Unless it was more of a collaboration.

"I hate driving on this," Sophie moaned, creeping along, cautiously centering the Mercedes on the wet dirt.

"Sorry," Callie said, as much for putting her innocent little neighbor in the midst of this mess as for the road conditions.

Somewhat maintained for a silt road, the one-and-a-half-car wide path took one sharp turn as they scouted left and right. Low, boggy, briny geography on the right with no hiding places, no structures, some growth. There was no scouring because the Jeep was either there or it wasn't. Thin and old from high tides, hurricanes, farm equipment, and years, the path turned into little more than ruts past an old ruined barn, rusted silo with a broken auger, and two slab foundations where a house and storage building used to be. It petered out at an algae-covered lagoon once used for irrigation when agriculture ruled the island.

Callie felt her nerves fraying, fretful like a mother losing sight of her child on a crowded beach.

"Don," Callie said into her phone, "does Colleton County have the capability to ping a phone?"

Static dropped in and out of Raysor's broken words to include a few four-letter ones she'd never heard him say before.

"Don?" she repeated.

Same, only with Raysor's voice louder. She heard *highway* and *coming*, then in a moment of clarity, *Where the hell are you*?

The incoming front was wreaking havoc with reception.

So she tried Colleton County Sheriff's Office. It rang once then the signal was interrupted. She needed a radio. Edisto Island was rural and signal often turned spotty, but having a cool front full of wet, saggy clouds didn't help either.

"Go to the highway, Soph. As fast as you can."

"If you'd listened to me, we'd still be on the highway."

Callie let the comment go.

Sophie's fast wasn't Callie's definition, but the yoga lady got them back to the highway.

Yes, a signal.

Raysor appeared to their right and pulled in beside them.

Callie gathered her gym bag and turned to her driver. "Sophie, I'm grateful for your help, but I'm going with Raysor."

Sophie's shoulders drooped, a contrast from the intensity of the last thirty minutes. Then pupils wide with fear, she tugged Callie by the sleeve. "Please, you'll catch your death of pneumonia out there, honey."

Already there, except for the death part.

Dredging up enough stamina to make her point, Callie took her friend's hand and squeezed it. "I'm okay. Raysor will get me to Charleston once I see that Seabrook's all right. Understand?" Sophie would no doubt tell the others pronto.

A consistent drizzle peppered Callie in her slipping trot to the SO patrol car. She fell into the passenger seat, her chest tight like a huge ice cube had taken residence. So short a distance had left her breathing fast and shallow.

"Can Colleton County ping a phone?" she asked between hacks.

"Sure can, doll," he said, and he reached for his radio.

She sat back, hooking her seatbelt.

Without asking, Raysor increased the heat in the car and focused a vent on her while he passed the request to his dispatch. A troubled worry in his expression, he seemed to analyze Callie, taking stock. Callie held her fingers over the vent, trying to get warm.

Dispatch returned. "Somewhere near Pine Landing Road," the lady said. "Need assistance, Don? That's Charleston County. An eighteen-wheeler wreck on 17 has their interest at the moment."

Jurisdictions mattered little in cases of emergency, but neither Raysor nor Callie were sure their predicament qualified. Pulling cars off an accident wasn't warranted for a hunch and a curious little reporter. Raysor declined the help and clicked off.

"Doll," he started.

"Can you identify Pittstop, Don, because I can't. Let's go. At least we can ID the Jeep and take it from there. Whatever's happening, we're interrupting the crap out of it."

His middle-aged, chunky-cheeked face stared at her, like determining whether she was trying to sell him a car with its odometer rolled back a hundred thousand miles.

"Seabrook's going to give me hell when he sees you," he finally said and pulled back on the road.

"Or thank you," she said, unzipping her gym bag and finding her Glock.

"Oh no, you don't," Raysor warned. "You're not leaving this car."

She slipped the weapon in the door pocket. "Even if I never get out of the car, this piece sits ready."

It was between six and seven miles to Pine Landing, and Raysor took the road like he owned it.

An old rotted limb dropped in the road before them. Raysor lifted his foot off the gas and plowed over it, a lifetime in the Lowcountry teaching him that a hard brake could slide them into soft ground and mire them for hours. The splintered wood disappeared mostly into a ditch on the driver's side, sending Callie's memory back to Sarah, the accident, and almost breathing water.

Avoiding the instinct to massage her clogged chest, Callie fought a worry of another kind. She cleared her throat, hiding any indication of how bad she felt to keep Raysor from changing his mind. He pressed the gas back again, and they sped down 174 toward Pine Landing . . . where she'd only yesterday met Seabrook. Where he'd talked her down from the frustration of learning she had two mothers.

Where he'd hugged her and made her feel better.

She braced herself against the dash when Raysor took a right turn at the Mount Olive Baptist Church without losing speed. A stone's throw from the gray cement structure, they raced past Calvary AME Church, a blue house, a shack, corn fields, then a sign announcing Future Charleston County State Park.

Though on asphalt, the area turned remote fast. Random corn fields baited deer for the season, but then scenery quickly became pines, oaks, myrtles, and scrub spruce dense and sardined. Moss, tons of it, heavy with rain like it fought to reach the jungle floor to lay down and nap on the leafy blanket. They reached where Laurel Hill Road veered left off Pine Landing, and Raysor followed the turn.

Callie craned behind her. "Wait, if they said Pine Landing, turn around and—"

Raysor dug in for a hard three-point turn. He got it. Faster than was safe but slower than Callie wished, he sped the patrol car from whence they came, tires hugging the blackness to Laurel Hill and its muddy, rutted road.

Nothing. No one.

Like pumping in cement, Callie's heart clobbered her ribs, constricted by lungs that wouldn't give. Tiny sparks tinged the edges of her vision, but she forced them back, pushing to see.

"Wait, stop," Callie whispered. Raysor shut off his lights, already slowing.

Though on a slight curve, she'd caught a glimpse of the copper-colored Jeep a hundred yards or more ahead, and Raysor had, too.

No other car.

No sign of the men.

No sign of exhaust, lights, or life in the Jeep.

The rain suddenly dropped out of the sky like a waterfall, and neither she nor Raysor was sure what to do.

What had happened with Seabrook? Callie recognized a trap when she saw one.

Chapter 23

THE DELUGE ON the hood, the wipers, their own exhales fogging the car seemed deafening at a time Callie wished it deadly quiet. No means to measure danger.

Raysor choosing to turn his headlights back on, they bounced off the heavy rain. He increased the wiper speed and eased the cruiser forward, leaning up to see better, his beefy hands throttling the steering wheel like a toy. In the half-second intervals she could see between wipes, Callie scoured the woods on either side of the Jeep ahead, her palm resting on the butt of her firearm in the door pocket. No sign of either Quincy or Seabrook, much less anyone else. Darkened by both weather and early night, visuals sucked.

"Whoa!" Callie flat-slapped the dash as the car slid a couple feet. The downpour had quickly turned a navigable road into one less sure, tires slipping.

"I can drive," his retort only adding to the stress filling the vehicle.

Callie reached for the radio, then remembered her limited voice. "Call it in," she said low, as if someone outside could hear.

"We don't know yet—"

Undoing her belt in a slow move, she repeated, "Call it in, I said." She hated to resort to her youngest officer, but she saw no choice. "Get Thomas out here. He's closest. Ambulance, too." For her if no one else. Hopefully no one else.

He didn't pause a second at the instruction.

Car still creeping, Raysor spoke low into the radio to Marie then hung up, taking him and Callie to within twenty yards of the Jeep's bumper. Unable to see through the back window into the front seat, they couldn't make out occupants, if there were any.

Suddenly Callie could hear her own heartbeat.

"Enough of this shit." Raysor unbelted himself and opened the door.

Retrieving her Glock, Callie reached for her own handle.

"No," he said. "Don't even think about it."

Suddenly the rain stopped, like a wet woolen blanket dropped on them and killed the roar. Though residual rain streamed off the oak leaves, nature turned quiet.

Raysor pulled his door back closed. "Listen, I don't need a liability out there, Callie. You're sick. A strong wind would blow you to the end of this road and dump you in the Edisto River. Plus Seabrook would whip my ass. Stay here. Hold your weapon if you want but keep your butt in this car . . . just in case."

Callie sighed and nodded.

Cap on, Raysor opened the door again and quickly shoved it closed, the rain dripping from the trees, leaving wet spots across his shoulders before he reached the front fender. The cruiser's headlights bounced off the chrome bumper ahead.

Quincy exited the Jeep, waving as if stopping traffic. "Hey, you can't be here! You'll screw things up."

Callie slid down in her seat and lowered her window. Quincy might question how Raysor found him, but the deputy was part of the original plan. No point in introducing herself into the mix until she had to, if she had to.

A chill whooshed in along with a whiff of rotting leaves on the autumn forest floor, the air temporarily cleansed of salt.

"What's going on, Quincy?" Raysor demanded, halting a few feet in front of the cruiser, so the light shined in the reporter's face. "We didn't agree to meet here."

The reporter waved frantically. "Shut those damn lights off. No, get out of here! He sees you and we're screwed." He turned to reenter the Jeep.

"Where's Officer Seabrook?" Raysor shouted. "I'm calling an end to this, Kinard."

Half in, Quincy snapped back around. "Pittstop redirected us *here*. Your man Seabrook said to follow through." He shifted too much, unable to look at Raysor.

Callie's nerves tingled. She wanted to call Raysor back, at least order him to assume his weapon. She placed a hand on the door, the other around her weapon.

Why didn't Seabrook exit the car?

She nodded as Raysor approached Quincy, hand on his Glock. "There," she whispered. "Just get Mike and let's go."

Raysor assumed a stance. "I said where's Seabrook?"

Quincy snatched a small weapon from the Jeep and shot. Head

snapping back, Raysor backpedaled two steps out of the car's lights and dropped.

Her heart kicked as an instinctive gasp stopped halfway down Callie's throat, in lungs that couldn't manage it. Caught between gasping and choking, she held her neck, fighting against a cough that would reveal her presence. Completely worthless to Raysor. A hazard to herself.

She'd messed up. Mike had messed up. And Raysor paid the price.

Shutting her eyes, she fought harder to contain the noise as much as the fear seizing her. An image of Francis floated across her vision in the murkiness. She recalled fighting to not breathe the water because if she did, then Francis already had. As long as she didn't die, he couldn't.

She peered down, only seeing dark, uncertain of her own consciousness. Her body involuntarily forcing her to inhale, a wet, rough cough escaped, and pain racked her torso.

When she regained a weak sense of control, she lifted her gaze to the windshield. Bathed in the cruiser's lights, a Ruger LCP aimed at her across the hood, Quincy behind the sights. "Come on out, Chief. Hands up and empty."

Then Seabrook's voice carried from the Jeep's passenger side, a weak eeriness to it. "Don't get out, Callie. Drive off!"

"Mike!" she called, grateful to hear him, but her feeble voice died in the air.

And for some reason, he couldn't move . . . or he would.

But she couldn't climb over the patrol car's computer to reach the driver's seat. Quincy had her. As much as she wanted to come out with her Glock, she knew better. She could barely hold it, so she laid it in the seat. Better he not know of her weapon than take it from her. She exited the car, her weight on the open window for support. A jelly feeling quivered into her legs, and she gripped the door tighter.

He motioned her from the car, and she struggled for balance before she let loose and did as instructed.

What about Mike?

He sounded hurt, and he couldn't get to her or he would've done so. *God, let him be trussed up, not injured.*

She studied Quincy, telling herself to remain calm, to study him now as a more proactive criminal than the simple nuisance he'd flaunted himself for the last few days.

Though her sense about him wasn't too far off, she deserved no pat on the back. Not for any of this. "Where's Officer Seabrook?" she demanded.

"Not your problem," Quincy said.

Now she was scared, in no shape to be left on her own.

Though not tall, Quincy stood taller than she, soft with fifty pounds in his favor. Her training far superior, at the moment she possessed no more strength than a three-year-old, and Quincy had witnessed those limitations. She studied him, wondering how well he could use his weapon. She dug for moxie. "I'd expect you to be carrying a little piece of crap belly gun, Quincy."

His menacing half grin didn't fit the unsophisticated role he'd displayed earlier. However, it slid into place as if comfortable in the sleaze. "Belly gun or not, it took down big boy over there." He waved it. "Come on out, further." He motioned toward Raysor. "See?"

The deputy lay on his back, legs bent as if they crumpled under his girth. She expected worse, almost grateful at the display. Laying on mud-covered leaves, his position and the low light made it difficult for her to see from twenty feet distant how much blood he'd lost . . . or if his chest moved. His head intact best she could see, he seemed almost asleep. By instinct she scanned for his weapon and noted it three feet from his gun hand. Ten feet from them. She moved toward him . . . just to try.

"Unh, unh, unh," Quincy said, and she stopped. He walked over to Raysor, lifted the deputy's weapon, and tucked it in his back waist band. Then he motioned Callie to the passenger side of the Jeep.

Pulse racing at the ability to see Seabrook, she sped over, slipping once in the rush, halfway expecting Quincy to stop her. He didn't.

"Mike?" The relief dropped her to her knees in the muck. "Are you hurt? What did he . . ." But then she saw blood. Another gasp, only a small one, but it sent her into another fit. She lowered her forehead onto Seabrook's leg, fighting again for air, and he rested his hand between her shoulder blades, rubbing.

"Shhh," he said. "You shouldn't have come, Callie."

She looked up and tried to smile, but in the dome light of the vehicle's interior, the shock of his paleness interrupted the effort. Blood blossomed across his shirt from his left side, trailing into the floorboard from under the seat. No smell of a recently fired weapon. Surely a knife wound. He'd seen Quincy as a victim in all this, let his guard drop, and been stabbed for the mistake.

"Raysor's down," she said, hunting for more damage. Seabrook's limp posture worried her. "Oh, Mike, how are you?"

"Not good," he replied, his thumb still rubbing. "Never saw him move. Happened when I questioned our unexpected detour. So stupid."

"Don't," she said. "We'll figure this—"

Grabbing Callie by the back of her collar, Quincy dragged her off, threw her to the mud, and aimed.

Seabrook roared, "No, Kinard!" and jerked himself upright and out of the car.

Quincy wheeled around, making Seabrook his target.

"No!" Callie screamed.

The officer slumped to the wet road with a grunt.

Quincy chuckled, the obnoxious chortle she'd come to abhor. "Damn, this is too frickin' easy. Bam," he said, and pretend fired his Ruger at Seabrook, then he whirled around. "Bam," he said at Callie. "It's like killing puppies."

Seabrook struggled to raise himself, holding onto the door. Semi-stable, he helped Callie to her feet. She took her time.

Come on, Thomas.

They never predicted Quincy. They focused on Pittstop. Someone named Pittstop existed, because she learned of him through Seabrook first. How would Quincy and Pittstop share the same world? Unless they didn't and the newspaperman did what he did best . . . making up stories.

She leaned against Seabrook, digging one foot into the mud, locking her knee. He maintained a grip on the door. Quincy held the Ruger on them, his aim unsteady from the adrenaline coursing through him. No matter, because she and Seabrook could barely stand, much less tackle the man. Only a weapon would balance the scales, and though she fathomed the answer before she checked, Seabrook's holster hung empty.

"So . . ." she started to say, but the word came out thin, desperate. Seabrook tried to tighten a hold around her shoulder. "What is all this, Quincy?" she said.

"A fucked up mess is what it is," he answered. "Why the hell did you come? You ought to see yourself. Damn, you're half dead."

She reshifted her sliding foot.

"Seems I treated his girlfriend in my ER years back," Seabrook said. "That's the deal."

But so long ago? "It went badly, I assume."

"You think?" Quincy yelled. "What would you call a coma? What would you call losing the person you loved more than life itself?"

Hell. She called it hell. Only she'd realized since coming to Edisto that hell had an exit she never thought possible. Sometimes it took a while, the journey not that pleasant, never straight.

Since she appeared on Edisto, in his calm, controlled manner, Mike Seabrook showed her the way back to sanity. Feeling the sticky on her sleeve, she peered over. Blood oozed through Seabrook's shirt.

"We were having . . . a chat when you arrived with Raysor," Seabrook said. With a grimace he peered over at Callie. "Is he—"

"Don't know," she said. "He hasn't moved. Can you tell how you are?"

"Jesus, people." Quincy rolled his eyes. "We need a solution here, not a reunion."

Seabrook shifted. "I take it the goal is to kill me for what you think I did."

Quincy saluted with the Ruger. "Bingo." His expression darkened. "You don't even remember the name Connie Winston, do you?"

Seabrook didn't answer.

Callie saw little rhyme to Quincy's reason. A herd of people saw him leave with Seabrook. Even if Quincy killed Raysor, Seabrook, and her, witnesses remained behind. He'd be the only one who came back. "Where's the getaway strategy?" she asked. "You're brighter than this."

Keep him talking, bragging, explaining. Thomas couldn't be more than five minutes from them.

Quincy delivered a flat-line smirk. Good. She'd snagged his attention, maybe hit a nerve. She needed him off his mark, distracted from whatever purpose haunted him. Time. This was all about time.

"You said you were meeting Pittstop." She made an animated effort to scan the area. "Yet we have no Pittstop. He wasn't even a part of the plan, was he?"

"Bad plan, huh?" Quincy said, rocking his head.

Duh? she thought, not caring to antagonize the gun-wielding fool more than she had.

He curled a finger.

Callie glanced up at Seabrook, who glowered daggers at the man.

Quincy gave a sarcastic laugh. "Um, that means come here, Miss Detective. You can't tell me no."

Making no move to leave the semi-safety of the car and venture into the open, Callie remained in place, Seabrook the same, apparently reading her body language.

The raised gun pointed at Seabrook's torso changed her mind.

Helping each other, they half-staggered to the back of the vehicle, Callie hoping this meant they'd have access to Raysor. And they kept heading toward him until Quincy shouted, "Stop. Not him. Here's what I want you to see."

He swung open the back of the Wrangler. A tarp draped across a bulk.

Stiffening, Callie tried not to forecast who might be under the material, but names raced through her mind, people from her house. People who couldn't possibly be crammed in the back of the Jeep.

Who hadn't she seen today? Thomas, Marie . . . Jeb. "No," she said before she could stop herself. "No." Nothing in her life could ruin her more than losing Jeb. She pulled loose from Seabrook and hurried to the vehicle, frantic to yank off the tarp, to confirm that whatever squeezed into the small space be anybody but her son.

Quincy backed up and let her.

Grunting with the battle, clawing, her strength so weak, she found an edge and exposed an arm. She released a moan. Hairy, older, not that of an eighteen-year-old boy. Tears streaming, her she prayed a thank-you the person was not her son. Dropping her head and leaning on the bumper, she needed a moment. She hadn't want to see who it was . . . just who it was not.

Almost sympathetically, Quincy aided her from the vehicle and back to Seabrook. "Y'all are really pitiful, you know it?" He yanked the black cover aside. The man underneath seemed in his late thirties, early forties. His lids fluttered in an attempt to awaken from whatever stupor Quincy put him in. A stranger to Callie, but she almost caved at the energy this game was extracting from her.

Seabrook whispered beside her. "Pittstop."

"Give the officer a prize," Quincy said, finger pointing to the sky. "Callie? Meet Pittstop. Pittstop? Meet Chief Callie Morgan."

"Huh?" grumbled the groggy man.

Thunder rumbled off in the distance. A light drizzle began. Pittstop tried to sort his location, the people, appearing to float inside his head without understanding.

Now Callie couldn't make heads or tails out of the scenario, and it must've shown.

"It was me, you dumb fucks," Quincy said. "I danced under your noses the whole time, yet you credited me with the IQ of a rock." He laughed once, then a string of laughter.

"You caught the man who killed my wife?" Seabrook asked, then shouted. "Why? To rub it in my face? To show how you could do something I'd been unable to do?"

Shaking his head, Quincy stopped laughing. "No, it was always me, you stupid cop, or shall I say doctor? Which do you actually prefer?"

Lilting to his left, an arm across his side, Seabrook's eyes were pinched in pain and anger . . . waiting. Waiting for a madman to own up to the purpose of his existence.

"Let's say doctor, then," Quincy said. He gave a slight bow. "Let me introduce myself, Doctor Seabrook. I'm the man who killed your wife."

Chapter 24

CALLIE FROZE AT Quincy's revelation, and Seabrook stared at the man who killed his wife. A hard stare. With a quiver in his jaw, he seemed to wrestle with their predicament in a cold, deep way. The individual who'd preened and strutted before them, even spent time in interrogation at the station, gloated. There was little Callie saw they could do other than wait to die . . . or die trying not to.

Tree frogs came out. The Pine Landing forest hung limp, wet . . . dead. No people close enough to hear a thing going down in their woods.

Mike breathed deeper than she thought him capable with a knife wound through his ribs, a hundred thoughts probably ricocheting through his head at how to take Quincy down.

But Quincy didn't appear to register any of these urges, though he surely connected. This entire scenario fed his hubris big time. A climax from an eight-year-old grudge.

"Glad you sent me to Florence to get this guy, Chief," he said. "The perfect segue." While he seemed to focus on the semi-conscious Pittstop, his wide-shouldered posture flaunted pride. The man fully understood what his announcement of being Mrs. Seabrook's killer did to his hostages. He quivered . . . Callie recognizing a perverted thrill when she saw one.

Nauseous at her connection to this business and the ultimate conclusion here at a muddy, middle-of-nowhere setting, Callie fought sinking to the ground. After Quincy completed his task, their bodies would disappear in the dark, black water Edisto River, with sharks and alligators making short work of the remains. "I sent you nowhere, you dimwit," she said.

Rocking his head in sarcasm, Quincy spoke like a teenager. "You *asked* me to help. Same thing. You were right, you know." His brows arched twice, in mockery. "A reporter seems a whole lot less dangerous than a cop. He let me right in the door, eager to have his poor story told about his upbringing, his time in jail, his misunderstood personality in a world of naïve, spoiled snobs. The stupid fuck didn't even realize Seabrook had been following him."

Callie almost cried at the last remark.

The man was a natural talker. The media dramatist in him yearned to be seen, heard, and appreciated for his dissection of current events. What journalist could resist a captive audience?

"You beat yourself up?" she asked.

"Wasn't as hard as I thought." He touched his Band-Aids and bruises.

Seabrook leaned heavier, fading fast. She prayed Thomas tore up asphalt getting there. The officer who'd fished her out of Scott Creek would have to save both her and Seabrook this time. Hopefully Raysor. But she'd rather be killed than see Thomas sacrificed for his effort. He wasn't used to this. Too many cops were dying in paradise.

Her shoulders wet from the forest weeping from the recent rain, her damp hair began to cling to her neck.

Quincy prodded Pittstop with the Ruger. "Losers can be led like kids to candy." Throwing a saucy grin, Quincy bobbed his head again. Callie wanted to rip his bobbing head right off.

A shiver extending from her chest into her arms, culminating in fingers that couldn't grip the back of Seabrook's belt very well, she combatted the weakness. "You met Pittstop in jail, while chasing other stories," she said. "While visiting your buddies."

Quincy shrugged one shoulder. "He heard I paid an inmate for information and sent me word he was open to suggestions. So I made one."

Seabrook wadded the back of her shirt in his grip, reminding her to keep it together.

"We have to regroup," Quincy said, addressing Seabrook. "We told everyone we were supposed to *meet* Pittstop out here. Nobody would deny you had the motive to kill him. And you'll kill him just as he shoots you. The honorable doctor avenging his wife after all these years, making the final stand . . . the ultimate sacrifice. Putting his mind to rest."

Then it all clicked. "You fucking did this for a front page article?" Callie asked, biting the words.

"Yes," he shouted, his free hand fisted and pumped. "Can't you see it? The poor bereaved husband meeting his wife's murderer in a standoff. They kill each other right before me." He grinned so damn wide. "The Edisto Beach Chief of Police put me on the trail!"

Muttering, "You sick son of a bitch," Callie covered her mouth and fought the bolus in her throat. Seabrook felt her sway and tried his best to hold her.

"Ooh," Quincy said, head nodding in fast jerks. "Callie, think about it. I paint the doctor a phenomenal hero, having him save me in the exchange. You do see it, right?"

She'd screwed up with Francis's sacrifice. Also with Raysor, Seabrook . . . she hung her head, sucking in air like it was syrup, but in her oxygen-deprived state she couldn't think. She needed options, but instead fractured ideas came and went, stumbling.

Seabrook spoke to her. "Callie? Honey, I can't hold you up any-more."

Yes, yes. She shook her head, blinked. Keep talking. "What would your fiancée think of all this?" she said. "What if she wakes up after all these years and sees you—"

Quincy's voice went cold. "She died three months ago."

For a moment all they heard was dripping rain, the frogs silent as if respecting what had been said.

The last piece fell in place to show the entire picture.

Quincy's fiancée sank into a coma, never expected to awaken. He killed Gracie Seabrook in retaliation, feeling somewhat redeemed . . . until the fiancée died. Then he decided to rain hell all over Seabrook and whomever he touched—until he killed him.

Gracious, what else had he prearranged for headline stories in some sense of justification, because from the sounds of this, he deemed him-self the orchestrator of all within his reach.

Callie recognized derangement. What else could they do to keep their captor engaged? Whether by design or happenstance, Quincy'd gotten off with his crime, giving him a carte blanche sense of freedom. Stoke his prowess. Yes, she needed to stroke the man. "The police never interviewed you back then, did they? Right there in the middle of every-thing, they never suspected you."

Quincy shook his head, grinning. "Nope."

"You sat at your" —she took a rattling breath—"fiancée's bedside, watching the story, having exacted your revenge."

Instead of beaming, Quincy's smile dimmed at the mention of the memory. "Until she died."

Yes. The mental trigger that told him his job wasn't done.

"You're *smarter* than I thought, Quincy."

Seabrook's body shook against her.

The reporter beamed. "I needed a distraction until I could think this through properly, so I paid Pittstop to brag about killing the doc's wife. A simple conversation to make a two-bit con proud. You should've seen him when I told him what to do. Not the why, mind you, but just a part in the play. Nobody could prove it. He made some cash. Win-win. Amazing what cops never see."

"Yes, amazing," she said. "But Sarah's car, Francis . . . chasing my mother."

"Pshhh," he blew out and shrugged a shoulder. "Only a reporter doing his job." He sneered at her, angled to the side for effect. "But that day-to-day work gave me the idea for all this! It inserted me into your lives. You never viewed me as a threat."

He was right. He'd been little more than background noise.

"Stop and think," he said.

She didn't have to.

Quincy counted down. "First, Beverly's political aspirations take me to Edisto, which leads me to Sarah—a great expose, by the way. Two mothers. Who'd of thought that?"

How did he know?

"If you killed my wife, then you broke into the Cantrell house," Seabrook said.

"Or paid someone," Callie said, "but something tells me you were hands-on in all this, except puncturing my tires on Edisto. I bet you had nothing to do with that."

He pointed at her. "That was the funny part. I didn't have anything to do with the first car, but it damn sure gave me the idea for the second."

A prank, an angry guy who probably got a ticket some time back. Totally unrelated to Quincy, her original instinct. Not listening to her guts had become a habit, a costly one.

Quincy laughed. "Yes, I break in, escape, and come back as the eager reporter only to wind up talking about Pittstop with the chief." He held his arms wide. "There must be a half dozen stories in there, every one of them primo. A friggin' goldmine of headlines!" He redirected attention to Callie. "Thank your mother for me. She's the catalyst for everything, after Seabrook, of course. I just stayed on her ass, behind the façade of needing election stories. The thing is, I kept finding other stories! When someone clued me in on the Cantrell musical wives deal, I had to chase it, beginning with the mistress. She wouldn't take my calls, but she damn sure changed her mind when I fished her out of the marsh." He gave a pretend swagger, as if astounded by himself. "But your mother! Jesus, she's a journalist's nirvana. Then suddenly I'm in your office, the girlfriend of the guy I needed to deal with. Add two and two and suddenly again, I come up with the genius of . . . this." His arms fell to his side. "Beverly will be so distraught. I'll spin it that her notoriety brought attention to her daughter and the island's favorite officer, and Pittstop found his window of opportunity."

The clear mention of her pending demise didn't matter. Not yet. It wasn't laid out in concrete as much as Quincy thought.

Please, Thomas, where are you?

"So Francis's death became a headline for you, too," she said, fighting against an anger that would only steal her strength and push Quincy to his conclusion.

"Unfortunate, I'm afraid. Impromptu decision, really. The old car sitting there. A bit of misjudgment with the brakes giving out on the causeway, though. Your officer? Collateral damage, and for that I'm sorry. If it makes you feel better, I asked my editor to put a special human interest piece on the docket for him. Hope to see it next week."

Callie tried not to stare up the road. At this point she'd break down at the sight of blue lights. But she did glance at Raysor. So undisturbed looking, but even if he peered at her she wouldn't know with him off to the side in the shadows.

Seabrook said nary a word. His shivering decreased, his shoulders no longer tight with the effort to stand. The occasional low grunt released involuntarily. If he fell, he'd take her with him, and she wouldn't be able to get back up.

That's the time she assumed Quincy would do them in. When discourse was no longer possible.

"You won't walk away from murder so easily this time," Seabrook said with a loathsome growl.

"Hey." The reporter did his head wobble thing again. "I did before." His fingertips tapped repeatedly on his chest as he relished the soliloquies. "I'll write this story, and instead of just Seabrook, I'll make everyone heroes. People will want to believe, in memoriam. A book even, once the story breaks."

He leaned a boot on the bumper and knocked Pittstop's half--covered shoulder with the gun. The body moaned and shifted under the tarp, trying to sit up.

Quincy tapped his head with the gun. "I've been rewriting the story though. Our friend here is going down for killing the three of you. Shot and injured, Raysor kills him in a glorious last stand before giving up the ghost. Hell, you'll have national news down here for the memorial service. Edisto Island celebrating the lost lives of four officers out of a force of, what, six?"

Tears silently flowed at the hopelessness and her not reading this man better than she had.

Quincy yanked her, disconnecting her easily from Seabrook. "Since our killer is waking up, we've got to finish this. I think it's best if you wind up over here—"

Raysor's blue lights lit up the small dark road. LED strobes bounced off the huge old trees.

A car horn exploded, in repetitive honks.

Pittstop sat upright.

Callie dropped to the ground.

Quincy high-stepped backward, arms spastic at the unidentifiable danger.

Seabrook rushed the reporter, taking him to the ground in little more than a clumsy collapse of weight. "Callie, run!"

Bolting toward Raysor, Callie jerked when the shot blast muffled behind her, but she kept moving. A second shot rang out, whizzing past her head into the woods.

"Stop," Quincy yelled, huffing from where Seabrook's hit sprawled him into the road. "Turn your ass around and look at me, Callie. See what your stunt just cost you."

Stumbling on feeble legs, feet sliding to a halt, she froze, still facing Raysor. He painfully opened an eye, the car's fob loose in his limp hand. Painfully she gasped, grateful he lived, crestfallen Thomas hadn't arrived. Scared to death what she'd find if she turned around.

"I can just as easily shoot you in the back, Chief."

No, no, no. She didn't want to. But tears pooling, she slowly eased around.

She met Pittstop's fear-ridden gaze first, the man standing backed against the Jeep. Then her gaze roamed over to Quincy.

The reporter shoved Seabrook off his legs with one foot, his gun trained on Callie.

"No," she sobbed, Mike's slack form scaring the shit out of her.

"You see what—"

"No!" she screamed and rushed to Seabrook as the blond officer's limp body rolled and settled to its back. "Mike," she said, using her sleeve to remove mud from his cheek so it didn't get in his eye. He could be like Raysor, unconscious. "Mike, open your eyes. I'm here, baby.

Thomas is almost here. We told him to bring an ambulance. It'll be okay." Rubbing her palm over his forehead, his cheek, she swore to herself he still could be alive.

Lowering, she kissed him. "Please don't do this, Mike," she whispered, touching his hair, his temple, as if her life force would help him keep his. "Please don't."

Scanning down his length, fingers feeling, she watched his shirt for movement and stopped when her hand met the gunshot wound in the center of his belly. *No. No.*

Her frantic search settled on his silver name tag, and she held her breath like she did stooping over Francis, hoping to see a rise and fall. She reached for his hand. "You're shot, Mike, but Thomas is coming," she cried. "Any second. Please hold on."

Laying her ear against his neck, letting his chin rest atop her head as he'd done times before on her doorstep, she listened . . . and listened . . . and finally, with a turn, she buried her face in his shirt and sobbed. She could hear nothing.

She felt a presence invade her sacred space. "See what you did?" Quincy whispered in her ear.

Slowly she twisted and whispered back. "We radioed this in, you crazy son-of-a-bitch." She pushed up. "You were going to get caught regardless," she said. Then she screamed, "This was not necessary!"

Quincy kissed her cheek then pointed at her with the Ruger to get up.

She lifted to a knee, swaying, and reached out to steady herself, her hand landing on Seabrook's chest. The touch almost took her down with grief, and for a second her vision wavered.

If she fell, Quincy would end the ordeal. She was sure of it. So she looked past the murderer and his horrible grin for a focal point. His fog apparently lifted, Pittstop stood stunned and stymied a few feet outside the Jeep, his tarp dropped to the ground in a stiff puddle.

Raysor's Glock lay barely a step ahead of him, dropped from Quincy's waist in the tussle with Seabrook.

Quincy's ruddy face shifted and blocked her vision. "It's time."

She collapsed again, draped across Seabrook. "I can't. I just can't," she said, fading the words to nothing.

"Hey, man," Pittstop said.

"Get up," Quincy told her again.

"Hey, what's your deal?" Pittstop asked.

Callie lifted her head.

Quincy glanced over his shoulder. "Listen, Roman. We've had an accident. Stay there. Help's on the way—"

Pittstop kicked the gun toward Callie. It fell short, landing instead beside the reporter's foot.

Quincy squinted, off guard, and in that split second, Pittstop dove at the man's legs and slammed him to the ground.

Callie went for the loose weapon, but with her reflexes slow, the wrestling preceded her, landing the two men atop the gun. Instinctively, she hunted for Raysor, the unarmed husky deputy struggling and failing to get to his feet.

Unsuited for street fighting, the reporter labored under the hits and twists of the thug. Pittstop made eye contact with Callie once . . . and that was all it took.

Mustering what she expected to be her last physical move, her body and mind bordering on complete disintegration, she clenched her muscles and stood, then ran limping, then floundering, fingers touching the mud once to stop herself from falling. The dozen yards to the patrol car seemed like miles.

Gripping the door, she hurled herself behind it and grabbed her nine millimeter on the seat. Heavy in her grip, her fatigue ruining any control, she dug deep and steeled her forearms and biceps, double fisting the firearm as she laid it atop the rolled down window. She used the door as her shield, a knee on the threshold of the vehicle to keep her stable.

Then reaching down, she called upon a yell that came out screeching and witchy. "Freeze, Quincy, and throw down your weapon."

The fighting stopped, both men staring like twins in the car's headlights.

Pittstop crab-walked back toward the Jeep. Quincy peered back at him, as if questioning the guy's movement while in the sights of someone who'd just hollered *freeze*.

Blackness threatened the edges of her sight. If she went for the radio, she was done. She had no help. Blinking, she honed on Quincy, a brief thought going out to Jeb, then John.

Quincy turned back toward Callie, clothes disheveled, wet and filthy, more scratches across his chin and nose. "Arrest me, then. The world . . ." he huffed, "will hear my story regardless. I'll preach what your doctor did to my fiancée. How after eight years I won my battle, and Seabrook won his. A hell of a story. This is goddamn movie material."

She put six rounds into the reporter.

A whoop-whoop sounded behind her. The gun fell from her grip.

A car door shut. More headlights gave her a clearer view of Seabrook. Her heart almost burst. Too exhausted to go to him, too strangled to cry for him, she gave it up and fell to the mud, one leg still hung in the car. As her cheek hit the muck, she shut her eyes, drawing inward, her only attention on getting air to her swollen, infected lungs.

But she'd pushed too hard and too long. Breaths wouldn't come.

Like back at Scott Creek, she thought she heard Thomas's voice, but this time she didn't care. She welcomed the blackness, expecting never to wake again.

Chapter 25

FITS OF URGENCY then others of pure fear consumed her despite the constant hum of the hospital room, but mostly she drifted for minutes she had no need to keep track of, unwilling to tend to the visitors silently coming and going. Hours muddied into each other.

The chills brought her to life several times, but then like a magnet, once the cold left, she withdrew. Warmth only spurred pain, mentally and physically.

Once, she assumed she'd finally died only to quasi-make it through the haze to partially remember Seabrook, possibly spurred by a person calling her name. Jeb maybe? But she hadn't the strength to awaken and cope yet. She gave up and fell to wherever she could fall and disappear.

"Enough of this, Callie. Wake up." The male voice grumbled, overbearing, somewhat angry. Though she fought the hospital smells, they infiltrated her head, helping to awaken her. She revived from where she'd hidden for who-knew-how-long, unable to elude her life anymore.

Whoever stood there smelled like cinnamon gum, despite the tube pushing oxygen up her nose.

"Wake the hell up," he demanded.

"Hold on a friggin' minute."

There was *that* voice again. Jeb.

"Don't talk to my mother that way," he said.

"It's okay, Jeb," she managed to whisper, and the effort brought her fully aware, every muscle reminding her she was still far from okay.

"Mom!" Then a body engulfed her, and she caressed his neck. "You scared the hell out of me," he said into her shoulder.

She patted him, but he didn't let her go, so she gently hugged her baby boy.

"Give her some space, son. Don't crush her."

As Jeb retreated, Callie focused up from under heavy lids.

Her old boss from Boston peered down from the opposite side of the bed, soft furrows creasing his forehead like when she'd lost some key piece of evidence . . . like he did when she announced her departure from the force. As if she felt the need to explain herself, when she'd done no wrong.

Only she'd done everything wrong.

"Stan, I . . ." she said, her chest thickening, a lump trying to rise. Visions of Seabrook . . . not moving.

"Welcome back."

The wet night of riddles, chases, and bullets poured over her like the rain that had soaked her and Seabrook on Pine Landing Road. Tears rushed to the surface and rolled down her temples and into the pillow. Covering her face, she released a tender sob, not wanting to connect to the present for the horrid pictures in her head.

The big, gruff man with his military salt-and-pepper cut, sat a hip on the edge of the bed and scooped her against his shoulder. "Shhh, Chicklet. I'm here." He rocked her smoothly, holding the side of her head, unlike a middle-aged detective native to shouting orders and dominating the roughness of Boston street crime.

An intercom paged a Dr. Black, and her mind pictured Seabrook delivering her pills and ginger ale. Then tending her broken rib after she saved Sophie in the church cemetery. Talking her down from a panic attack the day she moved to Edisto. Kissing her politely as they parted on her front porch, ever the gentleman. Their one solitary night in his bed.

"You can do this," Stan said. "I've seen what you're made of, remember." He pushed her hair behind an ear and coaxed her to raise her chin so he could see. "This time you nailed the killer on the spot."

How was that solace? She almost wished for some sort of revenge to fill her head and give her purpose. Anything other than this emptiness. She buried her head into his shirt. "I failed him. I failed them all. Just like John . . . Stan, I can't do this again."

Edisto, notorious for reconstructing broken lives, teaching souls they could leave the past on the other side of the big McKinley bridge, had rebuilt her with Seabrook's calm, assuring manner, underpinning each positive stride she made. And she'd ruined it.

"Mom, I need you," her son said with a hitch, standing on her other side, stroking her scarred arm.

Stan hugged her again and released her down to the linens, tucking the thin hospital blanket around her. "Jeb, go tell the nurse your mom's awake. They log that sort of thing."

The boy rubbed his nose and scooted out, nimble and eager to be of assistance.

Waiting for Jeb to exit, Stan turned back, Callie facing the wall. "We're alone, but we won't be for long."

She studied the closet.

"Seabrook is gone, Callie."

She stared back, angry at the obvious, hating to hear it said aloud. "I know that, Stan."

"Honey, you had to hear it. Listen to me."

"This isn't you and me on the job," she said, not bothering to wipe the drops, letting them wet her sheet.

"No, it isn't. It's worse. It's deep and personal, and you've had more doses of deep and personal than just about anybody I've ever known."

She sighed, her head so heavy, her heart forever frayed around the edges. A bright ray flared briefly between the slats of the blinds, then left, breezes off the Charleston water pushing clouds with their usual authority. The room lit up then went darker, like hitting a light switch.

Her last image of Seabrook appeared in her mind's eye, his body disgraced by the mud, the hole in his belly, the other in his side. Her tears renewed.

Cradling her once more, Stan talked into her hair. "You are going to make it through this, Chicklet. Jeb was right. People need you. And Mike Seabrook would expect you to continue with what you've accomplished, and do more. In his name if not your own. For your man Francis as well. I've lost men, too, Callie. It's damn excruciating, but you continue in spite of the hardship, and because of it. Don't let them die for naught."

At that she stared up with red-rimmed eyes. "But you weren't in love with any of your men."

With that his countenance melted, the boss-like demeanor defeated by her words. "I won't let you become a casualty, you hear me?"

A knock sounded. "Everybody decent?"

"Yeah," Stan said. "Come on in. She's awake."

The uniform entered, and she reached out to him. "Raysor? Oh my God, you're all right?"

Raysor's head sported a bandage above his ear. He came in, hat gripped, until finally he reached Callie's side. It struck her that the last time they'd shared a dangerous experience, she visited him in his hospital bed.

Pained at his expression, she took his hand, her heart in agony for this man who had enjoyed Seabrook's friendship for years. Turning his head to the side, he tried to sniffle without being heard.

"Don," she said, her voice choking. "I'm so, so sorry."

He wiped his nose and squeezed back. "Doll, I just wish I'd . . . I couldn't . . ."

"Don't," she said, shaking their grip. "You saved me with the siren." She placed her other hand on top and shook again, lost how to mend him and her both. "What would Mike say right now?"

He sniffed again. "He'd say have a nice day. He made everybody have a nice day."

A gingerly smile returned, and he released a soft chuckle. "The guy was definitely a looker." But then he dimmed a bit. "You two should've had more time. He cared a lot for you, Chief. And you deserved him."

Through a fresh round of tears, she kissed his fingers. "Thanks, Don."

Stan patted the deputy's sleeve. "Sorry, man. Sorry we had to meet again under these conditions."

A nurse came around the door, Jeb in her wake. "How's our patient doing?" she asked.

Beverly pushed in. "Callie? Oh, my baby, you're awake!" Stan stood and slid to the side to let her through to dote on her daughter.

Callie glanced over her mother's shoulder to see if the elder first lady sidekick had shuffled in, but she hadn't. Good. The woman reminded her of Quincy.

DAYS LATER, CALLIE rested on her porch, the side porch . . . her only view that of old Papa Beach's place next door, the foundation all that remained after a fire two months ago. All signs of her childhood neighbor officially gone.

The empty lot only widened the hole in her soul.

The front porch paralleled Jungle Road and traffic, and after seeing a patrol car go by twice, each time suffocating her with choked tears, she changed settings. She and Mike had relaxed at the front because it gave him a chance to watch over his Edisto while enjoying her. It had become their spot.

She'd waited too damn long to accept his advances. Raising a tea glass, she chased a wave of melancholy. A hint of her old fear stuck with her of late, clinging like it did when she moved in. She saw the signs, almost sensed one of her anxiety attacks brewing, thus her move to the side porch. Mike helped her through those, out of those, past those. She'd shame his memory caving again into that world of angst and dread. He helped her recognize those sensations for what they were: the fear of living and moving on.

She wasn't feeling the moving on part yet. She'd barely grasped the living.

On the side of the house, behind a screen, the air was cooler, the light darker in the shade of her own palmettos. Nobody able to see her, honk, shout, or wave.

Her health on the mend, she had maybe a week at most before she'd have to go to work. She'd tackle people then. But what was worse, the celebration of life ceremony for Edisto's fallen was scheduled at the Presbyterian church in two days.

Sophie flew into the screened room and set a tray on a small folding table beside Callie's Adirondack chair, the comfort food wafting a blended aroma of butter, tomato, oregano, cheddar, and toasted bread. "Vegetarian vegetable soup," she said. "And a grilled cheese sandwich, hot off the griddle."

Being October, the days ran from balmy to cool, this one being a hint on the chilly side. Callie huddled under a lap blanket. She withdrew out from under it and took a cut triangle of the sandwich. "Thanks." She took a bite, the cheese warm and gooey. "What's the difference between vegetarian vegetable and vegetable soup?"

Tucking sock-covered feet under her yoga-pants butt, Sophie assumed a pose in the settee across from Callie and shook her hair back. "No meat stock, silly."

"Ah," Callie replied, allowing a smile. "Of course."

Sophie empowered her with humor, positivity, and a fairylike attitude that life was what you made it. The pixie woman had filled a void Callie never thought she had. She reached for the soup, and keeping her legs folded in the chair, Callie nursed the heated bowl against her and tried a couple of spoonfuls. Her friend cooked quite well for a health freak.

Quiet poured in between them, Callie falling again into her thoughts, half-expecting Mike to pop in, uniform crisp, cheeks sun-kissed, blond hair out of place yet attractive enough to enter any restaurant and still be neat. He always looked neat.

"Your soup will get cold just holding it, honey," Sophie said.

"Sorry." Callie tasted another bite.

"It gets better," the yoga lady said.

Callie ate again. "It's fine, Sophie. Spices are perfect."

"No," Sophie replied. "I mean about . . . Mike."

All Callie could do was nod. It was already better. A scant scintilla better but nonetheless better. She didn't want it to be, though. She recalled the feeling from before. The moving on instilling a guilt that she was forgetting too much about her loved one when she didn't deserve to be the one left behind alive.

Her friend shifted to a cross-legged position, making her earrings tinkle. "Um, don't get mad, but I need to tell you something."

Callie gave a tiny gasp, a thump in her chest.

"Oh, no, nothing bad," Sophie said wide-eyed, reading her expression. "Sorry."

Her heart-shaped face sorted through several expressions, her mind apparently at work. "Girlfriend," Sophie finally said, "when you first moved here, I was a bit nervous about living so close to a cop with all that negativity and evil in her life. And gracious, you carried more than any ten people I knew!"

"Thanks, Soph. Love you, too."

"Just hush and eat your soup. Let me finish."

Curious at Sophie trying to be serious, Callie did as ordered.

"I credit fate for bringing us together," Sophie said. "And for bringing you here. Edisto needed you. Over the last few months I've been amazed at how the two of us can be so different, but be so close. Girlfriend, I think you've had echoes of Edisto in your being since childhood, and it took a series of events to ultimately bring you here." She touched Callie's blanketed knee. "Events good and bad, but the end result being you've found your life's mission."

But at what cost?

Callie thanked Sophie for the try and returned to her soup.

"By the way, I got rid of all the alcohol I could find."

"Including the Maker's Mark?" Her father's bourbon, the bottle he kept at Chelsea Morning for when he dropped in. Sophie didn't realize that.

"Sure," she said. "Especially that."

Callie sighed at the additional loss but understood her friend doing the right thing.

"Listen," Sophie said, "it's not that I don't think you can control things without alcohol, but . . . you . . . I just don't want the temptation to . . . and Jeb said . . ."

"I get it, Sophie. It's okay."

As badly as she wanted to suck down a fifth of gin, Seabrook had been her strongest ally in her achieving abstinence. He invariably caught her when she slipped, forever suggesting she join AA. Always reminding her to call him before she tossed back a few alone . . . on the porch . . . in this chair. She recalled his first visit to this porch, with Jeb. She'd been drunk out of her mind on gin and Neil Diamond.

Drinking wouldn't make her forget the pain. It would only raise its intensity. And she couldn't stand replaying Mike's words in her head about being better than that. She wasn't sure she could look at a bottle again . . . not without crumbling to pieces.

Drinking solved nothing. Today she was stronger, and she had to possess the faith she could carry that strength into tomorrow.

Chapter 26

THEY OPENED THE windows of the church to allow those who couldn't get in to hear the service. Colleton County's Sheriff offered the use of a larger Baptist church in Walterboro for the event, but Callie firmly yet kindly declined. Francis and Mike were Edisto officers, who died for their island.

The mayor didn't attempt to override her. Neither did Brice or anyone else on the council.

Callie went through the motions of donning her uniform like an amputee still feeling a phantom limb. The rank, the insignia, the name tag. The polished shoes and cap. The day she assumed the role of chief she had sat in her car outside the admin building, just as she sat now, watching the hubbub from a distance, less than eager to jump into the crowd. Her reservations before had been about diving back into law enforcement. This time, however, condolences, questions, and sad gazes awaited her. Her name was commonplace across the island these days.

She turned when someone walked by her car and glanced over at her. She'd beaten death while Francis and Seabrook had not. Some would hold it against her; others would deem her blessed. She sided with the former.

Little did anyone understand how horrible it was for her to forever wear that shroud.

Jeb ventured outside the church and stood on the top step, shading his eyes from the bright autumn afternoon sun. Callie gasped at how mature he seemed and how much he stood like John in that dark suit. Unexpectedly, guilt from that loss flushed over her, too.

Scanning the bumper-to-bumper cars covering the grounds, the clusters of huddled folk, he quickly settled on Callie's patrol car in a reserved spot. His frown softened, and he disappeared inside.

Callie sighed relief. She just couldn't be there for him at the moment. She could barely cope on this, her first public appearance since that day.

Stan appeared in his charcoal suit, shoulders broad, his presence striking. Boston all over again. Taking the steps dignified and with purpose, he approached her, and she thought she'd come apart at the déjà vu.

He leaned against the roof and peeked in. Shakily, she lowered the glass. "I'll be there in a second."

He stood back and waited.

The service began in five minutes. While she held notes on a piece of paper, she doubted if she would do the two men justice . . . if she could hold it together.

Raysor appeared on the top step. Then Sophie. Marie eased behind Raysor, worry in her expression.

Backing up from the car, Stan opened her door and held out his arm for her to take. "Time to do this, Callie."

Both officers had been buried while she was deathly ill, over two weeks ago, a bittersweet realization when Raysor broke the news while Stan stood beside her. But the island had saved the memorial service for her return, a nod to her. "You should feel honored," Beverly'd said over the phone.

Francis was laid to rest in Walterboro, near his parents. She hadn't visited yet but would take flowers and stop by the grandfather's home to pay her respect since he wouldn't be in attendance today. Seabrook, however, was buried behind the church. This church. And on the way inside, hand in the crook of Stan's arm, she focused only on the plain white church doors, a hitch in her windpipe at being so close to where her lover would endure eternity.

They strode up the aisle like a bride and groom, the front row reserved for speakers and special guests. Raysor, Callie, Mayor Talbot, Seabrook's father, and his brother who'd flown in from Nashville. She met the father just yesterday, the aftermath of seeing his pain putting her to bed early, until she had to rise today.

Stan sat near the aisle, at the end of the second row. Sarah, Beverly, Jeb, Sophie, Zeus, and Sprite . . . everyone she knew and many she did not. As the cars outside indicated, the place was packed. Even Miss Promise. With the dog.

Uniforms from Charleston, Walterboro, Johns Island, Hilton Head, some as far as Columbia. One from Spartanburg. The entire Edisto Fire Department and representatives from a half dozen more.

Florals jammed the front to bursting, leaving only walkways for the presenters.

She thanked the Lord there were no poster-sized pictures of the men. Nobody needed to be reminded.

A soft coolness pushed into the sanctuary through the open windows, the Spanish moss on the oaks outside swaying as if in mourning, bringing the salt air with it though the church lay six miles from the breakers, maybe four from the brackish Edisto River. A comforting scent to her.

Callie gave a small jump from her seat when the organist hit the opening bars of a new hymn, indicating the start of service. After one short verse, the minister presented somberly to the podium and spoke. He said something profound since several behind Callie mumbled *Amen*.

She stared down at her program, reading the bios written about the two men. Plain material full of facts, dates, relations, and general information itemizing what they'd accomplished in life.

Absent was Francis's sense of humor and his easy way with the teens. His Mickey Mouse watch. Seabrook's charisma and how he filled a uniform, bystanders parting with smiles when he exited his car.

Francis and barbecue. Seabrook and shrimp.

Their abilities to turn dilemmas into handshakes and thanks.

Not nearly enough. Not even close to the personalities they were.

"Callie," whispered Raysor.

She looked up to his chin jutting toward the front. Her turn to speak.

The room hung quiet, not even a cough. Two sets of rounded stairs made a dramatic entrance to the center podium. She took each of the twelve steps on one side with concentration, a grip on the railing, her stomach reminding her she hadn't been able to eat since yesterday morning. When she reached her spot, she unfolded her paper, but glancing out over the sea of guests, some damp, others stoic with jaws firm, she heavily remembered she was the last person in the room to see both men alive.

People were wondering how she'd pull this off.

She'd had her moment several days earlier. Alone for a few hours too long, her memories bottling, building, exploding with grief, she'd screamed and swiped a half dozen low ball glasses off the shelf. Then gripping each like a baseball, she slung them helter-skelter in the kitchen, one crashing her front window. Running over, Sophie grabbed her, took them both to the floor, and hugged her through the dark, deep sobbing she hadn't let herself do. For over an hour Callie poured out the anguish, then curled up on her sofa, exorcised, and plummeted into a sleep of the dead.

In spite of the weariness in her bones, she would do this. She found herself imagining Mike in the back of the room . . . grinning, proud, as he'd done during her swearing in.

Another breeze wafted through the church. Taking a second, she garnered a shot of courage from Stan's wink. Then she caught Thomas's eye. Bless him, he'd been there for her twice. Across the tops of so many people, she tipped her head at him, and the light from a chandelier reflected his tears. He nodded back.

"History gets heavier the older you get," she said. "And in law enforcement, that burden can take a toll."

She paused.

"Today, we remember Officer Francis Scott Dickens and Officer Michael Jenkins Seabrook, two men who made the ultimate sacrifice in law enforcement service. But, we also pay a very special tribute to the surviving family members"—she swallowed—"and to us, those who have been left behind."

She stood firm, trying not to lock her knees. "Please look around this church and see the extended law enforcement family standing shoulder to shoulder in solidarity. They will never forget your loved one, and they will never forget you. And I hope you never forget them . . . ever. Officers Dickens and Seabrook were exceptional police officers and exceptional human beings. Every single native Edistonian and most of Edisto Beach's visitors can say they are familiar with those two names. Their professionalism, their demeanor, their friendliness to tourists and residents alike, affected thousands in Officer Dickens' three short years and Officer Seabrook's six." She shook her head. "So little time, yet such an impact."

She cleared something thick in her throat as the sound of sniffles touched her ear. She gripped the dais harder.

"I have served but a few weeks in the role of Edisto Beach's Police Chief. My law enforcement dates fifteen years, and upon arriving on this beach, these two men were some of the strongest influences on me to take up the torch and contribute my training toward the protection of this community."

She smiled down, recalling conversations with Francis as he stumbled around the Jinx death at a summer party, ever ready to help, eager for orders, his second glance at the tight rear end of a blonde reporter covering the story.

"Francis was becoming like a son to me, only eight years older than my own child. The death of someone so young is doubly tragic. Mike . . .

well," and she had to swallow again. "We had developed an alchemy. Like minds, I guess." A tear spilled, and she let it hit the paper she hadn't read the first word off of. "He saved me in more ways than I can count. He convinced me how great I would be for Edisto . . . and how great Edisto would be for me." She glanced up through the filmy haze the lights cast through her tears.

She could speak of them for hours, but only because the words made her feel closer. Ending felt like a closed door, and while she wasn't ready for that, she had to move on.

She lifted her attention to the crowd, her legs so close to giving way.

"Grief is a process, ever evolving, that cannot be denied. It consists of two components. The most obvious is the loss. The second is the rebuilding of a shattered life. The loss is behind us . . . the rebuilding ahead. But that's why we are all here. To aid each other in beginning that reconstruction. Together we can do this. I'm here for you, and there will be days . . . I'll need you to be there for me. And we'll all remember Francis and Mike as long as we live."

She folded the unused note with shaking hands and returned to her seat. A pat on her shoulder, another her arm, yet someone else on her leg. She had no idea who did what, but without a doubt the camaraderie in the sanctuary aided her. And though almost sick with the grief she spoke of, she thanked the heavens for helping her through this stage. Maybe one day she could forgive herself, but today she couldn't imagine when that would be.

REFRESHMENTS WERE served at the nearby fellowship hall, but Callie preferred to wait outside, unrestricted and less confined. For an hour afterward, people thanked, women hugging her, the blue brotherhood tending to her as well as the Seabrook family represented. She weathered the attention, reminding herself it was all for them.

Stan remained on guard within a few yards at all times. He and Raysor exchanged words, sharing stories, finally managing to laugh, Raysor introducing Stan to various uniformed individuals.

Jeb hovered with Sprite at his side. Both her mothers brought Callie something to drink, and she couldn't count the number of times Sophie sneaked in and whispered, "You doing all right?"

Finally, as the crowd thinned, Stan wrapped an arm around her. "I think you've done enough. You've got to be exhausted, Chicklet. It hasn't been that long since you got home from the hospital."

He must've seen it in her, because she *was* tired. She let him walk her back to the church. From that side, the fresh grave caught her attention. Without hesitation, she headed toward it.

The stone wasn't in place yet, but she didn't need a marker to tell her where Mike was. A small tasteful marker next to the fresh plot indicated where his Gracie was buried. Callie never knew that.

Entering the wrought iron section marking the Seabrook family, she eased to the ground unable to resist touching the sod-covered grave. Fingers kneading the grass, she closed her eyes, hoping for a sense of his presence.

But this wasn't *her* Mike. He was elsewhere. Just like John went elsewhere. The fire left few remnants of her husband, and she always felt shortchanged without a body to bury. But here, only feet from where Mike's body lay, she learned that a grave gave no peace.

Gone was gone.

She let Stan help her to stand, and staring through the cemetery toward the parking area, she spotted someone she'd missed in the social greetings. Someone she hadn't spoken to since the day . . . that Quincy sent them on the goose chase that changed their worlds.

Miss Promise waited on a concrete bench, Beverly chatting with Sarah a few feet to the side. The old woman appeared not to be listening, but Callie knew better. This lady didn't miss a beat.

"Thanks for coming, Miss Promise," Callie said almost at attention, holding out a formal hand to the woman who felt no need to rise.

In Callie's reclusion, while trying to think of other than Seabrook, she'd thought of the ex-first lady, mulled over how this woman had inserted herself in her mother's world, and done more damage than anyone thought possible.

Promise took her hand like a limp fish. "Glad to see you with more pink in your cheeks, child. You had us scared."

"Callie," Beverly started, "do you want us to follow you to the house? Sarah and I were thinking—"

"Mother, do you think y'all could give Miss Promise and me a moment alone?" Opportunity made itself available at the most unexpected moments.

Stan discretely removed himself from earshot, relocating toward the front of the church, familiar with his old detective's nuances. Callie watched him go and turned back to Beverly. "I want to ask her opinion about something."

Today of all days, people would honor her wishes, and she was taking this impromptu moment to grab the privacy, while Miss Promise had to maintain her best facade.

It was the perfect time.

Pleased, her mother scooped Sarah around the shoulders and hustled her aside, the two appearing more like sisters than paramours for the same man. After inching Tink's tote bag a few inches to the side, Callie sat beside Miss Promise.

The lady gave her a tight smile, but Callie noted a smidgeon of caution in her eye.

"Ma'am," Callie started, "how's the election campaign coming?"

"Oh, dear, you'd have to ask your mother. She's the brains in all this. My days of active stumping are over, I'm afraid. Too much wear on a body. I'm just loaning her my name."

Understatement, the woman's forte. "Well," Callie said, "she seems quite grateful."

Miss Promise smiled wider, less reserved. "Glad to help."

"I imagine the effort gets harder from this point forward."

"The final leg, I think it's called. Only a month until November."

Taking the woman's hand in both of hers, Callie leaned in. "Exactly. So I must ask a favor, Miss Promise, assuming you don't mind. It's about taking care of Mother."

"Of course, dear."

Callie lowered her voice, keeping her smile intact. "Now that I've killed your reporter . . ."

Miss Promise tried to withdraw, but Callie held onto the thin hand , stroking as if conversing with a favorite aunt while in her head she was snapping that bird neck in two. "And since you can no longer feed private, personal, rather intimate material to Quincy Kinard . . ."

"Um, I—"

Callie clinched tighter. "Don't worry. I imagine if I seriously wanted to prove myself, I'd find numerous plain, benign pieces of ecru stationery in Quincy's residence, each with directions to one of Mother's appearances or informing you of Cantrell confidences and weaknesses. Timely, unidentifiable, probably prepared with Sunday gloves to avoid prints. No return address, typewritten and delivered by someone you royally tipped to remain silent."

"I wouldn't dream—"

"No, you didn't dream. You no doubt, straight-ass did it, Miss Promise." She let the woman retrieve her hand. "Mr. Kinard flashed one in front of me the day he died. I've seen too many of those notecards over the years, *ma'am*."

Promise released a thin breath and started to stand.

"Not yet," Callie said and took the woman back down by the sleeve. "You're going to listen to what I have to say, or I expose you clear across this state. Quincy Kinard was a murderer. For all I knew you held ulterior plans to dispose of my mother."

"Oh, oh . . ." The old woman gasped, rheumy eyes wide under her veiled pillbox hat. "I never knew that side of him. I just went to the paper, and . . . I mean . . . I was just . . ."

"Was getting even for whatever happened in the past? Something political between your husband and my father? A business dealing? Lack of support for a bill? Do tell, Miss Promise, so I can decide whether to consider charges."

Promise's pink-coated lips smacked once in resignation. "Lawton refused to endorse a business venture near the end of my husband's term. It cost us hundreds of thousands of dollars . . . it was to be our retirement."

"Why after all these years, though?" The sarcasm came so easily atop the fatigue.

Promise's mouth wadded into a pucker, anger flashing. "Because I'm broke, that's why. If your father hadn't been so high and mighty, I wouldn't be. Seeing your mother climb the political ladder, with an inheritance denied to me, well . . . you wouldn't understand."

"No, guess I wouldn't," Callie said, riled but not seeing the need to ruin the woman any further. Another day, another time, maybe, but Mike Seabrook's softer type of policing remained too fresh in her mind. She preferred not to sully this day. "Tell you what. I'll let you break the news to Mother that you're bowing out of her political campaign. I don't care how you disappear. However you maintain your dignity is up to you, but you'll absolutely, without question, preserve hers." She bent into the lady's line of vision and whispered, "Or I'll take you down, *ma'am*."

Promise Hollister, ex-first lady of South Carolina, tried to rock to her feet from the cold hard bench, a groan escaping. Callie aided her upright.

Beverly strode over. "Did y'all have a nice chat?"

"We did indeed," Callie replied, drawing upon a proper reserved smile for the occasion. "But I'm a bit spent, Mother. Mind if we forego the social time at the house?"

Her old mother wrapped her old familiar arms around her daughter. "Of course, dear. I'll call you tomorrow."

"Where to?" Stan asked, suddenly back at her side.

"The beach," she said, slowly walking to her car.

"The shore?" he quipped, the north versus south joke ever between them.

"Whatever," she replied. "Just point me to some impossibly soft-looking sand and waves that go on forever."

Chapter 27

SWINGING ON SEABROOK'S front porch, Callie watched dark clouds move further into the Atlantic. The storm had missed Edisto, barely hit Charleston with a dash of rain, then grumbled off. But it was beautiful roiling off above the slate gray sea.

There was something about the dark that made the light so much better.

She kept telling herself that in the three and a half weeks since the service.

Still in uniform, now over a new vest the town had no problem ordering once Beverly offered to cover the expenses, Callie had ventured down Palmetto after work as she had almost every day. Mr. Seabrook, Mike's father, was undecided what to do with Windswept.

Rubbing her face, Callie recalled the torment in the man's red swollen look, in spite of the dignity in his posture. A father grappling with outliving his son. She hadn't the nerve to ask if Seabrook had mentioned her. Maybe downstream she'd find the stomach to call. He requested Callie check on the beach house, as would any homeowner out here, so she made it her task to swing by each day. A cop doing her duty.

It took her two weeks to park at the place, another couple days to climb the stairs. Today, with thin resolve, she managed to sit on the porch. She hadn't been inside.

Just thinking about setting foot in that front door raised a massive tangle of emotions. Was the bed still unmade? Mike's uniforms in the closet? The porch alone veered her precipitously close to the edge. Inside, the smell of his clothes would kill her.

The swing was fine for the moment.

She hurt about Seabrook as badly as John, and she couldn't explain why. Her nights were so damn long. Like Stan said, Mike's murderer had been expunged on the site minutes after taking Mike's life, a good thing in anyone's book. But that also left her without motivation other than to live one day at a time until she regained purchase into a life that showed more promise.

Lots and lots of memories. So many in so few months.

A quick shot of a wind rushed in and through the porch, and she watched a pelican caught off guard try to regain control. She wished it were that easy.

Everyone had been remarkably great with her, and no question she lived in the right community. Jeb had Sprite, his best friend Zeus. Their mother Sophie, now Callie's sidekick, never let a day go by without checking on her. The silly little thing was one tough cookie.

Callie's refrigerator held vestiges of casseroles that continued for days after the memorial service. Some probably needed throwing out.

Callie didn't even remember what she said that day, but apparently it resonated. So had the events at the Town Council meeting while all hell broke loose on Pine Landing Road.

Sarah'd appeared on Callie's behalf that night and requested to speak. Her words remained hot gossip. The meek Sarah Rosewood kicked some council ass. Not only did the Town Council destroy Brice's request Callie be fired, but they hired two full-time temporary uniforms from Charleston and issued a call for applications for not one, but three new officers. Callie accepted the decisions with thanks, with the condition Raysor continue on loan from Colleton County. She'd do without an officer sooner than lose him from her force. He was the senior badge in terms of time on Edisto, with invaluable mental real estate.

Sarah later sent flowers to the hospital and food to the house, but she appeared little and then disappeared off the beach after the memorial service. Callie came home that day to a note that Sarah needed time to sort through things. She thanked Callie for accepting her in spite of the lies of the past but said she didn't want to intrude during this difficult time.

There was a reason Lawton Cantrell loved that woman.

Ben remained in the house. It would be some time before Callie could decide how to cope with him.

Annoyed with the thumps and prods in her lower back, Callie stopped the swing to remove her utility belt and weapon, setting it beside her . . . a sting in her heart recalling doing the same just inside this front door, right behind Seabrook.

Jeb had gone to Charleston for the day with Zeus, the two finally talking about college next fall, and they wouldn't be home until tomorrow. She had to shoo them off, her son scared of leaving her alone. He used to go places and assume Seabrook would be there in his stead. Jeb had come to like the man.

Beverly was rolling and steaming like a train toward Middleton's election day. Callie wished she could vote for her. Nobody'd seen a hair of Miss Promise. And the Middleton newspaper seemed remarkably amiable to Mrs. Cantrell after the news broke about their reporter and his past. The polls did an abrupt shift in favor of the Cantrell camp.

A car honked; the driver waved. One of the seafood restaurant owners. She lifted a hand to reciprocate.

Then she let her head loll back. Her mind played scenes like a film reel. So many actors, so many stories, so much color on this tiny little beach. She'd fallen in love with it along with one of its favorite sons. They'd all heal together . . . minus Seabrook. And Francis.

But not anytime soon.

"Chicklet?" a voice yelled.

She recognized the top of Stan's buzz-cut head as he clomped up the stairs. "Who else would it be?" she hollered back.

"Sophie said to check here for you."

Of course she would. Sophie was deeper than she let on.

He lifted a dried potted plant that had tipped and slid it back against the wall, then studied the four lone chairs, a settee, the rest of the swing.

She scooted over. "Sit here, but only if you don't break it. You're a big dude."

In easing down he stopped the sway, then started it back. She lifted feet off the floor and curled them beside her, leaving him in control.

He seemed almost native in his jeans, a long-sleeve polo, and somewhere he'd found a pair of deck shoes. Though they hadn't discussed his presence much, she was beginning to wonder about his extended stay. He had excess leave time, he said. She needed a shoulder, he said. Both made sense and suited her.

Some angel up there sensed she'd enjoy him being around.

"You're beginning to fit in, Yankee," she said. "Some kind of vacation you're taking down here."

His smile curled up on one side. "They stole my best detective. How could I not check this place out?"

Her arms stretched across the back of the swing, and she tapped him on his wide shoulder. "Hope you're not sticking around because of me." Lids closed, she breathed deeply of the scents in the air, the exiting storm having stirred up the ozone and salt.

"I came to chat about that," he said.

Apprehension snaked through her, and she sat up straight, feet down. "What, Stan?"

"I'm headed back to Boston in the morning."

She sank back into the swing's slats, relieved they weren't headed into a bossy lecture about her health or state of mind. "Of course you're going back. They're probably ready to replace you."

He sucked on his front teeth then pulled out a stick of gum, a sure sign that Stan had something on his mind. Always cinnamon. A habit from his smoking years. She waited while he unwrapped it in the same methodical manner, popped it in his mouth, and chewed it to the point he could speak.

"What're you so antsy about?" Callie knew this man. Though she'd been gone almost two years from the big city, he hadn't changed. His movements shouted nerves.

Twisting around, he threw an arm back over the swing, making her pull hers back to make room. "What would you say if I moved here?" he said.

"Wait . . . what?"

"I didn't tell you the whole truth after I left here back in June," he said.

"That . . . night . . . was a mistake, Stan. I had no right coming onto you when you were freshly separated from Misty. I was drunk. You pitied me. It was best she called you back, frankly. We might've messed up our friendship."

He stared out across Palmetto Boulevard, across the vacant lot at the white caps, working the gum.

"How's Misty doing?" she asked since he wasn't volunteering.

"We lasted a week."

She turned, concerned, but he continued to watch the waves. "You've been apart all this time? Why didn't you tell me? My gosh, we've talked, what, ten times?" Now she worried about *him*. Where had he been living? It pained her to envision him alone yet refusing to pick up the phone and call her. "Stan," she pleaded. "How are you handling it? How's Misty? All this time and you didn't tell me?"

He released a half-grunt, half-groan, focused on the water. "She found someone else. We filed papers. It'll be final in a few months."

"Oh my gosh, I'm sorry," she said.

"And I retired."

"Holy Jesus, Stan!" She stopped the swing.

He was the right age, by a couple months, but he was fit, smart, with years to go.

"It's all good," he said. "Don't flip out."

"You need to rethink this," she replied. She worried their roles had reversed. The boss/protector needing the attention now.

"Mr. Seabrook said I could rent this place," he said.

"What?" escaped before she knew it, her heart thumping as her worlds collided. She had hoped this place . . . how stupid. Surely the family had to dispose of it, rent it, financially make the most of it, but to Stan?

He patted her shoulder. "Don't worry. I told him no. That would've been cruel to you, Chicklet. I have enough sense to see that. I could tell you'd fallen for Mike Seabrook from the moment I spoke to you on the phone about him."

She wished she had realized it. "Thanks for not taking them up on the offer," she said, borderline irked that the subject had even been broached.

"Sorry," he said, rising. "Didn't mean to end this on a bad note."

She rose, too, and threw her arms around his middle. "We're good, Stan. We're always good." Resting her head on his chest, she inhaled, relaxing at the familiarity, the old history. Then she drew back. "So . . . when you come back, enjoy the lifestyle that my staff and I work hard to afford you. Sound good?"

The bear of a man grinned back. "You got it, Chicklet."

He left her there on the porch, waving once as he crossed Palmetto Boulevard to take a side street to where he'd been staying these last few weeks. In reality, it'd be nice having him around, not just long distance once a week. In a chummy, Raysor-kind-of-way.

She needed the foundation.

The light began to change. An awkward part of the day, this in-between time of dusk, and it always seemed to hang, lasting longer than it should. A time that had once been her nemesis, now a magic space loosened from the hours around it. Memories of her life in Boston, memories of Middleton, and fresh, raw moments of her time here. Like Sophie said, echoes entirely relocated to Edisto, bridging all those lives.

She'd do her best to use them to strengthen her present.

The future she'd worry about tomorrow.

The End

About the Author

C. Hope Clark holds a fascination with the mystery genre and is author of The Carolina Slade Mystery Series as well as the Edisto Beach Series, both set in her home state of South Carolina. In her previous federal life, she performed administrative investigations and married the agent she met on a bribery investigation. She enjoys nothing more than editing her books on the back porch with him, overlooking the lake with bourbons in hand. She can be found either on the banks of Lake Murray or Edisto Beach with one or two dachshunds in her lap. Hope is also editor of the award-winning FundsforWriters.com.

C. Hope Clark

Website: chopeclark.com

Twitter: twitter.com/hopeclark

Facebook: facebook.com/chopeclark

Goodreads: goodreads.com/hopeclark

Editor, FundsforWriters: fundsforwriters.com

CPSIA information can be obtained
at www.ICGtesting.com
Printed in the USA
BVHW030005150719
553418BV00021B/81/P